MEMORIES
OF
YESTERDAY

Rynn Ely

MEMORIES OF YESTERDAY

ISBN: 978-1-958626-66-5

Library of Congress Control Number: 2023921545

Copyright © 2023 by Rynn Ely

—Second Edition: December 2023—

Copyright Case Number: 1-12580288141

Cover Design 2023 by Isak Sjöström

Printed in the United States of America.

www.rynnely.com

In loving memory of Kaleb

You taught me what healthy love looks like, and for that, I'm eternally grateful. I hope you know how much I appreciated knowing you.

Contents

Playlist

<u>Zackalyn Songs</u> - Songs they listened to together

ALL WE ARE - OneRepublic

NOT OVER YOU - Gavin DeGraw

CAN YOU FEEL THE LOVE TONIGHT - Anston Seabra

SOMEWHERE IN NEVERLAND - All Time Low

OH, CALAMITY! - All Time Low

<u>Zack's Songs</u>

WAITING FOR SUPERMAN - Daughtry

BUY YOU A ROSE - AJR

FALL FOR YOU - Secondhand Serenade

THE MAN WHO CAN'T BE MOVED - The Script

CRACKS IN THE FLOOR OF HEAVEN - Oh Honey

FALLEN ANGEL - Three Days Grace

<u>Adalyn's Songs</u>

SOMEWHERE ONLY WE KNOW - Keane

CHOCOLATE - The 1975

SWEATER WEATHER - The Neighbourhood

PETER PAN - Kelsea Ballerini

PETER PAN - Kira Stone

LONG WAY HOME - 5 Seconds of Summer

<u>The Ending Songs</u> - Designed to compliment the ending

NEVER BE - 5 Seconds of Summer

AMNESIA - 5 Seconds of Summer

PART OF ME - Cian Ducrot

HOTEL CEILING - Rixton

NEVER FORGET YOU - Zara Larsson

CHAPTER ONE

August 2, 2016

Tragedy struck when a familiar car meandered through the lonely backroads of North America.

Disrupting that tranquil afternoon in August, an engine roared while it passed under tunnels of foliage with greenery towering as tall as the eye could see. The scent of pine trees permeated the air and birds chirped above, encompassing them with the comforting memories of home.

Gradually, jagged curves diminished and the road evened out to a straight path, though the pavement below became corrosive. Rocking the car against such conditions, the driver's eyelids fell heavy and the singular lane hazily became two.

Amidst the swaying, a picture frame that rested on the passenger's side slid in between the seats and down into the abyss. The clashing of its fall lurched the driver awake. Heart suddenly racing, they regained vigilance.

Reaching over for the picture, it was nearly in their grasp. *Just... a little... more...* they thought as they readjusted. Assessing the emptiness ahead, they shifted their focus from the road and began straining again.

In a flash, a massive object dashed out at the car. Catching the movement out of the corner of their eye, they glanced up to witness a silver truck pulling onto the road and colliding with the passenger side.

It transpired in an instant, but at the same time, in slow motion. They were helpless; at the mercy of the truck's damage. The realization of pain wavered as they struggled to comprehend what had occurred.

Eventually, the jolt struck, slamming the driver into the door and emitting a muffled *thud*. A crackling rang as the side window shattered upon impact, and the cracks filled with pooling blood. Unable to see, they listened to objects clattering about as the car tumbled and twisted. They waited until the world fell still, and when it did, they lay in fear.

Gravity pulled, forcing them to recognize that they were dangling upside down. Blood instantly rushed to their head while consciousness waned in and out. Feeling around them, their fingers brushed up against broken pieces of the car. They felt for the seat belt, attempting to pull their way free, but rapidly finding it useless. Beeping echoed from seemingly far away, yet it was their car registering numerous errors. Through the commotion, the driver listened as a pair of wheels screeched against the road, fading into the distance.

They were alone.

Without vision, panic set in. Unable to cut free, they felt for wounds. To their astonishment, there were more than they imagined. Up and down their arms, they brushed over millions of small glass shards that rested in the first layers of skin. As they worked their way down, they felt the seat belt that strangled them, cutting into their rib cage as a warm liquid melted onto their hands. *Blood*.

Continuing on, they made it to their legs. From the start, something was off. *I can't feel them*, they thought. Gently gliding a palm over their thigh, they realized it was for the best, as a sharp object dug into them. They inaudibly gasped.

Perhaps it was the excessive wounds or the blood that was pooling to their brain, but they fell momentarily unconscious.

When they awoke, they weren't sure how much time had passed. It was still warm out, so it couldn't have been long. Their vision still hadn't returned, though a stabbing pain erupted from the back of their head. Gently gliding over it with their hand, they felt it. Unsure how deep it went, an object slashed a large gash on the back of their skull, embedded at the base. The area began to throb.

Another spiking pain hit them in the abdomen as they felt their way to it with shaky hands. Nervously brushing over the diaphragm, they cut their finger on a piercing object's jagged blade. It was metallic.

They tried to scream, but nothing came out. Past the engine's hum and the endless beeping, they listened to the world around them, though it was eerily void of life. Losing consciousness again, they sank back under.

This time, when they woke, the air was cooler and the pain was far less tolerable. Perhaps it was the lack of adrenaline, but they understood that they didn't have much longer to wait for help. They listened to the blood drip like a faucet into the puddle beneath them. Trying to scream once more, nothing came out. Raising their hand in an effort to bang against the walls of the vehicle, they no longer could move.

Police sirens wailed in the distance and a sliver of hope bubbled in the pit of their stomach. *Help!* they tried to say. The police sirens neared, stopping beside the vehicle. *They heard it. They heard me!* Within no time, more sirens joined in and commotion encompassed the atmosphere as they listened to the voices that incomprehensibly echoed through the noise.

CHAPTER TWO

TWO YEARS EARLIER
August 2, 2014

Wind whirled in a haphazard manner, whipping the car in different directions as it coasted down the lonesome road. Howling and banging, there was nothing to do but increase the radio's volume to an almost deafening magnitude in an attempt to drown out the storm. Rain battered down, emitting loud splashes as it collided with the sunroof that protected her from the threatening downpour. The car shook as thunder rumbled overhead. Giving no trace of a break in the weather, the car drove on through the storm. When it finally passed, it left her in its place.

The storm had blown Adalyn Dawn in with the wind that year, appearing out of thin air and later disappearing just as quickly.

She'd moved briskly, rooting herself in everyone around her. Her presence was not one to forget, as she would never allow such an unmemorable performance. This mysterious being, majestic in look and soft in nature was only the beginning of a bittersweet ending.

Contrary to her grand entrance, she burned bright and faded fast, though her story was forever imprinted in everyone's mind. Her arrival altered time itself, as it ceased at her very command.

Before anyone came into her existence, there was Adalyn. Adalyn Rose Dawn came from a lavish reality. Her father was a powerful businessman in his previous years, while her mother became a successful socialite in their affluent community. The happy couple provided an opulent, sheltered upbringing for their three children. Being the youngest of the other two, Logan Dawn and Keisha Hyland, Adalyn was far more wild than them.

Described by those who were fortunate to know her as impenetrably powerful, confident, and perceptive in the way she held herself, she was similarly captivating, warm, and vulnerable. Words escaped her lips like dandelions after a child makes a wish, propelling them forward as the wind delicately disperses them amongst the sky. Her eyes radiated a golden hue, resembling dewy drops of fresh honey produced only by the purest of bees, and her silky brown hair waved like milk chocolate hot cocoa, drunk on a cold evening. However, her beauty lay much deeper than the surface; she was a flower if the rest of the world were weeds, a sunset-kissed sky if the whole world was achromatic. She was the cause for selfless change.

Living in a world of her own, she replenished the earth with her presence. She washed away its shadows, and with it, its worries. The universe she constructed became like a beacon of light amongst the trees, creating flavor in a bland dimension. Repeatedly drawn back to the same forest, she became engulfed as it called for her, trapped by its timeless spell. Compelled by its essence, a part of her vowed to always return.

And so it happened, on one warm, windy afternoon in August. The forests once more called for her. Absent for far too long, her voyages from home evaded the harshest of the winter months and most of the summer while she'd traveled south. Setting a path for home, the route consisted of just under a day's travel through backroads of luscious greenery. Cars quickly became scarce as her Range Rover drove onward.

Many hours had passed since she'd left the last city of East Bellvan, leaving only the forest in front of her. The grassy road she'd turned down came to an abrupt end, forcing the car to a brisk halt. Blocking off the road was a dense thicket of broken branches and vines.

"Dawn Hills!" She cheerfully exclaimed aloud, filling the voided woods with her voice.

Dawn Hills was the town she called home. Nestled in the heart of the forest, it was a sanctuary secluded by the towering trees, offering a sense of security to those that sought solitude. Established by her own brother, the Architect, it remained untarnished by the harsh impact of modern civilization.

Adalyn's car idled at the entrance, concealed by a thick curtain of vines that dangled from the tree branches. Interwoven, the vines serve as both a natural barrier and a veil to the world beyond.

Pulling them aside, she revealed the missing section of the road. In front of her, branches arched above the path, creating a tunnel of kempt flora and her eyes glistened at its beauty.

She was home.

The passage was short, and on the other side, the road began to transform. From the rugged, tattered dirt created by years of use, it flattened. Now paved with stones and gravel to avoid the harsh concrete for the forest floor, her car glided down the road as the small town finally came into view. Just moments before reaching the first building, however, she made a sudden detour. Taking the first right, she turned up the mountain road that led her home.

It was a brief drive, and as she pulled up, the crisp smell of the forest air struck her nose, sending a soft flutter through her stomach. Gazing up at her cozy abode, she couldn't help the smile that pressed against her lips as she admired the stunning wooden exterior and colossal windows that showcased a sleek, modern design.

A soft summer breeze brushed past her as she strolled up the broken limestone pathway leading to her front door. Nestled against the mountainside, the house's foundation was elevated, causing both the walkway and driveway to gently ascend toward the dwelling.

Familiar laughter rang through from the other side of the mahogany door, and that soft grin returned upon her lips as she pushed it open.

Greeted almost instantly with her friend's warm embrace, she casually dropped her belongings onto the floor.

"You're back!" the woman exclaimed.

Wrapping her arms around arguably her closest friend, Adalyn's hands got tangled in her cascading, black hair.

"Hi, Maddie," she greeted through soft laughter. Pulling back, Maddie's Latina features seemed to shine bright in her high-risen cheekbones as she smiled back at Adalyn.

"It's good to have you back," Maddie spoke with a sense of elation.

Opening her mouth, Adalyn was quickly silenced by the sound of more voices growing closer—those of which she hadn't heard in quite some time. Her attention was inadvertently diverted.

"Adam Stewart? It couldn't be..." Adalyn's tone rose as she questioned his presence. Peering into his unforgettable jade-green eyes, she smiled.

"It is, indeed," he responded as his lips curved into a soft grin.

She took in his striking smile, admiring the coarse stubble that shaded his jawline. There was a brief moment in time that Adam's grin would've thrown her heart into a frenzy, a time in which both Maddie and Adalyn had been head over heels for him. But those days felt as if they'd been eons ago, and it was possible that without that moment, the two girls wouldn't be as inseparable as they were.

Redirecting her attention, she turned toward Adam's new girlfriend, greeting the woman with an animated smile. "Arabella," she exclaimed. "It's great to see you again."

"It's good to see you too," the woman quietly replied. A soft blush formed on her cheeks, which she attempted to conceal in her blanket of long blonde hair. She was kind but excruciatingly shy; a wallflower that could easily fade into the background, which seemed to be her preference.

Rather delighted to see them, her head turned to Adam. "What brought you two back?"

"We just came back for the summer to see my sister," Adam responded.

"Right, of course," she replied, as if it was such an obvious answer. "How is Kayla?"

"She's well. You haven't seen her yet?"

Adalyn shook her head. Motioning toward her scattered belongings, she laughed. "I only just got back! How long are you in town?"

"We uh... we actually leave tomorrow." Adam's eyes shifted away for a moment, then landed back on her. "We're off to visit my dad's side of the family..." His voice trailed off at the end, and Adalyn's expression dropped.

"What a bummer," she replied, her voice dropping ever-so-slightly.

After quickly glancing up at the clock that hung near the stairs, Adam peered down at Arabella for only an instant before turning back to Adalyn. "You know, we should actually be going."

"Oh..." Adalyn responded, taken aback by his sudden hastiness. "Okay."

"I'm sorry," he pressed. "We just stopped by with Maddie to help take care of Rocky before you came home."

"Well..." Adalyn was practically at a loss for words. "Well, I'm glad I was able to catch you before you leave again."

"I'll be back," he teased. "I always come back!"

"That you do..." She forced a feigned giggle as he grabbed his keys off her entryway table. Exchanging brief hugs, they were off.

Closing the door as they descended down Adalyn's walkway, she turned back to Maddie. "What's with the rush?"

"Not a clue," Maddie said, shrugging her shoulders. Seeming unfazed by his exit, she glanced around. "Where's your luggage?"

Adalyn, caught up in the haste, struggled to reply. "Uh, it-it's still in the car."

Reaching for Adalyn's keys that had fallen onto the floor, one of her elated grins spread across her face. "I'll go get it while you settle in."

At times, Maddie could be immensely intimidating, but the loyalty and kindness she expressed toward her friends was virtuous.

"Oh—I..." Adalyn stopped her in her tracks. "Sure, but later. Catch me up first!"

"Okay." Placing her keys on the entryway table, they clattered against the mahogany. "What do you want to know?"

"Everything," she pressed. "How's my brother, for starters?"

"Your brother's good," Maddie began. "He's been pretty busy doing *Architect* things over the summer months."

"Oh yeah?" Adalyn giggled.

"Yeah... I still have no clue what that entails."

"I don't know a single person who does, but please continue!"

"Well... he's been helping with Rocky when he gets the chance, and Kalya and I have been assisting him on the council. But you just missed him; he left town for a few weeks." Contemplating further, Maddie gasped.

"What?" Adalyn pressed.

"Kalya finally got her bakery off the ground!"

"Oh, that's fantastic!" Adalyn exclaimed, slowly beginning to situate herself. "How's she doing with that?"

"Not bad!" Pausing for a second, Maddie corrected herself. "She's actually doing really great. It's been a hit throughout the community!"

"That's great!" Glancing around for the first time since arrival, Adalyn became instantly mesmerized by her home. "I see that the interior designer actually finished around here!"

As she walked down the hallway that extended toward the back of the house and expanded into the living room and kitchen, Adalyn's heels landed with a satisfying click on the new whitewashed oak flooring that covered the first level. The sun's afternoon glow shone into the house, reflecting off of the off-white walls and illuminating the rooms with natural light. Maddie followed behind her friend in silence, making her way to the back door where a cheerful golden retriever was patiently waiting to be let inside.

Walking into the immense, open floor plan, Adalyn set her keys down on the granite island that separated the kitchen from the living room. Staring at the new furniture, she admired the light gray fabric sectional and loveseat, evenly positioned around a cloud-gray wooden coffee table. On the opposite side of the table sat a polished fireplace, and above the mantle, a gigantic television was mounted on the wall.

Letting out a soft sigh, she twisted her head to her left. Past the living room were two doors: one was tucked in the far left corner of the room and led down to the garage, while the other was a glass double door that led to the backyard, which Maddie pushed open, allowing the eager puppy to bound inside.

"Rocky!" Adalyn nearly screamed with joy. Bending down to pet her dog, Adalyn ran her fingers through his golden, silky coat.

"He's really missed you," Maddie commented as she watched them reunite.

"I've missed him, too," she exclaimed. "He's so big now. What are you, eight months?"

"You'd know best," Maddie teased. "How was your trip, by the way?"

Adalyn glanced up before smiling upon her recollection. "It was marvelous!"

"What did you do? It's been a while since I last saw Henry. How is he?" Maddie wandered over toward the arching window, inspecting the wildlife bubbling below.

Henry had been a good friend from the earlier days, and an impactful individual for Adalyn. He was youthful at heart and brimming with adventures, always encouraging those around him to pursue the impossible, and Adalyn couldn't help but be swept up in his passionate ways of life.

Maddie's curiosity about the voyage was genuine; however, her opinions of the man were nothing but negative ever since he ran off to some island and left Adalyn's fragile heart shattered. She'd once considered him a friend, but now she saw him as nothing more than a cad.

"He's well. Oh, he says hi," Adalyn announced. She was clearly oblivious to Maddie's hatred. That, or perhaps she chose to ignore it. Regardless, she continued on. "After hours of sailing to the island, we arrived at this magnificent cove. It was magical, really! His new friends were interesting to say the least."

"How so?" Maddie questioned with a slight judgment in her tone.

"Oh, they were just very... natural, I suppose. I learned a lot about cast net fishing while out there, which was pretty fascinating! Oh and when night fell, they threw these wild parties with crazy bonfires. It was stunning. You really missed out."

"Sounds like it," Maddie lied. "I'm glad you had fun." Diverting the conversation, Maddie said, "Hey, do you want to grab your luggage from the car now?"

Adalyn glanced toward the front door and nodded. Rising off the floor, she fetched a few bags from her car.

"Need any help?" Maddie asked as she met her in the entryway.

"No," she shook her head. "I'm just gonna put these upstairs really quick!" To the left, just before the hallway, was a set of stairs that led to the second level.

"Oh, they got to the remodel in there, too," Maddie hollered. With that, Adalyn quickened her pace up the staircase.

Entering the small hallway, two guest bedrooms sat to her left, while the right side held the door to her master bedroom at the end of the hall. With a detached bathroom in the middle, a small office resided behind the door nearest the stairs.

Placing the luggage in her room, she gaped at the new changes. Fuzzy white rugs newly covered her light pine floors as a cream canopy bed sat against the center of the left wall. A chaise sofa rested at the foot of the bed. Across from it, a dresser stood with a small television propped up, along with photographs of her most precious memories.

Returning down the stairs, she met with Maddie once more. "Wow, it looks amazing up there. When did they finish?"

Still pressed up against the arched window, Maddie turned toward her. "I think they finished a couple weeks ago. They were at it all summer."

"Wow. Seriously, wow!" Adalyn repeated herself, unable to find a more adequate word to describe her astonishment.

In the entryway, the clock chimed five as the sun crept behind the mountain ranges. Maddie remained against the window, her shadow heightening as the sun set. She turned back to peer out one final time before declaring, "I think I better get home."

"No worries. Want a ride?"

"No need, the skies seem to have cleared. I think I'll walk. See you tomorrow?" Adalyn nodded, though Maddie was nearly halfway out the door.

Within no time at all, the sky had morphed into a navy blue. Galaxies of porcelain white stars twinkled in the distance as the moon illuminated the earth, bouncing off the treetops. She glanced out the large window in the living room, listening to the wind delicately whistle through the forest.

CHAPTER THREE

August 10, 2014

Upon the first week since Adalyn's return, she received a promotion. As Logan stepped down from the position, Adalyn became The Architect. Residents spent their days laughing under the summer's heat, enjoying barbecues and trips to the nearby lake. With the pleasant weather and vivacious combination of colorful leaves, campers journeyed through the forests, celebrating their last weeks before returning home for the colder months. The sun started its descent behind the trees, gradually disappearing and outlining the surrounding mountain ranges in a silhouette of tinted navy blue.

The tenth day of that month, in particular, expelled an electrifying sunset across the evening skyline. Mystic in beauty, plenty stopped to stare. Mesmerized by its allure, an unfamiliar figure slipped into town unnoticed. His hazel eyes scanned the settlement as he strolled its auburn-hued streets. Traveling alone, he passed through the expanding shadows. Nightfall inched closer, coating the land in the serene darkness.

The following morning, tunes played from the kitchen as cabinet doors closed shut and dishes clattered. Footsteps tapped against the wooden floors, and a faint jingle occasionally rang through the house as Rocky followed along. In but an instant, the garage door slammed shut as Adalyn left, and the sounds in the house ceased.

A faint ringing emitted from the clock tower as it struck eleven o'clock.

As a new Sunday tradition, Adalyn approached the front door of Kayla's shop, the Three Dog Bakery, which was located in the small shopping center that surrounded the town's only water fountain.

The bell chimed overhead as the door opened.

"Good morning!" Adalyn chirped.

Covered in floury dough, Kayla raised her head. Strands of her brunette hair that coiled like fusilli pasta fell in front of her face as she brushed them aside. "Good morning, Addy! How's it going?" Wiping her hands clean of the stringy dough, she met Adalyn down at the display case.

Inspecting the grand selection of assorted pastries, Adalyn motioned to a rather delicious-looking Cheese Danish. "Can I get that by chance?" Drawing her eyes back up to her friend, she responded, "And it's going well so far. How's the bakery?"

"Busier than ever! Now that I'm working as both the lead on the council, and a business owner, it's a lot... I'm angry at Adam for leaving so soon!" She reached inside the case, pulled out the Cheese Danish, and wrapped it in a paper sleeve.

"Why's that?"

"Well, he's off to visit our dad, but my mom's not pleased with his arrival... And aside from the family drama, he was supposed to help unpack a few things here, which he absolutely didn't!" She huffed. Contrary to their referral of one another, the two of them were only half-siblings, as Adam was a result of an affair had by their father. With an exhausted huff, she altered the topic. "I assume you heard about the newcomer?"

"No, no one informed me." Catching word of their presence was like a game of telephone, though news of their arrival became intriguing.

"I'm not too surprised, he hasn't really made himself known yet. I found out through the grapevine."

"Did you happen to catch a name?"

"I didn't catch it, just overheard a brief conversation."

"Oh. I'm sure I'll run into him eventually." Shifting the topic of conversation again, the two of them tended to take these quiet moments in the shop as ample time to gossip. "Did you hear about Maddie?"Adalyn questioned.

"No, what's the news with her?"

"Oh, nothing crazy. I believe she's seeing that new guy, Max, though."

"Well, good for her!" The bell jingled as the door swung open, bringing their conversation to an instant halt.

Adalyn's eyes fell upon the customer, then back at Kayla. "I'd better get going." She dismissed herself as the customer approached.

"Have a lovely day," Kayla called out, though Adalyn was nearly halfway out the door as she waved a farewell.

As noon hit, Adalyn stood outside the infamous ice cream shop to unite with her brother. Cathy's Ice Cream Shop became an iconic scene in the summertime, bringing in masses to its windows from open to close. Arriving a few minutes earlier than scheduled, Adalyn stepped in the extensive line to hold a place while she waited.

A soft tap on her shoulder drove her to turn around as she was met with a pair of soft hazel eyes. "Is this the line to Cathy's?" the unfamiliar man politely asked. His lightly tanned skin radiated as he peered up the line.

"Yeah, you found the right place," Adalyn replied as her eyes scanned the man up and down. Accentuated by the sun's golden rays, his hues assembled a vibrant masterpiece of blended color, and while so wild, they were equally kind and endearing. Just an inch short of six feet, he towered nearly half a foot over her.

"Thank you. I'm Zack, by the way." He gently brushed his short, dark-brown hair to the right side of his face as he spoke. The stubble across his cheeks emphasized not only a distinct jawline, but his high-risen cheekbones when he smiled at her.

"Pleasure to meet you. Are you new around here?"

Zack silently nodded. "Is it that obvious?" His thin nose faintly scrunched with nervousness.

"Oh, no. I just—it's just such a small town, you tend to know when you see a new face."

Nodding once more, he couldn't quite find the proper words to respond with. Coming to with a secondary response, he aimlessly commented on the line. "Is it normal to be this long?" There was a hint of a foreign accent to his voice, which vaguely intrigued her.

"Sadly, yes," she replied. Despising small talk, the novelty of this man's presence exempted him from her animosity as she carried on with it. "It's the only ice cream place around, and sort of a big deal here." Peering over at him, she softly grinned, followed by a gentle laugh.

"Ah, so it's tradition at this rate." Zack fed into the commentary with a joking undertone. "Then, I shall wait in this abnormally long line to get a taste of the culture!"

Facing forward again, a blushing smile crossed her lips as her phone pinged. A text message from Logan covered her lock screen. *So sorry, sis. Won't make it. Something came up. Rain check. Dinner on me?*

Emitting a heavy sigh, she had almost expected it from him, as even in retirement, his schedule remained packed tight.

"Is something wrong?" Zack probed from behind her.

"It's nothing." Frustration clearly filled her voice. Running her hand through her hair, she sighed. "My brother just rain-checked on our plans again."

"Sorry to hear."

"Yeah, me too." She glanced down at her phone again, checking the time. The clock was ten past noon as she emitted another heavy sigh. "I guess I don't need to be in line anymore, then."

"Well..." His dragging tone halted her before she walked away. "If you're already here, you might as well get some ice cream."

"But—" she began, her eyes scanning the enormous line. Recognizing her lack of hospitality to the newcomer, she caved. "You're right, might as well since I'm already here."

"What are you thinking of getting?"

"Don't judge... I'm super bland, so Mint Chocolate Chip."

"No judgment here," he exclaimed, squinting at the menu ahead of them. "I was gonna go for Cookies n' Cream; just as boring of a flavor."

Grinning softly, she allowed a few seconds to pass as she mustered up a proper question to ask that would continue to drive their discussion. "How are you liking it so far—actually, how long have you been here?"

"Got in late last night, but from the singular ice cream shop I've come across, it's pretty nice."

"Oh, so you're *new*!" Accenting on the last word, Adalyn's voice playfully teased him.

"Indeedly so."

"It's like," she took another glance at her watch, "half past noon and you've only seen this ice cream shop?"

"Admittedly, that was a slight exaggeration. Though, this is the first place I've stopped to check out."

"Well, it's definitely worth it for your first place."

"I'm sorry, but I don't think I caught your name?" Zack probed, having interacted with this woman for nearly a half-hour and hadn't learned her name.

"Adalyn," she replied, projecting a half-shrug upon the vocalization of her name. "Adalyn Dawn."

"Pleasure meeting you, Adalyn." Her name rolled off his tongue like maple syrup, daintily trickling down a stack of pancakes.

"And, I apologize, you told me but I meet so many individuals, I've become terrible at names. What's yours again?"

"I'm Zack. Zackary Blake in full."

"What brought you here, Zack?"

"I was traveling," he began, "and happened to stumble upon this place. I know someone here, actually."

"Oh, who?"

"His name is Max."

She held back an erupting grin, recollecting on her friend, Maddie. Collecting herself, she altered her posture as she dispassionately responded, "I think I've met him around. That's really nice that you know someone. Are you staying with Max, then?"

"No, I took a room at the Inn for now."

The Inn in reference was Mountain Crest Inn, the only bed and breakfast in town. Located out west, it sat at the cusp of the business district, positioned just before the town splintered off into large properties.

They were only two spots away from the front of the line as they'd gradually and unconsciously inched forward.

"Oh, Mountain Crest Inn. How is that?"

"It's alright. Quaint, but comfortable."

"Next!" the man at the booth hollered, gaining their attention.

Taking the initiative, he stepped forward, cutting Adalyn off. "Good afternoon," Zack stated. At first, she was partially annoyed by his rude gesture to butt ahead but was mature enough to concede. Zack continued, "I'll get the Cookies n' Cream, and she'll have the Mint Chocolate Chip."

Taking her by surprise, she smiled. "Oh, thank you."

"Of course," he replied, handing over her ice cream and setting down the cash on the counter. "It's the least I can do." Stepping out of the line to allow the next individual forth, she followed alongside him. Silently motioning to a table nearby for them to rest their feet, they took a seat. "So, are you from here?"

Taking a lick from the dripping ice cream, she responded, "Sort of. At least not far from here. How about you?"

"New York. The city of impolite people and large rodents."

"I was about to ask why you left, but I think your disgust answered that for me." Her head tilted sideways as she attempted to catch the ice cream before it dripped off her cone.

"Have you ever been?"

"No, but I'd at least love to visit."

"Well, it's a wonderful place to travel, but perhaps not too great of one to live in," he forewarned. A sense of curiosity washed over him as he pressed to know further about her past. "Have you ever left these woods? Like, to travel?"

"Of course I have!" she spoke abruptly. "My family raised my siblings and I in these forests, but I've traveled plenty since then. I was only recently lured back here when my brother presented his design for this town, a few years back."

Invested in what she had to say, he interrupted. "Wait, your family established this town?"

She casually nodded, "That's right. Adalyn Dawn... Dawn Hills."

"I don't know how I didn't put those pieces together." He chuckled, feeling fairly foolish for asking. "Do you have any other siblings?"

"I do! I'm the youngest of three. Aside from my brother, Logan, there is my sister, Keisha, who is the oldest of us."

"Oh. Is she here too?"

"No," Adalyn nervously laughed. "Last I heard, she was still in Shadow Mountain. I haven't spoken to her since—" she paused, hesitant to continue, though doing so anyway. "Since a few years after my parents passed. We used to live in Shadow Mountain together, until I left."

"My apologies about your family," he interrupted, recognizing the deep waters he began treading.

"No need, it was a decade ago."

Zack opened his mouth to speak, instantly shutting it closed.

"A wildfire," Adalyn interrupted, knowing all too well what the following question would have contained. "A wildfire swept the town when I was fifteen."

"Oh." Silence struck the conversation. "I'm sorry to hear." With efforts to alter the topic toward a more positive light, he informed, "I have a brother and a sister back home who are both younger than me."

"Really? I'd love to have a younger sibling to boss around."

"I admit, it was a lot of fun to do so."

"Any fun stories?"

A smile erupted across his face as he recollected the numerous memories of his siblings. "There was this one time," he began, expressively engaged, "my sister and I decided to scare our little brother with a frightening mask into doing our chores for a week. Unsure how we achieved it, and believe me, our parents weren't happy when they found out."

A vivid smile appeared across her face as he told his story. She laughed a genuine giggle when he finished, acknowledging the humor of the situation. Zack's gripping personality intrigued her as he continued telling compelling tales of his past. Something about the eager nature to which he presented himself allured her.

Long finished with the ice cream, she remained seated with the man as their absorbing conversations carried on. Ranging from personal interests and passions to atrocious family life, they fortuitously bonded. Time whirled past as they continued to chatter.

The clock struck a quarter to three as Adalyn's upcoming obligations crept up. Interrupting mid-conversation, she checked the time. "I really apologize, I am having a wonderful time getting to know you, but I have a friend arriving at three today."

"Oh, I'm so sorry," he unnecessarily apologized for taking up her valuable time.

"No, don't be." They rose from their seats. Glancing over at him, their gaze momentarily glued to one another. A sensation of butterflies fluttered in her stomach lining as she interrupted the silence. "I had a pleasant time getting ice cream with you."

"You as well. Maybe we can do a lunch next time?"

A grin appeared across her lips. She attempted to suppress it, but it overpowered her. Looking like a gorgeous fool, she mustered up the words to speak, "I'd love to."

"Sunday?" he urgently pressed before she could walk away.

"I believe that will work perfectly for me!" She gathered her belongings as she turned to leave.

"See you then." He waved her adieu as she took off, disappearing in between the crowded masses and boxy cars.

CHAPTER FOUR

August 17, 2014

Located at the southeast corner of Main Street and Maple Drive, Granny's Diner was not only the epicenter of activity year-round, but also one of the original landmarks in town. Set aside from the rest of its neighboring businesses, it maintained a Fifties-esque diner style, bringing back the timeless theme with neon signs, checkered flooring, leather booths, and priceless mementos scattered about.

Standing outside the turquoise-painted diner, Adalyn's eyes drifted toward the two neon stripes that ran across the top as she took a deep breath and pushed the front door open. A soft jingle emitted from the bell overhead, and she scanned her surroundings.

"Hey, Adalyn." Ruby's familiarly soothing tone greeted her. Her vision panned over to the hostess podium, and with a smile, Adalyn walked one step closer. "Your usual seat?" Ruby asked, reaching for a menu, though pausing when Adalyn shook her head.

"I'm meeting someone today. He should already be here..."

"Light brown hair, sweet smile, looks kinda like a lost puppy?"

Adalyn giggled at Ruby's description. "That would be the one!"

"He's sitting outside." Ruby stepped back from the podium, directing Adalyn toward the wooden picnic tables that rested out back during the summer months.

"Thank you," she replied as she followed the waitress's instructions through the back doors.

Seated under a patio umbrella outside, Zack was mindlessly staring off at a rabbit across the street when Adalyn approached. It wasn't until she hit his peripheral that he'd even noticed her presence. Jolting up, he greeted her with a delighted smile.

"Hey, you made it!"

She returned the expression as she took her seat. "Sorry I'm late, I got stuck at work!"

With the flick of the wrist, he seemed to pay her tardiness no mind. "Busy week?"

She simply nodded in response. "Have you done any more exploring lately?"

"Well, I checked out the town a bit, but I've mostly just been settling in," he responded. Adalyn nodded, feeling slightly foolish that she hadn't considered he would need time to acclimate. "And you? You mentioned a friend coming into town, right?"

"Oh yeah... my friend, Joyce, just moved back from the States. She's been staying with me lately."

"No one wants to be in the States anymore," he commented, chuckling lightly to himself. Not quite sure what he meant by that, she feigned a giggle nonetheless.

Approaching from their peripheral, Ruby stood beside their table, hovering over them with a pad and pencil in her hand. "Are you guys ready to order?"

"Uh," Adalyn glanced over at Zack for an answer, though his face was expressionless. "I-I'm ready if you are?"

He motioned a *yes* with the nod of his head, and watched as Ruby's pen took down a few letters on her notepad before craning her head toward him.

Just like every waitress at a diner, she slammed her pen against the pad when she was done, clicking it closed as she took the menus off their tables. With a synthetic grin, she promised to be back with their meals shortly before she walked off.

Avoiding another bout of silence, Adalyn asked, "So, are you looking to stay here more permanently or just for the season?"

Zack shrugged his shoulders. He hadn't thought that far ahead, nor been there long enough to make a conclusive decision. "I'm not sure. I'm still checking it out for now."

"Right, of course," she responded as Ruby returned, placing two glasses of water down in front of them.

Taking a sip, she continued. "It's a great place if you do decide to stay. Although I should warn you, it gets kinda empty during the winter months!" Taking a sip of his own water, he softly chuckled. "Nothing wrong with that."

"Yeah, nothing wrong with it," she repeated, though she didn't quite agree.

It wasn't much longer before two dishes clattered against the wooden table as Ruby set them down before promptly walking off.

There was this awkwardness that had washed over them. Perhaps they equally hated the small-talk, though it was practically unavoidable.

"So, what's your plan for today?" Adalyn asked, filling the void with yet another causal question. Having taken a bite, his mouth was full of food as he looked up at her with a stressed expression. "I'm sorry, finish first." She giggled.

Hurriedly swallowing his food, he took a sip of his water and calmly replied. "I was headed to the pet store next."

"Really? What for?" Her eyebrows furrowed, and she felt rather foolish. "I-I mean, do you have pets?"

He shook his head. "No... but I thought about it—adopting, that is."

Chewing a bite of her food, she covered her mouth as she asked, "So are you more of a dog or cat person?"

Without missing a beat, he chimed with a grin, "Definitely dog! How about you? Do you have any pets?"

"I have Rocky!"

"What's a *Rocky*?" he asked in a rather playful tone.

Emitting a soft giggle, she responded, "He's my golden retriever."

"Ah, so definitely a dog person," he teased.

She simply smiled. Unsure how to respond, she bobbed her head as she took another bite. "So you're thinking of adopting?"

she asked one more, remembering again what they were originally discussing.

"I think so. Nothing's for certain yet," he replied. Snacking on the meal in front of him, he asked after a moment, "What are your plans for today?"

"Um," she pondered, "I finished most of my work... so, I don't have anything planned."

Was this an invite?

"Would you like to come with me today?" he asked.

It was!

Rather pleased, she buried her excitement, wiped her mouth, and nodded. "Sure, I'd love to."

"Great! We can go after lunch."

Adalyn couldn't seem to finish her meal anymore. Anticipation ate away at her stomach, quenching the hunger she'd previously felt. She waited, though patience wasn't on her side. Time ticked by, perhaps slower than usual.

"Are you ready?" Zack questioned, a hint of enthusiasm seeping through his tone. Rising from her seat, her actions were enough to say she was. She watched him scan the patio, curious what he was looking for, though it was as if he heard her, because he then asked, "How do we pay here?"

"Oh, they just put it on my tab."

"Tab?" His brows furrowed. She'd spoken so nonchalantly, it stunned him. *Was she joking?* Her expression refused to move. *She was serious.* "Fancy." This time, his voice worded it as a statement, an expectation. He was doing his best to fit in.

Gathering the bits of their belongings and making their way to the exit, the two stepped out of the diner and onto Main Street.

It was but a few shallow blocks down, where the bell to World of Pets chimed as Zack propped open the door to step inside. A colossal selection of animals lined the store walls, housing a variety of pets.

In the blink of an eye, Zack vanished amidst the towering shelves, aimlessly wandering as he observed the captive creatures in cages. Occasionally, he would reappear at the end of an aisle, only to disappear just as swiftly.

Accepting this, Adalyn strolled down the dog aisle, in search of some knick-knack to bring home to her own furry companion.

"Anything catchin' your eye?" Zack questioned, surprising her from behind.

Startled, her heart raced as she attempted to calm herself. "Sorry, did I startle you?" He airily chuckled. "I didn't mean to…"

"No—" She fought to catch her breath. "It's okay, you're just… quiet."

"Sorry 'bout that." His hazel eyes met her for an electrifying moment, only to be pulled away as he looked at the shelf in front of her. "I found a dog."

"Oh?" Her tone raised in shock. "Show me!"

Just two aisles over, tucked in the back of the shop, were the dog kennels. Yipping erupted as they stepped closer.

"This one." He knelt beside the kennel and gazed inside. Following his lead, she did the same, only to come face to face with a youthful golden retriever-German shepherd mix.

Sophie, eight months old, the tag read.

Both of Sophie's ears bent down, just like Rocky's, yet her coat pattern familiarly matched a bi-colored red German shepherd. The infamous black saddle caped over her back, while her face appeared a muddy shade of tawny brown with a soot-black snout.

Smiling at the puppy through the window, Adalyn glanced over to see Zack's gaze completely captivated. "You should do it!" She urged his undeniable fixation with the dog.

"Huh?" He stuttered. Unsure why he asked, he covered up his mistake. "Oh—Yeah, you think so?"

Adalyn vigorously nodded her head. "Then maybe Rocky could have a friend," she teased.

He let out another airy chuckle. "Alright." Standing up, he glanced around for an associate. "I'll be right back."

She watched him as he walked off, disappearing around the aisle. A faint grin graced her lips, and she returned her attention to the dog. Before long, an employee appeared at the opposite end of the kennel to lead Sophie away, prompting Adalyn to rise from the ground.

"So?" Adalyn probed as Zack reappeared. "Are you—" Mid-sentence, she came to a halt as he held up a little leather collar and a few pieces of paper. A smile of surprise uncontrollably crept onto her face.

Rounding the corner only moments after, that charmed little personality in the window became but a ball of elation as its snout drove forward, nearly dragging the employee down the aisle. Tail vigorously wagging as she reached Zack, Sophie's soulful eyes beamed with admiration.

By the time they'd left the pet store, the sun had begun its descent in the sky, and with only an hour of sunlight left, there was no better place to spend such an occasion than Kane Park. Located at the end of the business district, and just past the school, Kane

Park stood to be one of the largest fields in town. There, the three blithely romped around until the heat slowly exhausted them and the evening grew darker.

Night's ascent upon the community forced the last of the sun's spell to plunge behind the horizon, resulting in orange and pink clouds bursting across the skyline. The evening concluded at Adalyn's doorstep with delayed farewells, prolonged until goodbye was the only thing left to say. From the doorsteps, she observed him walk off, disappearing into the faded darkness and devoured by the forest's trees.

CHAPTER FIVE

October 24, 2014

Adalyn's honeysuckle eyes jolted open. Adjusting to the light creeping into her room, her pupils dilated to compensate. Startled by an abrupt noise, her heart raced, unable to process reality in such haste. The noise ceased, leaving her curious about its origins. Currently unsure if she'd dreamt it, she pondered returning to her slumber, though instantly refrained when another knock pounded from the front door. Rocky's lawn mower snores overpowered his ability to hear the ruckus as he continued on with his deep snooze.

Arriving at the shaking front door, she cracked it open as the brisk air wafted in, shivering to its touch. Zack's proper, festive attire of a burgundy button-down and darkened jeans registered a forgotten obligation. *The Halloween Countdown.*

The Halloween Countdown was a traditional countdown that took place exactly one week prior to the end of the month. Though throughout the month of October, Dawn Hills crawled with enthralling fall festivities. From the carnival on Main Street and horror movies in the center of town to pumpkin patches and endless mazes, the community offered it all.

"Hey, Buddy Ol' Pal," Adalyn greeted through her sleepy haze.

"Hey Dear oh Friend of Mine." Zack's bubbly personality laughed off her frazzled introduction. As it started off as an aimless joke, they quickly adapted inane, endearing nicknames for one another. "Did you forget?"

With Zack recently becoming a part of the Council, his attendance became as vital as hers.

She gasped, "I am so sorry! I'll be ready in like, ten minutes." She began to close the door in his face, unintentionally planning to leave him in the cold, before halting mid-action and reopening the door. "Please come in. Make yourself at home!" The door bounced against the wall stopper as Zack stepped inside.

Taking a seat, he got comfortable on her couch while patiently waiting for her return.

Sooner than he was expecting, the clicking of Adalyn's heels against the wooden floors attracted his attention as he glanced over. Impressed with her swift dress change, he gazed at her with a soft grin. Wearing a darkened maroon dress with sleeves that fell off her shoulders, he watched as she adjusted the skirt, which, while shorter in the front, draped to the ground in back of her.

She interrupted the silence. "So sorry about that, I'm ready for the carnival now. Do you think we're late?"

"Well, you're the shining star, you tell me."

"We are *fashionably late*. Isn't that the trend nowadays?" Adalyn confidently insisted.

"Indeed!" He simply played along, feeding into it. "Fashionably late is exactly what we are."

"Plus how important am I to this, anyway?"

"Well, you are cutting the ribb—" he paused, shortly recognizing her rhetorical question. "You're always important."

Producing a large grin, she acknowledged his kind words, yet disregarded them. Retrieving her keys from the entranceway table, she finally declared, "Now I'm ready to go!"

"Fantastic!" he beamed, walking in the direction of the garage door.

"Wait!" Adalyn halted them in their step. "Whose car are we taking?"

"Do you want to drive mine?" he asked.

"Like, you drive or me—?"

"Why not you?"

"Well, I-I'm not very good..." she stuttered, confused as to why he was allowing her in the driver's seat.

"How bad could you be?" He was evidently unaware of her horrendous driving, as it was rather apparent he had never witnessed her behind the steering wheel.

"Alright..."

She provided little warning of the dangers he was about to be subjected to. Adalyn walked toward his mildly beat up, dirt-smeared, white '95 Chevrolet Silverado parked in the driveway.

Hopping into the Chevy, Adalyn fiddled with its buttons, adjusting both seat and mirrors to fit her small stature. "Hey, does this car have a working radio?"

"Yes. Isn't every car supposed to have one?"

"Not really run-down—" she paused, catching her slip-up.

A gasp emitted from his throat. "Riley isn't run-down. That's blasphemy!"

"You named your car Riley?" she teased.

"Yes, it's a normal thing. Look it up! And now, don't get off the subject that you just called my car run-down."

"I did not!"

"You did! Or you implied it. Either way, you did."

"No way..." Fully aware of her slip-up, she swiftly moved to start the car. An alarming cranking noise came from the engine as it turned over, though regardless of its rough start, the interior of the truck had managed to hold up nicely over the last years of use.

"*Lies,*" Zack softly mumbled under his breath as Adalyn threw the car in reverse to chug down the driveway.

An innocent grin appeared across her face while she slammed down on the acceleration, flooring it down the pathway and nearly off the side of the mountain that her house rested on. Immediately, Zack regretted his playfulness, as he was about to experience why everyone hardly let her drive.

Petrified, he emitted a soft scream. "I did not think this through!" He gripped the handlebar with both hands, wishing it would end.

"Never let me drive then." She thoughtlessly sped down the mountain road that led into town.

"I know that now…" he declared while watching the winding roads zap by. "Slow down!"

"What?" She couldn't hear him over the noisy acceleration of his truck. "I've got this!" Her voice held confidence as she shifted gears and slammed the gas pedal down again.

Turning onto the mountain road at an ungodly speed, Adalyn erratically swerved, forcing the car to tip to the right. Compensating for the shift, she began to teeter its balance as she sped down the road. Unwilling to slam on the brakes due to loss of control, she veered left and right, attempting to straighten out the car.

"No!" His heart pattered out of his chest. Knowing the impending ravine was ahead, she continued her effort to gain control.

With no success in doing so in time, the car went flying off the side of the road, missing the sharp turn as it chugged along in mid-air. Zack squeezed his eyes closed, and for a moment, he felt free, as if he was flying. However, he subconsciously knew it would come to a crashing end. An abrupt impact hit the car as Zack waited for more, expecting to tumble, twist, and turn down the side of the mountain.

Moments passed before he dared to open an eye, wondering if he'd died on first impact. Finally doing so, his surroundings were abnormally green as his mind took long moments to process his environment.

The car had managed to crash-land itself into a tree, just off the side of the cliff and inside the ravine. Strong branches encompassed the base of the truck, stopping it from falling any further. It remained there, nearly unscathed, though unbalanced and unable to be removed.

Immediately unbuckling his seat belt, his first instinct was to check on Adalyn, who was frozen in shock. Her eyes were peeled on the windshield, and both hands remained on the wheel. If it wasn't for her hyperventilating breaths, he could've assumed she was dead based on how still she'd become.

"Adalyn?" He tapped her shoulder. Her chest moved up and down rapidly, merely in shock. "Are you okay? Are you hurt?" Waving a hand in front of her face, he tried to catch her attention. "Should I call someone? 9-1-1?"

"Please, no need for either of those!" she finally screamed.

"Oh, thank god..." he muttered under airy breaths. "Don't scare me like that!"

"I'm sorry, I just—I thought I saw something, so I swerved and I just lost con—Zack, I am *so* sorry!"

"It's alright."

That was a lie, Zack was absolutely shattered over his truck. Finding it to be his pride and joy that had gotten him through plenty of tough moments, he was heartbroken inside. Disregarding his emotions toward the materialistic beater car, he assessed himself for any breakage or pain.

"Are you hurt anywhere?" he asked.

"I don't think so." She slowly peered over the driver's door window, reviewing the far drop to the ground below them. "But now what?"

Examining the passenger side window, he declared, "We slowly get out of this truck and climb down the tree."

"Then what? What about the steep ravine?"

"We climb out." Glancing back over at her, his tone was calm, forgiving. "Are you ready?"

"I think so."

"Open the doors on the count of three." Grabbing the door handle, he began counting down. "One... two... three. Go!"

Immediately, they both threw their doors open at the same time. The car teetered to the weight shifting, only to resettle moments later.

"You get out first—but slowly." Zack commanded, calculating that her lack of weight would make a lesser impact than his.

Doing exactly as she was told, she gradually scooted toward the open driver's side door, pausing any time the car teetered and resuming when it settled. Through numerous attempts of slowly moving outward, she wedged her way out of the car.

Easing herself once out, she peered back toward the passenger side. "Okay, that wasn't so bad. Your turn."

Remaining closer to the handlebars, Zack slowly scooted out, careful that his weight wouldn't topple the car. His final shift out the door lent to a massive teetering on the tree's branch as the car forcefully rocked back and forth, nearly tipping off the tree before it once more resettled and adjusted itself to remain locked inside the branches.

Descending from the tree's branches became the easiest part of their endeavor, as they had landed near the bottom of the ravine. "Now what?"

"Let's start scaling rocks now." Zack concealed his annoyance, valuing his friendship with her more. Peering around for a good, flattened area to climb, he asked once more since they were now out of the car, "Are you doing alright?"

Finding a shallower area of rock piles, he jumped on a few to start his upward journey. Following his successful, short climb, she responded in a nonchalant tone, "Eh, a couple scratches won't kill anyone. I'll have to call someone to tell them we can't make it today…"

"True, true. It'll be ok, they'll have to understand." He was surprised that was the first thought in her mind. "I think the top of the ravine will have better cell service." Misstepping, the rock he'd put pressure on slid down a few feet, taking him on a smooth elevator-like ride down with it. "Okay, so that one isn't a good option," he chuckled, playing his move off comically.

Peering back up, Adalyn had somehow taken a seat on a small ledge, further than she'd initially been. Her outfit was nowhere near hiking attire, though she managed to do it in heels, like a mountain goat. "You okay?"

"Yeah, I'm fine. Just took a ride down a rock. Say, how'd you get up there?"

"I climbed," she airily stated as though the answer was simple.

"I climbed. Why didn't I get up there?"

"You took the wrong path?"

She stared down at where he remained standing on the same rock which had tumbled down. Continuing the climb, he met her at the ledge, where they rested momentarily.

About eye-level to where the car had fallen, they sat side by side, glancing out toward the sky and his battered car.

"Well, if it wasn't a beater-car before, it is now," he playfully teased.

"I'm still so sorry, Zack. Maybe we can get it out?"

"Don't worry about it, really. It's just a car."

Internally heartbroken about his car's new state, he shoved his sadness down, refusing to provide any more guilt than she already felt. Had it been anyone else, Zack's rage wouldn't have been contained; however, Adalyn was different. Though it was blatantly and without a doubt her fault, he couldn't bring it on himself to get angry with her.

He remained on the ledge a few moments more, staring out at the vast ravine that they'd stumbled down, admiring its beauty. Mentally saying a final farewell to his car, he stood up, catching his balance against the angled ground. "Ready to get home? We're almost there." He extended a hand out to assist her up. Taking his hand in hers, she nodded, brushing off the dirt from her dress and leading the rest of the way out of the sloped ravine's deadly edges.

CHAPTER SIX

October 31, 2014

Halloween meant the town's annual carnival was on its last day. Storming the streets, residents bundled in layers and dressed in disguises as they marched down Main. Faux webbing and spooky ghouls hung from tree branches, while intricate ornaments that decked the houses billowed in the wind, waiting for onlookers to dare come near.

Night had begun to fall upon the district. This year's turnout was far greater than the last, implementing a drastic assessment of Adalyn's wardrobe. She'd formerly decided upon a matching set of angel wings with the Council body, though a few of them had disappeared for the time being. This left Maddie and Zack as the only representatives of the Council to proceed to the costume party with.

Unsure of the perfect attire to match the costume, Adalyn shuffled through her closet, skimming over the maroon dress and creating a mountain of discarded outfits atop her bed. Selective with her choices, the time ticked down before Zack's arrival at her door.

Finding herself aimlessly wandering about upstairs to procrastinate as time passed, she stumbled upon Kayla's mailed letter atop her office desk. Returning to her parent's estate, Kayla had abruptly fled town, leaving behind only promises to return soon.

Unable to write a complete response yet, the letter sat out, collecting dust. She stared it down for a moment, reading over the neatly written letters.

Pulled back to reality, a soft ding erupted from her alarm, pinging an alert of ten minutes until Zack's arrival. "Oh, shit." She returned to her room.

Standing in her closet once more, her eyes landed upon a fitting dress, and just in time. The roar of a familiar engine gave away his arrival as Rocky had already sprung to action, anxiously awaiting his appearance at the front door. Gifted by Adalyn as an apology for the previous week's accident, Zack pulled up to her villa in her very own Range Rover.

A few knocks slammed against the wooden door before the doorknob twisted as he pushed it ajar. Creaking erupted from the hinges, encouraging Rocky to emit a loud merry bark at his presence. Anxiously clomping about, Rocky slid into Zack on several occasions with a pleased grin on his canine face.

"One moment! Just putting the finishing touches on," Adalyn called out from above.

"No worries, I'll be down here when you're ready." Zack provided attention to Rocky in the meantime.

Rapid shuffling was audible from the floorboards while she swiftly rushed for the occasion, aware that once again, she was late. Trailing in and out of her bedroom to her bathroom, she applied the finishing touches to her outfit before meeting him downstairs. Examining the mess she'd made in the haste, she hesitantly halted, pondering if she'd have time to stop and clean it. Teetering back and forth, her lack of time management overweighed her obsessive need to clean as she began taking her first steps down the stairs.

Moving to the living room, he continued petting Rocky while awaiting her tardy presence. Rocky, acting severely deprived of attention lately, whined at any moment that all hands were not on him. Begging for more, Zack merely succumbed to his trickery, providing attention to the needy dog.

Adalyn's approach turned the heads of both boys. Captivated by her appearance, Zack examined the creamy beige pencil dress that fit snugly against her body and neatly-done hair. As she strutted down, a pair of white angelic wings dragged behind her.

"I'm so sorry, it's my fault again."

"It's no worries." He dismissed her tardiness with a grin. "I expect this out of you, now," he teased. Standing up from his seat on the couch, he brushed off the clumps of dog hair that piled on his black jeans and black button-down shirt.

"That's a terrible quality to have," she laughed. Watching him, she detoured to the cabinet, retrieving a lint roller to aid in the hair removal. "Let me help you with that."

"Oh, thank you!" He faced her, producing a cheeky grin as she traced the lint roller over his shirt. "Happy Halloween by the way!"

Glancing up at him, only inches from his face, she smiled. "Happy Halloween to you as well!" Noticing the lack of space between the two, she gradually took a step backward. "Where are your angel wings?"

"They're sitting in the car because it's hard to drive with them on. I'll put them on when we get there."

"Well, you better match with me tonight!"

"I will, I promise!"

She handed him the roller. "I got most of it off your shirt, the rest is on you! What time do we need to get going?"

Glancing down at his watch as he rolled his pant legs, the second hand was ten past an appropriate time to leave. "Well, um... Now..."

"Then let's get going," she rushed, fully aware that she was to blame.

"Alright." He set down the lint roller to draw the keys out from his pocket.

Taking a single look at his half-rolled pant legs, she picked up the lint roller and mentioned in her kindest way, "We can finish this on the way."

Zack took the lead toward the car, refraining from displaying his frantically hasty mindset, as he had never been an admirer of the tardy kind.

Their advancements toward the car were greeted with pleasantry, as she was rather glad not to have to drive anymore, having vowed to remain off the roads for the time being. He held the car door open for her as she boosted herself inside, sitting passenger in her own car for once. Taking a glance around, she was fascinated by the change of view.

"What's wrong?" Zack observed as she curiously checked out every corner of her side, evaluating each square foot of her own car.

"Nothing, just exploring." Reaching into the center console, she held an Altoids box in the palm of her hand. "Oh, I love these!" she exclaimed, opening the little tin container. Zack snatched it out of her hand, slamming it shut. It took her by surprise. "What was that?"

"Sorry," he apologized, placing them back into the center console. "They're nothing."

She had managed to catch a singular glance inside the box before it was snatched from her. Taking a mental note of the circular, white tablets, she kept quiet, refraining from any further questions. Silence took over as Zack carefully guided the car down the mountain road, leaving only the sound of gravel crunching beneath them.

"I have news!" Zack abruptly blurted, doing anything to avert her from the earlier mishap.

"What is it?"

"I found somewhere to stay that isn't the Inn."

"What? No way, that's fantastic!"

"Yeah, it's a small place just outside of town, near the Inn still."

"When do you move?" Adalyn asked.

"I move at the end of November."

"This is so great," she beamed with elation.

"I know," he replied in almost too calm of a tone. "It has a great yard out back for Sophie to roam in."

"Seriously, this is amazing news!" Adalyn compensated for his lack of external expression, displaying enough excitement for both of them. "Why didn't you tell me sooner?"

"Well, I meant to, but I completely forgot until I got the approval earlier today." Emitting a soft chuckle at her enthusiasm for him, he nodded, "I was thinkin', I'm gonna throw a housewarming party. Of course, you're invited!"

"Oh, that sounds spectacular! I can help plan it. We could do balloons, and cake, and—"

Zack interrupted her, "Dear oh Friend of Mine, are you ever just a guest?"

She fell silent, confused by his question. "What do you mean?"

He softly chuckled, "I know you like planning, but I got this one. Just bring yourself and your gleeful smile, and I've got the rest."

A soft smirk appeared across her face, as she'd never not been a part of the planning committee. It felt nice. Nearly bouncing in her seat, her excitement could hardly be contained while the car rolled into town. The clock on the dashboard read fifteen minutes past eight o'clock, once again late to the event.

Their belated arrival was greeted by Maddie's excited face, pounding on the passenger door as they parked the car.

"You're late!" Her screams sounded muffled through the car window as Zack shifted the car into park, allowing Adalyn to hop out immediately.

"I know, it's my fault. I'm sorry!"

"It's fine, you look stunning." Maddie's hasty expression eased as her eyes brushed over their appearances.

"You as well," Adalyn complimented.

She scanned her best friend's outfit as they matched in color, though differed in style. Her twin angel for the night possessed similar yet differently arched wings upon her back, designed uniquely by a local fashion designer for each individual. Adalyn's wings arched upwards, then draped down low, toward the ground, creating an ear shape. Whereas Maddie's arched similarly, but ended about where they started, creating a heart-shape to them.

Adalyn peered back toward the car, waiting for Zack's approach to assess his outfit. Listening to his shuffling through the back seat, he emerged fully dressed in the attire he was assigned to wear. Greeted by the matching girls, Adalyn was stunned by his celestial appearance. Although she'd seen him only moments earlier, his outfit had truly been tied together with the wings. Blackened like his outfit, the wings arched outward, similar to when a bald eagle lifts its wings before taking flight. Taking up plenty of space, his wings limited his mobility as he approached the two, crashing into the nearby cars while doing so.

"You look great!" Maddie complimented whilst stepping toward Zack.

"Really, Zack, you do look great!" Adalyn chimed in.

Blushing from the compliments, he grinned. Opening his mouth to speak, a large dinging struck the air from the carnival, signaling for them to get into place for the opening ceremony. "We better get going," Zack pushed, pleading to not be late for this as well.

The three of them joined the carnival lights. Marvelously stunned by what Adalyn had been missing out on, her vision became a blurry haze of warm-toned lights that encompassed the air. Shining pathways shown through the street as tents had been placed up along the sidewalks, presenting games and food.

Costumed children ran past them as they rapidly maneuvered down the street of crowded residents, pushing past to get through. Adalyn collided directly with a masked man, nearly knocking her to the floor. Grabbing her arm as she began to fall, he pulled her back upright. "My deepest apologies, ma'am," he grumbled through the distorted light-up mask.

"It's no worries!" she exclaimed as she pulled her arm free, looking to scurry onward and catch up with the others.

"Adalyn?"

Her name caught her attention as her gaze peered back toward the man, curious of who lay underneath the mask. Reaching behind his head, he removed the strap holding it together. His voice no longer warped by the mask, he became almost instantly recognizable to her.

Revealing the face beneath, she was greeted with a dopey smile that constructed wrinkles beneath his dark brown eyes. Covered by the shadows, they became nearly blackened, like charred coal, though gleaming like obsidian stones. The soft wrinkles created by his hearty grin traveled down his face only to hide behind the stubble that covered his jaw. A couple of gray hairs were slightly perceptible against his hickory brown roots, as he was about a few years shy of thirty. His lips were thin as he nervously pierced them together, awaiting her recognition of him to emerge.

"Ragnar?" She was pleasantly surprised by his impromptu appearance.

Nodding, he witnessed her expression go through the stages of confusion to pure joy. Arms unexpectedly wrapped around him as she took her dearest friend into a warm embrace, welcoming his return.

The final bell rang, coaxing her upstage. "I must—"

"Go!" he pressed, not meaning to disrupt her. "We shall catch up after. You'll find me in the area, I'm sure."

She expressed a soft grin as she slowly pushed through the crowd. "We'll catch up after," she repeated as her figure disappeared into the masses that flocked to the street for the final night's event.

Arriving backstage, where she belonged, Maddie questioned, "Where did you go?"

"Ragnar's back in town," Adalyn disclosed before the announcer began to call them onto the stage.

Strutting in, in a single-file line with Adalyn leading and Zack bringing in the caboose, they made their appearance in front of the assembly of festively-costumed residents, providing them with short speeches to kick-start the night. A roar of applause echoed through the trees after the final speech had concluded, commencing the grand activities.

Lights blasted off into the night sky, shining on until they dissipated into the atmosphere. The full moon shone even brighter than earlier, illuminating the entire street. The clamorous cheers from the masses slowly dissolved, reverting into jumbled chatter as the crowd that had suffocated the stage only moments ago dismantled.

Dispersing with them, the three of them stepped off stage and moved down to the front, where they remained chatting for a while longer.

"That wasn't too bad," Maddie admitted.

"It never is," Adalyn replied. "Anyone want to go do a carnival game with me? I really haven't had the opportunity since it arrived."

Stepping beside her, Zack stood only inches from her as their wings overlapped. "I'm in."

Noticing their closer attachment lately, Maddie refrained. "I can catch up to you later, but I promised a guy—a friend that I would show him around."

"Ooh?" Adalyn's *'oohing* pried to know more.

An uncontrolled giggle erupted from Maddie's lips as her gaze shifted between Zack and Adalyn. "I'll tell you later, I promise!"

"Alright. You promised, don't forget!" Taking in Maddie's embrace, the two friends parted ways. Watching her disappear into the crowd of ghouls, goblins, and vampires, Adalyn's full attention was now directed toward Zack. "What now?"

"Games!" Without missing a beat, he exclaimed with such a free nature.

"Cool! Lead the way, Buddy Ol' Pal!"

Pushing past the crowded street, it became nearly impossible to see over the costumed heads, nor hear past the dinging sounds of whirling machines. The brief walk introduced them to the only game that didn't have a line; Balloon Blast, a water pistol game with the goal to fill the clown-shaped balloon until it bursts.

"Make it competitive?" Adalyn asked.

"You're on!"

A blaring ding stemmed from the machine, sending the two off on their mission to win. Seconds ticked upward as they competitively raced for the finish line. Focused on their own, Zack's clown was in the lead, nearly at its height of bursting.

Defeated and aware, Adalyn's playful sport ceded as she turned the squirt gun toward Zack, aimed, and fired, blasting him with a stream of water.

Postponing his success, he squirmed at the shocking touch of the cold water. He had attempted to continue on with the game when another stream of water hit his arm, soaking it. Nearly even with Adalyn's balloon, he paused. Redirecting his shot, he fired water back at her. In return, she emitted a loud, laughing scream as he aimed right for her stomach, drenching her beige dress in a cascade of water. Once over the shock, she turned back to face the game. The two balloons had now scaled up to an equal size, racing after one another. Eventually, one popped, and Adalyn hollered with glee.

Stepping away after the round finished, she rung the tip of her lengthy brown hair out from the water and surveyed the prizes. Adalyn's win had granted her a small prize, in which she chose a miniature stuffed toy of a baby chick. Fluffy in touch and cute in looks, she was rather pleased with her victory.

"It's like you didn't even try!" she harmlessly teased, assessing his point score.

"It was a bad balloon, I guess." He observed as she boasted about her prize for moments more, enthralled by its darling appearance. "Whatcha gonna name it?"

"Not sure. Do you have any cute ideas?"

"Caiden!" he declared. "Or Kaleb?"

She deliberated for a moment. "I like Caiden."

"Caiden it is!" Enthusiastic that she picked a name he suggested, he glanced over at the little stuffed chick in a similarly dotting manner.

"We can share him, since we played it together." Her posture held pride as she strode around with the toy in front of her. In a fashion, he also grew attached to this little toy.

CHAPTER SEVEN

December 7, 2014

Over the course of a week, boxes in Zack's new cabin gradually emptied, while new furniture accumulated in the rooms and valuable belongings were methodically coordinated on the shelves. Slowly acquiring proper household items and decorating to his wishes, his new house transformed into a home. Filling the once bare rooms with a sense of character, he prepped his lodge for a rare celebration.

Without the assistance of Adalyn, Zack single-handedly assembled a gathering. Catered by local restaurants and streamed with subtle decorations, he ornamented his lodge with a humble touch. Keeping it modest, he invited only his closest of friends. In a small town, though, that just wasn't possible. What had started as an intimate gathering, quickly exploded into a vast party.

Sunset overturned the early evening sky as the newly stained, log exterior shone against the pockets of fresh snow that coated the grass around Zack's home. Located only a few miles northwest of Mountain Crest Inn, the cabin sat on top of a small hill that overlooked the road as guests leisurely sauntered in.

"Lovely place," each guest would compliment upon entering. He would respond each time with a simplistic, *Thank you*.

Leaning against the kitchen counter, Zack sipped on a cold beer, pretending to listen to yet another dull conversation from yet another nameless face that had uninvitedly entered his home. Seeping into his own thoughts to evade the futile conversation, he was whisked away by a familiarly raspy voice.

"Zacky-boy!" Max called out as he approached.

Cocking his head in the direction of his voice, Zack's face lit up with a vibrant grin. "Hey-a, Max!" Carelessly stepping away from the incessant jabber, he walked over to his pal.

"Zacky?" Adalyn teased, coming up behind the two. Zack shot her a playful grin that was immediately overtaken by Max's excitement.

"The place looks fantastic! Didn't think you had it in ya, buddy," Max teased, glancing around. "Hey, where did you get one of those?" Max motioned toward the beer in Zack's hand.

"Out back." With the neck of the bottle, Zack motioned toward the back patio. "There's food and coolers out there too. Help yourself."

"Thanks! Hey, Maddie should be right behind me, if you want to let her know I'll be out back?" Zack nodded as Max pushed through the crowd and out the back door.

Adalyn teased once more, "So, Zacky?"

He softly chuckled, "Yep."

"Any reason?"

"Not really. It started in childhood, and I just never could shake it. I got used to it."

She nodded it off. "So, him and Maddie are official now?"

"Yeah, as of last week. Aren't you her best friend?"

"Well, yes," Adalyn paused, recognizing how little she'd updated herself about Maddie's life. Changing topics, she asked, "I could use a drink, do you want anything? Er, well..." She quickly glanced down at his hand which was still holding the bottle of beer.

He followed her gaze, twirling the bottle. "Actually, I could use a refill. I'll go with."

Now flooding out of his house and onto the back patio, attendees were nearly multiplying in numbers. The two made their way out back, leading to the coolers of refreshments that lined up against the house. Stepping onto the wooden deck, Adalyn was impressed with the streamers of warm lights that dangled overhead. The warmth from one of the flame heaters sufficiently shielded them from the December temperatures. Adalyn picked out a hard lemonade from one of the coolers, as Zack replenished his beer.

"Cheers," she exclaimed. Their plastic glasses clinked together as the liquid inside sloshed onto their hands. "Congratulations on being an official Dawn Hills resident!"

A faint smile appeared as he brought the glass to his lips. Nearly emptying half the glass, he turned to face her. "I—"

"Hey! Zack, right?" Ragnar interrupted, sounding slightly inebriated. His obstructive timing ripped Zack away as he nodded, though curious as to who this man could be. "This party, 'tis brilliant! Adalyn's idea?"

"Actually, no. It was mine."

"Hmm," he scanned the backyard, admiring Zack's work. "Don't think we've had the pleasure. Name's Ragnar."

"Oh, so *you're* the famous Ragnar Adalyn talks about!" Loosening up, Zack produced a friendly smile toward the stranger.

"I suppose so. Speaking abouts, where is she?"

"Uhh," he pondered, glancing around. He'd hardly noticed she'd left during all the commotion. "She was right—"

"Right here! Sorry, Joyce just got here."

"I was just telling Zack that this is a nice gathering," Ragnar interjected, having assumed it was all to plan.

"Yeah, it really is. I'm thoroughly impressed, Zack!"

"Why thank you." Zack's cheeks gradually turned red from the plethora of compliments.

Tunneling her way through the masses, Joyce arrived beside Adalyn. "Hey!" she paused, recognizing she'd intruded in on the conversation. "My bad, I didn't mean to interrupt. I'm Joyce."

"No worries, we were just chatting," Adalyn said as she instinctively took a step back to introduce her friend. "I'm not sure if I've ever introduced you two. Ragnar, this is Joyce. She's an old friend of mine."

"Pleasure, ma'am. The name's Ragnar."

"Pleasure to meet you, Ragnar." Strands of her beach-wavy blonde locks sat behind her petite ears as a grin curved her bow-shaped lips into a plush smile.

"Joyce just moved back from the States."

Ragnar nodded in acknowledgment. "How were the States?"

"They weren't too bad, though nothing in comparison to here."

"I think that's agreeable. Are you from here, then?"

"No. I'm from the States, just lived out here for a few years," Joyce clarified.

"My apologies for the mistake."

"No need. What about yourself? Are you from here?"

"Yes, ma'am."

Adalyn tapped Zack on the shoulder. Leaning in, she whispered, "Let's give them space." Motioning with her hand to follow, she slowly crept away. "I was getting bored."

Zack nodded in agreement. He led the two of them off the deck and into the backyard. The volume of voices decreased the further they walked. "Are you hungry?"

"I could eat," Adalyn said, and Zack led them to the edge of his yard, where food catering stands encompassed the premises. "Hmm," she pondered, examining each.

"Anything catchin' your eye?"

"Well, plenty. It's just a matter of which."

His eyes scanned the surrounding vendors, landing on a stand. Motioning with his eyes, he slowly inched closer to it. "Pizza?"

"Pizza sounds great!"

Standing against the warm light of a pizza oven, they took their meals in hand and slowly inched back toward the center of the yard. Listening to the ambient chatter from the surrounding guests, a distant voice hollered, "Zacky, over here!"

Max motioned them over toward where he was sitting as they made their way through the sea of picnic tables that lay across the grass.

"Hey!" Zack took a seat across from Max.

"Maddie's inside, she'll be right out," Max spoke to Adalyn. Turning his attention back to Zack, he said, "I'm glad you decided to stay."

"Yeah, it's pretty great here. How could I not?"

"Loving the leather couch, dude," Max complimented. "Got any plans for the second bedroom?"

"Not really, no. Maybe an office."

Maddie crept up behind Max, swinging her leg around the picnic bench. "Office for what?" she snobbishly questioned.

Adalyn instinctively shot her a harsh glare from across the table, though Zack casually dismissed it.

Max immediately broke the taut atmosphere, "Oh, what about a pet room for Sophie?" He paused, looking around the yard. "Where is she?"

"She's at Adalyn's. A pet room isn't a bad idea, I'll keep it in mind."

"Are you gonna do any upgrades?" Max asked.

"Um, I don't really know at the moment, I just moved in. I'll figure it out," Zack responded, begging to move on from this conversation.

"Hey, I'm just really glad you're around permanently, man! It's been a long time. Remember when we were younger? Back in North Carolina," Max chuckled, beginning to reminisce.

"I thought you were from New York?" Adalyn interrupted.

"I am, sorta. I moved to New York when I was twelve, but I was born in Cherokee, North Carolina, on the reservation. Max, here, was an old mate from the reserve." Zack produced a hearty grin as he glanced over at Max.

"We used to ride our bikes around the reserve and wreak young havoc," Max said, chuckling at the memories.

"Where's your sister, um, Beka? That girl was crazy!"

Zack chuckled, "She's still back in New York with my family."

Max turned his attention to Maddie. "Beka and Zack were insane! They used to constantly get in trouble when they were little."

"Cute," Maddie responded, though she lacked actual care toward the conversation. Adalyn's gaze followed the conversation, listening intently to the stories.

"One time, Beka and I ran away in the middle of the night, ran about two miles through the dense back-woods, and knocked on Max's bedroom window for a midnight BB gun war."

"Did you do it?" Adalyn questioned.

"Of course," Max said.

Zack laughed, "Oh, we did, alright! I won."

"That's because you and Beka teamed up on me!"

"My uncle was pissed."

"Yeah, I didn't see you two around for like two weeks after the fact."

Zack grinned. He took a sip of his beer. "It was good times," he finally responded.

The table fell into a peaceful silence as they finished eating. Zack observed the miscellaneous guests that welcomed themselves into his house. He watched as they wandered about the open rooms, exploring it as if it was their own.

Scraping their paper plates clean of food, Max stood up. "We'd better get going. This was great, dude! We need to hang out sometime soon. The TV in there would be great for the games."

Joining him, Zack stood as well. "Of course. Next Friday, maybe?"

Max thought for a moment. "Should work."

"Let me walk you two out," Zack offered, slowly motioning them toward the front door.

"See you soon, Addy," Maddie called as she filed out the door.

"Bye, Maddie," Adalyn responded.

"Zacky, it's always a pleasure, man! And you as well, Adalyn." Max bid a farewell to the two as they stepped off the front porch and into the star-lit night.

Standing at the doorway, Zack and Adalyn watched as the last guests trickled out. Walking down Zack's long driveway, they disappeared into the navy blue darkness.

Adalyn stayed behind long after the last of them had left, assisting with the clean-up.

"You really don't have to stay," Zack mentioned.

"No, but I want to help. It's the least I can do."

"Thanks."

"It looked like you had a ton of fun."

He nodded with a grin. "Did you?"

She nodded back. Emptying contents of half-drank beer cans down the sink, she tossed them into a trash bag. "You never opened any of the gifts!"

"Oh," his gaze wandered over to the pile. "I'll get to them."

"Why not now?" she questioned. His eyes scanned over the messy house. "No, you're right. After?"

"Sure," he grinned. "We can open them after."

"Yay!" She continued on with the clean-up.

The house was near-spotless, cleaned from the cluster of cans and excess food as Adalyn's eyes gradually wandered toward the backyard.

"Do we dare?" Zack strained, dreading it.

"Well," she pondered, "maybe just the trash and the deck? At least so the forest critters don't come."

"Good point." He pulled the door open further, allowing her to step through.

Still lit up by the dangling lights, the backyard maintained a decent brightness that allowed them to work at ease. The nighttime brought out chirping crickets, though Zack filled the static noise with a familiar hum as he worked. Unconsciously, Adalyn swayed to his beat as she continued to pick up the trash. Peering up from his cleaning, a wide grin formed on his face as he gaped at her delicately dancing across his backyard.

His humming unintentionally waned, causing her to glance up. Making eye contact with him, she beamed one of her infamously vibrant smiles. Melting at her gaze, he foolishly grinned back.

"It's looking great out here," she interrupted the moment as her eyes left his, scanning the backyard, "I bet we could call it done and go open the presents now."

"Oh, yeah... Alright, sure!" He expressed a gallant grin as she bounded over to him, tossing the trash in the dumpster on her way in.

The coffee table overflowed with wrapped gifts, stacked high and cascading to the floor. They'd lit the fireplace, causing a soft ambiance of crackling embers and a soothing yellow tone that brightened the room.

"Which one would you like to see opened first?" Zack asked.

Adalyn pondered for a moment, scanning over the plethora of gifts. "Well, this one is labeled from Kayla. I have no clue what she got, but I remember her telling me to pick it up for her. Open that one!"

Softly chuckling at her persistence, he ripped out the tissue paper. Letting it flutter to the floor, he gently pulled out a bottle of 2013 St.-Emilion de Bordeaux. Softly twisting it in his hand, he examined the bottle. "Well, I bet that'll be worth something one day!"

Adalyn silently examined it as he twisted it, not daring to lay a finger on such a bottle. "She always goes big with her gifts."

"It's a great gift." He delicately set it down, away from Adalyn.

She sat in silence for a few moments more, not sure if many other gifts could top it. "Well, uh, what else is there?"

Fidgeting around the pile, he purposefully only chose the few from Adalyn's close circle—the ones that would interest her the most. "Joyce's?"

"Sure," she exclaimed, eagerly hovering over him as he unwrapped it.

"A toaster! I actually needed one of these." He twirled the unopened box in his palms, examining the toaster. Adalyn emitted a softened smile toward Zack's response.

"Okay, okay, not as interestin' to you. How about yours?"

"No, no! Save mine for later," she halted him. Scooting over a larger box, she presented it to Zack. "How about Max and Maddie's?"

"Sure." He ripped into the wrapping paper.

"Oh, a fire pit for the patio," Adalyn exclaimed. Her interest was piqued. "We could roast s'mores all the time!"

Her youthful excitement delighted Zack. Expressing an enthused smile, he nodded in agreement. "Yeah, whenever you want, come over and it'll be here."

She grinned widely, knowing well that she'd partake in plenty of s'mores nights. "Okay, who's next?"

"Well," he scanned over the pile once more, "yours is the last one we know."

"I guess..." She nervously held her breath as he tore into the wrapping. He froze as the ripped paper fell to the floor.

"What is it?" Adalyn pressed, moving closer to see around his arm, worried that it had perhaps gotten ruined in transit.

"Is that..." he spoke, unable to complete his sentence. "... Custom bookends of Sophie?" Nearly frozen in admiration, a smile slowly crept onto his face.

She silently nodded, almost nervous that he wouldn't like them as much as she hoped. "I got them hand-made with white marble... I hope you like them?"

"I—of course I like them!" Staring in awe, he delicately turned one of them in his palm. Inspecting the detailed brushing of each individual fur pattern, he examined its accuracy. "This is incredible. Truly!"

"I'm so glad you like it!"

An elated expression emerged across his face as his eyes dilated, lighting up towards her gift. Setting them back in the box, he reached over to hug her. Pulling her into a warm embrace, they stayed that way for a moment before she softly pulled away to gather her breath. Her gaze fell on his captivating smile, and she couldn't help but mirror it.

"I really must be getting home," she said, finally breaking the silence.

"Oh, right. Do you have everything you need?" he asked, slowly striding toward the garage door to take her home. She nodded and stepped into the cold garage.

The engine roared as the radio spoke at whispering volumes. The wind whipped in from the partially rolled-down windows while they chugged along in silence. Smoke rose from her chimney as they neared, while lights danced and flickered against the living room walls, made by the blazing flames of the fireplace.

Joyce must've been home.

Walking up to the front door, she turned to him. "Thank you for inviting me tonight. I've never just been a guest before... It was nice."

"Of course. Thanks for the help afterward!"

She flashed him a smile. Unlocking the door, she held it open a moment longer as if she'd been pondering over inviting him in. Eventually, she turned around one final time. "Goodnight, Zack."

CHAPTER EIGHT

December 12, 2014

Granny's Diner was the only sign lit up in town due to winter hours, becoming the hotspot for activity. During the cold months of November to February, it was transformed into a classier dining space on Friday nights, providing the community with a more up-scale location for residents to mingle and chat. Cleaned and prepped for visitors, the diner was altered from the modernized 'Fifties' ambiance to a more serene diner with orange-ish, warm mood lighting and tranquil music.

Adalyn and Zack had found themselves outside the diner that night, peering in at the guests chattering amongst each other. The exterior was lined with white Christmas lights and pine-green tinsel that dangled from the edges of the rooftop. Glancing over at one another, they inched toward the entrance, craving for liveliness to entertain their intrigued minds.

They ascended the three steps to the diner's entrance as the door flung open, faintly releasing slow, soothing jazz music from the speakers above. An unfamiliar woman stumbled out from the diner. She had clearly utilized the bar as she wobbled past. Mumbling and giggling, she nearly collided with the sidewalk. Adalyn and Zack both jumped out of her way in time, flinging themselves away from her before she took an unbalanced tumble. Following a short distance behind was her date. Holding a feminine shawl in his hand, he darted after her. Once more, the two of them sprang out of his way as he pushed past, hollering for her to wait up.

Adalyn's eyebrows raised as she witnessed the scene taking place. Peering toward one another, they forged onward, pulling the door open to reveal the transformed diner.

"After you." Zack motioned, holding the door open.

"Thank you!" Slowly prying the snow gloves off her fingers, she scanned the restaurant, evaluating its new design.

The interior contained the same artwork that lined its walls, continuing to provide a Fifties-esque nature to the place. Tables and booths had been neatly covered with white cloth, while dark fabric concealed the leather seats underneath. The decor created an elegant tone to the diner—as elegant as it can be, given the building's conditions.

"Just two?" Ruby gathered up two menus from a slot. In lieu of the fifties pin-up fashion she typically wore, tonight's attire consisted of a black pencil dress.

"Yes, just us. Thank you," Zack responded with a cordial smile.

Gathering their silverware, Ruby began to lead them to a circular booth made for parties of four. A headband of reindeer antlers jingled as she walked. Pausing in front of Adalyn's standing booth, reserved solely for Adalyn's arrivals, she placed the menus down. "Does this work for you, Ms. Dawn?"

"Yes, thank you." Adalyn took a seat.

Though the diner started its Fancy Friday trend over a month prior, at the start of November, this casual Friday night had been the first occasion Zack witnessed its transformation.

His eyes scanned the restaurant, engrossed in its newest designs. Aware of its winter alterations, Adalyn's voice imposed on his fascination. "It's pretty great, right?"

Nodding in agreement, his eyes landed on the menu in his hands. "Oh, look!"

"What?"

"The whole menu is different! They can do that?"

Evaluating the menu for herself, she giggled and nodded. "I haven't been here in a while, but I can confirm that the food is good." Her attention drifted to the surrounding environment, taking in the shift in scenery.

In the midst of her amusement, blurry figures passed her line of sight as her gaze flashed toward them. Across the diner, only tables away, two familiar faces took their seats.

Zapping Adalyn out of her glare, Ruby approached the table with a set of water glasses. "Are you two ready?"

Zack's attention turned to Adalyn. "Are you ready?"

"Yes, I believe so. I'll take the salmon with a glass of Pinot."

"Grigio or Noir?"

"Grigio, please."

Jotting it down in a scribble of acronyms, Ruby turned to Zack. "And for you?"

"I'll do the filet, medium rare, but make the pinot a bottle, please."

"You got it, I'll be back with that bottle." Pounding the back of her pen against the notepad, it clicked and retracted the ballpoint. Ruby dismissed herself from their table, moving on to the next.

Returning her glance toward Zack, Adalyn motioned with a finger toward a table at the other side. "Is that who I think it is?"

Equally, their gaze fell upon the table. "Is that... Ragnar and Joyce?" Overly curious, their eyes remained tied to the table, squinting for a better view.

Friday nights at Granny's Diner tended to be a romantic scene. Provided with soothing music and upscale dining, it was undeniable which crowd it attracted. Adalyn was aware of this when Zack had picked the place earlier in the evening and even provided notice of this, though, with that information, he continued to stand firm on his decision.

Returning with the bottle of wine, Ruby removed the cork and poured a taster into Adalyn's glass. "Let me know if this is to your liking."

Lips to the rim, she tasted a singular sip. Piercing her lips together, she pondered for a moment before nodding. "It tastes lovely."

Ruby grinned as she began to pour the wine into each glass. Setting the bottle at the center of their table, she dismissed herself. "Please let me know if there is anything else I can get you."

"Thank you, Ruby, I'm good for now," Adalyn stated with a pleasantly genuine smile.

Now sitting only inches from one another in their corner booth, Zack and Adalyn raised their glasses to toast. Momentarily gazing at one another, Adalyn raised the glass to her lips.

"Mm, delicious." Zack swirled the wine in its glass, like he'd witnessed most wine drinkers doing, while he examined the tornado of liquid from the side.

"I always love Pinot."

Adalyn's legs crossed over one another. Her plump lips were tinted red as her hands rested flimsily on the table in front of her. She positioned herself forward, hiding her nervousness, while comparatively, Zack, in his dark olive button-down and black polyester pants, positioned his whole body in her direction. A smile brightened upon her face, perpetually naive to Zack's admiring gaze.

Holding a confident pose, Zack was enthralled by her gifted existence. Moments passed before she'd gathered the nerve to glance his way again, to which he cowardly shifted his gaze away. It became a silent game of cat and mouse that their gazes played with one another, though absolutely unsuspecting or painfully a tease, she hinted at no notice of his apparent chase.

Soft banter could be heard from across the room as Adalyn occasionally fixated on Joyce and Ragnar, wary of their private evening. Drawing her attention back, Zack interrupted. "Did you know about that?"

She shook her head. "No. Are they...?"

Finishing her sentence, he interrupted her thought. "On a date? Looks to be."

Inaudible words were spoken between Ragnar and Joyce as the demeanor between them held tension; their body language made it blatantly clear that the two were on a date.

Moving her arm, a light *clink* erupted through the air as Adalyn's empty glass fell over on their table, slowly rolling toward the edge. Just in time, and seemingly out of nowhere, a hand clasped around the stem just before it hit the floor.

"My apologies," Adalyn's tone nervously wavered.

"No worries," Ruby politely smiled as she set the glass back on the table. "Would you like another glass?"

"That would be great."

Kindly dismissing herself, Ruby shortly returned with a new glass, which she filled with the Pinot.

Taking a sip, her gaze shifted back to Zack, who'd been watching the whole exchange. "I'm sorry, what were we talking about, again?"

He softly chuckled to himself. "Honestly, I forgot." His eyes drifted around the table before landing back on her. "How does the wine taste?"

Carefully setting the glass on the table, she glanced over at it as she re-adjusted in her seat. "It's good!"

"That's good," he responded, his voice fading out as a lump grew in his throat that he attempted to clear away with an *ahem*.

The table fell into a brief silence as they listened to the soft jazz that played overhead, taking this moment to recollect themselves.

At that instance, a chair's feet vaguely screeched against the flooring as Ragnar stood from his table. Apologetically dismissing himself, he turned toward his dinner company. "Just one moment, please. There is something I must do." A sly grin plastered across his face, knowing well that this moment would be worth it.

Approving his dismissal, Joyce nodded, though her gaze followed him while he made his way toward the bar.

Leaning over the bar's countertop, he flashed the unoccupied bartender his screen, "Hello sir," he politely interrupted, "would you mind playing this song next?"

Drying an empty glass with a rag, the bartender set it down on the table to examine the screen. "Sure thing." He nodded, accommodating the request.

Making his way back to his table, Ragnar silently re-seated himself in front of Joyce. Within moments, "Can You Feel the Love Tonight" began subtly playing across the overhead speakers.

Adalyn's head shifted the moment the lyrics began, as a confused grin crossed her face. The music incited a romantic tone, airily performing throughout the diner.

A hand softly tapped the top of her knee, drawing her attention back to the present and pulling her from her spiraling thoughts that were fixated on the song. Tingles erupted through her body, freezing her in place. Peering into his eyes, she became both bewildered and aroused, uncertain of his motive, but enticed by his confidence.

She didn't budge from her puzzled complexion when Zack leaned in closer; she was captivated by the moment.

Spellbound, her eyes fluttered as he gazed at her lips, watching them nervously closed shut. Heart racing, she'd been craving this moment, though always abstained from instigating. Zack took his free hand, gently pressing his index and middle fingers against the side of her chin, softly directing her toward him. Biting his lip, he took in the sight of this moment like a picture in his mind.

Leaning in, his lips delicately rested on hers, and she gave in to his gentle embrace, melting like butter upon his touch.

Moments elapsed before they pulled back. Nervousness reflected in their eyes, uncertain of where this instance would lead them. An uncomfortable silence encompassed their table as their bodies shifted back from one another.

"Are you still doing well over here?" Ruby inquired, her voice zapping Zack out of his perplexed immersion.

Glancing toward Ruby, Zack imposed on their behalf. "Yes, thank you."

Turning toward the seat beside him, Adalyn had disappeared. In doing so, he did the same. Under the warm lights of Granny's Diner, their booth was left abandoned. Dishes smeared across the cloth as their untouched meals remained, cooling down from the temperate air.

CHAPTER NINE

December 14, 2014

Adalyn's street was indistinguishable in the pitch dark. The headlights of Ragnar's '98 Volkswagen Passat illuminated the pale tree trunks in front of it, nearly missing each by seconds while carefully navigating the road. Chugging up the quiet mountain, his engine slightly revved.

"Remind me why you ran?" Ragnar probed, peering through the rearview mirror at the woman in his back seat.

Adalyn's gaze fixated out the darkened window as she briefly glanced forward, making direct eye contact with him. "I-I don't know."

"But, isn't it everything you wanted?" Joyce intervened from the passenger seat as Adalyn's focus shifted toward her.

"I think?"

"Well, how do you feel?" Joyce probed at her frazzled emotions.

"Honestly, I'm not sure..." Adalyn's mouth opened as if she had more to say, only to instantly shut. She failed to provide clarification, as she was muddled by her own decisions.

It was quite clear Adalyn's adoration for Zack, and vise versa, but her admission of raw emotions seemed to come few and far between. Knowing this, Ragnar simply gave in to her relentless stubbornness, turning his full attention toward Joyce now, as they continued on with their flirty banter while approaching Adalyn's abode.

Pathway lights had been shut off, leaving the home hidden amongst the cluster of towering trees and hardly seen by the naked eye. Ragnar's headlights illuminated the girls' path toward the front door as the car doors slammed shut. Calling out, they thanked him for the ride.

"So," Adalyn began, this time probing Joyce, "what's with you two?"

"Um, I'm not sure..." A blushed smile faintly appeared across her face as the two ladies stepped beneath the automatic porch light, brightening her smitten complexion.

"Do you want to?" Adalyn hesitantly asked as she fiddled with her keys, opening the front door.

"Date him?" Joyce pondered for a moment before answering. "Maybe..."

Four clomping paws rushed down the stairway to greet them as Adalyn dropped her belongings on the entranceway table.

Turning back toward Joyce, she concealed her lingering disapproval. Deciding that it was not the right time to discuss this, she temporarily dismissed the information.

Nights dwindled into morning as the mention of Zack's name became scarce in the household over the weekend. Unprocessed emotions challenged Adalyn's sanity as she barricaded herself indoors, doing anything to avoid facing them.

As Sunday, December 14th rolled around, the landline rang.

One after another, its lasting jingle incessantly buzzed through the phone. Adalyn's hand hovered over the unit, hesitant to answer.

"Are you ever going to get it?" Joyce pressed, tightening her grasp on the coffee mug each time it rang as if it were a stress ball.

"What if it's Zack? I don't even know where to begin."

"How about a *hello*?" Aggravated, Joyce shoved the landline closer to her. "You can't avoid this forever. It's already been two days."

"Fine." Grasping the phone in her fingers, she clicked the *answer* button. "Hello?"

"Finally!" the voice on the other end exclaimed frantically. "I've been trying to get a hold of you all morning."

"Maddie?" Peering toward Joyce, she clicked the speaker button on the base unit.

"Yes? Who else? Don't you have Caller ID?"

"You'd think," Joyce mumbled under her breath.

Holding back an eye roll, Adalyn responded, "What's up, Maddie?"

"Are you home?"

"You're calling my landline."

"Oh great, because I'm halfway up the mountain now. We need to talk! See you soon." The line clicked before either was able to speak another word.

Adalyn's focus pinned on Joyce. "You're right, that wasn't terrible... It was *horrible*."

"You don't even know what she's going to tell you."

"Did it sound like great news to you?" The sarcasm rang loud, puncturing the stale air. Taking a seat on the couch, Adalyn's mind wandered to far-off places.

Taking a seat beside her, Joyce concentrated on Adalyn's expression, reading her mind through singular glimpses. The room fell into a strained silence as the ball of anxiety around Adalyn's aura expanded. Spinning like an atom, it twisted and turned, sinking her into a black hole of negative thoughts.

Her anxiety had grown exponentially by the time the doorbell finally rang, exploding all the negativity into the air as she sprung from her seat. Nearly pushing the heavy couch backward with her force, she took off for the front door, swinging it open as it clashed against the stopper.

"What's the news?"

"Let me get inside first! It's cold."

Getting up from her spot on the couch with less haste than Adalyn had, Joyce met them at the kitchen island. "She's been a ball of anxiety. She won't stop until you tell her."

"Okay, okay. But you're not going to like the news. I suggest you sit down."

Swiveling her head, Adalyn glared at Joyce. "Told you!"

"Just sit down," Joyce commanded, fed up with her ticking anxiety.

Hesitantly taking a seat on one of the bar stools against the island, she centered her attention on Maddie.

Taking her sweet time to get situated, Maddie set down her belongings on the counter, fluffed up her wind-blown hair, and even fetched a drink from the cabinet, all while Adalyn watched her pace back and forth in her kitchen.

"Maddie..." Adalyn called out, growing rather impatient.

"Sorry," she said, taking one last gulp before setting her glass down. "Alright, so I was just leaving the bakery, right?" Maddie paused, awaiting their expressions. Receiving zero feedback, she continued, "Well, I saw Zack and—" Adalyn groaned with annoyance at the mention of his name. "What?" Maddie questioned.

"Nothing," she muttered. "Continue."

"I feel like I'm missing something important here."

"No, no, it's nothing," Joyce intruded.

"Okay..." She faltered for a moment, sensing the taut air. Hesitant, she continued. "Anyways, I was leaving Kayla's bakery earlier today and caught a glimpse of Zack with some girl." She took another pause, waiting for their reactions.

Adalyn furrowed her eyebrows and adjusted her posture, sitting up in her seat. On edge with where this seemed to be leading, she leaned forward. "Who?" Adalyn began to ask, only to be interrupted by Joyce.

"Was it someone we know?"

Maddie shrugged, returning to her glass for another sip. "It was that new girl, Rose."

"Who?" Adalyn repeated.

"You don't know her?" She asked, almost astonished. "God, you're lucky!"

"I'm gonna need some more context here, Maddie," Adalyn urged as anxiety spiraled in the pit of her stomach, twisting it into a knot with each daunting moment of uncertainty that passed.

"Sorry! I don't know much about her either. She got to town a couple days ago, I think, and she's extremely annoying," Maddie casually mentioned as she took another sip. "Like, this girl cannot shut up! I met her yesterday at," she paused, attempting to recollect *where* she'd first met Rose. "I think it was at the bakery, actually."

"Well, what were they doing?" Joyce probed, reeling the woman in from her tangent.

"Oh, right! Nothing much, but she was really touchy. They passed me at the fountain."

That spiraling anxiety that spun in her stomach halted and crashed to the floor; nevertheless, she did her best to mask it.

"Are you sure?" Joyce questioned, hardly believing it.

Maddie nodded. "I know what I saw," she insisted as she took a glance down at her emptied drink.

Taking a disheartened breath, Adalyn nodded along.

Fixating on Adalyn's frozen expression, Joyce tapped her. "Adalyn, are you okay?"

Refusing to move, she'd mentally sent herself off into space, orbiting the nightmare instead of existing within. As Joyce nudged her harder, she resurfaced. "—I'm listening, sorry." Her voice waned in tone, expressing no emotion.

"What do you want to do?" Joyce questioned.

Lifting her head, Adalyn peered over at the two. Senselessly, she debated the unprocessed thought aloud, "Can we run her out?" Her tone was stiff and perhaps sarcastic.

A soft laugh left Joyce's lips, though Maddie returned with a more serious tone, "How are you thinking?"

"You can't—" Joyce began to stay.

"Actually," Maddie interrupted, "You know, I have a cousin, Cara. She could definitely get the job done!"

Joyce shot her a questioning expression lined with worry.

"Back home, she's got this reputation of making people disappear without a trace, and could totally run her out of tow—" Scanning the expressions of the room, she registered that this perhaps wasn't the correct audience for this suggestion, as the two girls' faces scrunched up with concern toward the thought. "Never mind, back-pocket idea." Taking a step down from the planning board, Maddie fell back, recovering from her misjudgment.

Joyce intervened, attempting to bring reason back into the conversation. "How about we just wait it out? It won't last. Just two days ago, he was obsessed with you. That it doesn't just go away."

Adalyn nodded, though she didn't quite agree. Shrugging it off, the thought of it all was more saddening than she led on. Their voices faded out as she stirred in her momentary bout of grief. Gazing down the hallway, her mind sent her traveling to a problem-less land, where such trivial circumstances couldn't bother her.

Having had enough of Adalyn's wallowing, Joyce interrupted her daydreaming. "Hey Addy, how about we go out to eat?"

Twiddling her fingers around the empty drink, Maddie glanced over at her. "Yeah Addy, what do you say?"

"Granny's Diner?" Joyce jested.

Maddie shot her a glare, only to be interrupted by Adalyn. "Actually, I'm not opposed."

"Granny's it is," Joyce exclaimed, playfully reveling in her victory.

Rolling her eyes, Maddie reached for her purse and keys as she made way toward the front door.

The roads were empty during this time of the year, creating a tranquil aura to the forest that permitted animals to fearlessly roam in peace amongst the city streets. Aligning with the barren roads, the diner was nearly empty. The fluorescent lights buzzed as faint music played from the jukebox in the corner, having reverted back to its original design since Friday's event.

They were seated at the same table that Ragnar and Joyce sat only two days prior, with Ruby tailing closely behind. Dressed in her typical pin-up fashion with the same antlers as Friday, she asked, "Ready ladies, or do you need a moment?"

"Actually, we're ready," Joyce impatiently stated, her gaze falling toward the others for confirmation. Maddie nodded in agreement.

Taking their orders, Ruby wrote illegible notes on her pad, then reached for the menus to clear space.

The three ladies sat in sullen silence. Though they were able to escape the house, they couldn't seem to escape the situation.

They jolted up as Ruby clanked three milkshake mugs down onto the tabletop and set down their food, the wax paper of their burger baskets crinkling. "Anything else I can get you?" she asked.

"No, thank you," Joyce replied.

With conversation scarce, Maddie perked up. "So Joyce…"

Joyce turned to face her, raising an eyebrow. "Yes?" she questioned with unease.

"I heard you were here with Ragnar on a date the other night?" she probed.

A blushed grin formed across her face as she defensively asked, "What about it?"

"Is it true?" she pressed. "Are you dating him?"

"Maybe." Loosening up from her curt tone, she proceeded with a shrug. "I think so."

A playful smirk formed on Maddie's face. Opening her mouth, she was rudely interrupted by high-pitched vocal cords calling out to her.

"Maddie!" Their heads simultaneously cocked toward the noise, irritated by the abrupt interruption.

"Rose…" Maddie's dry tone dragged at the end, indicative of her irked state.

Adalyn momentarily perked up to the mention of her name, stunned by the woman's appearance. Rose was nothing like what she had imagined; sadly, she was prettier than Adalyn had hoped. Still, it was immediately obvious that she was a naive woman. Younger in maturity than she was in age, it was that lack of maturity that irked her most.

"It's such a coincidence to see you here!"

"Yeah!" Maddie's eyes were void of emotion as she feigned excitement. "It's a small town… I'm not that surprised."

"Oh, well sure." Fiddling with a strand of her fire-engine red hair, Rose glanced around the table at the other girls' stoic expressions. "Uh, do you mind if I join you guys?" she asked as she was already touching the back of the empty chair.

They motioned for her to take the seat. Wedging herself into it, she was clearly oblivious of her intrusion as her hair nearly slapped Joyce across the face when she sat.

Adalyn loved that Dawn Hills was small, but in instances like this, it was too small.

"So, what are your names?" the young lady asked, panning her focus between Adalyn and Joyce, who in return, silently stared at one another.

"I'm Adalyn," she finally spoke up, lifting her hand in a singular wave.

"It's lovely to meet you! I've actually heard mention of you all around town."

"Pleasure." Adalyn's tone implied otherwise. "This is Joyce." She motioned, directing Rose toward the other woman.

"Wonderful to meet you all. Zack told me a lot about you guys."

"How do you know Zack?" Adalyn asked with withheld emotions and feigned obliviousness.

"Oh, he's just been showing me around town! He's been very sweet. And you're his best friend, right?"

"I guess that's me," she mumbled.

"You know, we really must be going, Adalyn," Maddie intruded. Refusing to relinquish her glare at Rose, she tugged at Adalyn.

Picking up on the subtle queues, Joyce stepped in. "Yeah, we have that... *thing*."

Rising from the table, Adalyn turned to her. "It was a pleasure to meet you. Tell Zack I say *hello*."

CHAPTER TEN

December 16, 2014

A unique knock at the front door greeted Tuesday morning with a spirited figure. As Adalyn's heels clicked against the floorboards while they crossed the hallway, she stopped in the entryway when she saw the woman's silhouette bouncing around outside.

With an exhausted sigh, Adalyn took a deep breath and cracked open the door.

"Adalyn!" Rose's exuberant nature beamed upon arrival. Her energetic eagerness shrilled the placid air, compensating for her overbearing personality.

"Good morning, Rose." Adalyn's voice falsely simulated an equally merry tone. "Why are you on my front porch? Actually, how do you even know where I live?"

Rose simply giggled. "You're so funny!" Stepping into the house uninvited, she set her purse down on the entry table. "I actually need your help."

Adalyn was taken aback by the lady's intrusive nature, stepping back as Rose helped herself inside. "I was actually just about to leave to go get brunch..."

"Oh, great! I am so hungry, let's go eat!"

"I—uh..." It was no use. Rose was out the door and half way down the pathway.

There was a brief moment that Adalyn pondered just shutting it on her, though she feared the woman would just wait for her to leave, and with how insistent she was, it seemed more daunting than a brunch.

Grabbing her purse and coat, she followed the woman out of the house.

"So, where are we eating?"

"Well, it's winter, so that leaves us with limited options."

"Yeah, I noticed that around town. Why is that?"

Adalyn shrugged. "Not enough consistent residents to keep all the shops and restaurants open year-round, so we only leave a few open for casual dining and shopping." Rose scrunched up her nose to the idea. "You're from the city, aren't you?" Adalyn questioned with an irritated undertone.

Rose nodded. She didn't respond with words, which was a first, though Adalyn was smart enough not to question it.

The young lady's pink little Ford sedan beeped as it unlocked, and Adalyn's face cringed at the sight of it, but she got in anyway. It was a beater-car, to say the least, and she couldn't tell which was worse, the shot suspension as it drove down the gravel roads, or the dashboard that lit up like a Christmas tree.

Surviving the perilous car ride in one piece, they stood at the base of Granny's stairs.

"Hey, this is where we met the other night!"

"Mhm." Adalyn coldly responded as she hiked up the few steps.

Pulling open the front door, Rose's jade green eyes scanned the restaurant with wonderment, as if she hadn't just been there the day before. So much seemed to fascinate the young lady, both making it hard to stay resentful and just as equally causing a pit of hatred in Adalyn's stomach.

Locking eyes with Ruby, Adalyn motioned toward her reserved booth and took a seat.

"Okay," Adalyn started to say as she played with her napkin, "what do you need help with?"

Diverting her attention away from the consistent astonishment at every insignificant thing, she looked at Adalyn. "Oh uh..." For the first time since Adalyn had met her, Rose showed the first hint of insecurity as she compiled her words. "I am sort of being kicked out of the Inn..."

"And what can I do about this predicament?" Adalyn questioned with an annoyed confusion. Perhaps she was expecting something a bit more urgent.

"I was kinda hoping you could—"

At that moment, Adalyn could not have been more thankful for Ruby's intrusion. Interrupting their chatter by setting down two glasses of water, she pulled out her notepad.

"Hey ladies, are you ready to order?"

"Yes!" Adalyn urged as she played with the sides of the menu. "Can I just get a coffee for now?" Originally coming for a full meal, her appetite had incrementally depleted since Rose showed up at her doorstep.

"I'll take a cookies 'n cream shake, please!" Rose blurted. It was a noticeably odd order to request so early in the day, yet fitting for the young lady. Jotting it down, Ruby hastily dismissed herself, and a silence brushed over the two.

"You were saying?" Adalyn finally pressed after no advances were taken.

"Oh, right! I was hoping you could get me one of those job things somewhere."

"*Job things?*" Adalyn repeated, finding that verbiage rather peculiar for a grown woman. Rose nodded with a faded grin. Quirking an eyebrow, Adalyn tilted her head in confusion, knowing she would regret her next question. "Rose, have you ever had a job before?"

"Does modeling count?" she questioned with uncertainty.

Pondering it for a moment, Adalyn shrugged. "I suppose. Do you have any other experience?"

"Experience in what?"

"A job..." Adalyn uttered with a hint of contempt. It felt as if she was talking to a goldfish; something that couldn't seem to hold a thought for more than a fleeting second.

"Oh!" there was a pause. "No."

Furrowing her eyebrows, she was confused as to how this lady survived for so long on her own. "Ho-how do you manage to not have a job? You're what, twenty something?"

Quietly setting the two drinks down on the table Ruby smiled as she quickly sped off, careful to not interrupt the conversation.

Reaching for her drink, Rose twisted the red straw in between her thumb and index fingers. There was hesitation in her tone, a moment of timidity. "Twenty-one," Rose quietly corrected.

With this new information, Adalyn's demeanor softened. "Alright," she finally said. "How long do you have at the Inn?"

"Until the end of the week."

Adalyn simply nodded. "Alright then. Give me a couple days, and I'll see what I can do."

A content smile emerged across Rose's lips as she took her first sip of her shake with ease. Returning it with a half-hearted smile, Adalyn dipped her spoon in her coffee and stirred it, enjoying the brief period of silence. Knowing it would be interrupted at any moment, she was not surprised when Rose glanced over at her and asked, "So, what do you do for fun around here?"

Setting her spoon on the saucer, she took a sip as she pondered her answer. "There's a lot to do here—well, not really in the winter."

"Oh. Then what do you do in the wintertime?"

Thinking back to the previous winter, she replied, "Actually, I travel." Naturally, this answer introduced a whirlwind of questions.

"To where? Where all have you been? What's your favorite place?" Each question launched out of her mouth like a hailstorm of bullets, frazzling Adalyn.

"Uh," she began, not even remembering a singular question when she was done asking. "I guess it's been quite some time since I traveled last, but I enjoy making it out to visit my friend on his island."

"*His* island?"

"I misspoke," Adalyn interrupted. "Henry is a friend of mine who'd recently moved to some island in the Pacific. But again, it's been quite some time."

"Please tell me more!" Like a child at story time, she leaned in, resting her elbows on the table and her head in her palms.

"There isn't much else to tell. He's just a good friend; very kind and sweet. When he makes it onto the mainland, he stops by to say hello, and then sometimes, I go back with him for a few months to visit."

"What's he like?"

Without thinking, Adalyn bullet-pointed a brief description of him, "Tall, milk-brown hair, creamy-brown eyes, a glistening smile..."

Rose caught on to her dreamy stare. "Oh, I can imagine!"

Adalyn smiled, feeling almost uncomfortable with her comprehensive questions. Switching the conversation off her, she asked, "What about you? What do you typically like to do?"

"Hmm..." Rose pondered, and in that instance, Adalyn immediately regretted asking. "I really enjoy singing. My mom taught me when I was younger. I got pretty good at piano as a kid, but I'm not sure how much I remember of that...oh, and I love dating!"

Setting her mug down from taking a sip, Adalyn looked at her with a skeptical stare, though dismissed the comment. Adalyn opened her mouth to speak, but Rose casually interrupted.

"So, I met Ragnar the other day! Is he always that sarcastic?" she questioned as she took another sip of her drink.

Adalyn laughed. Perhaps for the first time since meeting Rose, as her laugh caused Rose to light up with delight. "I think so!"

Nodding, Rose went in for another sip. Her eyes naturally wandered, scanning the walls of all its memorabilia.

"Do you have family here?" Adalyn's question interrupted Rose's daze while she raised her cup to her lips.

"No, I don't really have a family…"

The sudden shift in mood quieted Adalyn as she recognized the masked dolefulness. "Oh. I'm sorry."

Rose shrugged the conversation into silence as she continued sipping her shake. Noise of thunderous slurping broke the still air, drawing attention to the redhead's drink as she sipped only air now. Glancing at the clock on the wall, the minute hand had hardly moved since their arrival, yet the event felt rather long.

"What are you doing after this?" Adalyn asked, feeling guilty of her previous question.

"I'm supposed to meet Zack. But I haven't heard—"

"Oh!" Adalyn cut Rose off, accidentally overlooking the last part. "Sounds lovely."

"It's exciting, but what new love isn't?"

"Yeah. What new love *isn't*?" Adalyn repeated with a mocking undertone that Rose didn't catch.

"I actually haven't spok—" Rose began, though Adalyn was quick to change the topic.

"How long are you planning to stay in town?" she asked, swiftly adding in, "I only ask so I know more details about your dilemma."

"I don't know! I was just passing through initially, but I wouldn't mind staying a minute."

Opening her mouth to speak, a rhythmic chime went off interrupting Adalyn's train of thought. Following the sound, their focus diverted to the young lady's phone. "I-I'm so sorry! I really need to take this," Rose said, reaching for the phone and sliding out of her seat.

Adalyn nodded with a forced smile in reply. Waiting for her to return, Adalyn glanced up at the clock on the wall. *Eleven-thirty.* Time was ticking by awfully slowly.

"Can I clear this off?" Ruby's voice interrupted, drawing Adalyn's attention.

Briefly peering over her shoulder, she watched Rose chat on the phone. The conversation seemed serious, though she couldn't bother to indulge. Turning back around, she nodded. "Yes. Thank you, Ruby!"

By the time Rose returned, her typically bubbly expression had faded.

"I'm sorry about that! I have an emergency. I have to run... would—"

"Go!" Adalyn insisted. "Don't worry about me!"

"Are you sure? I was sorta your ride..."

Adalyn had forgotten about that part, but perhaps it was better that she didn't have to listen to Rose all the way back up the mountain. "I'll be fine," she insisted. "I have to get back to the office, anyway."

"If you're sure... but this brunch has been so much fun! Can we do it again sometime?"

"It was a lovely brunch, we really *should* do it again," Adalyn replied, though not quite sure if she meant it. It hadn't been as horrid as she'd imagined, but Rose was still insufferable.

Sliding out of the booth, they both made their way toward the front door.

"Thank you again, Addy."

"I prefer Adalyn..."

"Okay, Adalyn." Pausing at the front door, she glanced back at the table. "Oh, did we need to—"

"It'll go on my tab," Adalyn clarified, brushing it off.

"Thank you!" She beamed.

Adalyn simply nodded her head. Watching the girl take off in a hurry, she turned to walk in the direction of the Architect building. She'd lied about having to get back to work so as to not make Rose feel guilty, leaving Adalyn to wander the streets instead, casually pondering how she'd get back home without the help of Rose's car.

Christmas lights strung overhead, bouncing back and forth from the building tops, creating a canopy effect upon the street below. Street lights were recently decked with red and white tinsel to resemble candy canes and wreaths hung from hooks all around. Potted poinsettias became a familiar sight around town, and plastic mistletoe was suspended above nearly every doorway, forcing the age-old tradition to continue on. The road was packed with small bundles of snow that lined the sidewalks as she strolled down.

Passing down the main streets, she stopped just before the alleyway of York and Main, where two familiar voices spoke in a hush. Curiosity getting the best of her, she crept just into listening range.

"We need to talk!" Rose aggressively asserted.

Ragnar tilted his head, "Hello, Rose. You know, it's always nice to show a little courtesy before rushing in, but very well. What do we *need* to talk about?"

"I just finished brunch with Adalyn and I need to know: Who is this Henry guy?"

"Bizarrely out of place, but he is an old friend of hers."

Despite being reclusive himself, Henry was admittedly an important piece in Adalyn's past. As the topic was out of place, it piqued Adalyn's interest, curious as to why the discussion's focus remained on her.

"Does she love him?" Rose pried.

"I suspect so. But if you ask her, she'll deny it, no doubt."

"Does he love her?"

"I couldn't know," Ragnar replied nonchalantly. "I don't know him that well."

"Final question," she stated as if playing a game of trivial jeopardy. "Is it true that you like Joyce?"

Adalyn scrunched her face in confusion at Rose's intrusiveness as she remained silent and hidden amongst the dumpsters against the brick walls, listening intently.

"Don't you find that question to be a bit imposing?" he replied with a smug tone.

"Maybe, but an answer?"

"If you want the truth, then yes. I do."

"Are you going to ask her out?"

"I already did." He remained clear in his intentions, revoking any abilities for her to tamper with his plans.

Believing that to be the end of her interrogation, Ragnar nearly turned to walk away; however, she asked one last question that halted him. "What about Zack?"

Surprised by the question, Adalyn's heart rate increased. She was almost fearful that the young lady had unraveled a capsule of emotions that both parties clearly buried.

"Miss, I thought that was your last question." Rose shrugged, clearly still expecting an answer. "What of him?" Drawn back in, Ragnar became uneasy as to where she was leading the conversation.

"Does she love him?"

He looked at her for a brief second before entertaining her curiosity. "Rose, you surely have acquired a *talent* for asking unanswerable questions. I *don't* know. Maybe you ought to ask her?" His response remained dutifully loyal to his friend. She nodded, defeated. "Why do you ask?"

She casually shrugged. "We've kind of been growing close lately and I've maybe been seeing him..."

This, above all else, truly piqued Adalyn's interest. However, a dull ache grew in her chest, sharpening with each beat. It was as if delicate fragments of her heart began to chip away.

Rose's voice cut through the air, reminding her of where she was.

"Thank you. You've been... *helpful*." Rose hardly meant it, but finally ceased her incessant questioning. As quickly as she'd come, Rose swiftly retreated from the alleyway..

Adalyn listened to Ragnar's receding footsteps following behind Rose as he, too, exited the alleyway, leaving Adalyn unaccompanied under the pale afternoon sky.

CHAPTER ELEVEN

December 17, 2014

About three blocks southwest of the center of Main, a tiny frontage road splintered off of Maplewood Drive, following the bank of Crystal Pond until it stopped just outside a dirt lot. To some, this was a second home, while others found it a grimy log building, well past its prime. This was the Rusty Saloon, a gritty dive bar of chipped paint and broken men. However, the pool tables that lined the center of the venue were a rather nice touch. On most nights, Adalyn wouldn't be caught dead in such an establishment, but tonight she made an exception.

Having borrowed her car back from Zack for the day, she pulled off Maplewood Drive and onto that frontage road. The dimly lit streets were typically filled with laughter and music, but this evening, they were eerily still. Continuing on, a sense of discomfort tightened in her chest.

Rounding the last corner, she was met with the unexpected glow of ambulance lights that flickered through the dense trees. Such a sight wasn't uncommon for the joint, but something about this occasion brought on a heightened sense of worry. Picking up her pace, she threw her car in park and stepped out, only to be met with the prominent scent of stale beer and damp perspiration.

Nearing the scene, her eyes scanned the crowd that had begun to gather around two ambulances. She was searching for a familiar face—a specific face, amidst the chaos. Shoving her way through the spectators with a sense of urgency, she spotted a figure she recognized. It wasn't the one she was looking for, but it would do.

"Mike!" she called out.

Turning around, it must've taken him a moment to place her unforgettable face amongst the crowd, yet when he did, he seemed to lighten up upon her appearance. "Well, well, well," he began with wonderment.

"Save it," Adalyn giggled as a soft blush formed on her cheeks. Motioning with a nod of the head, she directed them back to the ambulances. "What happened?"

"Two dudes started goin' at it inside the bar over some girl. The typical shit." He casually shrugged, displaying a lack of remorse.

"Jeez," she gasped. Straining her neck to see, she surveyed the crowd with an underlying sense of panic. Peering back over at him, she pressed, "Did you recognize any of them?" She watched his facial expressions change as he reflected back on it. However, the seconds were ticking by and she was growing impatient. "Mike?" she pried.

"Yeah, I think," he finally said. "No regulars by any means, but I think I've seen one come by every now and again, but the couple were new faces."

"Oh, there was a couple?"

"Yeah, that's what I said. Why are you so interested?"

"Well, I was supposed to meet a friend here... Maybe he hasn't arrived." There was an inkling of skepticism scratching at her tone. Although the description didn't quite seem to fit the bill, a gut-wrenching feeling of concern slowly trickled in, and her mind couldn't seem to depart from the idea that he could be hurt.

"What does he look like?" Mike questioned, pulling her focus back to the present.

"Uh," she began rambling her bullet-pointed list as her eyes continued to surf the crowd a moment longer. "A bit taller than me, but not by much with short, brown hair and intensely hazel eyes. He has a perpetual sense of bewilderment?"

An unpleasant expression formed on Mike's face as he quickly inhaled his breath through his teeth, letting out an inverted *hiss*. Her face immediately dropped and her heart started to race.

"Don't tell me..." Her tone carried a sense of pressing urgency, engulfing her with an overwhelming sense of panic.

"With a jawline that could cut raw steak?" Mike inquired.

She nodded with a look of solemn defeat as he mirrored her. Bobbing his head slowly, their gazes panned over to the scene. Rolling her head back in disbelief, one might perceive her as inconvenienced, however, beyond this visible response, she bore immense worry. Scoping out the area for an opening, her legs reacted before her mind could, sending her barreling through the crowd. It was luck that it spit her out on the other end of the horde.

Eyes locked on the ambulances' flashing lights, she ignored all the inaudible chatter and sprinted toward the commotion. With each stride, her mind skimmed over every worst case-scenario, until she saw him.

Sitting under the white modular lights that illuminated the grounds, he was wrapped up in a blanket on the bumper of the first ambulance, shivering against the December air. An unintentional smile crept onto her face as she recognized he was alright. Slowing her pace to calm her racing heart, she approached him.

Panning his gaze over to her, he must've seen her from his peripheral.

"Hey." A sheepish grin emerged across his face.

"When you said you'd beat me at pool, I didn't know you meant literally," she jested as she took a seat beside him. For such a shoddy joke, even he laughed. "You doin' okay?"

Looking over at him, she examined the damage. A couple gashes cut across his upper cheek, chin, and above the brow, his knuckles were bruised and slashed, and aside from the way he attempted to hide it, it was obvious he was avoiding putting weight on his left leg. She wanted to pry; she knew he was hiding the pain, but preeminently, she knew he'd deny it.

"I'm fine," he assured with a half-hearted smile. "How'd it go today with the car?" he asked, clearly averting from further questioning.

"Well, it's all in one piece!" she quipped.

"That's good," he said through a couple of breathy laughs.

"Thanks again for letting me borrow it." Readjusting her position on the ambulance's bumper, she leaned back against the doorframe. "What'd you end up doing today after I left?"

His mind scrambled from the past hour's events, what he'd done earlier seemed but a distant memory. "I just hung around town," he responded after a few moments. "I ran some quick errands, and what-not."

She nodded as a silence settled between them. Peering over at the building, she reverted back to the previous topic. "So, I heard it was a bar fight." Quirking her eyebrows in disbelief, she was inclined to ask more.

"Yeah, sorta. It's a long story…"

Glancing around, she looked back over at him with a sympathetic smile. "Well, we've got nothing but time." Picking up a damp cloth that rested in between them, she dabbed away a small bubble of blood that pooled from one of the cuts.

"Just to clarify, I didn't start it!"

"That's good," she laughed. "Who did?"

He motioned toward the other ambulance, where a tall and robust, twenty-some year old towered over a paramedic that worked to bandage a deep gash across his upper arm. She could've sworn Mike mentioned a female there, yet looking over, she found no trace—either she'd never been there, or was long gone by now.

Turning back to him, she furrowed her brows. "I don't recognize him. Do you know him?"

Zack nodded. "His name's Bryce." She waited for further information, but he abstained from answering.

Letting it be, she reverted back to her previous question. "So what on earth would warrant a bar fight with him?"

Adjusting the position of his injured leg, he let out a pained grunt. "Well…" he started to say, though there was some hesitancy tugging at his tone. He cleared his throat. "He was making these offensive remarks, and—"

"About what?" she accidentally interrupted with curiosity. A momentary stillness crept over them, and she questioned if he'd heard her. "Zack?"

Warranting a reaction, he just looked at her with a raised brow, asd if to say *you know;* as if to say, *you.*

For some reason, it astounded her that he'd to go to such lengths for her. A subtle smile emerged, and she tried to suppress it, given the circumstances.

Sniffling from the cold December air, he bit his lip. "I knew him from the last town I was in," he finally responded. Recollecting a more chronological timeline, he began to explain from the start of the evening. "I'd gotten here early and was waiting inside when he showed up and decided to run his mouth with a slew of—" he paused. Glancing over at the bar, he casually commented, "He can dish it, but he can't take it." Exhaling an airy chuckle, he looked back at her. "That's when he threw the first punch."

"Oh..." she replied. "Okay, not as bad as I was thinking." Scanning the scene, she asked, "So, are you in trouble or getting help or anything? What are we waiting on?"

He shook his head regarding both questions. "They were supposed to bring me water."

"That's it?"

He nodded, though he was lying. He'd denied medical attention shortly before she'd arrived. "Sorry."

"For what?" she questioned.

"I asked you to meet me here, and—"

A singular *ha* escaped her lips. "I don't mind." Glancing up toward the sky, then down at her phone, she pursed her lips together.

"What's up," he asked as he read her expressions.

"Well, it's only ten…"

"Yeah?"

"The night's still young, and I'm still hungry," she smirked. "How about take-out?"

"From where?" His question was answered as her eyes trailed over toward the bar, and he chuckled. "Really? From the place I just got kicked out of?"

"Why not? I didn't! I can go get the food."

With a raised brow and a shrug, he motioned toward the bar. "Be my guest!"

Hopping off the back of the ambulance, she dusted herself off and glanced back at him. "I'll be gone a minute, don't do anything stupid!"

"I can't promise that, Chica," he quipped.

"Chica? That's a new one," she laughed. "I like it." Turning around, she began her short trek over to the bar.

Sauntering up to the register, it was as if he was in two places at once.

"Mike," she exclaimed.

"Hey," he greeted. "Did you find the guy you were looking for?"

She nodded with a friendly grin. "I just came to place an order, if you're open."

"Definitely." Closing the cash register, he pulled out a notepad. "What can I get you?"

"Just a meat pizza to go?"

Jotting it down, he glanced up with a widened grin. "Comin' right up in five!"

With all the commotion happening outside, the inside was nearly empty; the emptiest she'd ever seen it, in fact. The pool table had remained untampered with from the previous game, and drinks remained scattered amongst the floor, drowning the hardwood in a sticky mess. Even the stools were still knocked over from the scuffle.

She explored the bar, perhaps inspecting what'd gone down during the fight. Starting in the far corner, the spills were the messiest, and cleaner as it spread further away. Stools were toppled, perhaps even purposefully shuffled during the commotion, and a few pool sticks were thrown about the room.

Pulled from her investigation, Mike hollered for her. "Your order's ready!"

Discarding the rest, she made her way toward the counter. Exchanging a small wad of cash for the pizza, she took one last look around the bar before departing.

Outside again, she held the box up like a trophy prize won, and Zack, in his poorly bruised state, laughed.

"Lookie what I got!" Her enthusiasm was met with an exuberant grin. Lowering the box back down to her side, she looked at him. He hadn't moved since she'd left, drawing realization to the suspicion that he may be downplaying his pain. "Are you sure you're alright?"

Rising to his feet, a subtle wince crossed his face, which he swiftly masked with a forced smile and a head nod. "I'm good, just a bruised leg."

"We can take it at your pace," she offered, but he refused. "So, you trust me to drive?" Her tone held a playful sarcasm as she reached for the keys from her pockets.

Jokingly side-eyeing her, he wasn't quite in the position to argue, though there was a hint of doubt in her abilities. Nevertheless, they began their walk to the car, leaving the pesky flashing lights and incessant chatter behind them, as if it was but a minute affair.

CHAPTER TWELVE

December 19, 2014

Smoke rose from Adalyn's chimney that evening while the light from the flames danced against the walls. There was something about the winter weather that brought on a particular mood for hanging decorations. With holiday tunes echoing throughout the abode, two silhouettes danced through the living room.

"Adalyn, where should I put this?" Maddie asked, holding up a vine of green garland.

"Across the mantle," she responded, peering over her shoulder as she began to unbox the Christmas tree.

Weaving it through the other decorations and photographs, Maddie ornamented the bushy garland. "Does this look good?"

Adalyn peered over once more and nodded as she unwrapped the faux tree from its box. Dragging its pieces onto the empty space near the window, she laid it all out. "Ready for the tree?"

Maddie hovered over, remembering how difficult it was to put up last year. "What time is Kayla supposed to get in tonight?"

Adalyn momentarily discarded the decorations and made her way into the kitchen. Setting the water kettle on the stove, she peered at the time. "In a few hours, I think. She left yesterday from her family's estate in Maine. We could wait for her before putting up the tree, if you want."

"I only think it's fair that we suffer as a team," Maddie joked, avoiding it at all costs. "You know, upscale Maine really suits her. Isn't it in the Eastern District?"

"Yeah," Adalyn responded as she cleaned off the counter.

"Is it true it's a mansion?"

"Would you be shocked? It's Kayla!"

The kettle hissed, interrupting their conversation. "In the meantime... hot cocoa?"

"Yes, please!" Adalyn gently slid a mug of cocoa toward Maddie. Standing around the island, they listened to the faint jingle of Christmas music that rang throughout the room. "What else is left for decorations?" Maddie asked, breaking up the silence.

"Since we're waiting for Kayla to get here, not a whole lot."

"Is she coming straight here?"

"I was under that impression."

"Without stopping at home first?" Maddie questioned.

"I don't know, she just said she'd be here, as in *here*, around six."

Maddie's eyebrows raised. "What do we do in the meantime?"

Adalyn's gaze flitted around, peering at the half-decorated living room. "We could finish hanging up all the garland?"

"That works!" Maddie set her mug down on the counter, leaving it to cool down.

Within no time, the floors became coated in the garland's faux leaves that notoriously flaked off. Following behind them, Rocky chased it around the house, nipping at its buds. His youthful play was rewarded with an abundance of laughter and merriment that dispersed through the atmosphere.

While they finished the last string, a soft knock tapped against Adalyn's front door. "I'll get it," she hollered, jogging into the entranceway. Cracking the door open, she emitted an excited screech. "Kayla!"

"Hi, Addy!" Kayla wrapped her arms around the woman, pulling her in for a tightened hug.

"Maddie, get in here," Adalyn hollered through constricted breaths. Running in, she also joined in the friendly embrace.

Pulling out of the group hug, Maddie stated, "We left the tree just for you."

"How fantastic," Kayla teasingly grunted. She gazed around at the decorations. "It looks great here, though."

"Thanks, we just hung the garland. The tree is for all of us!"

"It's tradition," Adalyn chimed in.

"But of course..." Kayla giggled, knowing well the hassle that that tree has caused them. "So, where's your new roommate, Joyce?" she asked as she scanned the house.

Slowly leading them out of the entryway and back into the kitchen, she peered over her shoulder. "She's with Ragnar right now."

"Why?"

"They're dating," Maddie casually commented, taking a seat on the island stool.

Kayla went wide-eyed. "Really? Ragnar?" She glanced over at Adalyn. "How do you feel about that?"

Adalyn groaned as she leaned against the kitchen island. "I hate it. I don't approve."

"You know, I've been meaning to ask, why don't you approve?" Maddie questioned.

"It's... weird. He's like my brother, and..." Adalyn curled her upper lip in disgust. "I can't explain it, but it's just weird to me. I hate seeing them get all touchy feely and making out in my kitchen."

The two girls subtly nodded. Suddenly, Kayla exclaimed, "Speaking of dating..." Her voice held intrigue as she panned over to Adalyn.

Cringing, she moaned. "Oh no... don't even go there!"

"Wait, what?" Maddie pressed, feeling out of the loop.

"Adalyn and I have been sending letters to each other, and let's just say that there's some interesting claims about Zack that she made in here."

"What! Addy, you didn't even tell me?" Maddie turned back toward Kayla. "What do they say?"

"Please..." Adalyn nervously giggled, burying her face in her palms. Her cheeks turned a bright cherry red.

"I'll have to pull them out of my bag," Kayla spoke, making her way toward the couch. Her satchel still dangled from her left shoulder as she moved toward a place where she could access the pocket better.

Maddie followed eagerly behind her, leaving Adalyn alone in the kitchen. "God, why did I have to send you any of those?"

"Please," Kayla protested, "they're fantastic. The most passionate I've seen you be toward someone." Adalyn groaned.

"Please, read," Maddie pressed.

Kayla fumbled through her purse in search of the letters. "Hang on. But while I look," Kayla's gaze turned toward Maddie, "Max?"

"You told her?" Maddie exclaimed, turning to Adalyn.

"Oh, please. It's talk of the town," Adalyn brushed it off.

"It's actually not the first time I heard about it, Maddie. Arabella and Adam even mentioned it. There were so many rumors that I picked up through the grapevine."

"Like what?" Maddie questioned.

"Well, the starting one is Adalyn and Zack." Adalyn groaned once more. "You can't deny it, Addy," Kayla teased playfully.

Adalyn attempted to switch topics. "Where are Adam and Arabella, by the way? Are they coming back?"

"They will, but they're actually traveling right now. Things got a little too heated at my parents' for them."

"How so?"

"My family can be a bit tough, and Adam is just my half-brother, so my mom's side was a bit harsh. It definitely strained their relationship."

"Well, hopefully they'll mend things," Adalyn stated.

After some time, Adalyn slowly crept into the living room, now leaning against the arm of the couch. "Last Christmas" faintly echoed in the background, seeming to grow louder as they fell more silent. Waiting for Kayla to dig through her bag, Adalyn nervously watched the television's screensaver which showed lush scenery as the fireplace cracked below.

"So, Addy," Kayla began, "how do you feel about Zack?" Adalyn groaned yet again. "Come on, it's just us! Admit that you like him!" Kayla pressed.

"Kayla..." Adalyn fussed.

"Oh Addy, it's so obvious," Maddie said.

"Most of your letters are about him. I have evidence here, somewhere."

"I don't even know if I like him anymore!" Adalyn argued, causing Kayla to raise a brow in question. Taking a deep sigh, she continued, "I overheard Rose talking about him, and I think they're dating..."

"Wait, when did that happen?" Kayla asked.

"Ugh, I haven't told anyone yet, but it was the other day after we got brunch together..."

"Ew, you got brunch with Rose?" Maddie quizzed.

"She invited herself..." Adalyn protested. "Either way, I think it's clear where Zack stands."

Emitting a defeated sigh, Kayla replied, "But you haven't asked *him*, and he obviously cares about you. Especially based on what your letters told me about the carnival, and the *car*."

"I know," Adalyn huffed.

"Oh," Kayla exclaimed, her fingers landing on the small stack of letters. "Got them!"

"Read, read," Maddie pressed. Adalyn grunted and glared at her friend in disapproval. "Addy, I gotta know!"

"Here! How about this line," Kayla began, holding up a piece of paper. "*I won't admit that I like him, but I'm not denying it.* Come on, Addy, just admit it."

Adalyn stuck her fingers against her ears. "You girls are insane!"

"How about this one? *I admit, he's not a bad kisser.*"

"Wait, when was that?" Maddie questioned.

Face buried in her palms again, Adalyn muffled, "That one was like, last week, after Zack and I kissed."

"See, you even kissed him. This is only a glimpse of what I have in these letters. You poured your heart out in these, and it's fantastic," Kayla exclaimed.

Adalyn's face remained a blushed pink. "You guys are the worst." She didn't mean what she said; however, the embarrassment sunk deep.

"Really, Addy, it's great. We give you so much shit, but it's because I've never seen you this passionate about someone." Kayla's playful tone turned kind.

"It's really great, Addy," Maddie chimed in. "Over the last few months that you've been spending time with him, you're like completely different—in a good way!"

"In the last three or four years that we've known you, we've never seen you this happy," Kayla comforted.

Adalyn lifted her head out of her palms, shaking her hands frantically. "No, no! Guys, it doesn't matter anymore. He's with Rose."

Kayla disregarded Adalyn's doubts. "Every single thing you've told me about him says otherwise."

"Like what?"

"Like, the carnival. No man acts like that and does that if they're just friends. And if you don't believe me, how about the time you crashed his precious car into a ravine and he didn't even raise his voice?"

Adalyn conceded, knowing well that Kayla was correct. Attempting to divert from the conversation, her eyes fell to the unbuilt tree that still lay up against the window. "We still have to put up the tree."

Kayla refrained from pushing Adalyn any further, as she knew that it wouldn't be long before she became closed off. Her eyes followed Adalyn's as she emitted a soft sigh. "We should probably get to that."

The girls rose from the couch and walked toward the disassembled tree, inspecting its parts.

"This doesn't look too bad," Maddie said, attempting to persuade not only Kayla, but herself, as well.

"We've done it once, how hard could it be?" Kayla optimistically replied.

Adalyn silently bent down beside its base and picked up the bottom layer, placing it on the stand. Attaching each layer to the last, the three girls fluffed the wired leaves that were stuck together, doing so until they reached the top.

Maddie paused and admired the work they'd put in, as the clock in the entryway chimed ten. Kayla glanced over and paused as well, admiring the familiar tree that they battled with every year. "Remember when we did this the first year Dawn Hills was established?" Kayla asked.

"I do," Maddie responded. "Remember when this house was hardly a home back then, Addy?" Adalyn nodded.

"So much has changed since then," Kayla chimed in.

Emitting a sigh, Adalyn simply replied, "The good ole days..." Her gaze returned to the undecorated tree. "Alright, let's finish this off!"

White Christmas lights adorned nearly every branch from top to bottom, and dangling in between the branches were ornaments of all shapes and sizes. Acquired over time, most ornaments were tied to a memory, while others held a place for empty branches. The tree stood directly in front of the enormous living room window. Emitting its festive glow, the girls placed wrapped presents underneath and an angel on top.

The clock chimed one as they'd stepped away from the tree. Taking in their accomplishment, they returned to the couch, where they sipped on spiked hot cocoa and nibbled on cookies. Curled under cozy blankets, they basked under the warmth of the fireplace. Eyes slowly drifting off to sleep, the lulling carol of "Winter Wonderland" jingled in the background.

CHAPTER THIRTEEN

December 20, 2014

The clock struck nine when the girls were whisked away from their slumber. Awoken by a pounding on the front door, their foggy minds sought to comprehend their surroundings.

"Who's knocking so early?" Maddie groggily asked.

Rubbing her eyes, Kayla gradually sat up. "Who's going to get the door?"

"I will..." Adalyn huffed, grabbing the side of her pounding head.

Wrapped in the cozy blanket, her bare feet touched the ice-cold floor. Shivers went up her spine, forcing her to walk on her tip-toes as she scurried towards the entryway. Cracking the door open, she stood behind it to block the crisp winter air.

Her expression widened at his unexpected appearance on her doorstep. "Zack?"

"Hey, do you have a moment?"

"I, um…" Her gaze wandered down the hallway. Repositioning, she braced herself against the chilly air as she blocked off the entrance.

"Or, maybe coffee or lunch later?"

She pondered it for a moment, his underlying sense of urgency intriguing her. "A-alright," she finally said. "Let's get coffee later."

"Great!"

"Can you come back in like an hour, though? I still have to get ready, and if you can't tell," she motioned toward the driveway packed with cars, "I still have visitors."

Hesitant, he obliged. "I'll be back in an hour, then."

"An hour," she repeated, closing the door.

She turned back toward the living room, where two eager faces stared her down. Nestled in their blankets, they sat on the couch, awaiting Adalyn's return.

"Who is that?" Maddie probed.

"Just Zack."

"*Just?*" Maddie insisted. "What was he asking?"

"To get coffee later," she dryly replied as she took a seat on the couch.

"Well, are you gonna go with him?"

Before Adalyn had a moment to respond, Kayla interrupted, "You better have said yes!"

She giggled toward the girl's reaction and nodded. "He's coming back in like an hour to pick me up."

"Okay, good." A relieved sigh left Kayla's lips.

"Which reminds me, can you lock up when you guys leave?"

"No problem," Kayla responded, readjusting under her blanket. "I'll leave around ten. The bakery is supposed to open on Monday and I haven't done a thing." Pausing, her eyes drifted toward the arched window. "By the way, was that your Range Rover he was driving?"

"Yeah. I told you how I crashed his car? That was my peace offering."

Finding it amusing, she let out a soft giggle. "Well, we should start getting you cleaned up for your date!"

"It's not a date," Adalyn interjected.

"Not yet," she insisted as she rose from her seat and began making her way toward the stairs. "Come on!"

Pressed and tidied, Adalyn returned down the stairs at a quarter to ten. Her foot hit the last step as Maddie's excited shriek shrilled the air. "You look stunning! I love that top."

"Thanks," Adalyn nervously spoke, running her fingers over the fabric material of her black plunge-neck.

Simultaneously, the doorbell rang as the clock chimed ten. Adalyn glanced over at the front door, then to the kitchen, seeking any last words of advice.

"It's time, Addy. You'll be fine," Kayla spoke, comforting her as she reached for her belongings. "Keep me updated on what happens," she hollered as she made her way toward the garage door to leave.

Standing in her kitchen, it was only her and Maddie now. "You got this," Maddie nudged. With a nod and a deep inhale, Adalyn hesitantly made her way to the entryway.

Peeling the door open, her gaze landed upon his. She feigned a welcoming smile as she stood there, but he wasn't making a move to leave. Instead, he held up two drinks and a brown paper bag from the French Express.

"I-I hope you don't mind," he stuttered, looking down at the parcels in his hands.

"Oh, I uh…" Adalyn bit at her lip as Zack eased a nervous grin onto his face. "I thought we were gonna go out to eat?"

"I was just thinkin' we could—"

"No, no, it's fine!" Moving aside, she made room for him to step inside. "This works better. Come on in."

As he entered, she noticed he retained a limp. Looking at him, she took in his cleaned-up features. His stubble was more maintained than the last time she saw him, though the bruises around his face were more prominent without the long strands to cover them.

"I'm sorry, I see Maddie's still here…"

"Hi," Maddie peeped from the living room. Taking this as a cue to leave, Maddie stood up. "I was actually just headed out. Max and I had plans."

Zack perked up to his friend's name, allowing for a delighted expression to seep in. "Sounds fun. Tell him hi for me!"

"Will do," she responded as she grabbed the last of her belongings. Bidding Adalyn an adieu, she hugged her tightly before heading for the door.

"Bye!" Adalyn hollered after her, and as she held onto the doorknob, she turned for one final wave.

"See you both for Christmas!"

Turning back to Zack now, Adalyn stepped over to the kitchen island, where he'd set down the drinks. "So, what did you get?" Impatient, she began reaching for the cups to read the sides.

"Uh, I got you a chai tea and I got some bagels. I-I hope that's okay?"

Looking up from the drinks, she smiled. "It's great! Thank you."

Plucking a blueberry bagel from the bag, she fetched the cream cheese from the fridge and began smearing it along the center. Following her lead, they quietly moved about the kitchen, dancing past each other every few steps to assemble their breakfast.

Finally settling, she took a sip of her drink. "So... What've you been up to?" she asked in attempts to break their bout of silence. He must've slipped into deep thought, because as he stared off at the specks on the counter while lightly picking at his bagel, he'd had no reaction to what she'd said. "Zack!" His name launched out of her mouth like a dart piercing the board, pulling him from his trance.

His eyes met hers, creating a rough lump in his throat that he struggled to swallow down. "Yes?"

"I asked what you've been up to."

"Oh, sorry. I've just been resting my leg, mostly. Oh, I finally hung a few Christmas decorations around the cabin!" Taking a bite of a piece of bagel he'd been holding in his hands, he looked at her. "What about you?"

"Well as you can see," she said, motioning toward the interior, "I put up Christmas decorations as well. Also, Kayla got back in town last night, so I spent time decorating the house with her and Maddie, per tradition."

"I saw the Christmas tree when I first pulled up. It looks really nice. Very Adalyn-esque."

"Thank you." She half-heartedly grinned while fiddling with the paper cup's lid. "How's Sophie doing, by the way?"

"She's well. It's been a bit hard walking her like I used to, but she still enjoys the backyard."

"That's great. You know she's welcome here for Christmas?"

"I won't forget her. Speaking of, should I bring anything, food wise?"

She shook her head. Falling back into a hushed state, Adalyn slowly gathered the courage to ask the looming question of the morning. "I have to ask... What is the purpose of all this?"

"What do you mean?"

"This..." Adalyn motioned toward the take-out scattered across the counter. "We never do take-out or anything, and you seemed kinda urgent to hang out..."

He expressed a casual shrug. There was something he was hiding, but she couldn't tell what. Finishing the bite he'd taken, he set the bagel down on his napkin. "I just thought it would be a nice thing after everything the past week, like that Friday night and the bar. Which, I am sorry for the other night, again."

She was taken aback by the mention of Friday night. It'd been just over a week, and this was the first she'd heard of it since it happened. Preferably, she wished it would never be mentioned, as she regretted her abrupt departure, but nevertheless, she powered through.

Ignoring his words like he'd never said them, she skipped over it. "Well, it's a nice gesture. I like the surprise!" Skimming over the food on the table, she returned her gaze to him. "And as for the bar, you really need to not be so worried. It didn't affect me in any way. I was really more concerned for you."

Recognizing perhaps she wasn't quite ready to discuss anything to do with Friday, he produced a strained grin. "I guess so. It's just really not like me..."

"Well, but you said you didn't even start it," she interrupted. Really not enjoying the sudden tone shift, she attempted to lighten the mood. Peeling off a chunk of her bagel, she plopped it in her mouth before asking in jest, "What does Rose think of your battle scars?" Her eyes inadvertently drifted toward his leg, which he was still refusing to put any pressure on.

Tension immediately entered the air at the mention of her name, with an even more serious tone washing over Zack. This did quite the opposite of what she was hoping it would do, and she instantly regretted it. Hitting the *undo* button in her mind, she watched his expressions with unease.

After enough of the taut silence, he finally glanced over at her. "You should know, Rose and I aren't seeing each other anymore."

"Oh. I'm sorry... Was it because of the bar?" she pried, and he shook his head.

"It wasn't ever gonna work out with her anyway, and we haven't talked since Monday." His tone was flat; one may even say that he lacked much sorrow for the situation.

She acknowledged his complacent stance toward the topic, though admittedly found hints of joy in the occasion that she buried.

"How's Rocky?" he asked, altering topics.

"Oh, actually he's great! He's found a new spot to lay. I don't know what it is about that spot, but he absolutely loves to lay in the corner, behind the tree." Adalyn's tone almost immediately reverted back to its normal, peppy expression.

"That's adorable." He chuckled.

She watched as he peered into his mug, which had now been emptied. "What else do you have planned today?" she asked.

Looking up at her, he pondered it for a moment before a realization struck him. "Oh, shit!"

"What?"

"I completely forgot I was supposed to meet Ragnar…" With an exasperated tone, he hastily started packing his belongings. "I'm so sorry!"

She let out a giggle as she walked him toward the front door. "I got a free breakfast out of it, I'll survive. Tell Ragnar I say hi."

Holding open the front door, a soft breeze blustered in, sending faint chills through her arms. Making her farewell brief, she watched with a giggle while he ran down her pathway.

It didn't take long to notice Rose's absence from town after the breakup. Like petals in the wind, she vanished, leaving behind only a brief memory of her existence; one that Adalyn wished to forget.

CHAPTER FOURTEEN

December 25, 2014

Flurries of white flakes fluttered to the floor on Christmas morning as a storm blustered in from the west. Glazing the ground with pale snow, the skies created a white haze over the town. Becoming a winter wonderland outside, the community filled with merriment and holiday cheer. Christmas carols echoed through the streets and snowmen appeared across town, while snowball wars were in full force and steamed cocoa permeated the air.

Inside, Adalyn kept warm as she sat in front of the crackling fire, readying herself for a jovial morning.

"What is that smell?" Joyce asked while she hopped down the last of the steps.

"Cinnamon rolls," Adalyn replied with a glistening smile as she checked the time on the oven. "They were a family tradition to make every Christmas morning."

"They smell great." Joyce made her way to the coffee maker and poured herself a cup before tiredly trudging over to the loveseat in the living room.

The front door slammed shut as a familiar voice rounded the corner. "Okay, I just finished hanging the wreath," Zack exclaimed.

Since Rose's absence, Adalyn and Zack's relationship was on the mend, placing the past behind them.

"Thanks! Coffee is brewed," she replied as she, too, poured herself a cup and joined Joyce in the living room.

While the oven timer ticked down, the three of them huddled around the crackling fire, indulging in tasty treats, toasty beverages, and holiday movies, patiently waiting to plunge into the heaps of presents that rested under the tree.

Holding his mug of cocoa up, Zack broke the silence. "Merry Christmas, you guys!"

"Merry Christmas," the other two chimed in.

"When do we want to start opening presents?" Joyce asked.

Adalyn shrugged as her gaze fell upon the five custom stockings that hung from the fireplace mantle. "Want to grab the stockings for us?"

"I got it," Zack offered, standing up from the other loveseat. Plucking them off the holders, he distributed them amongst the trio. Holding up the remaining two, he asked, "Adalyn, who do these go to?"

"The names are on the other side," Adalyn giggled.

He twisted the stockings around and lit up upon reading the names. "Rocky and Sophie? You got Sophie a stocking?"

She nodded, "Of course! They're a part of our celebration as well."

Dressed in holiday bandanas, the two dogs rested on top of one another, in front of the fire. Admiring it for a moment more, Zack gently woke Sophie from her slumber, calling her to his side to shuffle through her gifts.

Just as they finished trifling through the stockings, the timer dinged and Adalyn rose to tend to the kitchen. Returning moments later, she set a plate of fresh cinnamon rolls down on the coffee table.

"What's our plan today?" Joyce questioned as she picked up the knick-knacks she'd scattered across the floor.

"Well," Adalyn began, "I assumed we'd eat, start on presents, relax, and then everyone is coming over for dinner later."

"Who all is coming, again?"

"I have it down for Maddie, Kayla, Max, Logan, and Ragnar."

"Cool!" A faint grin appeared across her face as she took a bite of a cinnamon roll.

Adalyn exhaled, her eyes brushing over the mountain of gifts. "It's time! Joyce, do you mind passing them out?"

"Of course," Joyce replied as she began piling the gifts in front of the intended recipients.

Zack unraveled the first gift from Adalyn, revealing a leather wallet. Flipping it open, his hand traced over three golden letters, *ZLB*, engraved into its flap. "Wow..." He admired the wallet, taking in its condition. "This is nicer than I could ever fathom."

Adalyn nervously cupped her mug in both hands as she watched for his reaction. "You'd mentioned how yours was ripping, so I figured…"

Her voice trailed as he interrupted, "No, this is fantastic! This—it's great!" His eyes traced over its pristine leather as he muttered, "Zackary Lee Blake. I love it."

She blushed, pleased with herself. Her attention readily turned to Joyce, who'd begun unwrapping one of her gifts, as well. She peeled back the first strip to uncover the book that Joyce had spoken about for months, but had swiftly gone out of stock.

"Adalyn," she gasped in astonishment. "How?"

"I know someone…"

"This is amazing," she exclaimed, twisting it in her hand. Silently, she felt over its laminated cover.

"Okay, okay," Zack impatiently interrupted. He held out a box for Adalyn, and she set down her mug to grasp it. Prone to organization, she refused to rip wrapping paper as she slowly unwrapped the gift.

Peering down at a brown cardboard box, she questioned with a faint giggle, "Why did you wrap it twice?"

"So that you couldn't guess. Just open it!"

She bottled her confusion, diving back into the unwrapping. Folding back its sides, the interior exposed the bottom of a jewelry box. For some reason, she was careful as she removed it. Rotating it over in her palms, her eyes widened at the item. "You…" she began with wonderment.

"I did," he finished, proudly.

Throwing the top open, her gaze fixated on the necklace. London Blue Topaz hung at the tip of a diamond swirl pendant made of white gold. A round diamond lay above the blue gemstone as the swirl detail conjoined the design. The topaz was famously known to glisten under any lights. Proving to be true, the gem refracted all the light in the room, reflecting it in every direction. Adalyn held it in her palm for a moment longer, taking in its allure.

"Can I put it on for you?" Zack eagerly questioned.

"Y-yes, please!" She extended it out to him as she stood up.

Turning around, she lifted her hair out of the way. The pendant delicately sat on her sternum as he fiddled with its clasp. Dropping her hair, she inspected it in the entryway mirror.

"Wow," Joyce gawked.

"It's stunning. Thank you!" Adalyn gazed lovingly at the exquisite piece of jewelry. She took her seat on the couch once more, silently admiring it as the unwrapping continued on.

Each of them unveiled a plethora of wish-list items, their smiles widening as they plowed onward. The dogs happily leapt at wrapping paper as it flew around the room, crumpling and ruffling each fallen piece beneath their paws.

Basking in the fire's warmth and tranquil air, Adalyn jolted up. "Oh, I actually have one more gift for you, Zack!"

Without another word, she ran into the kitchen and returned with a small, white box, nicely wrapped in a red ribbon.

He curiously took the box from her and unraveled its bow as they draped over his lap. Wiggling the top off, his face was bewildered. "Is this..." He was more confused than she'd intended. Holding up the item, he dangled it in front of him. Sun shot off the metal engraving, blinding him as it twisted in the air. *Jeep,* he finally made out.

"It's a new car!" Adalyn played out the excitement.

His expression slowly altered to merriment as it all sunk in. "Oh my!"

She ushered him from his seat and led him toward the garage. "I hid it in here." The light flickered on as it slowly revealed a black four-door Jeep Wrangler.

"You didn't..." he stuttered. "Is this brand new?"

She nodded, proudly. "Brand new, never driven Jeep. Because I owe you a car."

"I mean you don't owe..." he stopped himself. "Thank you!" He turned to her and pulled her in for a hug.

"My debt is officially paid," she teased, gently pulling back after a moment too long. "I'm glad you like it!" She turned back inside, leaving him alone in the garage as he stood there a moment more, taking in the grandeur of his new vehicle.

By the time Zack emerged from the garage, the aura in the room had altered. No longer lazing around, the two girls had gotten to work in the kitchen. Clattering dishes rang on for hours as they prepped for the impending dinner, and a singular ding from the oven sent Adalyn gliding across the kitchen. Half past five now, the doorbell chimed, sending both Joyce and Adalyn into an overstimulated frenzy.

"I got it!" Zack shouted as he stood up from the loveseat he'd been resting in. Forced out of the kitchen on several occasions, he'd surrendered to watching television on the couch until guests arrived.

"Merry Christmas!" Zack greeted, opening the door for the guests.

"Merry Christmas," they each eagerly replied as one by one, they piled into the abode. First Max and Maddie, then Kayla, who each presented homemade desserts by the platter.

Finishing up in the kitchen, Adalyn strolled up beside him. "I got it from here, thanks!" Holding the door ajar, she playfully winced when she saw Ragnar strut up the pathway.

"You look like a bloody mess," he teased, not even bothering with an appropriate greeting.

"Merry Christmas, you Swedish bastard," Adalyn quipped, flashing him a grin. Turning around, she nearly dismissed Logan's arrival.

"Closing the door on your own family, eh?" Logan teased.

A gleeful smile appeared across her face. Pleased to see her elusive brother, she pulled him into a hug. "Merry Christmas!"

"Merry Christmas, Addy."

"I'm glad you made it this year."

"Yeah, my annual plans fell through. Plus I wanted to spend time with my sister." He stepped past her, making his way into the kitchen to join the others. Behind him, Adalyn shut the front door, expecting no one else to appear.

"Joyce, where are we at on dinner?" Adalyn questioned.

"Everything is ready. You guys can dig in."

Shuffling around the island in an organized manner, the guests loaded their plates with heaps of food and meandered into the dining room, where decorative name cards labeled seats around the rectangular table.

Taking a seat amongst the guests, Adalyn listened in on the discussions, though individual conversation faded into a hazy blur as she sunk into her own thoughts. The stress of hosting such a monumental dinner caught up to her, and she pondered her own wandering mind for a brief moment as she ate away at the morsels left on the plate.

Plucked from her thoughts, she was forced back into reality by Kayla's booming voice. "So, I have the annual truck coming into Three Dog in like two months; it's coming in February. Is there anyone that could potentially help with the unloading?"

"I can." Logan was the first to volunteer, though everyone else eagerly followed suit.

Maddie abruptly rose from her seat, interrupting the dinner table. "Dessert, anyone?"

"Actually, I'll join you." Joyce stood from her seat as well, helping Maddie as they bussed the table of empty dishes.

"Thank you, again, Adalyn, for inviting me tonight," Logan stated.

"Thank you for making it this year. It's great to have some family around this time."

"You know Keisha would love to be here for this."

"Do you..." Adalyn paused, "Maybe it's better not knowing."

"She's still in Shadow Mountain. Bridget is almost five now."

Five. It had been five years since Adalyn had seen her sister, but perhaps it was better this way. Five years was a long time, and in the span of that half-decade, that distance between them had become a necessary part of their story. Regardless, there were questions that even Adalyn couldn't quite evade. "She canceled on you this year?" she asked, perhaps prodding to know more.

Logan casually nodded, taking a bite off his plate. "You know she asks about you from time to time." A faint smile appeared across Adalyn's face, only to be interrupted by Maddie and Joyce's return.

"Okay, we have Kayla's cookies and my pie," Maddie announced as they set the platters down upon the center of the table, though the desserts were gone in what seemed like an instant.

Night fell upon the group as they gradually wandered into the living room. Everyone arranged themselves around the room, and the warm lights of the Christmas tree's glow illuminated the setting in which they conversed. Drinking like kings, they indulged in bottles of wine while mirthful chatter filled the house.

CHAPTER FIFTEEN

February 4, 2015

A supply truck piled into town that morning, making one of its many stops at the Three Dog Bakery, and just like promised on Christmas evening, eight individuals grouped outside of the bakery to assist.

Bundled in layers and still shivering, they contributed in rearranging and restocking the bakery, as it was past due time for an upgrade. Laboring through the workload, they busted through what would've been six hours of work, in a rapid three. The aftermath created a soothing appearance to the interior, with new furniture laid across the floors and fresh paint that embellished the walls. By noon, the team had begun wrapping up the finishing touches and conducted a walk-through to see their progress.

Adalyn strolled through the backspace, where the freezer of frozen dough stood, when a noise drew her attention toward the back office.

"Hello?" she called out.

No one returned a response. The main lights were off in the back office, and to Adalyn's knowledge, no one should've been back there. Hesitantly, she crept closer. A dim light illuminated the back door at the end of the hallway as Adalyn's heels clicked against the concrete floor.

"Hello?" she repeated. Once more, no response.

As she crept closer, she could make out a man's shadow through the door's slim window. She held her breath, careful not to make a sound. Watching his silhouette move from within, she observed as the man shuffled through the desk drawers. She pondered creeping even closer, when the office door finally swung open. Holding her breath and closing her eyes, she impulsively jumped out from behind the corner she'd hidden herself in. Surprising the man, they both jumped back.

"Ragnar?"

"God, Adalyn!" He exhaled deeply. Ragnar's right hand remained behind his back, while his left was placed over his racing heart. "You scared the shit out of me."

"The hell were you doing in the back office?"

His gaze momentarily peered back toward the office. "I was sorting through it for Kayla. She asked me to."

Adalyn quirked an eyebrow at his statement, questioning its validity. "Well, I hollered several times and you never responded."

"You try hearing in that room. The monitor's so damn loud, you might as well be deaf."

Giving in, Adalyn shrugged it off. She turned toward the door that led back out to the cars, taking a few steps before glancing back. "You coming?"

"After you," he responded, motioning for her to lead.

Squinting, they were instantly blinded by the sun's rays, which had descended in the sky since they'd first entered the bakery.

With all eight of them finished, they stood in front of their cars now, shivering and squeezing their coats together.

"Thank you so much you guys, really," Kayla spoke.

"You know we've always got your back," Maddie chimed in through chattering teeth as she huddled into Max's jacket. "Was there anything else you needed help with before we go?"

"No, I don't believe so. I think we can all go home."

"Have a great night, everyone," Adalyn hollered as she hastily ripped open the passenger door to Zack's new Jeep.

Though one of the first to pile into the warmth of a vehicle, the Jeep idled in the parking lot for a moment longer than the rest, as Zack fiddled with the exterior of his new car. Inside, Adalyn's snooping habits presented themselves. She shuffled through the dash, finding nothing but meaningless manuals and paperwork. Reaching for the center console, she hesitated. Peering over her shoulder, she watched Zack examining the back of the car, providing her ample occasion to continue onward with her nosiness. She flung the console open, shuffling through.

Near the bottom of the deep storage space, she'd about given up, when her hand brushed across the familiar tin box. Pushing all else aside, she quickly reached in for it, like a claw machine reaching for a toy. Lifting it out of the clutter, she examined the Altoid box. "It's empty?" she mumbled.

The car unlocked and Zack appeared beside the driver's seat. She tossed the tin box back into the console, slamming it shut. Her heart raced as he jumped into the car, completely oblivious to her snooping.

"Ready to go?" His cheerful tone warmed her as she forced her heart to settle.

"I'm ready."

"Back to yours?"

She nodded. The car finally backed out of the bakery and began its ascent up the mountain she called home.

"Thank you for helping today," Adalyn said.

"Of course. Anything for Kayla."

"I know she appreciates it." She immediately altered the topic. "This car is really riding nicely, though."

"You can't drive it," he abruptly stated.

She expressed a confused look. "I didn't—"

"Sorry, I mean, it's great. I really like it!"

"No. Backtrack," Adalyn playfully pressed.

"I'm sorry." He peered over at her as he drove up the mountain. "It's just..."

"Just what? That I'm a terrible driver?"

"*I* didn't say it..."

"But you thought it," she pushed, though she wasn't mad.

"No, no!"

"Don't lie."

"Okay, okay," he conceded. "It's not your strong suit." A grin appeared across Adalyn's face. "W-why are you smiling?" he asked, warily.

"Nothing. It's just the first time you were honest about it."

"Well, I didn't want to hurt your feelings before. And, I didn't really know how bad it was until you drove my car off a ravine."

"Yeah, I should've informed you better..."

"It's okay," he stated. The car pulled around the corner and onto her street. Slamming his foot against the breaks, the tires screeched. Inching closer, Zack's face was frozen in shock.

"Woah!" Adalyn screamed, nearly flying out the windshield at his abrupt breaking. Regaining her ground, she turned to glare at him, though stopped in her tracks as she saw his equally stunned expression. "What's going on?" Her eyes followed his gaze toward her abode. "Whose car is that?"

A red sedan parked outside of her abode, one she'd never seen before. It stood situated right outside of her garage door, really making itself at home. Zack drove his Jeep up the driveway leaving the tail end of his car hanging out in the street as he threw it in *park*.

"Stay here," he requested, stepping out. Leaving it still running, Adalyn cracked the window open slightly, in an attempt to listen in.

As he approached the car, the driver's side door of the sedan burst open and a woman slid out. Her brunette hair curled over her face, and the bombshell red dress she wore accented her tan skin. She stood in front of him, leaving hardly any room between them. Her stance was airy, flirty. Zack, on the other hand, seemed aggravated. He rested his left arm atop her car door, and even in his leaning stance, she could sense his tension. He was holding back. This was the most irritation Adalyn had seen out of him.

Adalyn had enough observing. Bursting open the car door, she stepped out. Utterly confused at this point, she approached the two with a false sense of confidence. "Am I interrupting something?" she questioned.

Turning around, the woman gently smiled. "My apologies for the intrusion," she began. "My name's Mia. I'm sure you've heard plenty about me."

"No," Adalyn coldly replied.

"Mia, leave her alone," Zack commanded. "Why are you here?"

"I come bearing surprises," she replied. A faint smirk crossed her face as she reached toward the back seat's handle. Moving aside, a young girl stepped out to reveal herself. "Zack, meet your daughter."

Too stunned to speak, Adalyn and Zack stood in deafening silence as they stared at the young girl. Standing just over three feet tall, the young girl's long caramel brown hair was tangled and unkempt as it shielded her eyes. She was shy upon first meeting, though the environment lacked a proper introduction. The girl clutched onto a small toy rabbit, her grip getting firmer as the environment got colder.

"Her name's Sky. Well, Skylar, but I hate that name, so it's Sky." Mia shoved the girl toward her father.

Zack was absolutely speechless. "When..."

"Well, she's four. Do that math. You're twenty-six now so what was that, twenty-two? Either way, Sky, meet your father." The young girl was silent.

"Why are you just telling me this now? We haven't been together in years," Zack protested.

"Four *wondrous* years, to be exact. But as much as I was refraining from this encounter, I recently realized that it was wrong of me. A girl should meet her father."

Adalyn stared at Zack with concern in her eyes, though he was too focused on the child before him. "I—uh, I think I should go..." Adalyn stated, slowly backing away from them. This felt personal, and rather awkward for her to be standing there.

Zack glanced over at her with panic in his eyes. "You don't have to go," he pleaded.

"No, but I really should... This is a lot to process, and—" she paused, stopping at the door of her car. "I'll be at Granny's. Let me know when this is done."

Even though it was her own house, she'd do anything to escape this bizarre encounter. Taking off down the mountain, she went to the only place that felt like a second home to her.

Stepping through the front door, the familiar bell rang overhead and she let out a soft sigh of relief. *Normalcy.*

"What can I get you, Mrs. Dawn?" Ruby's familiarly happy smile greeted her.

"Right now, I would love a cup of hot chocolate."

"Hot chocolate coming right up," she exclaimed.

"Thank you."

Returning quite quickly with the mug, Ruby quietly set it down as the front door's bell rang once more, casually drawing Adalyn's attention. *Mia.* The woman made her way toward the booth, sending Adalyn's heart racing. There was something about this woman that seemed intimidating. Her demeanor did not fit the way Adalyn felt.

"I came to talk." The woman's tone was calm, and Adalyn hesitantly motioned for her to sit.

"Where's Zack and the kid?"

"Back at the house. I wanted to talk alone." Adalyn nodded, pressing the woman to continue. "I know I don't know you very well, and clearly he's never mentioned me, but I can see in the way he looks at you that he cares a lot about you."

"What are you getting at?" Adalyn was uneased.

"Zack's not quite the caring type, though I'm sure he's never shown you that side of him."

"I guess not..."

"I just hate that I'm splitting you two up!"

"What?" Adalyn asked, more confused now than before.

"Well, now that Sky's in the picture, he's going to have to move back to help take care of her..." Adalyn fell silent for a moment. Glancing down at her cup, she pondered what that would mean for them. "I'm really sorry, Adalyn. I didn't mean to put you in the middle of this."

Looking up at Mia, she furrowed her eyebrows. "How did you know we'd be at my house? Why didn't you go to Zack's?"

"Honestly," Mia let out a sympathetic sigh, "I thought that was his house. I didn't know it wasn't until you just said that. I'd stopped at the gas station on my way into town and asked where I could find him and they gave me that address. But that makes more sense. He's always been a tufthunter."

"A what?"

"Class-climber," Mia corrected. "Someone who's always trying to climb a social ladder." Before Adalyn could ask any further, Mia continued, "Look, I am really sorry. Maybe it doesn't have to be that bad! We are only like six hours from here. Maybe you can make long distance work..."

Adalyn seemed to ignore everything she said. She didn't care; she didn't fully trust the woman. "You said he cares about me?" Adalyn asked, focusing on the one piece that actually piqued her interest.

Mia nodded. "Honestly, more than I've seen him care about a lot of people in the past. Probably more than me."

"I don't mean to be harsh, but how can I believe you?"

"I mean, you don't know me, so it's really up to you—oh, and this! Thank you for reminding me." Mia dug into her bag and pulled out her cell phone. "I got this recording during a phone call that he didn't know I was on. I was going to just delete it, but I never got around to it. Maybe it's a good thing I didn't."

Placing it neatly on the table between them, she pushed *play* on a voice recording.

"So, Adalyn," the audio began with an unfamiliar woman's voice. "Tell me why you won't tell her your feelings."

"'Cause... I mean, I want to, I really do. But she's *Adalyn*. I might scare her off, and also remember, she's not up for anything like that."

Adalyn talked over the sound, forcing Mia to pause it. "Who is that voice? That's not you."

"It's Zack's sister. It's besides the point. Just, *shh*."

Mia hit play once more.

"What if she was up for something like that and wouldn't get scared off, would you do it then?"

There was a long pause before Zack's voice responded. "I'd say, I'd probably be stupid risking our friendship, but I'd do it just so she knows."

"Why?"

"We've already been over this."

"Fine, then why didn't you snap at Adalyn when she completely demolished your car?"

"We've been over this too, and we both know what the reasons are."

"I don't remember them, so refresh my memory."

"I have a feeling you won't quit unless I do so." He took a deep breath. "Well, Adalyn is the only girl that has ever put up with my nonsense. She doesn't get mad at my constant blabbing about pointless, random things, and she's the only girl that can make me smile, even after the universe hits me hard. I don't get the reason I'm so scared of saying this stuff to her, but then I remember that there's nobody else out there like her, and if I say one wrong thing, that'll all be over. So, the harsh reality is: I would be sad and heartbroken inside when she found someone that wasn't me, but then I'd make myself be happy because I love her enough to watch her be happy with someone else; someone that'll treat her like the *once in a lifetime* girl she is."

"That was touching, Zack," the female's voice said as Mia paused the audio.

"Wow..." Adalyn deeply exhaled. "That-that's a lot to take in."

A piece of her wondered its validity, though it was clear as day that it seemed to be true. Of course she cared about Zack; liked him, even. However, she'd never thought about what she'd do when it came time to tell him this. Though, perhaps a part of her wondered, if she told him how she felt, would he stay?

"I mean at least now you know how he feels. I'm sorry it's all coming out at such a poor time," Mia apologized again.

"I'm confused," Adalyn began.

"What about?"

"All due respect, Mia, you're his ex. Why are you sitting here, telling me about how much he likes me?"

"Just because we are no longer dating, doesn't mean I don't want the best for him." A sympathetic expression washed over the woman's face. "I didn't mean to overstep. I came here to talk with you and apologize for creating this rift with the news of a child. I'm sure it's got to be a lot to process."

Adalyn took a deep breath. "When would he leave?"

She shrugged. "I think that's more of a question you'd have to ask him."

Nodding, Adalyn silently ran her fingers along the rim of her mug. It would be selfish of her to force him to choose, so she refrained. Now disheartened, she continued to spin her finger around the rim.

"Hey, I know this interaction was short, but I really must get going..." Mia stated, standing up. Stopping beside Adalyn, she towered over her like a looming gray cloud. "Good luck." The woman's tone was haunting, as if to challenge her. Though when Adalyn glanced up, a widened grin was plastered to the woman's face.

CHAPTER SIXTEEN

February 11, 2015

Speeding through the forest, Adalyn passed the tree where Zack's truck remained entwined in the branches. As she drove up the mountain road toward home, Mia's conversation a week prior echoed in her mind, and memories clouded her vision like a montage. Recollecting Halloween and the housewarming party, a smile crept onto her face. She recalled the way she felt as they kissed in Granny's Diner that one Friday night.

The car accelerated at a rapid pace while she whipped through the forest. With the engine at full throttle, she neared the last turn before her abode. Adalyn took deep, hyperventilated breaths while she drove the last hundred yards toward the house.

His Jeep sat in her driveway as she pulled beside it. She was significantly late. Throwing the Range Rover in *park*, she bolted for the front door, and it slammed against the wall as she entered, swinging back around to nearly hit her.

"Zack?" she frantically called out. "I'm so sorry!"

Her keys fell out of her hand, clinking against the hardwood floor, and the commotion caught his attention as he glanced over. Their eyes met. His hazel eyes shimmered against the living room lights; she could just melt. Letting out a delicate chuckle, he stood up and smiled.

"You're okay," he reassured. "I just got here like ten minutes ago."

"Phew," she sighed with relief as her racing heart began to calm. Walking further into her own home, she set her belongings down on the counter. "Do you still wanna go for lunch?"

Both their eyes drifted toward the clock, which read three now. "It's a bit late, and I kinda ate when you said you were running late," he admitted.

"That's okay!"

"I was thinkin' we could go for drinks later, around five?"

Beginning to walk over to the living room, she shrugged. "Sounds fun to me. A show in the meantime?"

"You read my mind!"

Both reaching for the remote, his hand grazed over hers, and though it sent her heart racing a million miles an hour, she involuntarily pulled back. He must've sensed it too, as his hand lingered over the remote for a moment more before grabbing it.

"*Friends*?" he checked.

"Of course," she replied.

Leaning back into the couch, she watched a few seconds of the show before turning to him with a mischievous smirk. "Rusty's Saloon for drinks?" she teased.

Sarcastically side-eyeing her, he chuckled. "I think I may be banned from there for life."

"No way." She shook her head. "Do you know how many fights break out there? Yours was nothing in comparison."

He let out another airy chuckle. "How about Oak Lounge?"

"Isn't that..." She didn't quite want to say the word *pricey*, but it was, and that was coming from her.

"Why not?"

She shrugged. She wasn't opposed, though she wondered about the occasion.

The television played on, leading them into a momentary lapse of conversation. In the distance, Rocky's footsteps could be heard pacing around the entryway, his nails tapping away at the hardwood floors.

Repositioning herself on the couch, she furrowed her eyebrows to a fleeting thought. "Where's Sky?" Her question interrupted the void, causing him to stare over at her.

"She's with Mia," he responded in a casual tone.

"I don't mind if you bring her," Adalyn interrupted, and Zack faintly smiled.

"I'll keep that in mind." Turning his attention back to the television, there was a short pause before he added, "It won't matter soon enough."

This comment drew her attention as her heart rate began to pick up. "What do you mean?" Her voice wavered, though she attempted to conceal her concern.

"She's headed back home in a few weeks with Mia."

"Oh..." *A few weeks*, she noted to herself. Faltering for a moment, she swallowed the lump in her throat before asking, "Are you going with her?"

He looked over, his hazel eyes piercing her under the television light. It was intimidating. Not him, but the anticipation that grew greater every millisecond he didn't answer—and there were a lot.

"I don't know. Why do you ask?"

"No reason."

That was a lie.

"I thought about it," he admitted.

"Yeah?"

He shrugged his shoulders, brushing it off as if it was a minor decision. "It would be easier to be there for her, and Mia said she'd help get me settled if I did."

"That's sweet of her." She shifted in her seat, though no change in position could make her feel more comfortable. "Why did you two split?" Adalyn pried.

"Uh," he let out a chuckle. "She was a little crazy toward the end."

"Oh..." She refrained from asking further. Reverting back to the prior conversation, she probed, "Do you want to? Go with her, I mean."

Zack expressed a look of uncertainty. It wasn't a plan that even he'd thought through much yet. Answering on a whim, he nodded. "I think so."

"Oh... wow."

"What?"

"Nothing! That's great. I think you should, if it'll benefit Sky."

His face showed complete disassociated indifference. Perhaps it was that he was too upset at the idea that he couldn't bother processing at this time, or maybe he just didn't care that deeply, but it upset Adalyn.

Rising from his seat, he glanced over at her. "I'm gonna get a drink, want anything?"

"An ice tea, please?"

"One ice tea comin' right up, Chica!"

She aimed a synthetic grin toward his enthusiasm to conceal any discontent. There was a tiny voice in the center of her stomach, telling her, yelling at her, *gnawing* at her, to tell him. Opening her mouth, the words stuck like a bubble at the top of her throat, clinging on for dear life as she tried to propel them forward. They wouldn't budge. Three little words. *I like you.*

She tried again, but nothing. Peering over the back of the couch now, she watched him pour the glass of ice tea.

She tried again. This time, the words launched out of her throat and into the air.

"I like you."

Perhaps her words hadn't hit his ears yet, as his expression had yet to change. Though, it was in that moment of silence that it hit her. All that logic and reasoning that had been suspended, struck down on her. She felt delirious, hysterical for disclosing this. *What was she doing?* She couldn't seriously have believed that if she admitted her feelings, he would stay. She couldn't have been so *selfish*. That child needed him, and she was hoping he would pick *her*? *Shit.*

"I-I'm so sorry…" Rising from her seat, she quickly started walking toward the back door. "I think I need some fresh air, actually… I'll be back soon."

"Wait what?" It took another second before his mind finally processed, and by then, she was halfway across the back patio. Headed toward the front of the house, she began to beeline toward a small trail that hid on the other side of the road from her driveway.

Bewildered by the sudden drop of information, he set the pitcher down on the counter and took off after her. "Running from this, really?" he hollered. "Please don't make me chase you!" Talking to himself, he mumbled as he picked up his pace, "And you're going to make me chase…"

She didn't particularly mean to run, but lately she'd gotten quite good at dropping bombs of emotional impact and bailing. Standing on the other side of the road, she looked back at him.

"It was wrong of me to say that," she hollered.

Reaching the end of the driveway, he opened his mouth to respond, though it was no use, as she'd already begun descending down the trail. He was unfamiliar with this path, as it was one they'd somehow never walked before. Though, based on its wear, no one else had, either. The path was brushed over with bushes and grass, and the dense canopy of trees above made it rather dark. He was at a disadvantage with his limp, though it didn't stop him from going after her. He wasn't going to let her leave like last time. Stopping in his tracks, he listened for any movement. A twig snapped in the distance, and he took off after the sound.

Cutting behind some trees, he managed to cut her off in her tracks. "Wow, laziness really paid off for me," he mumbled again to himself. Catching his breath, he looked at her. "Okay, stop running away now, please." He bent over, resting his hands on his knees.

Glancing over at him, she stopped. "Okay..."

"Now, you said you like me? Did I hear that right?" he asked through panting breaths as he worked to stand up straight again.

"What? No..." She attempted denial.

"Adalyn, I know what you said, I wanted to see if you'd own up to it."

"Blame Mia," Adalyn blurted, though it wasn't really Mia's fault. Perhaps she could've purposefully planted that thought in Adalyn's head, though it seemed a bit out of place for someone who'd been so kind. *Or was it an act?*

Now she felt delirious.

Taking a seat on a nearby fallen tree, she felt exhausted as the last bits of adrenaline began subsiding. "That's not true," Adalyn began again. "She told me last week that now that Sky's in the picture, you were leaving to go back with her, and with all the talk today, I thought that maybe..." she paused, feeling disgusted for even thinking that way. "It was wrong of me to spring that on you."

"Mia," he cursed under his breath. Turning back to Adalyn, his eyes grew compassionate and he took a seat beside her. "She had no place sayin' that stuff."

"Well, clearly she wasn't too far off," Adalyn scoffed. Standing up again, she slowly began the trek back home.

"Oh no you don't!" He quickly rose up and began walking beside her, not letting her get away again. "Just tell me if you meant it. It's fine if you said it on a whim."

Adalyn continued the walk in silence, deciding it best not to answer to save herself from further humiliation.

"C'mon. I promise I will not make you feel embarrassed, okay?" he pressed.

She hesitated. Turning to face him, she casually shrugged and continued walking.

"Oh, no. You can't just shrug me off! Fine. I'll speak first, then you tell me the truth, okay?" Adalyn stopped walking. She stared at him, prompting him to continue. "Okay. I like you. Now I've said what you said. Your turn."

Adalyn stared at him, hesitant to speak. Every fiber in her body pushed her to talk, but something within her blocked her from doing so yet again.

Finally finding her voice again, she huffed, "Fine. Yeah!" Adalyn peered down at the forest floor for a moment before continuing to walk again.

"*Fine, yeah*, what?"

"Yeah. I do." Adalyn picked up the pace in her stride.

"*Yeah you do*, what?" She stopped to stare at him for a moment, finding him completely obnoxious that he was forcing her to say it all.

"Fine. Yes, I do like you."

"You do?" he coughed, choking on air. She rolled her eyes, sheerly out of nervousness. "Okay, so let's get this whole you liking me and me liking you thing sorted out."

"Oy," she huffed, finding another dead tree to sit on. "What is there to talk about?"

"I would love it if this could be the part in my life where I actually had a normal relationship, but apparently that's not in the cards.

Okay, you like me, I like you. What do you want to have happen now?"

"I don't know… this is why I've been avoiding the situation since day one."

"Day one?"

"I'm exaggerating," *She wasn't.* "Look, it was wrong of me to say that right now."

"It wasn't though," he corrected. "I'm glad you did. We should talk about it," he pressed.

"I-I don't think I have it in me right now. There's so much to process still, I don't even know where to begin."

"Okay, I respect that. But we do need to talk about this eventually, Adalyn."

"But it'll be so awkward," she protested.

"I-I'll think of a way for this conversation not to be completely awkward, and we'll come back to it later."

"Or, we just drop it…"

"Nope, I'm Zack. I don't just drop stuff."

Ignoring him, she turned to leave. Walking back in silence, she hadn't remembered going this far, and she was feeling the tension build between them.

Finally, her house fell into view. Stopping at the tree line, Adalyn watched as Zack walked onward. Observing him, she thought back to the last time they'd stood there, when Mia first made her appearance in Adalyn's driveway.

"You comin'?" Zack hollered back at her from the driveway. Nodding, she continued walking.

There was something about Mia that irked her, something awry. She couldn't quite place it, but she was admittedly beginning to feel forever altered by the parasite that was overtaking her empire.

CHAPTER SEVENTEEN

Mia's infiltration struck Adalyn's world, shaking it like a boat that weathered the storm. Preoccupied with Sky, Zack's presence was few and far between as of late, and Adalyn missed her friend. She missed their frequent outings and lifted spirits. However, when he did come around, he'd appear with the same wholesome smile he always had. Though, Adalyn knew better than to trust that false grin, as she saw it in his eyes when he arrived that afternoon.

Adalyn had been wrapped under a blanket, sipping on a glass of piping hot apple cider in front of her fireplace, when a sudden knock on the door yanked her from her thoughts. She peered down the hallway, toward the noise. Part of her lacked the motivation to tend to it. Another knock hit against her front door. This time, she didn't ignore it.

Zack's figure could be easily made out through her sidelites as she approached. "Hey, Dear oh Friend of Mine," his voice chimed.

"Hey, Buddy Ol' Pal!"

"Can I come in?" Adalyn stepped aside as he entered.

"What can I do ya for?" she asked.

"So, I was thinkin' we go out today."

"But it's cold out?"

"When has that ever stopped us?"

"I suppose." She pondered for a moment. "Where?"

"Wherever you want."

"Well, wherever we go, I'm really hungry."

He motioned toward the front door that still remained ajar. "Ready to go?"

She reached for her purse on the entry table, nodding. "You still haven't told me where, though."

"Can it be a surprise?"

"What if I don't like it?" She took large strides toward the car, in efforts to dodge the chilly weather.

"Then, where did you want to go?"

"Somewhere with warm food."

"I can do that," he confidently replied.

Entering the passenger seat of his car, she immediately turned to him. With such excitement, she teasingly hollered, "Floor it!"

A soft grin appeared across his face, "I rather not. The five-o would catch me."

"Aw," she sighed, buckling her seat belt, "You're no fun."

"I am fun! Just rather not go to jail."

"But it would be such an adventure…"

"Fine, but bail me out if I do get arrested," he teased, stepping on the gas pedal for once.

"Wouldn't I always? Anyways, vroom-vroom!" Jeeps weren't known for their speed, though the thrill of the acceleration excited her. He couldn't help but chuckle at her enthusiasm.

Music filled the car, and though their voices were hushed, they both hummed along to "All We Are," one of the top tunes on Zack's infamous playlist. Adalyn was pleasantly surprised when the car took its slow turn into the parking lot of The French Express. Hardly containing her eagerness, she unbuckled before Zack had even parked.

"Easy, there," he exclaimed, shifting the car into park, though she was already nearly out of her seat.

"Hurry, it's cold!" She waited for him on the sidewalk. Inside, Adalyn took a brief scan over the menu before placing it back down. "I'm getting hot chocolate. How about you?"

"I think hot chocolate, same as you."

"That's it?" she questioned.

Zack nodded, peering over at her. "I don't know anything else I'd want."

"How about a cupcake, or a cake? Oh, what if we share a slice of cake?"

"A cupcake," he responded. "If I got one cupcake, will that make ya feel better?"

"Sure."

"And we can share a piece of cake."

"Sounds great!" Her eyes became fixated on the display case.

Stepping up to the cashier, Zack announced, "Can we get two hot chocolates, a slice of the coffee cake, and I'll take the chocolate cupcake." Zack nudged Adalyn to gain her attention. "Which do you want?"

"Oh, that one." Her finger wavered over a vanilla cupcake with pink frosting and colorful sprinkles. As bright as she was, it was only fitting that she chose such.

The two of them sat near the patio, though today had not been the most ideal for such a position, as the gray clouds held up, hazing over the land and making the mountain ranges nearly impossible to see. The landscape was rather achromatic.

Adalyn took another bite of the coffee cake, getting lost in her thoughts. Her gaze drifted onto the land outside, though her mind wandered much further.

"So," Zack interrupted the silence.

She snapped her head in his direction, zapping herself out of thought. "Yes?"

Nervousness played a part as he shuffled the slice of cake around his plate. "I've been meaning to bring up last week..."

"Oh. What about it?" She played naive.

"Well," he began.

She automatically interrupted, "I don't know."

"What do you mean?"

"Well, I clearly... *yaknow*..." She couldn't bring herself to say the three simple words again.

"Sure," he stated.

"And I don't deny what I said... I just don't know."

"Okay, and can I ask, why?"

"I suppose, I value our friendship too much." She lost her appetite. So much from Mia's encounter whirled in her head, though she tried not to let it show. "I worry it'll change, I suppose. You know... How it did with the others."

"The others?"

"Rose..." she clarified. He was coming to a clear understanding now. "And, I don't know if I'm ready to date anyone yet. Dating isn't my thing." She shocked herself with the blunt response. Though she indubitably cared, it had only been a week prior that she'd even found out about Sky, or about his feelings.

"Then, we don't have to." He comforted her, easing her stressed tone.

"Really? I mean, I really do... you know. I just need time."

"Really," he reassured. "Nothing has to change. It isn't a big deal, I promise." His falsified grin beamed in her direction, though even in the dimmed light, she could still read the sorrow that seeped behind his hazel eyes.

They continued on in an awkward state of silence as ambient cafe chatter loudly encompassed them. Plunging into a state of perplexity, they contemplated the *next*, muddled by the *now*. After some time had passed, she zapped herself out of thought, only to witness that Zack had fallen into a similar trance.

"So, your twenty-seventh birthday is coming up next month," she exclaimed, getting his attention.

"Oh, yeah." His tone was dry.

"What do you mean by that?"

"Well, I never celebrate my birthday."

"That's sad. Why not?"

He shrugged, "It's not something we celebrate in the Blake household."

"Well, it is in the Dawn family! We have to do something for it."

"Hmm," he contemplated, "like what?"

"Perhaps a party?" His face inadvertently cringed to the thought. "I suppose not that."

"It's ok, really. I like—"

Adalyn interrupted, "No, I refuse to just dismiss it. If you could do anything right now, what would it be?"

A gust of wind blew through, sending chills up Adalyn's arms as goosebumps grew mountains on her olive-colored skin. Zack shivered at its touch as well. "Go somewhere warm."

She sipped her hot chocolate. "I don't think I've had to brace for a cold winter in years. I've always traveled during these months." Thinking to herself, she emitted a soft giggle. "Yeah. In fact, last year, around this time, I was on an island."

Zack was huddling into his coat, freezing against the nippy air. His teeth quietly chattered as he muttered, "Lucky."

Another gust hit her skin, shaking her out of her rumination. "I could *totally* be somewhere warm right now." Stirring something inside her, the cogwheels of her inner thoughts began to twist. "Actually, that's just it!"

Zack glanced up, startled by her sudden excitement. "What?"

"What if we go somewhere for your birthday?"

"Like where?" His voice held some hesitation, but she plunged onward.

"I dunno." She began pondering over the idea. "Logan has a place out by the lakes that don't freeze over. We could go there?"

He contemplated for a moment. "When?"

"For your birthday, of course!"

"The fifteenth is so far away..." he grumbled.

"Well, when?"

"Sooner," he urged. "I miss the warmth. It's cold here. I don't think New York has *ever* been this cold."

She giggled, "How about the first week of March, then? I have some matters to attend to at the end of this month."

"That would work. My sister gets in at the end of March for a few weeks. Oh, but Mia is about to be gone until the second. I'll be watching Sky until she returns."

"Your sister is coming to town?" Adalyn's tone held excitement, as she'd heard plenty of the woman.

"Yeah, you'll like her. She's your age," Zack responded. "But, the trip?"

"Oh right. Hmm, the fourth, then?" she suggested.

"The fourth is a Wednesday, would that work?"

"Why wouldn't it?"

"The Council... Won't they need us?"

"Zack," she pressed with a giggle, "it's winter. Nothing happens in winter that they'd need us for."

"The fourth it is, then!"

Zack smiled and brought the mug of hot chocolate to his lips. Sipping on the last drops, it concealed his elated expression.

CHAPTER EIGHTEEN

February 28, 2015

Adalyn had wandered into Granny's Diner late that morning, finding comfort in the stillness that surrounded the forest. Sipping her casual cup of coffee, as she did most mornings, she stared off into the treeline that surrounded the diner while slowly tracing the rim of her cup with her middle finger.

She enjoyed moments such as these, where the world was silent, yet nature rang loud with activity. She could've sat like that forever. As the cold touched her lips, she watched her breath dissipate into the chilled February air.

Sitting there until the cold became too unbearable, she finally retreated to warmer ground.

"Thank you," Adalyn waved to the waitress as she was halfway out the front door.

A part of her didn't seem to want to return home quite yet. She idled in her car for a moment more, pondering over anything to extend her time away from home. Between Rocky and Joyce storming the abode, it had become quite chaotic lately. Eventually shifting her car into drive, she traveled deeper into the town. She parked in front of the local market, Teddy's. There wasn't much she needed, nor craved, but she wandered the aisles anyway.

"Adalyn?" Zack's familiar voice spoke from across the aisle.

Piquing Adalyn's attention, she immediately turned toward him. Her gaze fell upon Zack's familiarly welcoming grin with Sky by his side.

"Hey," Adalyn replied as they neared.

"How're you doin' lately?"

"I'm alright! Just grocery shopping…" Adalyn held up the box of pasta that rested in her left hand. Moments like this reminded her why she hated going to the store: she despised the awkward small-talk she was continuously forced into.

"Who's that, Papa?" the young girl asked.

"Sky, this is Adalyn!"

"Oh," the young girl replied with amazement dancing in her eyes. "You're friends with my Papa?"

Adalyn nodded as she smiled at the girl. A ringing emitted from Zack's pocket, disrupting their stale meeting. "Uh, I should get this… Can you watch Sky for a second?" Zack dismissed himself before she had the ability to decline.

"You're pretty," Sky said. Her voice was as sweet as her caramel hair.

"Oh, thank you, Sky."

"My Papa talks about you a lot. He says you're nice and pretty!"

"Oh, that's very sweet of him." Adalyn felt out of place now.

"Do you like ice cream?" Sky asked.

"Yes, of course."

"Sorry about that," Zack interrupted as he approached. "Sky, are you ready to go home?"

"No! Adalyn said she'd take me out for ice cream."

Adalyn's expression said it all, as she clearly never agreed to such.

"I don't think she did," Zack argued. "Plus we said we can get ice cream later."

"I-I could take her, if you'd like." Adalyn instantly regretted the words that escaped her mouth, though Sky was nearly jumping for joy.

"I—you really don't have to."

Adalyn shrugged. "Just meet us there when you're done. Are you ready, Sky?"

"Well, don't you need to check out?" Zack motioned to the singular box of pasta that she still held onto.

"Oh." Her cheeks lightly blushed as she placed it back on the shelf. "I don't really need it." Adalyn held her hand out for the young girl as she discarded the empty cart.

While they walked, Sky skipped along in front of her, pulling Adalyn's arm as she did so.

"What's your favorite flavor?" Sky asked.

"Hmm," Adalyn pondered for a moment, "Mint Chocolate Chip. How about you?"

"Mine's Cookies n' Cream! Just like Papa's. Why won't you date Papa?"

Adalyn's heart skipped a beat, stunned by the abrasive question. "Wha-what? Where did you get that info, Sky?"

"Mama and Bryce says that Papa will never find love, but Papa says he loves you."

"I—uh... She says that in front of you?" *Bryce? Bryce? Why did that name ring a*—it hit her. "Who's Bryce?" she casually asked.

"That's Mama's boyfriend," Sky exclaimed. "And Mama says you'll never date Papa in a million qua-trillion years!"

Adalyn stopped in her tracks to that news. Things were starting to piece together, but now wasn't the time. Squatting down to Sky's height, she attempted to address the situation in the friendliest way possible. "Sky, I love your Papa very much, but sometimes you just aren't ready."

"Why?"

"You don't rush greatness," Adalyn replied. She stood back up.

"You don't rush greatness," Sky repeated. The cogwheels in her young mind were whirling out of control as she grasped its concept. She emitted a brightened smile once she finally did.

Unversed in such blunt conversations, she redirected the topic. "So, are you going to get any toppings on your ice cream?"

Sky shook her head and returned to her innocent skipping. Snow caked the ice cream store's red exterior, and even then, the *Open* sign remained lit.

"We're here," Sky exclaimed as the door's bell chimed overhead.

A young figure appeared from the back, approaching the cash register. "What can I get for you two lovely ladies?"

Adalyn made her way toward the display case. "Can I get a Mint Chocolate Chip cone and a Cookies n' Cream cone?"

Sky became fascinated with how they scooped up the ice cream. She hardly blinked as she watched, fogging up the sneeze guard. Handing her the ice cream, Adalyn observed as Sky smeared it all over her face, barely making it to her mouth. Holding back a smile, she cleaned the young girl up from her messy eating.

The overhead bell chimed once more. Adalyn had been cleaning up yet another mess from Sky when his voice loomed overhead. "Good, you guys are still here."

Jolting to the surprise, she twisted her head in his direction, only to be met with Zack's two vibrantly hazel eyes beaming back at her. "Hey!"

"Hey," he beamed in response.

"Have a seat." Adalyn motioned to the seat across from her.

"Papa," Sky cried with joy as she ran into his arms. He picked her up, hugged her tightly, then set her down on his lap.

"How's it goin'?"

"We've had fun so far. Right Sky?"

Sky vigorously bobbed her head. "Can she babysit me all the time?"

"I don't think—"

"I don't mind," Adalyn interrupted. Sky climbed off of Zack's lap and skipped off once again.

Once out of earshot, Zack turned to Adalyn, "You really don't need to."

"No, it's really fine! I think bonding would be good for Sky and I. Plus she's kinda fun to be around." There was a brief pause, and Adalyn took this opportunity. "So, Bryce and Mia," she mentioned in a low tone with a raised eyebrow.

Her words caught Zack off guard as he froze. "I—"

"Save it," she interrupted. She wasn't mad. Not after recollecting that he'd gotten into the fight to defend her, or at least that was her take-away from that conversation. Producing a slight grin, she made a dismissive gesture with her hands.

He wearily smiled, abstaining from saying much more. Embracing a moment of placidity, he altered the topic. "Are you ready for the trip in a few days?"

"I think so. I really haven't packed at all, but I think I'm prepared. I got the keys from Logan for the cabin, so we're all set there."

"Oh uh, whose car are we taking?"

"We can take mine," she offered. "It has comfier seats, and quite a bit of wiggle room for the dogs and us."

"Alright, that sounds good."

"Papa," Sky interrupted, "come look at this!"

Zack flashed Adalyn a playful eye roll as he stood up. "I'll be back."

Adalyn sat back in her seat as she observed the two of them. Inaudible laughter echoed in the parlor as a soft grin formed across Adalyn's lips. Her honey-dipped eyes lit up with a similar joy of her own.

She eventually stood up. Gathering her things, she made the executive decision that it was time to head home. Her hand rested on the door as she peered over her shoulder at the two of them, and without saying a word, she pushed it open. The bell chimed, though by the time Zack would've glanced over, Adalyn was halfway to her car.

CHAPTER NINETEEN

March 4, 2015

Adalyn stood at the window, overlooking the mountainside below. Luggage packed, she waited on Zack's tardy arrival. Her eyes fixated on the road like a hawk's, flinching at any movement on the ground. She was eager; eager to leave.

Her ears perked up to the low rumble of a car rounding the corner. With irritatingly slow caution, Zack's black Jeep gradually trailed toward Adalyn's abode. Fleeing the window, she hastily took off toward the front door, throwing it open just as he stepped out from the driver's side.

"You're finally here," She hollered from the doorstep.

Carrying her luggage down the limestone pathway, she met him at the bottom, where the path converged with the driveway. Her Range Rover sat idle in the driveway with its trunk popped.

"Sorry, I was getting Sophie ready." Opening the door to the back seat, Sophie hopped out and Rocky emitted a loud bark from the doorway as he piled down the path to greet his furry companion.

"You're fine." She handed Zack her suitcase.

"Are you ready?"

"Just a moment." Without saying another word, she turned around and walked back inside. She returned moments later with a blanket draped over her shoulders and a pillow in her hand.

"You know it's not *that* far away?" he teased her.

"Yes, I'm aware," she giggled as she tossed him the keys and jogged around to the passenger side.

As the ignition started up, he gripped the steering wheel with both hands and sarcastically quipped, "Ah, such a fancy car... With no scratches. We'll see how long *that* lasts..."

She playfully scowled. "Don't even *think* about it. Now floor it, and don't break my car."

"No promises there, Dear oh Friend of Mine! Also, how far away is East Bellvan?"

"It's about three hours until the main city of East Bellvan, Buddy Ol' Pal!" She giggled after calling him such. "But another two until Logan's cabin. Just start on the only road out of here, and it's pretty much a straight shot down."

Zack nodded. As the car rolled out of her driveway, Adalyn shut her eyes. Curled up in her makeshift bed, she began to drift off to sleep as she listened to him hum along to a tune that had been caught in his head. He sang to fill the void of silence.

Driving this way for many hours, drowsiness sunk in. Tapping Adalyn on the shoulder, he woke her from her beauty sleep.

"W-what?" she mumbled, shuffling about in her seat.

"Adalyn, I'm kinda getting tired."

She began to stir, slowly lifting herself into a sitting position as she watched the road in front of her. "How far are we?"

"About three hours in."

"Have we passed East Bellvan?"

He shook his head. "It's comin' up in about ten miles."

"Let's pull over when we get there." He nodded and let out a long yawn as he continued on. Adalyn observed the road as she struggled to wake up. "Why is it so quiet in here?"

"Oh, the radio doesn't work well in these parts. It's all static-y."

"So, plug in the aux," Adalyn exclaimed as she reached for the cord to start up the music.

The miles to East Bellvan flew by as the Range Rover parallel parked against a random curb. Switching seats, Adalyn's gaze drifted off to the distance, briefly taking in the sights of the small town.

Pointing out a shop across the street, she said, "You know, I used to work at that coffee shop over there."

"Really? I thought you'd never lived outside of those woods."

"I did for a time—it just wasn't a *long* time." Diverting the conversation, her hand hovered over the gear shift. "Ready to go?"

"Are you gonna drive us off a cliff again?" he teased as he buckled his seatbelt.

Producing a razor-sharp glare in his direction, she rolled her eyes and shifted the car into drive.

The drive was off to a smooth start for once. A soft tune hummed from the speakers and Zack turned the volume up, whispering along as it lulled him, though sleep never came.

Long roads of paved concrete gradually transformed into rattling gravel as they turned down Lake Shasta Drive, the last street before the lake house came into view. Zack yawned, exhausted from being trapped in the car. Peering behind him at the sleeping bundles of fur, the car ascended the long driveway.

"We're here," Adalyn exclaimed, shifting the car into *park*.

Zack immediately threw the car door open, springing out of it. He was in dire need to feel the ground again. As he did this, Adalyn nearly sprinted toward the front door, leaving Zack to fetch the luggage from the trunk.

"I'll meet you inside," he hollered to her, though she was already halfway there.

The cabin was enormous. Within the two floors, it had three bedrooms, a large, open kitchen, a rustic living room, and three bathrooms. The backdoor of the first floor opened up to a raised balcony that overlooked Shasta Lake.

"Zack," Adalyn hollered from the top floor as she peered over the mezzanine.

"What?" Zack held the last of their luggage in his arms as the dogs nearly tripped him while running under his feet.

"Come check this place out!"

"Just a second," he replied, setting the bags down before hiking up the stairs. Reaching the top, his eyes scanned the rooms. "Logan's livin' large here!"

Adalyn nodded in agreement. "This used to be my parent's vacation home, but they gave it to Logan and he did some renovations. I haven't seen it since I was a kid." Amusement twinkled in her eyes as she scanned the remodeled cabin.

Zack stood silently beside her, observing as she reminisced. Her twinkle caught his attention, finding her excitement rather enchanting.

Having had that moment, she eventually snapped out of it. "Should we unpack?" she asked, turning to face him. He nodded. "After, I was thinking of going to The Light Maple?"

"What's that?"

"It's a nice restaurant in downtown Shasta."

"Sure. One, two, or three?"

"What do you mean?"

"Well, which room do you want?"

Standing against the railing of the mezzanine, she teetered between the three rooms. Pointing to what was admittedly the master bedroom, she stated, "I call this one."

He scanned the remaining two. "Okay, I'll take the one next to you then."

"Where's the luggage?"

"It's downstairs." He peered over the railing, toward the entryway. "I'll go get them..."

The dogs piled up the stairs as he sauntered down. Returning moments later, he carried all bags in one trip, like a pack mule against a steep hill. Nearly collapsing under the weight, he set the bags down at the top of the staircase and exhaled a deep sigh of exhaustion.

"Thank you!" She picked up her bags as he worked to catch his breath. "I'm going to unpack. Do you want to meet back at the stairs in about an hour for dinner?"

He nodded in acknowledgment, finally managing to catch his breath as he retired to his room for the hour.

Adalyn shuffled around the bedroom, opening and closing drawers and doors. Listening to music in her ears, she hummed "All We Are's" melodic tune aloud.

In contrast to her, Zack didn't bother unpacking. He rested upon the bed in his room, listening to the ambient noise of the fan circulating overhead. After many hours spent crammed in a boxy car, his eyes began to give up on him, plunging him into a delicate slumber.

Adalyn's bedroom door slammed shut, jostling Zack awake from his nap. She softly knocked against his bedroom door, whispering, "Can I come in?"

"Y-yeah," he spoke, disoriented.

"Neat! Are you ready to go?"

He yawned. Reaching over the edge of the bed for his shoes, he nodded. "I'm ready."

"Great!" Nudging the door open as she exited, it swung against the stopper and emitted a loud *thud*.

Zack followed her down the stairs and toward the front door. Unable to keep up with her energetic strides, he eventually gave up and watched her prance off in front of him.

Stepping through the door of The Little Maple, Zack's eyes strained to focus under the warm, dim tones of the incandescent lights.

The world felt like a fever dream, zooming past him in a thick haze. Still straining to regain consciousness, he simply existed. Drifting in and out of reality, he followed Adalyn like a blind man to a seeing eye dog as she took the lead.

Taking their seats, Adalyn peered around in awe as numerous flashbacks struck her memory. "It's a lot like what I remember."

"You came here often?"

"Yeah, with my family."

Older and rustic in style, The Little Maple was well-maintained. It was a tucked-away treasure just outside of the main square of downtown Shasta; something only locals tended to know about.

"It's nice here," he commented. The waiter brought out two glasses of water, managing to not interrupt their chatter.

"It used to be tradition that when we came up to the lake house, we'd come here. Actually, I used to go by the name Shasta when I lived back in East Bellvan."

"Wait what?" Zack's full attention drew toward her.

"Yeah, It was right after I turned eighteen. I wanted to start a whole new life and escape that whole *tragedy* that struck my family, so I changed my name and moved out of the forest. Obviously, that *did not* work out!" She nervously chuckled as she picked up her glass of water and took a sip.

"City life just not for ya?"

"No, probably not."

"What can I get you?" their waiter asked, interrupting the conversation.

"Oh, the salmon, please?" Adalyn responded without missing a beat. She knew her order by heart.

Having forgotten to look at the menu, Zack picked it up and shuffled through the pages in a hurry. Peering up, he was frazzled. "I'll get the, uh... The ribeye, please. Um, medium rare."

"You got it," the waiter replied. Removing the menus, he cleared off their table.

"Thanks." Zack drew the conversation back to its previous state. Taking a sip of the water in front of him, he asked, "So, what brought you back into the forest, then?"

"Which time?"

"There were multiple?"

She nodded. "Two times. The first time was after I turned eighteen."

"Okay, let's start there. Why did you move back after that?"

"Sit back, because it's a doozy," she teasingly joked. He leaned against the back of his chair. "Okay well, I met this guy back then, named Dray, and his daughter, Delilah. They're the reason I packed up my belongings and moved back into the forest—into Shadow Mountain." She began twiddling with her cloth napkin.

"Really, Shadow Mountain? I'm—wow. Okay. Anyways, what next?"

"Well, we ended up getting married."

"You were married before?" She simply nodded, finding that information to be ahead of the point. Shrugging to her placid response, he pressed on. "And then?"

The conversation momentarily faltered as two plates were set down in front of them. Pausing until the waiter walked away, Adalyn continued. "Well, about two years later, Dray passed away and Delilah's aunt took custody of her. Oh, and the estate—oh my god, how could I forget to mention this enormous estate. It was this white mansion in the valley. Absolutely stunning! Anyways, the bank took it since I couldn't afford it... And then Keisha, the only family I had in Shadow Mountain, gave birth to her daughter, Bridget. She had no room, meaning I was back on the streets again. That's when I went back to East Bellvan."

"Oh, I'm sorry... That's really tragic."

She shrugged it off, cold to its memory. "It was five years ago... It felt like a lifetime ago."

Zack nodded at the momentary silence. He shoveled a few bites into his mouth before asking, "Alright, what about the second time?"

"Oh, that's a better story!" Her spirit lightened up, beaming with her usual glow. "I was working in that coffee shop again. It had been a few months since I'd left Shadow Mountain and Logan somehow scouted me out. That was when he proposed the idea of Dawn Hills."

"That's a much better story!" He grinned. "That's a lot to have happened in less than a decade." He took another bite, peering over at her nearly untouched plate.

"It feels like forever, though," she replied, plunging them into another lapse of silence. Taking a nibble of food, she finally disrupted the quiet ambiance. "So, what's your family like?"

"Huh?" He was taken aback by her question, now glancing up from the table.

"Well, you've never told me anything about them at all. What are they like?"

"Oh, they're alright. Probably more dysfunctional than most."

"How so?" She asked, casually picking at the salmon on her plate.

He shrugged. "There was a lot of fighting and screaming, growing up."

"Oh... Sibling fights?"

He shook his head as he began to shuffle the bits of food around his plate. "Typically between our parents, actually."

She glanced up, now drawing her attention toward him. "Really?"

"Is that not normal?" he questioned with genuine concern. She shrugged, uncertain either way.

"I wouldn't know any difference. My parents hardly spoke to one another, and when they did, they were passive aggressive. How did yours fight?"

"Well, my dad was a raging alcoholic..." A sudden realization struck his eyes as he recalled a specific time of his childhood. He set his fork down on his nearly empty plate and took a long breath. "There was this one time when I was younger that my parents were in yet another fighting match, but for some reason, something really angered my father. He went crazy... I don't think I've ever seen him so angry..."

"What happened?" Adalyn questioned. She was on the edge of her seat, but perhaps for all the wrong reasons. His past intrigued her, as she knew very little about it.

"I have no clue what had washed over me that day, but I guess I'd had enough?" Zack's voice raised at the end of the sentence, as if he questioned his own actions. He let out a soft huff of disbelief and continued. "I don't remember too much of what happened, but I recall waking up in the hospital because he'd thrown me across the room and broke several ribs. CPS got involved, my father got arrested, and they took me out of the house that night."

"What about your mom?" Adalyn was vastly wrapped up in his story, hardly taking her eyes off him as she scanned his expressions.

He let out a deep sigh and picked up his glass of water, taking a sip. "My mom sided with my dad and blamed me for sending him to jail, so she let me rot in foster care for a few months."

"Wow..." She exhaled deeply, processing the spew of information, though a piece of her felt a hint of triumph that he confided in her."I-I'm sorry. I didn't mean to pry."

"It's alright," he spoke with a gentle grin. He lifted his head and his eyes met hers. "I don't think I told anyone that story."

A gentle smile appeared on her lips as she focused back on the last morsels of food that rested on her plate. There was something more humane to him after he told his story; something more enticing to her. No longer this kind stranger that had fatefully wandered into town all those months ago, he had given a piece of himself to her, and she to him—something she'd come to cherish. Altering the topic to something lighter, she asked, "So, how old are you turning again?"

He peered off into the distance, mentally counting away at the years that had passed. "Twenty-seven, now."

"Wow, you're old," Adalyn teased.

Zack playfully rolled his eyes. "You're not far behind. What is it, one more year?"

"I'm only turning twenty-six this year. I'm still young and spry," she spoke with peppy confidence.

"Well, I'm not twenty-seven *yet*."

"No, but you're eleven days away. You might as well just consider yourself old." He let out a soft chuckle. Placing her napkin atop the table and checking the time, she let out a yawn. "Are you ready to go?"

"What do you mean?" he asked. She motioned toward the door. "Oh, yeah."

Rising from her seat, she picked up her card from the checkbook and gathered her belongings. Continuing their chatter, they gradually began to stroll toward the exit. At this point of the night, the restaurant was nearly empty, signaling that it was past time to bid their evening adieu.

CHAPTER TWENTY

March 5, 2015

Wednesday morning, speedboats zoomed past the cabin at bright hours, sending waves crashing against the shoreline. Lake Shasta was actively known to be a hotspot for summer activities, as well as for some in the deepest of winters.

Sitting up on the balcony, the two sipped their morning coffee in bathing suits as they overlooked Rocky and Sophie romping around the backyard.

"You know, I've always wanted to ride on a speedboat," Adalyn said, interrupting their tranquility.

"You never been?"

She shook her head. "Logan has a Bowrider down at the marina, I believe."

Zack pondered for a moment, taking a sip of his piping hot coffee. "Wanna mark something off your bucket list today?"

"How do you suggest we do that?"

"Your best friend here once mastered in hot-wiring just about anything."

"Or... I'm sure Logan has a key laying around here?"

"Sure, if you'd like to do it the boring way," he joked.

Adalyn smiled as she rose from her porch chair. "I'll go dig around and if we can't find the key, then *maybe* I'll let you hot-wire it."

"Deal," he exclaimed, perhaps too excitedly.

Adalyn rummaged through all the drawers in the cabin, not quite knowledgeable of the key's shape, but hoping that she'd recognize it when she saw it. Clattering through miscellaneous clutter in the kitchen, Zack quietly snuck up beside her.

"Find it yet?" His presence startled her as she jumped. Before she had a chance to answer, Zack reached an arm across her. Her gaze followed as he picked up a ring with two keys, dangling them in front of her face. "Actually, I believe these are what you'd be looking for."

She raised an eyebrow from confusion, "How did I miss those?"

He shrugged. "Oh well. Are you ready for the best day of your life?"

An expressive glow illuminated her eyes. "Lead the way!"

"Actually, I'm gonna need you to lead the way. I have no clue where the marina is."

"It's not too terribly far." She shoved the drawers shut as she made her way toward the front door, reaching for her packed beach-bag on their way out.

Just past the driveway was the main gravel road that wrapped around the lake. Not long into their walk, the marina's water fell into view, glistening through the trees. Holding most of the community's personal boats for the off-season, the pier sat about seven properties down from their own.

Taking in the rows of boats, Zack's eyes gleamed with admiration. "Which ship is it?"

She pointed northwest from where they stood. "The one that has *Dawn* painted on the side, of course."

"But, of course!" Strolling up to its port, Zack twirled the key ring around his middle finger.

As they boarded onto the boat, the fresh scent of the salty lake wafted into their noses. Amused by his skill set, Adalyn watched as he flipped and twisted different gears before plugging in and turning the engine key.

"What's our next step, Captain? Do you know how to steer this thing?" Adalyn took a seat in the passenger side of the boat.

He glanced over his shoulder at her. "No, not quite, but it can't be that hard." Flipping the choke, the engine roared.

"Hey, you did it!"

"I told you, I've done it before." He glanced around, inspecting the ship's gadgets as he assessed the tools needed to properly drive it. "I think if I pull this... and do a little..." He spoke to himself as they slowly maneuvered away from the dock. "Neat."

The boat drove toward the center of the lake, though not very speedily. "Hurry this thing up," Adalyn insisted. Shades now covered her eyes as she leaned against the back of the passenger seat, basking in the sun's faint warmth.

"Alright, alright, I'm working on it." He pushed the lever forward, sending the boat throttling at a faster speed. "Is this better?"

She nodded, nearly being thrown from her seat as it did so. Regaining her balance, she stood up and made her way toward the bow. Adjusting her hair, she sat on the bench and peered over the boat's edge, admiring the lake below.

"See anything cool?" His voice became muffled against the roaring waves, though she heard him. She shook her head. Heaving the boat, it came to a soft halt as he joined her up front.

"How about you? See anything cool?" she questioned, playfully teasing him.

"Depends. What's your definition of *cool*? It all looks pretty cool to me."

"I don't know, sometimes these decently large salt-water fish hang out in the middle of the lake... Though they typically are deeper in the water."

"And, how do you expect me to find that, then?" he teased.

"I dunno, jump in and look!"

He wavered for an instant before confidently responding, "Alright." Before allotting time for any doubts, he rose from the bench. Ripping his shirt off and discarding it across the boat's deck, he dove off the bow's edge.

"Zack! What are you doing? Are you insane?" she hollered as she leaned over the rim. He popped out of the water, shaking his head as water sprayed in all directions. "How do you plan to get back *on* the boat?"

"I live in the present, Adalyn," he responded as he tread the water. "I'll figure it out when I get there."

"Oh my..." She tracked him as he swam laps beside the boat.

Diving under the water for a brief instance, he rose, spitting out a small stream of lake water. "It feels great, you should come try!"

"No thanks. I'll stay where it's dry."

He chuckled. Now scanning the boat's walls, he thought out loud, "Okay, how do I get up onto the ship?"

"Already?" she giggled.

"It's colder than I thought it'd be," he said, and Adalyn smirked. Her expression said what she didn't need to; that she told him so.

She let out a low *hum*. Scanning the interior, her eyes caught a glimpse of some rope. "Can you climb a rope? Because I found rope."

"Didn't do so well last time I tried, but okay, let me at it!" She threw the rope down and knotted it to the railing of the boat.

With some struggle, Zack climbed the rope. Hoisting himself onto the deck, he rolled over, lying motionless on the ground for several minutes in efforts to recuperate. As he did so, Adalyn hauled the line of rope back onto the boat.

"God, I'm freezing," he spoke through shaky breaths. She let out a faint giggle as she threw a dry towel in his direction.

"That's why I don't jump off boats in March, silly!" She took a seat beside him as he shivered.

"It was your idea!" Through jittery teeth, he altered the topic, "Now, what's next on this bucket list of yours?"

She deliberated for a moment as her eyes scanned the lake. "Well, I've always wanted to go to the Bermuda Triangle and drink coconut juice out of a coconut on a beach. I've never been cliff diving, parachuting, or carried bridal style—like they do in the movies."

"Haven't you been married?"

"Yeah, why?"

"Well, didn't you get carried bridal style on your wedding night?" She shook her head, causing him to terminate further questioning about the topic. "Okay, how about we head back into land and see what else we can scratch off that list?"

Her eyes lit up with excitement. "Okay!"

"Give me a moment more to warm up and then I'll take us back." He still shivered against the gentle breeze that occasionally wafted in from the surrounding mountains.

"In the meantime, you can tell me what *you* want for your birthday."

"Hmm. Nothing."

"That's not a viable answer, Zack."

"But, this trip is more than enough," he contested.

"Why is it that you don't ever celebrate?"

"It's just never been a Blake family tradition. My dad hated to celebrate anything."

"That's so sad," she exclaimed. He shrugged, not minding so. A cold breeze hit, sending another shiver down his spine. Fidgeting with her fingernails, she shifted the conversation. "How do you know how to hot-wire stuff? Was that from your time in New York?"

"Well, parts of it, yes. My parents moved to New York when I was around six, and I lived with my aunt and uncle in North Carolina for a few years before joining them."

"That didn't answer why you knew how to hot-wire things."

He hesitated before speaking, but inevitably continued, "I used to work at a motel and hot-wire expensive cars on the side, for trading purposes, when I lived in the Bronx."

Completely missing what he'd meant, she asked, "Oh, you're from the Bronx? Isn't that one of the worst places to live?" Adalyn inadvertently scrunched up her nose.

"Yeah. Wait, you didn't know I was from the Bronx?"

"No, I didn't. I didn't know much of either place you grew up in."

Zack's focus turned to the floor of the boat as he responded. "Oh, well, I am from Cherokee, North Carolina, the Native American reservation. Then I moved to the Bronx with my mom." His insecurities grew as he spoke, and his leg nervously shook, waiting for her reaction. Adalyn casually nodded. Though his heritage didn't linger on her mind, Mia's words sat in the back of her throat like a sour taste. *Class-climber. Tuffhunter.*

She ceased the discussion as her gaze had wandered off now, peering out at the surrounding mountains. Yet another strong breeze struck the air, and Zack had had enough being on the boat. Drying himself off more, he crawled into the driver's seat and revved up the engine. "Ready to head back to shore?" She gazed over at him and with a soft smile, she nodded.

The engine had hardly stopped when Adalyn reached her hand out for the dock. "Easy, you're gonna hurt yourself," Zack warned as she instantly pulled her hand back. Shutting off the engine, he hopped out to tie the speedboat up the way they'd initially found it.

Hesitantly, Adalyn reached for the edge of the wooden dock once more. Balancing herself on the rim of the boat, she swayed against the rocking waves. As she lunged for the pier, the boat dipped away causing her to misstep. Tripping herself on the dock's rim, she lost her balance and began to fall backwards, toward a watery landing.

Instinctively flailing her arms, she felt his hand reach for her. Grasping her at the last second, he quickly pulled her up and into him.

Now resting against his chest, Adalyn listened to his heart beating through her shaky breaths. Regaining composure, she peered down at her cold foot. "Oh shit," she mumbled through a trembling voice.

"What is it?"

"I just lost my shoe..." She dwelled for a moment as her gaze fell upon the lake, though her shoe had already begun its trip to the bottom.

Zack let out a quiet *hum*, contemplating what to do next. Still holding Adalyn against his chest, he took his free arm and spontaneously swooped her up. Holding her like a bride on their wedding night, she wrapped her arms around his neck for balance.

"Hmm, this is new... I like it though." She nervously giggled as her gaze teetered from the ground, up to him. "Say, why am I getting picked up like *this*?"

"Well, Adalyn, I've learned you love the single-lady life, meaning you don't want a boyfriend for a while, but I do believe every girl deserves to be carried bridal style at least once. So, I am taking it upon myself to be the one who does it first."

Adalyn's face lit up with an uncontainably widened smile as she gaped up in adoration. "Zack..." Her tone was longing. She was speechless, yet her mind sped at a mile a minute. Gazing up at him, the tone of his hazel eyes whisked almond brown and shamrock green together, creating a kaleidoscopic masterpiece of vivid color. She was lost in them.

The short trek to the cabin was peaceful, as he managed to carry her the full way. And when they got back, he gently set her down upon the chilled, wooden floor, where the dogs eagerly greeted their return.

"Thank you," she replied. Taking off the other shoe, she tossed it to the side, acclimating to the cool hardwood.

"Of course."

"I was gonna go get cleaned up, then I thought we could figure out dinner?" He simply nodded in response as she disappeared up the stairs.

Upstairs, Adalyn sat on the edge of the bath. Waiting until the steam rose from the water's surface, she flipped the nozzle to the shower head and stepped in. Squirming under the hot temperatures, it nearly scorched her skin. However, no amount of boiling water distracted her racing thoughts from roaming right back to *him*.

She let out a disgruntled groan that was silenced against the running water. Reaching for her phone on the counter, she checked the time. *Four-thirty*. An hour had passed. Realizing this, she quickly stepped out and got dressed.

Creaking the bedroom door open, Adalyn peered over the mezzanine. The television illuminated the room, and the sun was on its hasty descent behind the frosty mountaintops.

"Sorry," she apologized as she descended the staircase.

Twisting his body toward the back of the couch to face her, he expressed a vibrant grin. "No worries. Oh, I didn't know this was a fancy dinner? I'll go get ready."

"Wait, is that what I think it is playing right now? Is that *Friends*?"

"Yep! The episode is half-way over. C'mon, wanna join in?"

Without hesitation, she joined.

As the episode came to an end and turned over to the next, Zack rose from his seat. Without a word, he disappeared up the stairs. The television roared loud enough to deafen her darting thoughts. Laughing along, time sped by her, and before she knew it, another episode came and went. Footsteps made their way across the upstairs as a voice echoed down to her.

"Ready for dinner, yet?" Freshened and tidied up, Zack stood against the railing, looking down at Adalyn. Dressed in a denim blue button-down and black pants, he playfully grinned as he took his first steps down the staircase.

Mesmerized by his appearance, his hazel eyes twinkled with a shimmer of excitement against the television's blue light as he reached for his coat on the back of the couch.

"I'm ready," she finally responded.

Out the front door, their silhouettes flickered while foggy clouds of steam rolled off their lips from the frigid air.

CHAPTER TWENTY-ONE

March 30, 2015

Staring out the window of Granny's Diner, Adalyn sipped her morning coffee in her reserved booth. Amidst the freezing temperatures, the smoky steam that wafted from her piping hot drink enlivened her, filling her spirits with a sense of joy. Bringing it to her lips, her body warmed as the liquid trickled down her throat. She emitted a soft *ahh*.

Her serene moment, however, was suddenly and abruptly cut short.

"I thought I'd find you here." Adalyn turned toward the familiar voice. "It's Beka, Zack's sister."

"Oh, right! Hey. It's a pleasure to see you again." Adalyn's expression lightened up in the woman's presence. They'd had the pleasure of briefly meeting one another a couple days prior, when Beka had first arrived.

The woman's platinum blonde hair swished behind her as she gleefully approached the booth. She was average in both height and appearance, though kind at heart.

"You as well." Beka's burgundy tinted lips curved into a genuine smile.

"How've you enjoyed the town so far?"

"It's been so great! I've spent most of it exploring."

"That's great to hear. Remind me, are you here for a while?"

Beka nodded. "A couple weeks, about. Mind if I take a seat?"

Adalyn motioned to the spot in front of her. "Be my guest. What brought you to Granny's? I assume your brother must not be far behind?"

Beka shook her head. "No, he won't be joining us. He's meeting up with someone today, so I came looking for you. Figured I'd take you up on your previous offer to show me around? I went to your house, but some blonde told me you'd be here?"

"Ah, Joyce..." Adalyn replied, sipping her drink. "Yeah, I can do that. Any particular place in mind?"

"I was hoping you'd actually tell me of places, since I really don't know this town."

"Sure thing. Let me finish this coffee, and we'll get started with Main Street Shopping Center? It's not a whole lot to see, but it's quite pretty, and the closest nearby."

Beka nodded. "I heard there's a carnival there in the fall time?"

"Yes! The Halloween carnival is extremely popular in this town, though you missed it. It ended in October. Are you thinking of moving here?"

"Goodness, I wish. No, I have a life back in New York. Though, I thought about it. With the surprise of Sky, and all... And, I am really not a fan that Mia is still around."

"Oh yeah. That's actually kind of new for me too..."

"I thought he'd ditched that witch a long time ago."

"What do you mean?"

"Oh, she's still coming off as a sweetheart to you, isn't she? Yeah, she and I used to be close friends. We were almost inseparable, until I found out she was using me. All I can say is, beware. She is *not* what she seems."

"Good to know," Adalyn replied, really unsure how to take that news. Glancing down at her mug, Adalyn took a final sip, emptying it. "I'm ready whenever you are."

"Oh, perfect!" Beka immediately jumped to her feet, collecting her belongings. "Since we are going on Main Street, I had my eye on a little boutique around the corner that I'd love to check out, if you don't mind."

"No, no. Not at all. Lead the way." Adalyn encouraged, pleased with her enthusiasm. She followed the woman out the diner, nearly running to keep pace. She was coming to understand how Zack felt every time she'd skipped off ahead.

Beka came to an abrupt halt outside of Little Sally's Boutique, one of many that rested on Main Street. It was about a block from the diner and stocked with alternative, grunge style clothing—fitting for Beka's personality. Tugging at Adalyn's sleeve, she led them inside.

"Thank you for coming with. Zack refused to step foot in here with me."

"Why's that?"

Beka shrugged her shoulders. "He hates shopping of any sorts. Truly, you'd be lucky if he'd even be willing to go to the grocery store with you." Shuffling through the racks of clothing, Beka was gaining a stack of items that draped over her forearm. "Do you mind if I go try these on?"

"Go ahead," Adalyn encouraged.

She walked the aisles as she waited, not actually looking through anything, but rather just deep in thought about nonsensical ideas. She pondered about Rocky, and advancing his training. She thought about her friends, and how little she'd visited them lately. Her mind raced over many topics as she waited, though lately, her thoughts couldn't seem to shut up as they flooded her head.

Beka popped up beside her like a silent mouse. "Are you finding anything?"

Adalyn jolted from her thoughts and shook her head. "No, I wasn't looking."

"Too bad, you'd look so good in some of these!"

"I don't know… It's not my style. I think it looks better on you."

"Whatever you say."

"Did you find everything or are you still looking?"

Beka glanced down at the pile in her hands. It was thinner than before. "No, I got everything I could ever want. I forgot how much I love small-town boutiques."

"They really are great," Adalyn commented as she followed Beka towards the front. "So, I was debating ice cream at the famous ice cream shop or heading up north, toward the town's small lake. It's frozen over for the season, but they serve some amazing hot chocolate and you can watch residents ice-fish."

"Isn't it a bit cold for ice cream?"

"Well, that's up to you. Most residents around here wouldn't pass up the chance. It's great ice cream; you can't knock it till you try it."

"I'm not knocking it, I just don't know how bearable it'll be in this weather."

"So, hot chocolate and ice-fishing, then?" Adalyn proposed.

Beka shrugged, happy to go along with Adalyn's ideas. "Sounds lovely!"

The drive to the community lake was short, though filled with scenic beauty, as Beka's focus remained glued to the window. With the crisp winter coming to an end, it brought on gentle blankets of snow that coated the tree branches and created a winter wonderland, which seemed to intrigue the woman.

Little was spoken between the two during the car ride, though Adalyn hardly minded. The backroad led straight through to the main lodge that oversaw the lake, and as Adalyn pulled on to its paved road, she parked in the nearest spot she could find.

"We're here," Adalyn announced. Beka's fascination muted her as she slowly slipped out of her seat. "You coming?"

"Sorry, I'm coming," Beka finally replied, closing the car door and racing over to Adalyn. "I just—you don't get to see this much nature often in New York."

"Aren't you from North Carolina?"

"Sure. But I left when I was like ten or eleven. I hardly remember anything like this!"

"I guess that makes sense. Ready to go inside?" Adalyn nudged her, finding the air to be quite nippy.

Beka followed Adalyn up the steep ramp that led to the elevated lodge. A grand hearth crackled in the corner, emitting a candescent glow from its core. Adalyn took a seat on a nearby couch, leaning into it as if it were her own.

"This place is..." Beka began.

"Stunning," they said together.

"I know," Adalyn replied. "I don't come up here often enough, but this is probably one of the coziest places in town. It's just a rough drive in the winters, having to kinda off-road it."

"Yeah, I bet you guys get piles of snow..."

"Oh, absolutely. The lodge is owned by the Connors family, who kinda outlives my own around these parts. Their son, Pax—I believe, just recently took over the family business, and remodeled the lodge over the summer."

Beka grinned, amused with Adalyn's avidity. "It all sounds so lovely! Maybe if I get time off one of these summers, I'll come back up for a visit."

"You really must," Adalyn exclaimed. Her body began sinking into the couch. "The summer is actually the best time to come. You can swim in the lake, and a ton of residents have barbecues along the shore. It's a whole ordeal!"

"How do you order, here?"

"You go up to the counter." She pointed behind Beka, to a small booth near the entrance that offered a slim selection of pastries and beverages.

"Sweet, I'll be right back. Can I get you anything?"

"Hot chocolate?"

"Sure thing."

Beka returned with two to-go mugs in hand, placing one down on the coffee table in front of Adalyn and taking a seat in a chair across from her. "Okay I have to ask, what do you do as an Architect around here?"

Adalyn giggled as she took a sip of her scalding drink. "Well, there isn't much to do in the winter time because everyone has either skipped town, or is hiding away indoors. However, I get extremely busy in the summers. I keep the town in order. I help with business upkeep, maintain a record of all the individuals that travel into the town, get a census of those who become residents, assist the Council with statistical data charting progress of business, and ensure safety. Of course, I also host and coordinate most parties as well. It's a lot more work than I lead on, but I get swamped during the summer-time."

"Oh, wow. I genuinely wasn't expecting that answer. Though, I really had no clue. Not even Zack could tell me!"

"Zack doesn't even know the half of it. He joined the Council at the end of the summer, so he completely dodged the shit-show."

Beka laughed. Taking a sip of her drink, she set it down on the coffee table between them. "Okay, so tell me one more thing... What's with you and my brother?"

"Oh..." Adalyn took a sip of her hot chocolate in efforts to conceal her concern. "What about him do you want to know?"

"Like, everything about you two. Are you two seeing each other? Sleeping together? What's the deal? Because he does *not* settle down in one place, yet here he is. A *homeowner*? I've never seen him more head-over-heels for someone. What magic love potion did you place on him?"

Adalyn was flattered. She hid her cheeks that burned scarlet red. "I-I really didn't do anything."

"No seriously, Adalyn! I don't mean to frighten you, but I've never seen him show as many emotions as he does."

Taking nervous sips of her drink, she tried to ignore that it still scorched her tongue upon every sip. "I mean, I really like him too, I suppose."

"You suppose?"

"Well, I do. A-and I've told him that once. I just... I don't know if I'm ready yet. But I really do like him a lot!"

"It's just odd how both of you are so *hush* about your feelings and yet you feel so strongly about one another."

"I'd like to believe it's because we both don't want to risk what we have," Adalyn began. "We both know that dating would risk our friendship, but every now and then, we will take a step forward. It's a process."

"But you both want something more than just a friendship?" Beka pried.

"True, I won't deny that. But we also stay in that friend zone to avoid any slips that could harm our friendship."

"Why does it have to be that difficult? Why can't you two just admit what you're feeling and take that leap of faith?"

Beka's words stuck with Adalyn, as she had no real excuse. She took another long sip from her drink. Trying not to wince from its heat, she held it near her mouth to conceal the pain.

"That's a good question," Adalyn pondered, feeling lost within her own reasoning.

"See. I mean, sure it's scary at first, but imagine the outcome." Beka leaned back in her chair, holding the cup in her hand. She hadn't taken many sips from her drink, as she was doing the smart thing and waiting for it to cool.

"I have imagined every possible outcome."

"And are they good?"

"They're moderate."

"What's so bad about them?"

"Honestly," Adalyn thought more, "nothing."

"And you can't just take a leap of faith?"

"I took the first leap!" Adalyn protested. She sat up, feeling vulnerable in her slouched position.

"Yeah, because saying *I like you* is *such* a big leap of faith..."

"It was the first step."

"Inch. It was the first inch," Beka corrected. "Well, I'm just saying, and maybe don't listen to me. I'm only his sister. I *only* know him like family, and what-not... But maybe give him the room to say something sensitive, or something sweet. I know he wants to speak up, but he's too shy."

Adalyn quirked an eyebrow, listening to the woman's advice. "Alright. What would you propose I do or say to initiate that?"

"Did I just sway you to date him?"

"No." Adalyn dropped the woman's hopes in an instance. "It was a sweet thought, though. But I don't mind hearing your advice at least."

Beka playfully rolled her eyes and grinned. "If I were you, I would just say what was on your mind. I know it's scary, but I guarantee, after listening to him endlessly talk about you, it'll yield pretty great results. But that's all I'm gonna say! The rest is on you."

Pleased to be ending this conversation, she nodded in agreement. "Understood. I'll take it into account when I speak with him next." Adalyn didn't quite mean it, though she wasn't about to tell Beka so.

"Alright, well I came up here for hot chocolate and ice-fishing. Though it's pumpkin spice instead, I've gotten a hot beverage. Now it's time to watch ice-fishing!"

"Gladly! Step right up," Adalyn exclaimed. She rose from her seat and led the two of them to the east side of the lodge, where in the center of the enormous glass panels was a double-door that led to the balcony.

Venturing through it, the chilly air struck them. Adjusting to the temperatures, Adalyn pulled her jacket sides tighter around her waist. Pointing out in the direction of the lake, she motioned to the buckets of fish that residents had gathered.

The lake was frozen over with thick blankets of ice. Against the glassy water, the pine trees glistened as the sun's gentle rays refracted off the snow. Adalyn sipped her drink beside Beka as they silently stared off at the lake, enjoying the calming sport taking place in front of them. After some time, even Beka had had enough of the nippy air.

As Adalyn returned Beka to Zack's cabin that evening, Beka stopped and leaned into Adalyn's driver side window. "I had a lovely time, thank you. Please consider everything, though. I promise you won't regret it!" She began to walk up the long path toward the front door. "Goodnight, Adalyn!"

CHAPTER TWENTY-TWO

March 31, 2015

Adalyn's lips curved into a gleaming smile, forcing her cheeks to rise and delicate wrinkles to form around her mouth. Her eyes lit up with admiration when he greeted her at the door that late morning. Zack's surprise visits always seemed to enliven her spirits, and she encouraged them with her optimistic twinkle.

"What can I do you for?" She hugged the front door, continuing the expression of glowing excitement.

"Just stopping by. I met with Max for lunch, down at Granny's, and figured I'd stop in to say hi!" A gentle grin appeared across his face. He wasn't nearly as expressive as Adalyn, though no one could ever match her. However, he meant more than he showed, and he showed it better in his actions.

"Aw, that's sweet. How's Max?"

"He's doin' well. I don't know if you heard…"

"Max and Maddie are moving in together," they simultaneously spoke, only to pause and laugh at their sync.

"Yeah, I heard," Adalyn responded. Her elated grin continued to shine as bright as the sun, creating a warm tingle inside Zack's stomach.

Pleased he'd stopped by, she enthusiastically suggested, "Say, if you're not busy, let's do something today."

"Alright, sure. Beka is watching Sky right now while Mia is off doing… *Mia* things. Whatcha got in mind?"

She deliberated for a moment, turning some ideas over in her head. "Hmm, perhaps we could go down to the lake again before the ice turns to water?"

Though she'd just been there the day before, she was determined to appreciate every lasting moment of the frozen waters before the warmer weather swept in to melt it all away.

"That sounds like a great idea," he happily replied.

Smiling, the cold air began nipping at her. "Oh, come in," she offered, stepping aside. "I just have to clean up and let Rocky out before we go. It'll be quick, I promise!"

He stepped inside her front door, instantly blasted with the familiar theme song. "Is that *Friends* playing?"

"Yeah! Ever since we watched it together, I've kinda been obsessed."

"I always told you it was a great show!"

"I don't disagree," Adalyn responded as she picked up the last of the dishes that had been spread across the counter. Moving to the living room, she straightened the blanket that rested on the back of the couch. From her peripheral vision, she watched a blurb of golden fur chaotically bolt past the back door. Rocky had slipped into a zooming frenzy outside, only prolonging Adalyn's ability to leave.

Finally panting from exhaustion, Rocky's cheerful face appeared at the back door. Letting him back indoors, she reached for her purse. "Sorry 'bout that, I'm ready now."

Zack's attention was glued to the infamous sitcom that projected on Adalyn's television, hardly hearing her as she spoke. "Wha—oh. Great, let's go!" He hesitantly shuffled into the entryway, occasionally peeking back behind him as the laugh track echoed through Adalyn's abode.

Prying the car door open upon arrival to the lodge, they were immediately hit with March's brisk weather.

"You comin'?" he hollered from the sidewalk.

Adalyn hurried out of the passenger side, jogging over toward Zack. "Sorry, I couldn't find my wallet."

"What do you need that for?"

"Oh... I guess nothing." She swung her purse over her shoulder as she followed him up to the lodge.

The warmth from the fire hit her rosy cheeks as she stepped inside, warming her at its touch. Taking a seat against the windows that faced south, she removed her jacket and placed it behind her.

"Hot chocolate?" Zack asked as he rested his jacket on the back of the seat across from her.

"How did you know?"

"C'mon Adalyn, is that even really a question?" He valiantly smirked as he turned to walk off.

Shifting in her seat, she peered out of the vast window beside her. The southern windows had a direct view of the lake below, to which she mindlessly gazed out upon, surveying the flock of geese that rested atop the frozen lake.

Zack returned with two cups and handed one to Adalyn. Taking a seat across from her, he sipped his drink and winced. "Oh god, that's hot!"

Adalyn couldn't help but giggle as she held the cup in her hands for warmth. "What did you expect?"

"I dunno, honestly." He set his down on the table between them. Rising up again, he wandered toward the window to peer out at the lake. "Remember when we ice skated on this?"

"Oh goodness, we did, didn't we!" She didn't know how she could've forgotten that. It was an eventful moment that inevitably landed Zack in an urgent care with a light concussion after playfully chasing the geese and colliding into a snowbank.

"Not one of my best moments," he chuckled.

"Definitely not one of the best moments, but sure was a funny one—looking back of course."

Peering over her shoulder, she glanced over at the seating that she and Beka had sat in the previous day. Recollecting on their chat, the talk of Zack lingered in her mind, churning as she ran it over again. Curling up in her chair, she held her drink in her palms.

Appearing beside her seat, Zack held out a blanket and set it on her lap. Amidst her deep thoughts, she'd hardly noticed he'd even wandered off, though she gladly took it and wrapped herself up.

"Oh, thank you!"

Another moment of silence wafted over them as Adalyn reheated herself under the warm blanket and Zack finally sipped away at his cooled drink.

Minutes passed as his gaze remained on her for a moment too long before he finally choked up the courage to ask, "Well hey, I have one mere question to ask..."

Adalyn perked up. "And that is...?"

"Ya know the whole thing where I like you, you like me?" he asked. She quirked an eyebrow, curious where he was going. "Well, answer me honestly. Why aren't we dating?"

"Wow, I had a sense you were about to ask me something like this. Umm..." She pondered for a moment, unable to come to a single reason as to what held her back anymore. "Honestly, I don't know..."

"Really? I was expecting a whole list of reasons." Zack nervously chuckled, perhaps trying to lighten the mood.

She laughed as well. "Yeah, I really don't know why we aren't."

"I see..." He paused and pondered. "So we aren't dating for no reason... But we could be dating?"

"Uh, yeah. I guess. And yeah. We could be; yes. I see no reason why not..."

He fell silent for a moment more, gathering the proper words to say. "So... If I just asked you to be my girlfriend, and if you agreed, then we'd be dating... Interesting." He spoke to himself, though he spoke it aloud.

"Yeah, that's how it works." Adalyn proceeded with caution, as she was partially caught off guard with such questioning.

A widened grin appeared across his face. "Well alrighty, miss!" A burst of confidence washed over him; something she'd never seen before. "Will you do me the honor of being my girlfriend?"

Adalyn couldn't hold back the soft giggle and wide smile that followed his question; the way he asked was wholesome. Her stomach lurched—not with butterflies, but rather a sense of excitement. A twinkle glistened in her eyes as she lightly bobbed her head. "I would love to."

Taking the final sip of his drink, he grinned as he placed the cup on the table between them and let out a loose sigh of relief. "Hah, wonderful!"

Taking another sip from her drink, a wave of warmth washed over Adalyn as she felt rather pleased. It felt *right*.

CHAPTER TWENTY-THREE

April 3, 2015

Shortly after the sun's early descent behind the mountains, Zack's familiar Jeep pulled into a parking space outside of the fancy, new Italian restaurant. First of its name, La Regale made its appearance as one of the more lavish dining experiences the town had ever seen.

Four days had passed since Zack had popped the long-awaited question, and the couple had become more inseparable than before—if that was even possible. Filled with excitement and delight as of late, it was only fitting that he finally took her on an official date.

Outside the restaurant, Zack grasped the passenger-side door handle and yanked it open. A beaming smile appeared across his face as he was met with her honeyed eyes, which glistened against the dangling lights that hung from the establishment.

"Thank you," she said while she emerged from the car. The edges of her pine green, satin dress clasped around her thin stature. Even in early April she wore no jacket, as she was afraid to taint her elegant look. Suppressing a shiver, she crossed her arms over one another, hastily following alongside him.

Zack pulled open the front door to La Regale and stood aside, allowing Adalyn to walk in first, her stiletto heels clicking against the wooden floorboards as she did so. A warm breeze blew through her hair, waving it behind her as she approached the hostess stand. Lacking the confidence, she peered over at Zack, who was fixated on adjusting his black button-down shirt that had been ruffled from the breeze.

"Do you have a reservation, sir?" the hostess asked. Gaining Zack's attention, he glanced up.

"Uh, yes. It should be under Zack Blake?" Adalyn could sense the nervousness in his tone as it wobbled and wavered when he spoke.

The hostess scanned over a list of names in front of her. "Oh yes, Mr. Blake. Right this way."

A lurching churned in Adalyn's gut as she began to follow the woman down a long aisle of occupied tables. Nervousness exacerbated the butterflies that fluttered in her stomach, though she couldn't quite seem to pinpoint *why*. As she stepped further down the aisle and away from the podium, she felt the eyes of a thousand souls searing holes into her. Keeping her head high, she paid them no mind.

Distracting herself, her focus ventured toward the exquisite paintings that lined the walls. Vivid colors danced off their tapestries as she strolled past. Positioned in the back of the establishment was a luminescent wall filled with bottles of the most expensive wines—perhaps emptied, that illuminated the restaurant with a turquoise hue.

The hostess came to an abrupt stop in front of a table that rested in the heart of the dining hall. "Does this work, sir?" she asked.

"Yes, thank you," Zack responded. Adalyn could read it across his face that he'd hoped for something more secluded, though found it rather pointless to argue in such a busy setting. Caving in, Zack pulled out a chair, motioning for Adalyn to take a seat.

"Thank you."Adalyn smoothed out her dress as she sat.

"Wonderful. Here are these. The waitress will be right with you if you need anything else." Placing down two menus on the table, the woman dismissed herself.

Silently situating her silverware on the table and positioning the cloth napkin in her lap, Adalyn pondered what to say—anything to say that would rupture the silence. But for once in their entire friendship, she couldn't think of a single thing to talk about. She felt out of place, out of her element, as they sat there; something she'd never felt before.

She peered over at Zack for potential answers to the tension that was fizzing inside her, though he'd been obliviously scanning over the menu.

Okay, he seems fine. Perhaps it's just me. Turning her gaze on to the sea of customers, she took a deep inhale. *It's just me,* she reassured herself. Picking up the other menu, she began looking it over.

"You look really nice," Zack finally spoke up, interrupting her racing thoughts. The presence of confidence in his voice soothed her; it grounded her as a gentle glistening rested in her eyes.

"Thank you! You do as well." She'd inconspicuously scanned his handsome attire earlier in the night, making note of its elegance.

"I'm gonna run to the bathroom real quick. I'll be right back." He set his menu down and dismissed himself.

Adalyn picked her menu back up as she scanned over it, though nothing on it truly seemed to catch her attention. She continued to look it over until she'd nearly memorized its contents.

"Look at her over there," a woman spoke just loud enough for Adalyn to hear. Unsure who the woman was referring to, she simply dismissed it.

"Wait, Melanie, which one do you mean?" a second woman asked.

"This restaurant was so nice until she decided to bring some tufthunter into it."

Adalyn's attention rose. Now well aware of whom they were referring to, she eavesdropped from behind her menu.

"How can you tell?"

"Did you not see him! He reeks of it. Now it's going to be stuffed with these lowlifes, thinking they can just come here—Oh, shh. He's coming."

"Hey," Zack cheerfully greeted upon his return.

Adalyn set her menu down, producing a warming grin. "Hey!"

"Did you find anythin' good?"

"Actually, not really. You'd think this place would have a better selection."

Zack opened his menu and scanned its contents. His face scrunched up with confusion as he was unable to find a single dish that stuck out to him; better yet, a single dish that he actually understood. "Oh yeah. All the ingredients have weird names. Like, what is *foie gras*?"

Adalyn laughed, "Okay, that's actually pretty good. It's like goose or duck liver, I think. But you know what I don't see on here that I'm *craving*?"

"What?"

"Pasta! I do not see a single pasta dish on this menu. It's absurd!" Though sincere about her disappointment over the lack of pasta, she spoke with a faint smile plastered on her face. "You know, I could really go for your homemade meatballs right now..."

"Really?" Though confused about her sudden change in plans, his tone held a sense of relief that she notably played off of.

"Really! Plus it's so loud in here. I know we got all dressed up to go out, but I really wouldn't mind just going home, turning on our show, and making a homemade meal together—Only if you want to, of course!"

A delighted grin broadly appeared. He had little interest to be in such a place, but he did so to try and impress Adalyn. "I—yeah, that sounds great," he said, trying not to sound too relieved.

"Really? Okay, great!" Adalyn swiftly rose from her seat. Producing a side-glare in the women's direction, she pushed her chair in and they silently raced through the aisle of tables that led to the exit.

Swinging the front door to Adalyn's abode open, the couple sauntered into the kitchen. Feeling more at ease, her shoulders relaxed for the first time all night, and she placed her belongings down on the island counter. Immediately turning toward the refrigerator, she let out a melodic *hum* that coincidentally concealed the sound of her stomach grumbling.

Zack casually moved beside her. A sense of tension gradually dissipated from his aura as he'd returned to familiar grounds. Letting out a soft sigh, Zack glanced over at her. His lips unconsciously rose into a delicate smile as he admired her outline that shone against the refrigerator lighting.

"I have ground beef and I know I have spaghetti noodles around here too," she spoke, completely oblivious to his gaze. Remaining entranced by her essence, he was unaware that she'd spoken to him. Peeking over her shoulder, she lightly furrowed her eyebrows. "Zack?"

"Sorry, I-I was just remembering all the ingredients I needed."

Good save, he thought as he took a few steps to his left and began washing his hands in preparation.

"No worries. What all do you need?"

"Any chance you have peppers and onions?"

She scanned the shelves. "Oh, I have some peppers, but I don't think any onions. Oh, but I may have onion powder? I don't know if that'll do it justice."

He airily chuckled. "We can give it a shot!"

"Want me to boil the pasta?"

"Sure. You're on pasta duty and I'll man the meatballs."

She giggled at his comment and retrieved the box of pasta from the pantry.

They fell silent for a moment while they fixated on prepping the kitchen for their meal. In a matter of minutes, the island became a disarray of ingredients, thrown about in no sense of order.

Adalyn jumped as the clock chimed seven. Falling out of her absorbed trance, she recognized the near-soundless environment, filled only with the chopping of peppers and sleepy snores from the two dogs cuddled up in front of the fireplace. Setting the wooden spoon down beside the stove, she quietly made her way into the living room. "Want to watch something?" she asked, peering back at him.

He glanced up. Nodding, they simultaneously spoke, "*Friends*?" She laughed and turned back toward the television. Turning it on, she pulled up the DVR full of their favorite show and clicked a random re-run. It began to play aloud as she returned to the stove.

Water drained in the sink from the pasta in the strainer, and at that moment, Zack stepped beside her to search the spice cabinet for paprika. An idea formulated in her head as she playfully hip-bumped him. Biting her lip, she looked up at him to note his reaction.

A bit confused at first, he noticed her spirited undertone as he mischievously smirked. Bumping her back a bit harder, she dramatically stumbled.

"Ah," she laughed, this time lightly shoving him with her hands. The smirk remained on his face as he went to shove her back, only to be surprised with flying strands of spaghetti hitting him. Pasta fell to the floor as he grasped a few more strings and flung them at her.

Before they knew it, pasta was slathered about the kitchen, sticking to the walls. In the humorous scuffle, Zack had managed to grab hold of Adalyn, ceasing her cannon-throwing fists of pasta.

Meekly wrestling her, she dropped the spaghetti, now weak with fits of laughter.

Uncontrollably giggling, she slid to the floor, her sides now in pain.

"Oh, Adalyn," he playfully groaned, though he couldn't hold back a mirthful grin toward her excitement. "You're sitting on smushed pasta!"

Tears were nearly rolling down her cheeks as she looked at him through watery eyes. Behind him, pasta was glued to the cabinets and fridge. "Well, at least I cooked the pasta, right!"

With a smirk plastered on his lips, he extended an arm out for her. Helping her back up, the timer dinged. With her hand still in his, he gaped at her. Their eyes connected as a thousand sparks emitted in between them. A lump gathered in her throat while she admired the gleam in his radiant eyes. Allured by his attraction, she was drawn in by him.

There were no butterflies, no fear, and no tension. She closed her eyes to the comfort of his presence and felt his warm breath as he leaned in closer. Gently pressing his lips against hers, he grabbed at her waist. Taken aback by the passion, the sensation of an electric fire shot through her system as she wrapped her arms around his neck, pushing into him.

The timer dinged again, tugging them from their moment.

"I gotta..." He hesitantly pulled away. Letting him go, her arms sank down to her sides and she returned to what was left of the pasta.

"How much longer on your half?"

"I think everything's ready over here. Is there even any pasta left?" he questioned after assessing the destroyed state of the kitchen.

"I think there's just enough," she laughed, stepping back for him to evaluate.

Peering over her shoulder, he shrugged. "Looks good enough to me!"

"Great," she exclaimed as she reached above her for two bowls. Setting them down on the counter, she began divvying out scoops of pasta into the separate dishes.

"Wine?" Zack asked, hovering over the fridge. She glanced up from scooping meatballs onto her dish and nodded. "Pinot Grigio good? I know white isn't really fitting for spaghetti, but—"

"I don't think I have any Pinot," she began, only to be interrupted by him pulling out a chilled bottle from the shelf. Smiling at his bubbly smirk, she watched as he poured two glasses.

The clock chimed nine when they plopped down in front of the television with their dinner. Situating the dishes on the coffee table, he raised his glass in the air. "Cheers!"

"Cheers!" Their glasses clinked together, and they took a sip of the white wine.

Placing his glass on the table, he caught a glimpse of the two dogs still sleeping in front of the fireplace. "Ya'know, we should set up a date for Sophie and Rocky."

She followed his stare to the dogs. Enthralled by his idea, she exclaimed, "I think that would be so cute! What if we made them dog-friendly spaghetti and meatballs, like Lady and the Tramp?"

He chuckled, knowing well that she was serious. "Yeah, we can get a little picnic set up for them and everything."

"Okay, it's gonna happen! We are *absolutely* setting up a puppy date for them." Satisfied with the plan, she triumphantly leaned back against the couch, allowing her focus to return to the television.

The episode played on, and the food gradually disappeared from their plates. Now entwined in one another on the couch, they cuddled up under a warm blanket. Somewhere in the passing time, they'd turned off the lights, leaving only the television to illuminate the room. Before they knew it, light snores emitted throughout the house as Adalyn's head rested soundly on top of Zack's shoulder, and his on top of hers.

CHAPTER TWENTY-FOUR

May 25, 2015

Summer rush came early this year as streets bustled with pleasant greetings, returning the forest to a state of liveliness.

Amidst the chaos, Adalyn found herself inside a bridal boutique, delicately grasping onto the hand of her former roommate, Joyce, who presented a rather large stone upon her finger. Against the frosting cream walls and LED lighting, the diamond gem nearly blinded the room.

"Okay, give us one more twirl, Joyce," Maddie hollered from the couch.

Modeling on the platform, Joyce gave the white gown another twirl. Snugly wrapped around her figure, the skirt cascaded to the floor like Cinderella's ball gown.

"Stunning!"

"How do you feel about it?" Adalyn asked.

Joyce turned toward the mirror. Giving it another twirl, she ruffled the skirt of the dress. With a gleaming smile, she looked over at the girls, "I think this is the one!"

Erupting into a frenzy of excitable screams, they all sprang with animation.

"Okay, so did we ever decide the date or where the wedding will be held?" Maddie asked.

"Well, it's still being discussed, but we were thinking about July twentieth! We still don't have a place picked."

Adalyn immediately stepped in. "It'll be in my backyard."

"Wait, when—"

"Ragnar and I talked about it. We haven't finished finalizing everything yet, but since you asked..."

Her face lit up with a luminescent gleam. "Oh, thank you, Adalyn!"

Adalyn's lips curved into a smile as she saw her friend's merriment. Joyce turned back to the mirror and swayed the skirt back and forth a few more times. She felt whimsical in it; like a princess at the ball. She paused mid-twirl and her face sunk into a nervous grin.

"What is it?" Adalyn asked.

"Well, weird question, but do you know any priests?"

"Uh, actually Ragnar said he was hiring Zack to officiate."

"Should I be worried?" Joyce half-teased.

"Probably... But whatever." The clock ticked one-thirty and Adalyn's phone buzzed, interrupting their moment. "Sorry, it's my alarm..."

"Is it time?" Joyce asked with dolefulness in her eyes.

Adalyn dismissed the alarm. "No. I've got a little longer."

"Then let me go change back, before you go."

Hopping down from the platform as Joyce ran off, Adalyn took a seat beside Maddie on the guest couch.

"Are you sure you don't need me there?" Maddie asked.

"You're all good, really. Kayla said she'd step in for you."

The alarm buzzed again, and she shifted her gaze toward the clock. Joyce broke through the fitting room curtains, just in time.

Silencing the alarm once more and collecting her belongings, she glanced over at Joyce with a gleaming smile. "I'm so excited for you! Are you sure you'll be okay today?"

"Yes! I have Maddie to help where help is needed. Now, go!"

"Okay, if you're sure." Hugging her friends goodbye, Adalyn hurried out of the bridal shop door.

Against her black winter trench coat, the temperate May weather heated her like an oven as she made her way toward the Architect Building. When she'd left her house this morning, the air was brisk and frost covered the grass; however, by midday it had warmed significantly.

The Architect Building fell into sight as she picked up her pace. Speed-walking down the last block, a familiar voice called for her.

"Adalyn?"

Her heart sank. *Rose?* she thought to herself. She knew that voice from anywhere.

"Adalyn," the voice hollered once more. Adalyn halted in her tracks.

Turning around, she squinted in confusion. Across the road, a young woman was flagging her down, though it wasn't Rose—it couldn't be. This woman had aqua blue hair and was of healthier weight with refined makeup skills, unseen in Rose's previous appearance. In addition, her clothing style was too disparate from what Adalyn knew; this woman dressed in a grunge style with black ripped jeans and fashionable, gothic clothing. Admittedly, this woman was far more attractive than the young, red-headed girl that Adalyn had seen last December.

This was not Rose. It couldn't be. As the woman crossed the street, her unforgettable jade green eyes fell into view. *Oh, yeah. That's Rose.*

"Rose..." Adalyn said, less than amused.

"Violet, actually."

"What?" Her tone held a mixture of confusion and annoyance.

"I go by Violet now. Violet Quinn."

"Oh." Adalyn spoke, unamused. Checking the time on her phone, she began to walk away.

"Look," the woman blurted for Adalyn's attention, "I came to apologize and... I don't know, maybe start over? I know I was young and stupid and honestly, *weird* last time we saw each other, but I'd like a restart." Adalyn stopped walking for a moment. Attempting to hold her attention a little longer, Violet said what she knew would gain her focus. "Zack didn't like me, he liked you. Even my own eyes could see that. Look, I don't expect us to be friends right off the bat, but I'd love a second chance. I promise, I am not as young and dumb as I was. A lot's happened since then and I'd like to believe I've grown."

Adalyn turned around to face Violet. "I have a meeting in about five minutes."

"Okay..." Violet spoke, unsure where she was going with this.

"...And when I get done, I'm willing to grab coffee with you—but *only* coffee. A singular cup of it, and we can catch up," Adalyn replied. She had no direct intentions of becoming friends with the woman, as last she remembered her, she was insufferable. However, the woman piqued her curiosity, and she was willing to give her a shot.

"Okay," she enthusiastically spoke.

"I'll meet you at Granny's at," Adalyn glanced at the time, "four-fifteen. It gives me time in case the meeting runs late."

"Typical place," Violet giggled. "But okay. I'll see you there." Violet's jade eyes glistened with excitement as Adalyn turned again to leave.

Now sprinting down the last block, she was nearly late for the meeting. Climbing up the building's stoop, she swung open the heavy door and ran inside.

"Sorry I'm late!" She flung herself into her desk chair.

"You're fine. It's only five minutes 'till two, you're not late yet," Kayla responded as she peered up from the stack of papers in front of her.

"No, but later than I wanted to be."

"Is it just us two today?"

"Yeah. Zack is busy with Sky, Maddie is with Joyce, helping pick out everything for the wedding, and I have no clue where Adam is."

Kayla sarcastically chuckled, "Yeah, me neither. But okay, we've got about three minutes to debrief before we walk into that boardroom, so let's get started."

Within no time at all, the front door to the building slammed shut and thin heels clinked against the floor. Adalyn and Kayla stared at one another with an inkling of fear circling their auras. Like a wolf to a bear, no matter how powerful Adalyn seemed to be, she cowered to the chief of Shadow Mountain.

The doors to their conference room swung open and Lilith took her first step across the threshold. The woman's saffron yellow eyes burned past her onyx black hair and blared into Adalyn's soul as her and her selected disciples took their seats around the oval table.

It was their annual Conference of Architects—really just composed of the two women, since no other towns neighbored them. This meeting was set in place to discuss effective policies and financial standpoints, but if you asked Adalyn, it was just trivial. Each year, it was the same discussion; the same arguments, that no one could ever seem to agree on. *Demolish this. Incorporate this. I don't get this.* Quite frankly, she didn't get why they even bothered to meet. The two women ruled so vastly different, this meeting was just a concoction for a major migraine, rather than a solution to anything.

It seemed like a lifetime passed before the clock ticked four, and Adalyn assisted Lilith and her entourage out the front doors. Waving a farewell to the unnerving woman of Shadow Mountain, she hung back for a minute before making her way toward Granny's Diner.

Flinging the door to the diner open, she scanned the restaurant, looking for the fire-engine red hair that she'd grown familiar with. Not seeing such, she sighed with relief, only to immediately tense back up when the woman's recognizable voice echoed across the diner.

"Adalyn!"

Adalyn turned her head toward the source, locking eyes with the woman. Pressing on a smile, she slowly meandered over to the table.

"Hello, Ro—Violet." She took a seat across from the woman and removed her belongings, setting them on the chair beside her.

"Hey, I didn't think you'd show."

"Part of me didn't either," she jested, though there was some truth behind it.

Ruby approached the table, interrupting the reunion. "What can I get you ladies?"

"A coffee, please," Adalyn instantly responded.

"Same, please." Violet handed over the menus that rested on the table. Turning back to Adalyn as the waitress left, she said, "Well, thank you for giving me a second chance."

"I haven't yet."

"Right, of course…"

Ruby quietly returned with two cups of coffee.

"So, why are you back?" Adalyn went straight to the point, removing any room for meaningless conversation.

"Uh," Violet nervously began, "Believe me when I say, it wasn't up to me. I'm um… I'm married now." She held up her left hand, presenting a luminous diamond ring.

"Who?" Her tone didn't hold back the disbelief she had that someone would agree to marry her.

Ignoring it, she replied, "His name is Kian. He moved me and his four year old daughter, Copeland here. We, uh… We just moved in today."

"Oh."

"I'm also pregnant," Violet blurted, drawing Adalyn's full attention.

"What?" Adalyn's heart skipped a beat as her eyes inadvertently fell to the woman's stomach in astonishment. Doing the math in her head, her mind raced. "Who's?"

"Kian's. Who else—oh." Silent tension washed over the table, though Violet's words did happen to mitigate her stress. The woman spoke again. "Hey, I know you're uncertain about me, but I'd really love it if we could try again, I remember being extremely invasive and naive—and I can't say I'm not still naive, but at very least, I'd love a chance to truly get to know you, without stepping on everyone's toes. I know I really messed with the *balance* of things." Adalyn scowled, thinking back to how annoying it felt, dealing with the *old* her. "I heard about you and Zack."

She shot a confused glance. "How?"

"News travels fast. I'm happy for you, though. You two were always the perfect couple; even I knew that. He wouldn't shut up about you when I was... Anyways... You two will make amazing parents!"

Adalyn stared at her with utter confusion. "I—We're not having kids..."

"Oh, I just heard about a kid now, I thought—well, I guess that timeline wouldn't have made sense..."

"Nope, that's his ex," Adalyn clarified, though her explanation seemed to do the exact opposite.

"His...?" Violet furrowed her eyebrows.

Adalyn scoffed at its thought. Leaning in, she began to explain Mia's disposition. Leaning back out when she finished the story, Violet's jaw had nearly dropped to the floor.

"Jeez." That was all that Violet could say.

"You're telling me."

"Sounds like I missed a lot," she jested.

"Well, maybe if you stick around..." Adalyn gleamed. Admittedly, in the few minutes that she'd spent with the woman, she was impressed.

The woman's face lit up. "Does that mean we're—"

"Well... Let's not get ahead of ourselves. Let's just maybe try out this acquaintance thing first."

A twinkle of hope sparkled in Violet's eyes. "Thanks."

Looking up at the clock on the wall, she noted the time. *Five o'clock.* Glancing back at the woman, she asked, "So why the name Violet?"

"Why not?" she casually shrugged. "I think it's more fitting now."

"Is there anything else I can get you two?" Ruby asked, checking in on them.

"The check, please?" Adalyn asked.

"You got it!" With a beaming smile, she walked off.

"I like Violet," she responded as Ruby hastily came back with the bill.

"No tab this time?" the woman jested. A laugh tugged at the side of her lips as she placed her card down.

"I have a new card that I haven't bothered entering yet." Signing the merchant copy, she glanced up at Violet with a delighted grin. "Look, I really do need to get home, I promised I'd meet—"

"No, you're totally okay!" Violet genuinely beamed. "I'm really glad you gave me a chance. Maybe we can do this again soon?"

"I'd like that," Adalyn responded with a genuine tone as she picked up her belongings in a haste and made her way out of the diner.

While her hand rested on the door, she glanced over her shoulder to where Violet sat, only to see the remnants of an empty table. Inhaling, she held her breath and pushed the door open as a heavy gust of wind blew past.

Stumbling into her home that evening, she exhaustedly made her way toward the kitchen. The lights remained dim around her house and an unusual silence crept in as Rocky's enthusiastic presence was nowhere to be found. Hair raised on the back of her neck while she fumbled to find the light switch.

Flipping it on, the lights flickered before they illuminated. Unexpectedly, her eyes widened to the trail of red rose petals that led from the kitchen. She dropped her belongings on the floor and walked along the petaled pathway that trailed up the stairs. From the third step, she listened to the familiar tune of "All We Are" coming from her bedroom and watched light flickering underneath the doorway. Peeling the door open, the rich smell of vanilla hit her nose.

The room had been lit with rows of candles on nearly every surface and her bed became blanketed in red petals. In the corner, Zack stood over the nightstand, lighting the last cluster of candles. He was completely oblivious to her entrance, only making note of it when Rocky and Sophie barked to her presence. Turning around, he froze in shock.

Adalyn's elated expression was beyond comparison. Her honey brown eyes glistened against the candlelight as they locked eyes with his hazel orbs.

"You weren't supposed to—"

She took her first steps into the room, scanning it with admiration. "I'm sorry, I got home early from—it's not important. Why did you do all this?"

"I uh—Well it was supposed to look better than this. I haven't finished setting up." His eyes nervously darted around the room.

"Even so, this is so sweet! What did I do to deserve this?"

"Well, it's your birthday today and I thought you should come home to something nice." Zack sheepishly grinned.

"How did you know? I don't tell anyone."

"Logan accidentally told me at Christmas..."

"This is absolutely *amazing*. I-I'm at a loss of words. Zack, seriously this is—" Adalyn walked to the center of the room, now illuminated by the glow of the candles.

Her ecstatic expression alleviated his nerves. Meeting her in the middle, he had picked up two glasses of red wine from the nightstand and placed one in her hand. "It's Pinot," he chuckled.

"Zack, I—" Finding no other words to quite complete her train of thought, she kissed him.

CHAPTER TWENTY-FIVE

June 21, 2015

A soft breeze wafted through the air, sending ripples through the calm, turquoise water, while rays of sunlight glistened off the surface, twinkling like a pool of stars. Summer solstice brought life to the lake as creatures of all kinds rejoiced at its banks. To the west, canoes and paddle boards coated the surface, while the east harbored gentle waves for the ducks and deer that chose to visit that afternoon.

The morning had started out with an enthusiastic Sky vigorously jumping on their bed, eagerly seeking adventure. Reining in her youthful energy, Adalyn put together a last minute trip to the lake.

Standing against the lodge's balcony railing that looked out to the eastern sector, Adalyn and Sky admired the forest life below. "Addy, look! There's duckies!" Sky lit up with elation as her tiny finger pointed out to a flock of ducklings that had gathered on the bank.

"Aw, adorable!" Adalyn bent down to the young girl's level and looked through the railing. Peering just to her left, she proceeded to point out another paddle of ducklings waddling along the bank. Tottering behind their mother, they made their way toward the shore's edge.

"What're they doing, Addy?"

"That mama's gonna teach them how to swim."

"Can you teach me one day?"

Adalyn just smiled. The balcony's door noisily shut as she cocked her head in its direction and stood up. Approaching with a drink carrier in his left hand and a bag in his other, Zack interrupted the girls' moment. "Hey, sorry it took so long. They were out of the raspberry tea, so I got you iced chai."

"Oh, no worries. Thank you!" With a smile and a peck on his cheek, she took her drink out of the carrier.

"Papa, what did you get me?"

"I didn't forget you, Sky." Zack plucked out a small cup and handed it to her. "Here, it's chocolate milk."

Taking the cup with both hands, she beamed. "Papa, Addy and I saw duckies!"

"They're right over there." Adalyn pointed to her left at the flock of ducklings beginning their descent into the water.

"Addy says she's gonna teach me how to swim!"

"Is that so?" Zack asked with a curious expression, to which Adalyn responded with a silent shrug. Sky ignored him, newly distracted with her chocolate milk.

He picked the young girl up in his arms, holding her above the railing as she gazed off into the distance, feeling like a bird perched at such enormous heights.

"Do you want to feed the ducks, Sky?" Adalyn asked. The young girl perked up with a gleaming sparkle of excitement. "Your papa brought duck feed. We can go down to the lake and feed them!"

"Yes pwease!" Sky squirmed to get free of her father's grasp, extending her arms out toward Adalyn. Zack set her down, and she immediately grasped for the woman's hand, taking it in her own as they descended the staircase.

By the marsh, geese and ducks paid no mind to the few residents that had wandered down to the edge, though the deer had long taken off by the time they'd arrived.

"Okay, you have to be very quiet," Adalyn whispered to Sky. "You don't want to scare them, or else they may run off."

"Okay, I be quiet," Sky repeated back as she squeezed Adalyn's hand tighter.

She glanced down at the young girl with a gleeful grin, then over at Zack who walked beside her. "Do you have the feed?"

"Yeah, here you go." He handed her the bag. Taking it in her free hand, she crouched down to Sky's level.

"Give me your hands." Sky let go of Adalyn and cupped both her hands together. Pouring a pinch of bird feed into her hands, she looked at it in awe. "Okay, don't give it all to one area. Spread it out!"

Sky took the bird feed and slowly attempted to approach a family of ducklings. As she grew near, they began to waddle away. "Why do they run away?" she asked with disappointment.

Adalyn held in a giggle while Zack answered, "You're big and scary to them." Sky giggled and ran back to them.

Adalyn sat down in the grass and patted the ground beside her. "Here, come sit next to me." Both of them joined her in the grass as she tossed the bird feed in front of her. "Now we wait."

"Wait for what?" Sky asked.

"Well, if we stay quiet, they might come up to us."

Sky complied and sat there in silence. A few minutes passed and the young girl crawled into her father's lap, fiddling with a piece of grass she'd plucked. Adalyn rested her head on Zack's shoulder while a duck quacked as it began to feed on the seeds.

"Look! Look," Sky exclaimed.

"Shh, don't scare it away, silly," Zack whispered as the duck froze. Sky quieted, though she silently bounced with joy.

She beamed when the duck came closer. Behind the mother, a few ducklings began to waddle up. Excitement lit in both the girls' eyes as they looked at one another.

"Hold your hands out, Sky," Adalyn whispered while she poured another pinch of bird feed into the young girl's hand. Turning to Zack, she poured some in his as well. "Now, when they get near, hold your hand out and be still."

"How do you know about this trick?" Zack asked.

"All creatures are the same around here; they're very trusting if you can bribe them. I learned this from an old friend, years ago."

Holding their hands out, they remained silent as the ducks approached. Pecking at Zack's hand, the mother duck was hesitant of him. The ducklings, however, were not so cautious. They arrived with curiosity, nearly crawling onto Sky's hand while they ate. More ducklings eventually joined in.

A goose squawked in the near distance, startling Sky as she flinched. Her attention turned toward it. "Do they want bird food, too?"

"No, Sky. They aren't as nice as the ducks are," Zack responded, holding the young girl in place on his lap.

"Aww, but they look hungry!"

"Here," Adalyn poured a pinch more into her hands. "Continue to feed the ducks before they get full and go home."

Sky immediately turned her attention back to the ducklings in front of her. "Okay!"

"Well, that was easy," Zack chuckled. "You're good with kids!"

"I took care of a few in my day," she quipped as she poured more feed into both of their hands.

"Thank you." He grinned, turning back to the ducks in front of them. Pouring half of his portion onto the grass around them, he held the other half in his hand.

Within no time at all, more ducks surrounded them. Gaining trust from the cluster, the birds inched their way closer until they, too, were eating out of everyone's hands.

"Addy, this is the best," Sky whispered with sheer fascination.

Zack leaned over and gave Adalyn a peck on the lips. "This is fun. Thank you."

Adalyn smiled from the compliments while more ducks flocked over to see the commotion. Quacking emerged from all around them. To Sky, this was a magical, memorable experience; one she'd cherish for ages. She felt like a princess of animals as they encompassed her. It was exactly how Adalyn intended this day to go.

The afternoon sun surged, and was now scorching down, making it hardly bearable to continue. Lucky for them, they were nearly out of bird feed. "We should probably head off before the birdies get angry," Zack announced after some time.

"Awww…" Sky complained.

"It's getting hot, silly," he attested.

"But I'm not hot! I wanna keep doing this!"

"Sky, we've been doing this for the past two hours."

"Nuh-uh," she protested.

"Oh well, let's go!" He picked her up in his arms regardless. Maintaining a rather fun voice even as she fussed, it somehow soothed her; she began to giggle. "We'll be back to see the ducklings soon," he promised.

"Okay!" She squirmed in his arms. "Let me down, Papa! I wanna walk."

He set her on the ground as she took off toward the lodge. Waiting back for Adalyn, Zack held out his hand and the two of them followed behind the ecstatic girl that had skipped off ahead of them.

CHAPTER TWENTY-SIX

July 20, 2015

Wooden chairs were placed in two symmetrical rows, and strung from tree to tree, lights dangled above the yard with vines entwined in their wires. Down the middle row of tables sat the arbor, draped with white chiffon fabric and laced with flower vines. Leading up to the arch, two wedding staff frantically sprinkled white lily petals down the path.

"T-minus two hours," Adalyn hollered at the staff as she stood on her back patio with a clipboard in hand. "And, an hour until the bride arrives. Chop-chop!"

"Miss..." A worker approached to her left.

"I don't want to hear it, just fix it," she commanded, not even bothering to look up from the clipboard as they staggered off.

Food caterers began setting up in the southwest region of the yard, emanating sweet, delicious scents into the air, and exterior design staff placed the finishing touches on the yard. Now alluring—and indubitably magical, the venue shifted into a whimsical oasis.

The doorbell rang in the distance as Adalyn checked the clock. *One-thirty*. She ran to answer the door.

"Joyce," she exclaimed. "You're early. Why?"

"Maddie said to meet here for makeup."

"Since when!"

"I—"

"Sorry, I'm here," Maddie interrupted.

"When did we move the makeup and hair to here?"

"Sorry, Addy! It's a long story. Can we just use your bathroom, please?"

"I genuinely couldn't care enough to hear the 'long story'. Just go get ready, please!" Annoyed now, Adalyn irritatedly motioned toward her bedroom.

"On it!" The girls sprinted up the stairs as Adalyn disappeared out back.

Smells of fine cuisine and flowers now permeated the air, making Adalyn sneeze upon first exposure. Exploring the grounds, she inspected each sector until she couldn't spot a singular flaw. Recognizing the decorous conditions, she wandered back inside to check on the bride.

Climbing the staircase to the bedroom, the doorbell rang and she groaned, turning back down to answer it.

"Hey," Zack greeted, kissing her on the cheek. "You look stunning."

She rolled her eyes, knowing well that he was just saying so to be kind. "You know this isn't even my outfit for the event, right?"

"Oh... Well, you look cute anyways. The pantsuit really works for you."

She laughed. Pecking him on the lips, she moved back toward the stairs. "Well, I have to tend to the bride, since she and Maddie decided to switch up plans on me, but your outfit genuinely looks very handsome."

"Why, thank you! I'm glad you think so, I borrowed it from Max." A dorky smile appeared on both their faces as she climbed the stairs and disappeared into her bedroom.

"Okay," she barged into the bathroom, nearly startling the two girls. "Where are we at?"

"Finishing hair now, then moving over to makeup," Maddie responded.

"Anything I can help with?" Maddie shook her head. "Well, Zack is here."

"Is Zack's outfit bad? Should I be worried?" Joyce quizzed.

Adalyn giggled as she'd taken a seat on the bench in her bathroom. "No, he actually looks very handsome. Apparently he's wearing a black suit he got from Max?"

Maddie laughed. "I know exactly which one that is. He came over a week ago to try it on. Trust me, I can confirm it looks good!"

Joyce let out a sigh of relief. "Okay, good. Hey, Adalyn, genuine question..."

"What's up?"

"How much do you value your toaster oven?"

"Wha—why?"

"Uh, we kinda need a toaster at the new place..."

"Oh. I mean, I hardly use it—"

"I know."

Adalyn pondered for a moment before answering. "Consider it a wedding gift."

"Really? Thank you!" Her eyes skimmed over the clock on Adalyn's counter. "Hey, does anyone know where Ragnar is yet?"

"He should be here—" The doorbell rang. "I bet that's him. I'll go get it." Adalyn sprung from her seat as she nearly flew down the stairs. Meeting her at the door, Zack and Adalyn answered it together. "Ah, look who finally decides to show up," Adalyn teased.

Ragnar rolled his eyes. The nervousness overcame his ability to handle her witty remarks. Nevertheless, he returned it with his own quip. "Shut up, Addy. I'm still a minute early." She ignored him and moved aside to let him in.

"Where should we..." Zack began to ask.

"Umm, let's try upstairs in either of the guest bedrooms. Does that work? Joyce is already upstairs, getting ready in my room."

"Okay." Zack led the way up the stairs.

Closing her bedroom door to avoid the boys seeing the bride, Adalyn gasped.

"What? Does it look okay?" Joyce nervously asked.

"It looks *perfect*!" Joyce beamed as the worry seemed to wash away.

Without a word, Maddie grabbed Joyce and sat her down on the bathroom stool. "Close your eyes," she instructed.

By the time Joyce was able to open them again, she was transformed into fully-done hair and makeup, and Adalyn had changed from her pantsuit, into a heather purple A-line dress that draped the floor.

Dithering in her room as the time passed, Adalyn checked her watch once more. *Two-forty-five.* "Five more minutes till. Put your shoes on. I think I heard the boys go downstairs already and I know the guests are here." She nervously rambled.

The Wedding March echoed through the house as ambient chatter from below ceased. The signal was in place; it was time. Placing the last of her jewelry on, Adalyn helped clasp Joyce's necklace before she extended her arm out for the bride. "Are you ready?"

Joyce took a deep breath to ease her nerves as she linked arms. "Ready."

Adalyn beamed as she pulled open the bedroom door and they took their first steps down the stairway. Guests gathered outside, sitting in their seats.

"Hmm, my maid of honour is giving me away," Joyce teased to lighten the air.

Arriving on the final stair step became Kayla's signal to let go of Sky's hand, sending her down the aisle with a basket of red flower petals that she dropped along the pathway. Organ music began up as Joyce took an even deeper breath than before.

"Wow," she mumbled under her breath as she peered over at Adalyn.

Adalyn smiled back at her friend and gently patted her hand for reassurance. "You've got this."

Taking her first step down the flower path, the sensation of love began to overpower the fear she felt. Melting at his gaze, Joyce involuntarily smiled brighter than the sun as she approached the end of the aisle. There, Ragnar stood in a black tuxedo with his hands folded in front of him, watching with adoration.

Flower petals crinkled underneath the girls as they stopped in front of the altar. Adalyn kissed Joyce's cheek before taking her place beside the bride. The music faded out and inevitably ceased as Ragnar briefly glanced over his shoulder at the priest.

"You may all be seated," Zack began. His gaze fleetingly shifted between Ragnar and Joyce. "We've gathered here on this wonderful day to unite this beautiful couple in matrimony. In this holy estate, these two come here today to be joined. Now Ragnar, do you take Joyce to be your lawfully wedded wife, to love and to hold, for sickness or for health, for richer or for poor, till death do you part?"

Ragnar longingly gazed into Joyce's sapphire blue eyes. "I do."

Zack now looked over at Joyce. "Now Joyce, do you take Ragnar to be your lawfully wedded husband, to love and to hold, for sickness or for health, for richer or for poor, till death do you part?"

She stared into Ragnar's dark brown eyes with a gleaming smile. "I do."

"Now, before this beautiful couple is to be married, does anyone object? Speak now or forever hold your peace." The air was silent. Eyes darted around the room, searching for anyone that could possibly object. "Since no one spoke, let's get the rings!"

Kayla rose from her seat nearest the altar and handed Adalyn the two rings, who then handed each to the couple. Taking the initiative, Ragnar clasped her hand and placed the ring upon her finger, in which she mirrored the action, slipping the band onto his ring finger.

Zack grinned as he became mesmerized by the exchange, nearly forgetting his next line. "Oh! I now pronounce you Husband and Wife. You may kiss the bride!"

Leaning in with brightened smiles, the couple kissed.

The hour following the ceremony was crammed with professional photographs as the guests casually dispersed and the staff prepped for the reception.

Transformed from the previous wedding arrangement into the reception, wooden tables were covered by white cloth and placed throughout Adalyn's backyard with bouquets of purple and white lilies resting in the center of each. Surrounding them were fancy, white plates and floral name cards neatly placed on top.

Spending most of the evening alternating between the dance floor and chatting with their guests, Ragnar and Joyce finally took their seat at a table of their loved ones, ending the night surrounded in merriment. Champagne corks popped, spewing foamy bubbles into the sky, and food was served on fancy plates while laughter permeated the summer atmosphere.

CHAPTER TWENTY-SEVEN

August 30, 2015

Teddy's, the local marketplace, was devoid of customers that Sunday afternoon as Adalyn aimlessly strolled the fluorescent-lit aisles. Following behind Zack and Sky, the plan was to be in and out in a quick minute. Forty-five minutes had passed now, and all Adalyn could hear was the soft whirling of the fans overhead and Sky's clobbering feet slamming against the white epoxy floors.

Adalyn had fallen into a sort of daze at this point. When she finally came to, she had no clue how much time had passed, just that they were back in the pasta aisle as Sky debated over which box she craved most. Zack's phone rang for what felt like the fiftieth time since they'd arrived, to which he silenced it.

Opening her mouth to ask who it was, a voice hollered in the distance, interrupting her train of thought. "Adalyn?" she whirled her head in the direction.

"Adam?" she spoke in astonishment. It had been at least a year since she'd seen him last; since he'd run off without even a proper goodbye. She was hesitant to approach him, though he made that rather difficult to avoid as he abruptly ran up on them.

"Yeah. I'm back in town, finally!"

"Why for?"

"Uh, it's a long story. Care to grab drinks and catch up?"

"Sure, I have drinks with Logan tonight, though. Maybe another time." She peered over at Zack. "Oh, Adam, meet Zack. He's my—"

Zack stuck his hand out. "I'm her boyfriend!" His voice was friendly, obliviously friendly.

"Pleasure to meet you," Adam responded with a grin. "Let me know any time you're free, I'd be glad to catch up sometime."

"Will do," she emptily replied, having no real intentions to reach out. Taking the hint, Adam turned to leave.

"Who's he?" Zack asked, merely curious.

"That's Kayla's step brother, Adam."

"Oh! I think I've heard his name a few times before, now that you mention it." Adalyn silently nodded. Turning his attention on Sky, Zack glanced down at the conflicted child who'd still not been able to choose one macaroni box over another. "Still unsure?"

She looked up at him with more uncertainty than needed over such a decision. "I can't pick!"

"Here, how about the unicorn ones? They are cuter." Adalyn butted in, having had enough of standing around.

"Oh, okay!" She beamed a smile as she placed it gently in the grocery cart. *If only it was that easy.*

"Thank you," Zack mouthed as he made a beeline toward the checkouts before she held them up any longer.

As the Jeep pulled into Zack's driveway, a gut-wrenching feeling hit Adalyn's stomach upon seeing the infamous red sedan.

"What is she doing here?" Adalyn asked.

"I, uh... Shit, I think today was her day with Sky." His seat belt clicked as he hopped out of the car in a hurry, leaving Adalyn behind to gather their belongings.

"It's about damn time you got home. I called only a million times with no response!" Mia's angered, though rather justified tone startled Adalyn.

"I'm sorry," Zack began as he made his way toward the door to unlock it.

"Save it," she growled.

Grabbing the groceries and unbuckling Sky, Adalyn refrained from involvement.

"C'mon, Sky," Zack called from the doorway. "Let's go see your Mom."

Sky looked up at Adalyn as her Papa called for her. There was an inkling of worry in her expression. "Go on, you're not in trouble," Adalyn assured her. It didn't seem to vanish with her reassurance, but the young girl ran toward the door, anyway.

Dropping the last of the groceries on the kitchen counter, a commotion rumbled from the front yard, only growing louder as the minutes passed. Quietly shuffling through the bags of perishables, Adalyn listened in, though it was only inaudible yelling.

Silent as a mouse, Sky snuck out of her bedroom and made her way to the kitchen. Standing on the other side of the island, she glanced up at Adalyn, who'd now completely stopped putting groceries away and was listening intently through the kitchen window. "What's Papa and Mama doing?" Sky asked.

Startled by the young girl, she whirled around to face her. "It's nothing, Sky. Go back to your room and play."

"Is Mama gonna take me from Papa?"

"Huh? Where did you get an idea like that?"

"She told me."

Adalyn slowly walked over to the young girl and bent down with concern. "How so?"

"She told me yesterday to say bye-bye to Papa because I'll never see him again."

"Why would she say that?" Adalyn spoke, instantly regretting it, as it wasn't appropriate to ask a child. Sky shrugged. "Well, let's go back to your room. I'm sure she didn't mean it."

"Okay!" Sky gleamed and turned to head to her room, only the bickering voices grew louder as she got closer to the door.

"Actually Sky, why don't we go play out back," Adalyn urged. "Get your shoes on!"

"Yay!" The young girl sped off to fetch her shoes.

From the back, the bickering was but an inaudible noise. Outside, the hot sun beat down, instantly causing them to break a sweat, though Adalyn would call it a *glow*. The air was muggy with humidity. Hot temperatures suffocated them as Sky romped around the newly-cut grass that sat within the back fence line. Being chased by Sophie, she didn't seem to mind the thick air.

"Addy," Sky hollered.

Adalyn rose from her seat on the back patio, curious if the young girl's calls were of any urgency. "What is it?"

"Lookie! A butterfly landed on me!" Sky slowly spun toward her, displaying a monarch butterfly that rested on her shirt.

Adalyn produced a genuine elation to the girl's discovery. "It's very pretty! The butterfly chose you." The girl beamed as it took off, flying into the baby blue sky. Returning to her seat, Adalyn sat there for a while longer.

Momentarily slinking inside to evade the heat wave, Adalyn's eyes scanned over the microwave clock. *Two-thirty.* It had been just over an hour since they'd started bickering, and time was ticking down before her dinner with Logan.

A sense of sadness began suddenly gnawing at her as she watched the young girl frolic in the yard. *Would this be her last time to watch this?* That feeling grew like a plant in her chest, though she pressed it down. It wasn't her child, but sometimes she wished she was.

As the hour passed, the sun's strength only seemed to grow. Even Sky felt it now, becoming quite sluggish in contrast to earlier. Laying in the cool grass beside Sophie, she gazed up at the afternoon clouds.

"Sky," Adalyn called from the doorway. She perked her head up. "Come on inside really quick, let's get some water!" She complied, finding the thought rather pleasurable.

Taking a long gulp of ice cold water from a plastic cup, she looked up at Adalyn. "Do I have to go back outside?"

Adalyn smiled and shook her head. "No, of course not!"

"Sometimes Mama makes me keep playing, even when I'm too tired," she casually said in between sips.

"What, that—" Just then, the front door swung open and slammed against the stopper as Zack stepped into view. Glancing over, she read his solemn expression, though behind him, Mia's footsteps pounded against the hardwood floor. Nudging Sky toward her room, Adalyn remained in the kitchen, uneased by the tension that suffocated the air.

"Sky, pack your things," the woman hollered as she barged her way into the house.

"Mia, you're not thinking straight," Zack argued.

In that moment, Adalyn shrunk against the cabinets as they continued to bicker.

"No, I think this is the clearest I've thought in a long while. I came here to talk civilly at first, but between your lack of time management and Sky's evident lack of proper care, I think that talk went out the window. We're moving and she's coming with me. And honestly, it's best you don't follow."

"You can't just take her away like that," Zack pressed.

"Says who?"

"If you do," he began.

"*If I do*, you'll what? Go to the courts? And they'll believe you, a druggie with a record?" She scoffed. "You have no case."

Before Adalyn could adjust to the barrage of revelations hurled across the kitchen, Mia made her way to Sky's room.

Reaching for her arm, Zack urged, "Mia, wait!"

"Let go of me," she hissed, ripping her arm out of his grasp. "Don't touch me!" Turning to face him, she stared him dead in the eyes. There was something about that glare that even seemed to scare Adalyn; something sinister in the way she looked. "Touch me again and I'll break the other leg too." Her eyes motioned toward his limp.

Adalyn just quietly watched from the corner, her eyes panning back and forth between the two like a match of tennis, except instead of a ball that was being knocked around, it was pieces of information being hurled across the court. At first, it startled her. Most of all, the revelation of drug usage, and around Sky?

Perhaps she pondered if all she'd ever known was a drugged Zack, which that thought irked her; it disgusted her. However, about three insults later, it all became so much to take in, that she sunk away.

Mia must've seen this, as her laugh, though it sounded more like a heinous cackle, disrupted the air, drawing Adalyn back to the current situation. "You still haven't told her, have you?"

Adalyn's eyes shifted over to Zack now, and his scanned the room. Looking for an out, there wasn't any. "This should be good," Mia sneered.

"A druggie? Is it true?" Adalyn asked.

"Adalyn," he began, though his tone only confirmed it.

"I love when I ruin a good relationship with secrets," Mia cackled, reaching for her purse that rested on the end of the couch. "You know what, I'll just leave you two to it! I'll be back later for Sky."

"There's your true colors," Zack snarled, though she just smirked.

Her hand grasped the door handle, throwing the front door open. A gust of hot air plowed through, sweltering the taut air, only to cease as the door closed behind the woman.

Looking over at Zack, their eyes met, though he was unrecognizable to her now. Without a word, Adalyn, too, made her way toward the front door.

"Where are you going?" he asked.

Adalyn silently shook her head as she collected her belongings. "Away. Away from *you.*"

"Are we over?"

She scoffed, and it echoed throughout the cabin. "I don't know. I don't feel like I know who you are anymore."

"Can I explain?"

She shook her head. "I don't think I can sit here and listen right now." Turning to leave, she looked back one last time. "I trusted you." She shook her head again in disbelief. "I need space, Zack."

"How long?" he pressed.

"I don't know." The words were scratching against her throat as she struggled to say them.

CHAPTER TWENTY-EIGHT

September 7, 2015

"Can I get you anything?" Adalyn asked her house guest.

"A Manhattan Cocktail?" Ragnar inquired as his charcoal brown eyes shimmered at the thought of a drink. Preparing his drink and sliding the glass across her island counter, she picked up her own tequila soda and took a seat beside him. "Is that...?"

"Shut up. After the week I've had, I'd like you to refrain from judgment." She took a long sip. "Now, how was your and Joyce's honeymoon?"

Ragnar involuntarily smiled widely as he recollected. After taking a sip of his drink in an effort to mask it, he took a second before responding, "It was grand! We traveled a bit, did some island hopping."

"That's wonderful."

"Hey, uh, thanks again for that toaster."

"No problem. I hope Joyce is enjoying it."

"She's been putting it to use," he responded with a grin. "Did I mention to you that we adopted an owl as of late?"

Adalyn nearly spit out her drink. "A *what*? Like the bird?" He nodded, rather pleased. "Like, a live bird?"

"It's white!"

"Is that even legal?" Ragnar shrugged. "Where did you find it?"

"I acquired it from an old member of mine, who recently passed. They left me the bird in their will, and I admittedly grew quite keen to it."

"Ragnar! What if it's diseased?" He brushed off her concern and she inevitably conceded. "Fine... What did you name it?"

"We've decided on the name Boris."

Adalyn rolled her eyes and took another sip of her drink. "So, you got him from a will?" Ragnar nodded in response. "Ya'know, I should get me one of those."

"Why for?" he asked. "Are you planning to die on me soon, Adalyn?"

She laughed and shook her head. "No. But doesn't everyone have one of those, nowadays? Don't you?"

"Hm? Oh, yes! I scribbled it out a year or so ago. I should update that." He turned back to her. "Hypothetically, who would get which valuables?"

She shrugged. "I don't have too many valuables to hand away other than maybe this house and Rocky."

"I'd take Rocky," he interjected.

"Really?" She was astonished by his offer.

Ragnar peered down at the sleeping dog by his feet and with a gentle smile, he nodded. "He's a good boy, I can't see why not."

"Fine, consider it done!"

Returning to her previous statement, he took a singular scan of the room and found plenty of valuable items to contradict her statement. "And that seems rather valuable." He pointed toward a painting. Examining further, he pointed out a few more items of value. "And about your position as Architect?"

"Okay, okay! I see your point..." She contemplated for a moment. "I think I'd give the rights to my house to Maddie and Max. My position, I'd most likely hand back to Logan, though if not him, perhaps Kayla. Apparently my dog goes to you! And probably send my car with you as well..."

"Who knew I stood to gain so much upon your death." He awarded her with his notorious sarcastic smile, but in a warmer tone than usual.

"Don't get any ideas, Ragnar."

"And for Zack? None?"

"Right now, he can get this..." She picked up a paperclip off the kitchen counter.

"Is it meaningful somehow?"

Adalyn giggled and shook her head. "No, I just found it on the floor earlier today."

"Oh, but I thought he—" Ragnar paused, feeling he was becoming invasive.

"Well, you thought wrong. He sucks!"

"Might I ask, why?" She let out a grumble and she rolled her eyes. "I regret asking..."

Sarcastically glaring at him, she began hashing out her side of the situation. Ragnar finished his drink in a timely fashion as her story came to an end. Setting down his glass, Adalyn instinctively picked it up to refresh it. Sliding a refilled glass back over to him, he took another long sip before letting out a vocal ahh. "Perhaps you'd like my two cents?" he finally questioned.

"Fire away..." She wasn't sure whether she'd regret this, as their friendship was most valuable in the plethora of honesty they provided, regardless of the situation.

"You mentioned you never queried more? So as I do understand your perspective, I must further, how can you be upset with a man when you've yet to hear the whole story?"

She sighed and took a sip of her drink. He'd had a point, though his words did not void her feelings. "Well... I suppose. I just... It was very off-putting!"

"Of course. News like this is never *good* news, and this Mia does seem like a, in other words, witch... But does it provide a right to hold it over his head without his side?"

"Ugh..." she groaned. "I suppose... It's still upsetting, regardless. I can't comprehend how he can have a child and do this. I mean, what if I've never met the sober Zack, and all I've ever known was some *druggie*?" Adalyn shook her head in disbelief. "I mean, he only just got Sky in his life, but still..." Ragnar took a long sip of his drink as she vented. Setting it down, he opened his mouth to speak. "Ugh, I hate men," Adalyn interrupted, too riled up to notice Ragnar's attempt at responding.

"Might I intrude once more?" he finally managed to slink in between her breaths.

"Go ahead..."

"As I do take your words with a grain—no, a *bucket* of salt, I must confess that you make some decent points that could bode well to address." She quirked an eyebrow of curiosity as he continued. "Did you ever see something like this coming?"

"No," she immediately insisted, then paused, recollecting back to that strange Altoid box in his car. "Well..."

Quirking an eyebrow, he watched her deep in thought. "Do tell."

Letting out a sigh, she should've seen it. It was right there. "He had this Altoid box in his car. Well, I think I first found it in my car? But it traveled to his new car, and they had these little white tablets that did *not* look like Altoids." Pausing, she screamed, "I should've known!"

"You seem quite upset over this," Ragnar verbally noted. "Of course with good reason... But—" He piqued Adalyn's attention with that last word. Quickly cocking her head in his direction, she stared daggers at him, waiting to hear the rest of that sentence. Admittedly, it slightly intimidated him. Nevertheless, he continued. "You've found yourself at some crossroads. My true piece of unbiased advice stands with the notion that you'll have to answer for yourself. *Is all this worth it?* I simply ask in your best interest, as you're my dearest friend—"

"Brother," she corrected. "You're like family to me, but continue on."

He widened a grin. "As your *brother,* I ask you to evaluate for yourself the worth of all this, or if you find it's time to let go."

"Let go?"

Ragnar glanced down at the watch on his wrist as it read five before two o'clock. "I must be going soon. The wife calls." Taking another sip of his drink, he pressed to continue. "Where were we before I depart?"

"You mentioned if it's time I let go?"

"Oh, yes." Ragnar collected his thoughts before continuing. "I think you ought to evaluate to which extent you'll bend for both of them to make this work. I know you, Adalyn. Like iron, strong and unrelenting, you'd break before you bend—or kneel for anyone." His finger trailed around the edge of his now empty glass. "Don't let this situation tell you any different." Ragnar rose from the hightop around the island counter.

Struck silent by his words, she churned it over in her head for a moment as she walked with him to the front door.

It was lunch time when she pulled open the door to the French Express. The strong scent of freshly brewed coffee permeated the air, and ambient chatter filled the cafe. A warm breeze blew in from the open patio as Adalyn searched around for an available seat. She'd come with a purpose; one that didn't involve a mug of coffee.

Her ears perked up to the familiar voice at the register. "I'll get a hot chocolate with a shot of espresso, please," he spoke, still oblivious to her presence.

Finding a seat near the patio, she took a deep exhale in efforts to wash away the anxiety that pooled in the pit of her stomach. Straightening her posture, she focused on anything but the impending conversation she was about to initiate.

Over the past week, she'd contemplated leaving. She'd pondered time and time again if this was worth it, but there was something that told her to stay; something that told her it *was*. So, here she was. Was she a fool? Perhaps. Ragnar had admittedly gotten in her head. *He'd had a point.* She nervously fiddled with her fingernails as she contemplated what she'd say.

Raising her head up, their eyes met. She held her breath as she listened to her heart pound. Fear-stricken, she watched the confusion circulate in Zack's eyes as he froze in his stance.

"I, uh..." he stuttered, "C-can I take a seat?" She nodded and motioned to the seat across from her. Quietly exhaling the breath she'd held in, she witnessed his confused expression instantly turn to sorrow. "I, uh... Okay, before you say somethin', lemme just explain..." he waited to speak, perhaps giving her an out, but she didn't take it.

"Carry on," she replied.

"It's not what you think," he started, but she scoffed. Letting out a sigh, he continued to explain. "What she said was true, a long time ago." There was a pause. He was holding back about something.

"And?" she pushed.

"And... a bit recently too," he hesitantly admitted.

She just quirked an unamused eyebrow. She had plenty of questions, though she figured she'd let him play out most of them. "So what Mia said was completely true?"

"Sort of. Sort of not." His response was confusing. She watched his eyes drift away for an instance, but he continued. "I don't anymore, though."

"Oh, that's good." Sarcasm cut through the air like a box cutter to a fresh piece of tape. "But you used to?"

"I was clean for about a year before I came into town, but started again after the fight."

"The fight orchestrated by Mia and her partner, Bryce," Adalyn harshly noted. He nodded.

"I completely stopped again when Sky came into the picture."

"That's good at least," Adalyn coldly replied. She began nervously picking at her fingernail. A million questions swarmed her mind, but at the same time, she truly didn't want to know their answers. "What was it?"

"The?" He looked at her, though her expression said what he was asking. "Uh, they're called dilaudids."

"What?"

"Pain killers," he clarified. She just nodded. All she could seem to do was nod.

"Why?"

"Why did I take them, or why..."

"Why did you first take them?"

His eyes drifted away again, obviously noting that this conversation was painful to him, though Adalyn didn't care. She needed to know that the man she fell for was in there, somewhere.

"My dad," he finally spoke. "When I told you about the time I defended my mom and went into the foster system? That's when it started..." He paused for a moment, collecting himself. "I took them on and off for years after that."

She nodded once more, processing the information. "Were you ever high on them when you were with me?"

"A few times..." A disgusted look surfaced on her face, and he instantly regretted it. He watched the respect she'd had for him drain from her body as he talked. "Not often, though."

She didn't believe him. Why would she? Though she'd had enough; she'd heard enough. It wasn't that she was letting it go, but perhaps she figured that the less she knew, the easier it would be to move past it. *He wasn't doing it anymore, and only sometimes in the past,* she reminded herself.

Perhaps in this moment, ignorance was bliss.

Diverting the conversation, she asked, "What about Sky and the move?"

A part of him felt relieved about the topic change, though he shrugged his shoulders. "I don't know. I genuinely haven't heard from her since. It's been bizarre."

Silence washed over them as she took another sip of her drink. Disrupting it, Zack asked with hesitation in his voice, "Did you have any other questions?"

She nodded again. "Will I have to worry about Mia coming after me now?" He immediately shook his head, and quite vigorously, too. "I refuse to be caught in the crossfire of your war," she bluntly stated.

"I know," he responded. "That's valid."

A faint smile of hope wavered over her lips as she attempted to conceal it. "Okay," she finally said.

"Does that mean we're..."

She hesitantly nodded. "I think we can work to get past it." She said it, though she even questioned how easy that would be. Nevertheless, she wanted to try.

"Alright, that's fantastic!" Gaping at her complexion, he couldn't help but express a valiant smile.

"What?" she asked, shrinking under his gaze.

"Nothing," he responded, taking a sip of his drink. "I just—I'm glad that we'll be okay."

A delicate smile crossed her face, though a soft buzz from her pocket startled her. Her one o'clock alarm pinged and she gasped.

"Oh crap, I didn't even realize the time! I have to get going." She hastily rose from her seat and collected her belongings.

"Oh, uh... I'll see you soon?" he asked. She looked at him and nodded. Turning to go, she didn't bother to look back as she departed the French Express.

CHAPTER TWENTY-NINE

October 31, 2015

Once more, the carnival's shimmering lights danced through the thickets of trees. The distinct tolls of game bells rang through the forest, and laughter sang along to its chimes. Slowly accumulating throughout the month of October, faux webbing lined the houses and frightening creatures made of plastic dangled from the eaves. On the thirty-first night of the month, little ghouls gathered in the dimly lit streets. Haunting the dark roads, their blithe laughter filled the air as they packed their buckets tight with sweet candies.

Night winded to an end as the little ghouls slowly dispersed along the streets, leaving the world bare of their haunted laughter until the next year. Though, the carnival still chimed in the far distance, illuminating the sky. Three costumed figures could gradually be made out as they traveled down the shadowy streets toward home. A soft light in the distance glistened through the trees, and a tiny Tinkerbell skipped ahead.

"I don't wanna go home yet," Sky whined as she stopped in the middle of the road.

"Well, everyone else went home." Adalyn extended her free hand out for Sky to grasp, which she did.

"But, what about the carnival?"

Zack pushed aside the Captain Hook cufflinks and peered down at his watch. "It's past your bedtime!"

"Bu-but!" Sky quivered her bottom lip, hoping to appeal to her Papa's better side. Perhaps he would've fallen for it if she'd done it just a moment earlier, because as they turned that last corner to his cabin, that familiar red sedan idled in his driveway.

"What's she—"

"I have no clue," Zack interrupted, letting go of Adalyn's hand and walking ahead.

"Mama's here!" Sky went to skip ahead, only to be held back by Adalyn. Something was awry, and she could sense it. Tightening her hold on the young girl's hand, Sky settled. Looking up at the woman, she felt her wariness, instantly becoming confused. "What is it, Addy?"

Adalyn did her best to stay quiet and listen in, but from the dogs barking in the distance, it made it nearly impossible to hear clearly. She turned to the young girl and shrugged. Bringing her finger to her lips, she quieted her. Beginning to walk again, she silently led them around the house and through the back door, in efforts to shield her from whatever fight would soon erupt.

The back door gently closed behind them. "Sky, go play in your room, okay?"

"What about Mama and Papa?"

"They'll be okay. Just go play and I'll come join you soon."

"Oh-tay!" And with that, she mirthfully skipped off to her room. Staying in the living room, Adalyn listened from the window.

"So now you show up," Zack's voice echoed. "You were supposed to be here hours ago to pick Sky up for the night."

"I felt it was only fair to give you one last moment with your daughter before I took her away."

"What are you talking about?"

Under the light of the house, Adalyn could visibly make out a packet of papers being exchanged between the two; she knew what that meant, she'd seen it before. *Custody Papers.*

"What do you think it means? I'm taking her with me. She's my daughter. We leave tonight."

"Wh—"

"You couldn't possibly be asking me *why?* You knew this was coming!"

"I didn't think you were serious..."

"Serious as ever. Now, where's my child?"

Hesitating, he let out a defeated sigh. He couldn't argue with the law. "Inside."

Mia stormed past him. Busting open the front door, it swung into the wall and shook the cabin. The sound jolted Adalyn as she'd since backed away from the window and taken a seat in a nearby chair, casually flipping through a magazine that she'd found in an effort to seem as though she hadn't just been snooping.

"*Adalyn,*" Mia sneered as she rested her eyes on her.

"Always a pleasure to see you too, Mia." Her heart pattered out of her chest, feeling wildly intimidated by this woman. She turned back to her magazine, hoping that it would drain the attention off of her, and it did.

Mia shifted herself toward Zack again. "Sky! Pack your things!"

It was déjà vu.

"Again with this?" Zack protested.

"This time, I have the papers. She's no longer in your custody, at all."

"So, I'm supposed to never see her again?"

"Well, if you *read*, somewhere in this thick packet, it says you get visitation rights every few months. If I decide to keep that, that is."

Adalyn could sense his heart shattering as she spoke, but he did well concealing it. It's the only thing one could do against her wrath.

"Sky, come here," he called.

Two little feet came clomping out of the bedroom. Unaware of what had just gone down, she burst into the room in a storm of liveliness. "Yes, Papa?"

He bent down to her level. Even that low to the floor, Adalyn could still make out the tears that welled in his eyes. "Look, you're gonna go to Mama's for a little while, okay?"

"Oh-tay! And then I come back here next week?" Zack shook his head and Sky looked at him with confusion.

Doing his best to conceal his dolefulness from her innocent eyes, Zack turned to Adalyn. "Can you please help her pack?"

Setting down the magazine, Adalyn silently nodded. Taking Sky by the hand, she led them into her bedroom. There, she grabbed

Sky's suitcase that she'd take to travel in between houses and began loading it with all of her favorite things.

"Addy, why are you packing everything?"

Tears now welled in her eyes. She'd taken quite a liking to the young girl, and Sky had seemingly taken a liking to her. Goodbyes were never easy for Adalyn. Sniffling back the tears, she cleared her throat. "Uh, because you'll want these at your Mama's house."

Still oblivious to the situation, she sat up on her bed and dangled her feet. Recollecting on the night's fun, she sat in her Tinkerbell outfit. "Addy, what was your favorite part about tonight?"

She enjoyed the child's sense of wonderment, even in the darkest of times. Smiling, she answered. "Umm, I liked the carnival a lot."

"Me too! The Big Bad Wolf and Little Red Riding Hood were scary, though!"

Adalyn giggled. "You know that was just Ragnar and Joyce, right?"

Sky nodded. "It was still scary!"

"Who's costume was your favorite?" Adalyn asked. Sky just pointed at her. "You liked my Tiger Lily costume the best? Not Maddie or Max's?"

She shook her head. "Cruela DeVil is evil!"

"Okay, what about Merida or Robin Hood?"

"You mean Kayla and Adam?" she giggled. "I really liked Captain Hook!"

"You mean your Papa?" Adalyn gently laughed as she folded a few of Sky's shirts and placed them into the suitcase. Sky vigorously bobbed her head up and down.

"What about you, Addy? Who was your favorite?"

"I really liked Tinkerbell," she exclaimed with a beaming smile.

"Hey Addy…"

"Yes?"

"I loves you," Sky announced as she wrapped her small arms around Adalyn and a singular tear dropped down her cheek. Sky pulled back and hopped off the bed. Running across the room, she grabbed a beaded bracelet off her desk and placed it in Adalyn's hands. "I want you to have this. I made it for you!"

Adalyn took a moment to admire the bracelet of multiple colors before placing it on her wrist. "It's lovely!"

Around Adalyn's neck dangled a simple golden chain with a little heart charm at its tip. It was given to her by her mother years ago. They'd found it at the market, and Adalyn had cried until her mother bought it. She unclipped it as it collapsed in her hand.

"Sky," she called out. "I want to give you this. My mom gave me this when I was a little older than you. I want you to keep it close to you, and don't ever lose it, okay?" Nodding, Adalyn clasped it around her neck.

Running over to the mirror, she held it in her hands and looked at its tiny charm. "I love it!" Skipping back, she wrapped her arms around Adalyn's neck.

"Hurry it up in there," Mia barked.

Releasing her embrace on the young girl, Adalyn zipped up the suitcase. "Okay, are you ready to go?" Sky shook her head, but Adalyn stood up anyways. "It'll be okay." She lied. She didn't know if it would, but it soothed Sky.

Walking her out, Adalyn watched from the doorsteps while Zack said his goodbyes. He stepped back and the car door closed as the red sedan pulled down the driveway, disappearing down the darkened street.

CHAPTER THIRTY

November 4, 2015

East Bellvan was known for plenty of things. It was known for its small town coffee shop and government buildings, such as the Courthouse and Post Office. It was known in the summers as the central hub for expeditioners to rest before setting off on their next adventure, and in the winters, it was known as a ghost town. Most importantly, at least for Adalyn, it was known for its ability to service private taxis to the neighboring forest communities, no matter the weather.

The evening train *choo*-ed in the distance as it roared past, and a yellow taxi drove alongside with its windshield wipers whipping against the falling snow. Aboard that taxi, Adalyn sat in the back seat, making her way back to Dawn Hills. Peering out the window, she observed as white powder piled up along the road, and all of a sudden, the car came to an abrupt halt in front of the vines that hid the arched passageway to home.

"I'm sorry, miss. This is as far as I can take you," the driver spoke.

"O-oh, okay." She hesitantly gathered her jacket and briefcase and exited the car. "How convenient," she mumbled as she watched the taxi disappear into the white haze and reached for her phone. Pressing the dial button several times, one finally answered.

"Hello?" The voice on the other end was groggy, as if they'd been asleep all day.

"Vi? Hey so, I'm at the town line... Do you maybe have the motivation to come and pick me up?" She instantly wondered if it was a mistake to call Violet, given how far along she was in her pregnancy, though part of her was glad she did.

A lot had been amended since Violet came back to town. Setting aside their differences in the past, Adalyn not only acknowledged the growth she'd made, but also took a liking toward spending time together, and as of the recent months, the two had grown rather close.

Violet couldn't hold back a giggle. "The town line? Yeah, I probably should get out of the house anyway. I'll be there soon!" The line clicked, leaving Adalyn alone in the still forest.

Hiding under a tree, it shielded her from most of the snowy downfall until Violet's new SUV's headlights barreled through the vines.

Faint laughter emitted from the car as she rolled down her window. "I don't pick up hitchhikers," she teased, though the audible sound of her doors unlocking rang through the silent air.

"Vi!" Adalyn quickly hopped in the car and turned toward her with a gleaming smile. "It's so great to see you. You look huge!"

"About six weeks left," she replied with a relieved smile.

"Oh, how exciting! Do you know the gender yet?" Violet shook her head. "Okay, how about names?"

"We have a couple in mind, but we really want to surprise everyone."

"Fine, fine!" Adalyn sat back in her seat and warmed her hands against the hot air that blew from the vents.

"So, how was your trip? Why were you in East Bellvan?"

"Ugh, it's a long story. But hey, Kayla and Maddie are about to come over. Wanna head to my house, pour some win—water, and just catch up?"

She laughed at Adalyn's slip, though kindly dismissed it. "When are Kayla and Maddie coming?"

"They should be headed back from the lake right now, if you wanna head to my house?"

Violet happily shrugged, finding nothing better to do than lazy around with her friends. Without further question, she drove toward the mountain. Tree branches sheltered the road from the storm, and the car gripped its slopes with ease. A soft glow from her house beamed through the hazy air as they approached it.

It wasn't long after they'd warmed up that Maddie's car piled through the same road. Turning around the last corner, her blue car fell into view. Adalyn's focus panned back to Violet as she pulled four mugs from her kitchen cabinet and placed them on the island.

"Hot cocoa or apple cider?"

"Oh, hot cocoa, please," Violet replied. Groaning from the baby, she positioned herself on the stool.

As Adalyn began to heat up the water kettle, the front door pushed open, sending a gust of snow to drift in with it. Violet shivered to the chilly air's touch and pulled her shawl tighter around her. The door immediately slammed shut as two voices chattered at its entrance.

"Sorry, I didn't think it would be so windy out!" Maddie's voice hollered down the hall. Connecting eyes with Violet, she audibly gasped. "You look absolutely radiant! Kayla, look at Vi."

Amidst hanging her coat up, Kayla halted in the entryway and turned toward Violet. "Vi, you look amazing!"

"Oh, stop you guys..." Violet blushed. Holding onto her stomach, she attempted to get out of the stool.

"No, no! Stay there. We'll come to you," Maddie declared. She didn't take that offering lightly, as she did just that. Too exhausted to move, Maddie came to her. "How the hell did you get here?"

"I drove."

"What! Why?"

Violet glanced over at Adalyn, who was silently organizing four drinks in the kitchen. "She was stranded at the town line."

"Addy, why didn't you call us?"

Adalyn peered up at them. "Hmm? Oh, I did. Check your phones. My call went straight to voicemail."

"It's because we didn't have any cell service while heading down from the lodge," Kayla stated as she entered the room. Maddie took a seat on the stool beside Violet while Adalyn passed out the four drinks. "So Addy, why were you out of town?"

Adalyn shrugged as she took a sip of her drink. "I had business to take care of."

"Elusive," Kayla declared as she raised her eyebrow in curiosity.

Softly laughing, Adalyn dismissed it. "Not the interesting type of business."

"Okay, well I haven't seen or heard from you since Halloween, and word around town is that Zack just lost Sky?" Kayla inquired.

"Straight to the point, huh?"

"Actually, I haven't heard about it. That sounds awful, what happened?" Violet questioned. As of late, she'd been bedridden by pregnancy, making her oblivious to the happenings outside.

"Custody battle with his psycho ex. It's a whole progressive thing," Maddie stated, giving her a brief run-down of what she'd recently missed.

"Well, before we start feeling pity for him, I need to put it on the table that I've been contemplating leaving him..."

"Okay, did Kayla not just say he just lost his child?" Maddie pressed.

"Yes, yes! And that's sorta where my dilemma lies."

"I say don't do it," Maddie interposed. "He just lost his kid, losing you might throw the poor guy over the edge."

"And I thought about that..." Adalyn stirred her cider with a teaspoon, growing more and more perplexed.

"Okay, well what makes you want to leave him right now, so urgently?" Kayla asked.

"So, I've told you all about some of Mia's antics and how cruel she is. Well, about two months ago, we almost broke up, and sometimes I regret not going through with it... I really do like him, don't get me wrong, but I did *not* sign up for this. Better yet, I don't think I was ever ready for a relationship, and I jumped into this one without recognizing the baggage it came with."

"Okay, that's a valid reason to break up," Violet exclaimed.

"Sure, but I still say no. It's something that can be fixed."

"Well, and I thought that too, Maddie! And I did try, I really, really did try." Having stirred her drink for far too long, Adalyn finally took a long sip of the cider. "Kayla, how about you?"

Kayla let out a low *hum*, pondering a proper response. "Personally, I think there's more to the story."

"Wha—" Adalyn huffed, but inevitably, she was right. "Okay, there is." The girls audibly gasped, and Adalyn ignored it. "So, don't judge..." Her eyes immediately fell on Kayla.

"Ah," she defensively huffed. "I—fine. Continue and I'll do my best to refrain."

She flashed a smile. "So, I've been chatting with someone lately—"

"Like male, or female?" Maddie interrupted, though Adalyn shot her a slighted glare.

"Male. *Anyways*, he and I have been chatting, and I've confided in him a bit about the situation. He's been so sweet about it and so caring. It's hard not to want something like that. But it got me thinking. If I were to date, I'd want something like that—something easy. Not necessarily *easy*, but like... simple. Things just feel right with this guy, and I can't help but feel that I've made the wrong decision."

"Wow, Addy! Who's the secret lover?" Maddie pressed.

Her face turned red. Hesitant to speak a name, the girls continued to pry. "Okay, it's obviously someone we know," Kayla finally deduced.

"Ragnar?" Violet asked.

"Ew, no! I did talk to him about Zack a couple months back, but no! He's with Joyce, and he's like my brother."

Violet giggled. "I don't know, I always found Ragnar extremely attractive."

"Vi," Adalyn screamed, not wanting to hear it.

"Well if it's not Ragnar, Zack, or Max, then…" Kayla's eyes widened with realization. Looking over at Adalyn, she shrunk under Kayla's glare. "It's Adam…"

"What," Maddie and Violet simultaneously screeched as they stared at her, searching for any hint that Kayla was wrong.

"Please don't tell me you two—"

"No, no, no!" Adalyn swiped at the air as if to wipe away even the thought of such. "No. I'm not the type to do that to Zack."

"So, what is your plan? To date my brother?"

"I don't—no. I mean, I don't know. But it's just easy with him. He gets it; he understands. He understands *me*…"

"Yeah. He has that appeal." Kayla scoffed.

"Oh come on, Kayla… Who hasn't had a crush on Adam around here?" Maddie giggled. "So our little Addy has a crush."

Kayla paused for a moment, finding logic within herself to be against such, but she couldn't. "Okay. I'm not swayed yet, but I will accept this enough to listen." To that, Adalyn beamed a soft grin.

"So then Zack?" Adalyn inquired, still uncertain what to do.

"What do you mean? Are you actually trying to break up with him?" Kayla quizzed.

"You were all for it a minute ago," Maddie reminded her.

"And you weren't."

Violet grew a headache, trying to listen to their back and forth. Finally, she'd had enough. "Adalyn, what do you want? What would make you happy?"

Adalyn stared at Violet with pained eyes, not quite sure of an answer to either of those questions. To one degree, she felt she'd be better off single, but to another, she did love and care for Zack. "I-I don't know... But I have another trip with Zack to Logan's cabin this weekend, and I'd at very least like to avoid it. I don't think I could handle being on that trip with him."

"Okay, so say you broke up with him. How?"

Adalyn pondered it over for a minute, only to inevitably shrug. "I haven't bothered planning so far in advance."

"Oh, okay. This could be fun," Maddie chimed in.

"What do you mean?" Violet questioned.

"Hypothetically, Addy, how would you do it?"

Adalyn pondered the thought. Opening her mouth, she began to plot. Perhaps it was all too real of an idea for her, because each word that escaped her lips only seemed to deepen her desire and solidify her fate.

CHAPTER THIRTY-ONE

November 6, 2015

On that brisk afternoon, a bluster of wind sent fallen leaves tumbling through the desolate streets. Trees had grown bare and snow glazed the brown grass as the turning of the seasons commenced. Dawn Hills, and most nearby communities, became haunted by the emptiness of the winter months.

The sun was at its peak as Zack readied the Jeep for their departure. Warming under a blanket with another glass of Merlot, Adalyn listened from her living room as he slammed the trunk closed. Knowing well that that was her cue, she waited a minute longer, until he called for her. She listened to the stomping of his footsteps as they traveled up the pathway, and the jingling of his keys as he twirled them around his finger. Finally, the front door blasted open, carrying a chilly wind through her abode.

"Everything's packed," he exclaimed from the doorway. "Are you ready?"

With a forced smile, she rose from her seat and met him at the front door. "That was quick."

"Yeah. It didn't take long, but the car's warm."

"Oh wonderful! Thanks." Leaving a peck on his cheek, she headed off down the pathway and stumbled through the chilly air.

Zack stood at the doorway for a moment, admiring as she took off to the car. There was something in her carefree essence that delighted him as he couldn't seem to hold back a soft chuckle. Locking the front door, he fell only a few steps behind her.

"Hurry up," Adalyn whined through chattering teeth. She waited for him at the car as he slowly trudged down the pathway.

He chuckled once more. "I'm comin'!"

Sprinting down the last few feet, he unlocked the car and climbed aboard. In the back seat, two dogs paced around, settling in for the long ride ahead.

"Lake Shasta, here we come!" Zack beamed.

"Yay!" She was false in tone, though she didn't let it show. Extending her seat back to rest, she faltered for an instant, then lurched forward. The sudden movement alerted Zack as he glanced over to inspect what she'd been doing, only to see her fiddling with the aux cord.

A sudden burst of sound transmitted from the speakers, startling Zack as he flinched. Adalyn couldn't help but let out a soft giggle. "You good?"

He nervously chuckled, feeling rather silly for reacting that way. "Yep."

"Okay," she teased as she rested back in her seat. "Well, it's all set up for you now."

"Are you going to sleep?"

She shook her head, paused, then shrugged. "I don't know. I just have a splitting headache, so I figured I'd close my eyes."

As upbeat tunes emanated from the speakers, Adalyn's eyes softly drifted shut. Tossing and turning in her seat for what felt like hours, comfort became nearly impossible. She let out a minor groan, finally giving up on the idea of rest.

Opening her eyes for the first time since they'd driven down the mountain, she sat upright in her seat and silently peered out the side window.

"You okay?" His voice ruptured the still air, sending an unexpected wave of irritation to trickle through her system. Perhaps it was the bottle of wine she'd downed earlier, but annoyance pooled in her throat as he spoke.

"Yeah, I'm fine."

"Oh, okay. Are you excited for the trip?"

"Yep." Her voice grew harsh.

"Whatcha thinkin' of doing while we're there?" She simply shrugged, not bothering to answer. "I was thinkin—"

"Zack," she snapped, "Can you please just... *shh*!" She wasn't sure what had gotten into her, and never intended it to be so harsh, but she couldn't take it anymore. *The incessant blabbering!* Her head pounded in her skull and dull pain fixated behind her eyes. She covered her eyes with both her hands. Taking a few deep breaths, she finally lifted them. "I'm sorry..."

He was rattled by her curt manner. His voice was quiet as he spoke, fearful of angering her again. "It's o—"

"It's not, but thanks." Her eyes focused out on the world past the car. Shiny from the ice that coated it, the road glistened as they passed over. The scenery around was veiled in white snow, masking the greenery and concealing any nature that lurked beyond. "Honestly," she finally began.

"Yes?" He glanced over at her, nervousness accumulating in his gut.

"I don't know anymore..."

"What do you mean?" He did his best to stay calm, but the uncertainty and anxiety began eating at him.

"*This*, Zack... Us!" She abstained from making eye contact, keeping hers peeled on the road ahead, though even he could see the tears welling in her eyes as she spoke.

Was she being sincere? His heart began to shatter, and with it, his focus. Hitting a puddle of black ice, the car began to swerve.

"Zack," she screamed as he immediately set to correct it.

"S-sorry..."

"I just..." She took a deep sigh. "I'm not happy anymore... I wish things were easier." Stuck in her throat like food when eating too fast, she choked on her words.

"I get it."

"I-I..." She looked over at him as a single tear ran down her cheek. "I don't want it to be over, I really—you have to believe that... Maybe we could keep trying?"

"Okay," was all he could muster. He knew better than the words that escaped her lips.

"I just wish things were easier… I wish that we could go on nice dates without worry, and hang out until wee hours, like we used to. Like before—" she stopped. "Like how we used to…"

It was then that he knew. Perhaps it was that bottle of wine that he knew she'd downed before getting in the car; perhaps it was just the right amount of liquid courage she needed to finally be able to tell him the truth.

"Okay," he finally said after a long bout of silence. "I get it, but I think you'd be better off. I think we should break up."

"O-oh. Okay…" she spoke. The tears stopped falling for an instance as she processed his words, only to instantly return the moment she did.

Though they were stuck in limbo, the car traveled onward in silence. Holding in all the sorrow that filled his chest, he softly gulped, hoping that it would subside. He wasn't used to this feeling that punched him in the gut. He never cared like he did now; like he did for her. Uncertain whether or not to turn the car around—or rather what this meant for them, he continued on.

The sign for East Bellvan came into view, indicating that it would only be a mere ten miles until they reached the town line. Both their eyes scanned the sign as a wave of tension circulated in the car.

Finally, she spoke. "You can drop me off at the coffee shop."

"Wh—Oh, okay… How are you gonna get home?"

She glanced down at her phone, then back up at the road, still avoiding eye contact. "Maddie's in East Bellvan right now, she'll give me a ride back."

"Oh… Okay." He was clearly disheartened.

Another awkward pause washed over them as they listened to a soft hum of music that expelled from the car speakers, though none of them dared to touch it. One of the dogs stood up to readjust, startling the two with the jingle of their collar and reminding them of their presence.

Finally, the car came to a slow halt in front of the coffee shop.

"Here we are," Zack spoke, perhaps giving her an opportunity to take it all back, but she didn't.

As he shifted the car into park, he hopped out to assist her with unloading her belongings from the trunk and released Rocky from the cramped back seat. When that was over—and it was finished quite quickly, he stopped to look at her. Taking in the woman on the side of the road with a dog in one hand and her luggage by her side, a pit grew in his stomach. Making eye contact with her, he watched as tears welled in her eyes, doing everything in his power to not do the same.

"I'm sorry," she spoke. The dam of tears burst as they flooded down her cheeks. He wasn't sure what the appropriate thing to do was, so he held her. He held her in his arms, embracing her through the November air as if it was only them again; as if it was the last time he'd ever get to hold her. He didn't want to let her go.

A horn honked in the distance, and she pulled away from him. Tears still streaming down, she backed up.

"I-I have to..." Adalyn motioned to leave. "Goodbye, Zack." With that, she turned away and got in the car.

Unknown at the time, it was the last she'd see of him for a while, as he didn't turn around, but rather continued onward.

Zack Blake didn't leave because of her callous commentary during the car ride, he left because he understood her performance.

Heartbroken that it was too good to be true, he recognized that to her, he was no longer enough and she wanted out. To which, he simply set her free.

CHAPTER THIRTY-TWO

November 25, 2015

Under the string lights that dangled over Main Street, soft jazz echoed through the town. Originating from the park, a local band strung along through the cold, bringing tunes to the community as they prepped for the holidays.

Adalyn and Adam slowly strolled down the street, taking in the merriment and laughter while they made their way to La Regale. Since Zack's sudden disappearance from town, she'd taken a liking to Adam's cheerful, yet sophisticated nature—it was different, but in a good way. Passing by the park, the music grew louder as Adalyn hummed along.

"Do you know this song?"

She paused and cheerfully looked at him. "Nope! But it's the same few notes constantly playing. It's become easy to guess what comes next."

"Ah!" With a faint laugh, he teased, "I just thought you were some musical genius."

"Yes, *totally*," she sarcastically replied. Playfully nudging him, she caught him off guard as he misstepped, nearly tripping. "Oh my god," she gasped, "I'm sorry, I thought you had your balance." A delicate giggle escaped her lips once she'd assessed he was fine.

He brushed himself off and gave her a coltish glare. "Oh so you think that's funny?" His voice attempted to remain serious, though a crack in it deemed otherwise. Gently nudging her back, she toppled sideways.

"I didn't mean to," she spoke through cracked giggles. He laughed alongside her as he grasped her arm and pulled her upright, allowing her to regain balance. "You know, I've had fun the past few weeks." Adalyn beamed. Spending nearly every day beside him, she'd grown quite keen to his presence.

"I have as well." He kissed the top of her forehead as his eyes glistened under the artificial street lights, and a gentle smile arose. "Alright, let's not be late for our reservation." Delicately taking her hand in his, he led them to the doorway.

Stepping over the threshold, she looked back at him with a playful smirk. "Careful, Adam. There's a raise there. I'd hate to see you fall!"

"I didn't fall," he protested.

Floating down the aisles of white table cloths and pretentious guests, Adalyn's fascination was caught up in the grandeur, her eyes scanning the infamously illuminated casing of expensive wine bottles, something she hadn't had the ability to admire the last time. Lined with priceless pieces of art and decor, the restaurant's upscale atmosphere never failed to impress.

"What do you think?" Adam asked. He enjoyed her admiration for the finer things in life—something they had in common.

"It's lovely."

Adam pulled the chair out for her as she straightened the back of her pine green, satin dress and took a seat. Drawing her menu close to her, she scanned over the plethora of options until she found something that even remotely made sense to her.

Beckoning her attention up from the menu, the waitress hovered over them. "Alright, are we ready to order?"

"Yeah, I'll be getting the Anatra with a bottle of Rosé." Adam spoke with such a flow to his words, it was captivating to Adalyn.

"And for you, ma'am?"

"I'll get the, uh, the tag-lita de..." Adalyn stumbled as she tried to pronounce it.

"Tagliata di Manzo?" Adam corrected as a soft chuckle left his lips.

"Umm, yes. Please." Clearing the menus off the table, the waitress disappeared into the sea of guests.

"Do you not know Italian?" he spoke with a teasing grin.

She gave him an embarrassed look. "I was taught it as a kid, but if you don't use it, you lose it." Adam simply smirked. Producing a cheeky grin, Adalyn reached for the glass of wine that had just been placed on the table and took a sip.

"What do you think of the wine?"

"It's..." Adalyn swirled the liquid in the glass and took another sip. "I like it!"

"Well, that's good, because that was a thousand-dollar bottle."

"W-what!" She nearly spit it out.

"Kidding! I was kidding. I—" He began to chuckle at her reaction. "I'm sorry, I didn't think you'd take it so seriously." Reaching for his own glass, he took a sip. A long moment of tranquil silence passed the time as they dove into the bottle of wine, shortly followed by their meals.

"Okay, so hear me out," Adalyn spoke up. "I have been craving s'mores lately. I don't know why. Perhaps it's the cold season? Anyways, I propose that after this, we go back to mine and roast marshmallows over my fireplace. What do you think?"

Adam pondered it for a moment. "Alright. Sounds like a solid plan to me."

Returning to the rest of their dinner, Adam finally set his fork down against his empty plate and looked over at her with a hint of confusion.

"What? What is it?" Adalyn insisted.

"Nothing, I'm just—I'm shocked..."

"About...?"

"That you've never been here."

"Well, okay. I've been *here*. I just haven't eaten here." He silently quirked an eyebrow. "Okay well, Zack and I had our first date here..."

"Wait, what?" Even Adam was astonished by that. He wasn't one to create a bias based on social class, but he was well aware of who dined at La Regale, and Zack just wasn't one he'd pictured on the guest list.

"Well... We started to, but guests got really judgy because, well, it's Zack." Adalyn picked her fork back up, nervously moving around the morsels of food that sat on her plate. "So instead, I insisted we leave early and we went back to my place."

"Yeah, sounds more like it," Adam chuckled.

"What's that supposed to mean?"

"No, no! Not that. I just—Sounds like the type of crowd to really kick out someone that doesn't fit in."

"Oh, yeah." Adalyn let out a soft laugh as she recalled a prior memory. "Yeah, he doesn't exactly have class. He's a bit too childish."

Adam chuckled. "I wasn't going to go that far..."

"No, seriously! Try having a serious conversation with him; he acts so immature."

"Oh, I'm not doubting you. I just wouldn't go as far as to trash your ex in front of you."

She smiled. "I appreciate that, but really, it's okay if you do. It failed for a reason."

"I'll keep it in mind," Adam chuckled. Reaching for her hand that delicately rested on the table, he held it in his own and beamed a genuine smile. "Are you ready to go, then?" She nodded, and they rose from their seats.

The car ride to Adalyn's was quick. So quick, the car hadn't even managed to heat up, leaving Adalyn shivering in her seat as her breath became a shallow puff of steam against the cold air. Coming to a smooth stop in front of her abode, Adam strolled around to Adalyn's side and held open the door for her.

"Oh, thank you." She kissed his cheek as she discarded the warm layers and stepped out of the car. Taking him by the hand, she ascended the sloped pathway.

Inside, Adalyn stirred the wooden logs as the fire crackled. She'd moved aside the coffee table and set up two cushions in front of the fireplace. In front of them, rested the basic ingredients to make s'mores.

After positioning the firewood, Adalyn took her seat beside Adam, who wrapped a large blanket around the both of their shoulders.

Longingly gazing at her side profile, she finally turned to face him, nervously breaking out in a blush. "What?" she pressed.

"Nothing." He was unable to shake the smile off his lips.

"No, come on! What is it?"

"Nothing. I just... I've really enjoyed myself lately with you. I... I really like you, Adalyn." She expelled a timid giggle as her cheeks only darkened in the shade of red. Unable to look at him, she bowed her head and lowered her gaze toward the floor. "What?" he finally asked.

"Well, it only took you a year," she teased. "Not to mention, your response was un-Adam-like for you to say."

"My bad." He chuckled softly, holding his smile as his gaze fixated on the flames ahead. He felt nervous against her confidence, but was equally enticed by it.

"I liked that you said it." She paused before adding, "Because I like you too. However—"

"That's never good," he interrupted.

She gave him a sympathetic smile. "*However*, I have to stop you there... I don't know if I'm ready to leap into another relationship. I just got out of one."

Hurt from the rejection, he smiled through the pain. For her, he would do just about anything, and for their friendship, he wouldn't dare to jeopardize it. "That's alright. I can wait."

Appeased by his caring nature, her smile grew genuine as she kissed his cheek. Turning back to the fire, she gently rested her head on his shoulder, wishing to stay that way for just a moment longer.

CHAPTER THIRTY-THREE

December 3, 2015

A breeze swept against the trees, sending branches scraping against Adalyn's living room window. To the east, the sun crept in, illuminating the couch as she rested her elbows down on her kitchen island, waiting for the kettle on the stove to hiss. A sudden knock thudded against her front door, drawing her into the entryway. Pulling her sweater tighter around her body, she opened the door.

"Ragnar," she exclaimed, moving aside for him to enter.

"That took you bloody long enough, it's freezing out here," Ragnar quipped as he shook off some of the snow that had gusted upon his navy blue woolen coat.

"My apologies." She closed the door and made her way into the kitchen, where the tea kettle hissed. Tending to it, she joined him around the kitchen island. "So, what brought you by?"

"I realized I haven't been here in a short while, so I thought I'd pay you a visit since I was in the area." He smiled, and with his foot, proceeded to shove some of the loose gravel from his shoes to the edge of the kitchen counter while she wasn't looking.

"It's a pleasure, as always. Can I get you a drink? A Manhattan, perhaps?"

Ragnar's smile widened even further. "You know just the way to start a morning."

As she concocted the drink, she turned to him. "How've you been? How's the owl of yours treating you?"

"The owl is still alive, believe it! And doing rather well, in case you were worried." He picked up and curiously inspected her choice of whiskey for his drink. "Good choice," he insisted as he placed the bottle down next to her other ingredients.

"Can't say I wasn't worried about him for a while there," Adalyn jested. "How's Joyce been? I haven't seen much of her since Halloween."

He turned away from the counter and eyed around her home in curiosity. "Oh she's good. I assume that means you haven't heard that she's gone back to the States. She's tending to some family matters."

"Not at all. And you didn't go with?" Her question was met with a headshake.

"No, I had some of my own matters to tend to." Ragnar's charcoal eyes gave a gleam, and while peering along her walls, caught sight of something familiar. He took a few steps to inspect his findings. "Tell me Adalyn, I am not interrupting a *special guest* am I?" he spoke in a teasing manner, laying Adam's jacket back on the chair where he'd found it.

Presenting him the finished drink, her eyes followed him as she blushed. "No, Adam's long gone. He left early this morning."

"Oh, staying over already? Am I sensing a romance in the making?" Ragnar quipped as he took a sip of his cocktail.

She exerted a soft giggle. "Sorry Ragnar, I may be single again, but I don't feel like dating anyone at this moment."

"I must say, I'm fairly shocked."

"What does that mean?"

"You've grown close, it amazes me that you don't pursue anything. However, it's your choice, of course."

A soft, pink blush formed on her cheeks. "Perhaps I'm just not quite ready yet. Not after Zack, and all..."

Nearly emptying his drink, he proceeded to swirl the cup in his right hand, watching the ice spin around in circles. "So, I assume you heard about Zack?" Adalyn furrowed her eyebrows in response. "I'll take it as a no."

"No. I haven't spoken to him since he dropped me off in East Bellvan."

"Then perhaps it's best not talked about." The granite clinked as he placed his empty glass on the kitchen island counter. "It's up to you," he concluded.

She shrugged as she swept her hand across the air. "Carry on."

"Well, I happened to spot him in town earlier this morning."

"Oh?" Her interest piqued, and she did her best to disguise it. However, Ragnar knew her all too well to see through it. Picking up his glass, she asked, "Do you want another?"

Feeling as if he had already had two, Ragnar politely shook his head in response. "I must say I thought he looked quite rough though."

"Did you speak with him?"

"I didn't. We were never that close."

"Oh... I didn't even think he'd return."

"He has a home here, does he not?"

"I suppose... I just never knew why he left, and it's been almost a month. I guess I wasn't expecting to see him again... Based on how we ended, and all."

He toyed with her words in his head before responding. "Do you wish that he wasn't?"

She pondered. "No, I'm glad he returned. I think as little as I want to admit this, I miss him." Ragnar raised an eyebrow, expecting her to continue, which she did. "I know that everything was falling apart, and not all of it had to do with him, but I miss him. More importantly, I miss his friendship. I don't think many can equate to that." At that instance, Adalyn's phone lit up, spending a loud buzzing as it vibrated against the counter. "It's Vi, I'd better get this." Dismissing herself, Ragnar watched as she walked off.

Something seemed off in her demeanor, though he couldn't quite pinpoint it. He turned back to his empty glass, rattling it a few more times as he respectfully attempted not to listen in to the faded conversation. She returned only moments later with a synthetic grin plastered all across her face.

"Everything alright? Something important come up?"

She nodded a response. Reaching for her purse and coat as she spoke, "I'm sorry to cut the morning short, but Vi needs me to pick up some things from the market for her."

"Oh, sure. Not to worry. Send her my well wishes, will ya!" Somewhat puzzled over what could possibly be so urgent this early in the morning, he stood up, gathered his belongings and followed her out.

"Will do," she spoke as she closed her front door behind the both of them. "I'll make this up to you, though. I'd hate for you to have driven over for nothing. How about dinner later this week?"

"Sounds like a plan," he agreed as they parted their separate ways.

To arrive at Vi's, Adalyn would've had to take a left turn onto York Street, but instead, she kept driving straight. Uncertain what she was doing, or if she'd even go through with it, she carried on. To her right, Mountain Crest Inn's sign flashed past, and within a short time after, so did the French Express.

Parking her car at the end of the long pathway, it tucked behind a tree just to the left end of the property. She sat idle in the car for a moment before finally turning it off and stepping out. Beginning to make her way through the dead, yellow grass, she stopped in her tracks as an infamous voice rang through the property.

"You have a daughter to prioritize, Zack. So get over your stupid little heartbreak, recognize she didn't, and *never* will care about you, and move on!" The back door slammed shut and in the distance, two figures marched into the driveway. "I really hope that Sky didn't get attached to her. It would be really unfortunate if you had to explain to her just why she, and everyone else, leaves you. Then again, if she's anything like her father—and she is, she'll have to get used to it, too." Mia's car door slammed shut and the sound of her engine starting up resonated through the property. Adalyn ducked behind a bush, fearful of getting involved in the quarrel.

When the red sedan had passed by, she stood from her position. Peering over at the cabin to her right, she froze. *Nothing's changed,* she reminded herself. No matter how deeply she came to miss him, her idolization of him was truly that; an illusion. Unable to proceed any further, she turned back to her car.

The mid-afternoon sun hung low in the sky as she slid into the driver's seat. Taking a deep breath, her phone buzzed. Seven missed calls from Adam. She pressed redial.

"Hey!" Adam's cheerful voice rang through.

"Hey, sorry."

"I was getting worried. We had plans today, didn't we?"

She peered down at the clock on the dashboard. *Three-thirty.* "Shit," she mumbled under her breath. "I'm so sorry, Adam. I'll be right there. I'm like fifteen out."

"Okay, cool. I'll—" The line clicked as she hung up.

A typical drive back from Zack's house averaged fifteen minutes, but Adalyn drove at an abnormally slow pace. Perhaps contemplating her initial decision to go to his, or even the ultimate decision to not go inside, her mind was everywhere else but the road in front of her.

Slamming the car door shut in her driveway, she was immediately greeted with Adam's perpetually merry smile and a delicate kiss. Though this time, his jade eyes didn't sparkle to her like they used to.

"Busy day, I presume?" he questioned as he held open the front door for her.

"Uh, yeah. Ragnar stopped by, actually."

"Oh, that's nice. How's he been?" Adam sat down to greet Rocky, who'd dozed off on the couch while Adalyn set down her belongings on the counter.

"He's been well. I'm really shocked that he still has that owl of his. Also, did you know Joyce was back in the States?" A text pinged across Adalyn's phone, drawing her attention to a group chat of her close girlfriends.

"Yeah, I believe Kayla mentioned it to me. Oh, I ran into Maddie and Max today at the store."

"Hm?" she asked, having not been listening as she texted.

Adam peered back at her. Television remote in his hand, he'd been surfing through channels as they spoke. "I saw Maddie and Max in town. They seem well. Oh, did you hear—never mind." He paused, turning back to flip through channels. "Anything in particular you care to watch?"

"No, what were you going to say?" She stared over at him, curious about how he would proceed. Dismissing his second question with the wave of her hand, she responded, "And uh, I don't have a preference. Whichever."

"It's nothing." Adam clicked on a channel and rose from the couch, making his way beside her in the kitchen. He poured both of them a glass of ice tea and placed hers down in front of her. "Uh," he finally ceded, "word has it, Zack's back in town."

"So I heard." Her voice was monotone as she raised the glass to her lips. The cell phone pinged several more times, its screen filling up with notifications from Violet, Maddie, and Kayla.

Adam kissed the top of her forehead and glanced down at the screen. "Miss. Popular," he teased as he began to walk back to the couch. Looking back at her he stopped. "Coming with?"

"Hm?" She drew her attention away from her phone for a moment and glanced over at him. "Oh, sure." Picking up her glass and phone, she made her way to the couch.

"I was thinking of heading back to Maine in a couple months for a week or so to visit my family."

"Oh?"

"I was wondering if you'd be interested in joining?"

"I, uh—" Adalyn was taken aback by his question. "Uh, I'll have to double check, but maybe." She wasn't quite sure what to say in such an instance. When she was supposed to be growing these wild feelings for him, she wasn't. Admittedly, the beginning was intriguing; it was something new, but now, as that spark died, so did the rest. The warmth she'd initially felt for him altered, and he was growing to ever-so-slightly annoy her lately.

"Wonderful," he beamed, completely oblivious to her hesitation.

"You aren't worried, though?"

"What do you mean?"

"After Arabella, you aren't worried about me coming?"

"Well, you're Adalyn..."

"What does that mean? Didn't your family cause you to detach from her?" Adalyn was frank with her questions, leaving him no room to sugarcoat it.

"Wow. Straight to the point," he nervously chuckled. "It was a failed attempt all around with Arabella and I. Everyone has a failed attempt for a relationship."

"I don't have any failed attempts," she bluntly stated.

"Well, sure you do!"

"Name one," she pressed.

"How about Zack? You said that it crashed and burned, and that you were ashamed of him."

"It wasn't a failed attempt, and I most definitely don't feel ashamed by it." Her voice grew stern, plunging them into a moment of silence. Directing their focus onto the television in front of them, they sat this way for a few minutes in efforts to distract themselves from the conversation of differences they'd had.

Jiggling his empty glass of ice around, Adam stood. "I'm going to refill my drink, can I get you anything?"

She peered over at her empty glass on the coffee table. "Uh—" Before she could speak, he reached for the glass.

"One ice tea, coming up." Kissing the top of her head, he dismissed himself.

She looked over her shoulder at him. "I'm sorry," she hesitated to speak. "I didn't mean—"

"Don't worry about it," he interrupted. "Would you like anything to eat?"

"No, I'm alright." She felt his eyes searing into the back of her head. Turning to him, she met his gaze. "What's up?"

"I just—tell me again why you don't want a relationship."

"Adam... We've been over this."

"I-I know, but just for shits and giggles, tell it to me again."

"Adam—" She pleaded with him to not go down that road.

"No, I'm sorry... I just—we are so good together."

"Sure, but—"

"We have an amazing time when we are together!"

"Sure, but—"

"I really, really admire you, Adalyn."

"I'm just not ready," she finally blurted out. Silence washed over the room and her eyes drifted to the clock on the microwave. "What time did you need to get going?" she asked, hinting at his unwelcomeness.

Catching the hint, his eyes followed hers to the clock. "I can head out shortly."

"I'm sorry," she looked at him. "I just have a really early morning tomorrow, but I promise to meet for lunch?"

"Sure, that works great." He poured them another glass of ice tea. "After this, I'll head out."

"Okay." She smiled. "Again, I'm sorry."

"Don't be!" He set her glass of ice tea down on the coffee table and took a seat beside her for the last of the episode.

Curling up to him, they sat in silence as the screen shifted to black, rolling the credits and dimming the lighting in her living room. He was hesitant to leave, taking his time to pack his belongings back up, though she continuously insisted it was for the best, and eventually drove him out the front door. Standing at the doorway, she waved as he descended down her driveway and his car disappeared into the dim of the night.

Careful to leave enough time in between his departure, she waited a moment longer before descending down the same path. Cautious, she traveled through the backroads, behind town. It was all on a whim for her, just as it was earlier. She wasn't even sure if she could proceed, or if she'd be sitting outside his property once again, but she knew she had to try.

Rolling up, his living room was illuminated with lights and the faint flickering of the television could be seen through the window. This time, the property was void of the red sedan, though Zack's black Jeep sat in the driveway. She took a moment, assessing what she was doing, and with a deep breath, she got out of the car.

That night, she somehow ended up back on Zack's doorsteps. Hesitant to even knock, she stood there for a moment, eventually finding the courage somewhere in her to do so. She couldn't tell if he was shocked or happy to see her when he finally answered; he stood absolutely astonished in the doorway.

"C-can I come in?" she finally asked.

"I—" he stepped aside to let her pass. "What are you doing here?"

"I... I don't really know..."

"Well, uh, can I get you something to drink? Maybe a hot tea?"

"Um, yeah. Please. That sounds good." Her eyes scanned his home as she made her way to the couch. Nothing changed inside since she'd last been there. It was sorta comforting. "I heard you got back in town this morning?"

"News travels slower than I expected," he commented as he placed the kettle on the stove. "I got in yesterday evening."

"Oh." She bobbed her head. "Where, uh... Where did you come back from?"

"New York." She watched as he fiddled with the refrigerator and poured himself a drink. "I went out to visit my family."

"Oh. I hope they're well."

"Not quite," he mentioned as he took a drink.

"I'm sorry to hear." He simply nodded. The kettle hissed and he brought her a mug of her favorite, Chamomile with extra honey.

"Oh, thank you." She took the cup from him as he sat in a seat across from her.

"How have you been?"

"I've been well." She couldn't tell if she was lying when she said that anymore.

"I heard about you and Adam."

"Oh... Which part did you hear?"

"Well, what isn't there to? You can't go into town without it being talked about." He chuckled, though she couldn't tell if he found it funny.

"Well, you should know..."

"You don't have to explain, Adalyn. It's alright."

"No, really. We aren't—God, you really never listen to me, do you..." He looked at her, stunned with her sudden temperament change. "You always do this. You always think the worst of me, when it simply isn't true, but you refuse to hear anything else."

Bewildered, he ceded. "I'm listening."

"I just—Adam and I are *not* dating. I couldn't date him... Not after us."

"I'm sorry?" he questioned. She took a deep breath and a sip of her tea, calming herself. "I didn't mean to ruin anything. I want you to be able to be happy."

"God, of course you do..." She rolled her eyes and took another sip, attempting to conceal the tears that began to form.

He moved over to sit beside her and looked at her. "I didn't mean—"

"It's not you—it's not your fault, I mean. I just..." She looked over at him, her eyes meeting his soft hazel hues. "I'm glad you're back."

"What are you trying to say?"

She took a deep breath, potentially searching for her words, or any words to describe how she felt or why she was there. "I-I still love you."

"Oh?" He was taken aback, though not shocked. "I mean you know—"

"But I'm not ready to be with you again," she interrupted.

"Okay." A hint of confusion formed in his tone, but he kept an open mind.

She took another deep breath. "I hate admitting anything remotely sappy, but I missed you... I missed *us*. How we were before Mia came in, I miss that... At very least, I want our friendship back, and I know, we just broke up. I can give you ti—"

He interrupted her this time. "I would be lyin' if I said I didn't miss everything, too." His words eased her racing thoughts. Leaning back against the couch, there was a comfort to him that she missed. It soothed her.

The day's events finally began to catch up, and her eyes grew heavy. She did her best to fight the urge, though only seemed to be losing the battle. The last she'd remembered before she slipped into dreamland was the warmth of a blanket being draped over her as she rested her head against his black leather couch cushion.

CHAPTER THIRTY-FOUR

December 30, 2015

White cotton curtains danced in the wind as natural light beamed in through the open window, warming everything it touched. In the distance, the sounds of the forest resonated through Adalyn's abode. It was a bright and sunny day, in contrast to the unfitting circumstances of the morning.

It had been nearly a month since Adalyn reentered Zack's life, and a couple weeks since they began to build back what little was left of their tattered relationship. However, a mournful silence filled the thick atmosphere. Standing against the mirror of Adalyn's bedroom, she adjusted Zack's black blazer. Patting out the remaining dog fur that embedded in the worsted wool, he eventually swatted her hands away.

"Thank you," he acknowledged as he turned to the mirror to complete the rest.

"I-I am at a loss of words…" she began, recognizing the bottled tears that slowly crept to the surface. "I'm sorry."

He turned to her with a melancholy expression as he forced a feeble smile across his lips. Muted, he turned back to the mirror. Downstairs, the clock struck nine-thirty. Only thirty minutes until they had to leave. She moved to sit on the chaise sofa that rested at the end of her bed while the sun's creeping touch warmed her legs.

"So, Violet had her baby," Adalyn spoke as she nervously played with the fabric of her dress.

"That's good news."

"Yeah, a healthy baby boy named Mitch." He just simply nodded. Perhaps under any other circumstances, he would be cheerful for Violet, as they'd recently re-mended a friendship, though given the situation, he remained somber. She peered over at him, seeking any form of communication. "Look, I know it's not easy right now, but I'm here if you're ever ready to talk…"

"Thank you. It means a lot." Zack's tone remained stiff and desolate. His mind had traveled to far-off places; anywhere but here, because *here* was cold and heartless.

An invasive buzz erupted from atop Adalyn's dresser for the dozenth time, drawing both their gazes toward it. She rose from her seat to retrieve it, only to read it was yet another message from Adam. Silencing her phone, she returned to her seat on the chaise again.

"I know it's not much of a consolation, but I loved her a lot…" At this rate, Adalyn was grasping at straws, trying to bring forth any form of emotional clarity. His eyes teared up for an instant, though he sniffed and they disappeared. "Y-you don't have to be strong for me—for anyone, really. We all are here for you, and we more than understand..."

He turned to face her, and she held her breath. She wasn't sure what he was about to do, but for some reason, she feared that unknown. Sitting upright, she watched his every move as he walked across the room and over to the open window. Moving the white curtain aside, he glanced out at the forest below.

"I just don't understand *how*," he finally spoke.

She exhaled and relaxed her shoulders. "How do you mean?"

"The report didn't make any sense."

"What did it say?"

Zack stared off into the abyss of trees, as if he were searching for something on the ground below. "The last time I saw her was Thursday, when I picked her up from school and dropped her off at Mia's house for the night. I was supposed to go and pick her up the following day, and come Friday, I woke to a sickening feeling—more so than usual. A gut feeling, maybe." He shook his head in disbelief. "I sped to her house that morning, and when I arrived, the feeling only got worse..." He paused to regain composure before continuing.

"I'm sorry," Adalyn spoke in an attempt to comfort him, but he continued on with the story.

"Police cars and ambulances were swarming the house and parked all across her yard when I pulled up." A singular tear slid down his cheek. "I asked several cops that were standing around the front yard what happened, though no one seemed to give me a straight answer. It wasn't until I walked inside that I finally started to learn bits of the truth."

"Did you see—" Adalyn stopped herself from continuing, instantly regretting its inappropriate nature.

Answering regardless, Zack shook his head. "A cop inside informed me that she'd wandered off in the middle of school and her teacher found her wounded from a mountain lion attack."

"I'm *so*—" Her concern was overrode by his search for answers.

"It doesn't make any sense... I just don't get—" He took a deep inhale. "She's not one to wander off."

"Do you have any other ideas about what happened?" Her question was met with a headshake.

"The case is closed. It's written off as an animal attack, and there's nothing further." For the first time since the story began, Zack twisted his head to look over at her. Sadness surfaced on his face as she moved closer to him. She didn't know how to react, but she did the best she could. She couldn't deny that heartache pooled in her own chest, though she reminded herself, *this isn't about me, it's about him,* as she stuffed her feelings into a bottle and saved them for a later date.

Zack wasn't actively crying, though she wiped away the singular tear that had fallen down his cheek.

He gently grabbed the hand that had brushed away his tear, holding it as he looked at her. His eyes pooled with so much emotion, nearly taking her under its thick waters. She stared into them, like a window to his soul. Downstairs, the clock in the entryway chimed ten. Letting out a deep exhale, she took a step back.

"I believe it's time..." she spoke.

He sighed and bobbed his head as he conceded to the inevitable. How could anyone be ready for such an event? He was ready as he'll ever be. Holding the bedroom door open for her, they stepped out.

The Jeep was cold upon first entrance, but no colder than the atmosphere that encompassed them, or the ground that they walked across as they approached the small plot of land atop the hill.

The service took place at the cemetery, though due to the town's newer establishment, it was more or less a field. Grass crunched beneath them, and in the distance, a small crowd of attendees in black attire twisted their gaze as they drew near. Solemn expressions washed across their faces upon eye contact. Even in such a crowd, it was nearly silent.

Ragnar and Joyce, who'd just gotten back in town, were the first to step forth and give their condolences, followed shortly after by Kayla, Maddie, and Max. It was a small gathering, exclusively filled with the important individuals that had tended to her daily life in one way or another.

The coffin that they congregated around was empty. It was merely a representation for the service; a pawn to tug at heartstrings, while her real youth was captured in an urn that sat on the mantle in Zack's living room.

Max stepped forth and embraced his friend. "I'm so sorry, man." There was a hint of sorrow in their tough expressions as they did their best not to crack. Where they'd grown, it was emasculating to cry, but given the circumstances, it was nearly impossible not to.

"Thank you for coming."

Through the dreary atmosphere, a pair of heels approached, drawing everyone's attention back toward the road. *Mia?* Adalyn's heart raced as she glanced over, though it wasn't. It took her a moment to pin the woman's familiar beauty to a name. *Beka.* A faint smile escaped Zack's lips to see his sister, to whom presented a pitied smile back at him.

"It's good to see you. Thank you," Zack spoke.

"I couldn't miss this. I'm very sorry." She embraced him, then took her place around the circle.

The service began. It was brief; however, throughout the ceremony, Zack remained stiff, stuffing every ounce of his emotions into a bottle that he planned to bury. He was clearly wretched over his bereaved daughter, though something inside him had gone numb.

At the end, he stayed behind a moment longer than everyone else, paying his respects while he stared down at the lowered coffin.

It became a caravan around town, as cars that hadn't even taken part in the service all slowly trialed up the mountain to Adalyn's abode, where the reception was to take place. Regardless of their exclusion from the service, plenty more guests arrived to mourn the passing of a young girl whose livelihood brightened the town.

The afternoon was far from cheerful, though Adalyn did her best to keep the atmosphere leveled. She had earlier prepped and decorated, leaving the first level of her home a timeless memorial of the bright young girl. Even over such little time with Sky, she'd managed to capture the young girl's essence. Images and memories of the finer times hung along Adalyn's walls, and bouquets of white tiger lilies and pale blue daisies rested on nearly every surface. It was a perfect representation of what Sky would've wanted, and she recognized that as Zack's eyes glistened upon viewing.

"Adalyn, this is stunning," Beka spoke as her heels slowly clicked across the floor, fading into the living room. "Did you do this yourself?"

"Yeah. I mean, I had some professional help, of course…" She nervously chuckled, attempting a modest tone to the praise she was receiving.

Beka returned to Adalyn's side. Now leaning up against the kitchen island, she provided her with a warm hug. "It's good to see you, even under such awful circumstances."

"I'm just glad you could make it… Are you the only one from Zack's side to make it out?"

With an exhausted sigh, Beka nodded. "None of my family were happy when they found out about her. Plus, Zack's not close with them anymore. Actually, I don't even think they know where he lives." She gently chuckled in disbelief. "Also, did you notice who else didn't show?"

"Mia," they both said at once.

"I noticed that, too. I wish I could say I was surprised," Adalyn replied with disappointment. "It truly shows how little she cared." Fiddling with a fallen daisy petal on the countertop, she glanced up with a look of mild disgust. Talk of Mia always irked her.

"It's alright. It's better that she's not around. Maybe it'll really solidify the hatred this time," Beka said as she spun to face Adalyn with a pleasant smile. "Thank you for supporting my brother."

"Oh, of course." Adalyn flashed a faded grin as she pushed herself away from the counter. Grabbing a bottle of empty wine that rested on the counter, she held it up. "I should go get more. Please feel free to look around and chat. I'll be back shortly."

Passing from the kitchen to the entryway, something caught her arm. Looking up with confusion, she met Adam's jade eyes that burned with an anxious stare.

"Hey, can we speak?"

She peered over her shoulder, briefly looking into the living room. Yanking her arm out of his grasp, she declined. "No. Now's not a good time…"

"Then, when? I've been trying to reach you."

"I'm sorry, but given the circumstances…" She sighed, recognizing it was simply not an excuse. "What is it?"

"What's going on?"

"Nothing," she replied immediately, shutting down any availability for a conversation.

"I know you, Adalyn. This isn't like you…"

"I appreciate the concern, but really, I'm okay. I have to go get some more wine, so if you'll excuse me…" She barged past him, simply evading his baffled stare as she walked away. In the distance, the front door slammed shut, but she refused to look back as she hurried to fetch more wine from the guest room upstairs.

Returning from her brief moment away, the party had grouped in the living room. Setting the bottle down on the counter, she quietly watched from afar. The room fell into a blurry haze, or at least that's what she remembered, as her mind did its best to block out the thing it frankly couldn't handle.

She stared up at a singular picture of the young girl in her final days; one that would be immortalized for the rest of history, and by the time she glanced back, or at least by the time she'd come out of her daze, most of the guests had departed. Only a few sparse, but close friends remained behind.

Finding herself in the kitchen again, she stared at that singular image.

"Thank you for today." Zack's voice startled her as she jumped back. She peered over with another faded smile.

"Of course. Anything for Sky." As little as she voiced it, the loss truly got to her; it was something even she was finding harder and harder to conceal as the afternoon drug on.

He gently kissed the top of her head as he began to walk away. Though it wasn't much but a fleeting moment, a genuine smile flashed across her lips.

"You know," she whispered, drawing him back in, "I know I didn't know her for long, and it's not about me, but I *really* miss her..."

He turned back to her. "She really did love you. You have every right to mourn."

"So do you," she responded. He nodded in return, though it wasn't enough for her. "You don't have to be strong. She was your daughter..."

"I know," he replied. Solemn in tone, he lingered for a moment more before turning to go once again.

"Zack," she spoke, stopping him in his tracks.

He didn't bother to look back as he replied, "People grieve how they grieve..." She let out a deep sigh as he continued off.

CHAPTER THIRTY-FIVE

January 7, 2016

The tiny heart-shaped pendant rested atop Zack's dresser ever since it had been returned, along with the rest of Sky's belongings. That necklace was one of the few items the young girl held close to her in her final moments, and through a brief crack in the gray clouds, sunlight beat through the window and onto the charm, refracting light like a beacon. It beckoned her. Adalyn finished adjusting her black midi dress and walked toward the necklace.

It'll be okay. Her own voice played back in her head, recollecting on the last memory she had with the young girl, and just how wrong she came to be. *It wasn't okay.* Tears welled in her eyes, though she refrained from letting them drop. Holding the necklace in her fingers, she admired it as she moved back to the mirror and placed it around her neck. It was fitting for the day.

"Are you ready?" Zack hollered from the other room. His tone was stiff, once more burying what he couldn't seem to handle. She glanced in the mirror at the charm that dangled from her neck. Even though it was her own, it felt foreign to her, as if it wasn't really hers anymore.

"Coming!" Taking another glance in the mirror, she rushed out of the room.

In a black button down and leather coat, Zack waited for her by the front door. Stepping into the main room, she took in the sight of him as she made her way over. He was rugged lately; partially unshaven, worn, and drained. His eyes drooped and bags sagged underneath, while his crooked smile hardly glistened with its unique charm anymore. In one hand, he held up her black trench coat, and in the other was the small urn. For a brief second, his eyes fell upon the necklace, though immediately shifted away as he held open the door.

The car ride was absolutely silent. There was nothing to say—at least nothing they wanted to say, as they traveled up the long back roads that led to the lodge. Adalyn's eyes wandered to the forest that drifted beside them.

Though they were together, she could not feel further from him.

Since the service, Zack had hardly spoken to anyone, and a part of her felt as if she was losing him. She glanced over in his direction, watching his eyes focus on the road ahead. Reaching for his hand that rested on the gearshift, the touch gained his attention. It was a fleeting moment that they made eye contact, though it was the first time in days that he'd even looked in the direction of anyone.

A faint, yet fake smile crossed his lips, then his eyes went back to the road as the lodge fell into view.

Wishing not to draw attention to themselves, they snuck around the side, reaching the lake in no time. Zack halted at the same spot that they'd fed the ducks only months prior, taking in the memories that had been created in that very spot, though a cold breeze reminded him to keep going. It was the middle of winter now, and the lake had grown over with a thick layer of ice.

Stopping at the bank, they peered across the untouched forest ahead. Across the waters, the land was sectioned off to preserve the wild animals' habitat. With no bridge to get them over and the ice too thin to trek, Zack scanned the surroundings for any path. To his luck, a few feet up, rocks emerged from the iced-over stream.

"I think if we're careful, we could make it."

"Well, are they slippery?" Adalyn asked. Testing it with his own foot, he nearly lost balance but continued onward anyways.

"A little bit... But the water isn't deep enough to get swept away." He was persistent on his idea to travel across the lake and set his daughter to rest there. Though Adalyn couldn't fully make sense of his logic, since they'd never gone over to that area, she followed along anyway.

Perhaps it was his determination, but he made hopping over rocks seem much easier than it was. As if it was as simple as walking across land, Zack crossed the lake, assisting Adalyn with every stone she stepped on.

This side was noisier. With the lake acting as a filter that drowned out nature, birds chirped even louder than before. But there was tranquility to this atmosphere.

Taking it in, a sudden *pop* sound drew her back as she glanced over at Zack, who'd opened the urn and began spreading the ashes about the cold ground. With his heel, Zack chipped away a hole in the ice at the bank and sent some flowing down the stream. They remained silent, not daring to break the serene moments of Zack's goodbye.

He stood there for a minute more, reminiscing on her beautiful, youthful essence. Adalyn could've sworn she'd seen a tear fall, though in this cold, there was no telling for certain. She questioned reaching for his hand or letting him be, but she did it anyway. Gently grasping his hand in her own, he glanced over at her. His kindred eyes held pain as he looked at her. To her surprise, his hand clasped over hers, tightening his grip.

He took a deep inhale. "Okay."

"Huh?"

"Okay," he repeated. "I'm ready."

"Oh, uh... We can stay a bit longer." He shook his head and with that, led them back across the lake. For some peculiar reason, crossing back over seemed easier than the first time.

Zack stopped at the bank, where Adalyn had taught them both how to feed ducklings. Taking an audible breath, he continued walking back to the car.

"Oh, wait." Adalyn stopped him. Releasing her grip on his hand, she began to undo the clasp to her golden necklace. Walking over to the bank, she broke away a small piece of ice to reveal the lake below. Holding the necklace in her hand, she clenched it in her hand one last time before setting it afloat down the lake.

"Until next time," she whispered.

Standing up, she rejoined him back at the trail. He didn't question her; he knew. Reaching for his hand again, they walked back to the car.

By the time the Jeep pulled into the driveway, gray clouds had completely obstructed the sun and a small red sedan sat out front. Adalyn took a deep sigh. Never having attended the funeral, she was astonished by the woman's audacity to show up now.

"Well, well, well." Mia's unpleasant voice cut the air. "Look what the cat dragged in. Adalyn, you're back!"

"And here to stay this time, Mia," she coldly stated as she closed the car door. This time, the woman had nothing—not Sky, not fear; nothing on her.

"Oh, you've got some bite this time," Mia snickered.

"What do you want?" Zack intervened as he began to walk inside.

"I came to collect Sky's belongings that the police gave you and any valuables from her room."

"No." Zack was blunt. The steam expelled off his breath as he stopped in his driveway. His stern response shocked Adalyn, causing her to peer over in disbelief.

"No?"

"You heard me. No. You couldn't even show up to your own daughter's funeral."

"Oh yeah, I want her ashes, too."

"You're about thirty minutes too late for that, sorry." He extended his hand back for Adalyn to grab, motioning that they go inside where it's warm.

Mia exerted a huff. "Excuse me? What did you do to my daughter?"

"I gave her the proper send-off I know she'd always want, and if you knew her any better, you'd know what I did."

"You just... The *nerve*," she growled.

"We're done here, Mia. It's over."

"The hell we are! Are you forgetting about a little weapon I—"

"What could you *possibly* do to me at this rate?" Zack interrupted, his voice raising an increment this time. Ignoring her astonished expression, he glanced back at Adalyn. "C'mon, Adalyn. Let's go." The tables had turned in ways she thought were unimaginable, and she couldn't deny that her respect for him instantly shifted.

"I'm sure you thought of Sky as your daughter, too! And just like Delilah, she also left you." It was as if she was grasping for straws now, saying anything that could hurt her.

Adalyn halted her in tracks. Anger and pain boiled in her heart, ignited by the hatred of a petty woman. She opened her mouth, but Zack interrupted. "You have nothing left here, Mia." Solemn in tone, yet harsh in demeanor, Zack stood his ground for once in his life. "If I ever see you again—"

"*What*? What will you do?" she pressed, though her voice came out shaky. Admittedly, Mia felt afraid of him. A man with nothing to lose was a dangerous man.

Zack sensed her unease, as a long pause followed her question before he simply responded, "Goodbye, Mia."

The front door slammed shut and Zack made his way into the bedroom, where Adalyn sat at the edge of the bed, fiddling with her fingernails. She glanced up at the doorway when she heard the sound of his footsteps approaching. "Is she gone?" He nodded his head. "For good?"

"I'd like to hope so." He took a seat beside her, and they sat in silence for a long moment, perhaps uncertain what to say or do next.

CHAPTER THIRTY-SIX

February 16, 2016

And there he was, dancing about his kitchen. Life had carried on in Dawn Hills for just about everyone involved, and he continued to slide carefree about the wooden floors in a pair of socks.

It had been upwards of a month since they'd spread Sky's ashes, and with Mia in the wind, Zack officially solidified his place on the Council. Better yet, for the first time ever, he sat down and introduced himself to a therapist. Though he was nowhere near finished mourning, this was his earnest attempt at appreciating the good in life. He was beginning his own journey of recovery.

Song and merriment tolled throughout the cabin as a bell chimed at the front door. Pausing the music with a simple press of a button, he went to fetch whatever had come to his porch step that February night.

Tugging open the door, the brisk winter air struck his bare skin as he held his breath to adjust.

"Adalyn?" he immediately questioned, staring at the woman who stood at his doorstep.

"I, uh... I come bearing food in hopes you'd let me stay for dinner?" Holding up a dish of food in her hands, she scrunched up her nose in nervousness.

Without question, he stepped aside to let her in. Crossing that threshold, she let out a gentle sigh and began to relax her shoulders. Taking off her jacket, she hung it on the coat rack and looked over at him with a smile.

"What'd you bring?" He'd moved to the kitchen by then, watching as she made her way over with the covered dish.

"Oh, uh..." Setting it down against his countertop, she uncovered the tin foil that kept it warm. "Homemade meatballs... I know it's a lot to insinuate since I sort of invited myself over, but I was hoping you'd have spaghetti pasta? I'm all out at my place, and—"

"I think I've got exactly what you need," he interrupted as he began rummaging through the cabinets. Pulling out a half-empty box of spaghetti, he walked back over and set it down on the counter.

A widened grin crossed her lips. "That'll do," she vibrantly exclaimed.

"Perfect-o!" Turning back around, he fetched a pot to begin the cooking. "So," he began. His voice drew her attention to him. "How are you? How've you been?"

"Uh, I've been..." she paused, pondering over the previous weeks. "I've been well." *Suppose, as well as she could be.* "Busy, really." She hadn't been, but she *had* been avoiding him. A lot pressed her mind lately, and with the turmoil he was going through in his own world, she'd chosen to step back.

"All good things, I assume?" He was teasing her. Perhaps if she wasn't as tense, she could sense that.

"N—uh, yeah. Work things, really." Adalyn began fiddling with her keychain, doing just about anything to avoid looking at him. He casually nodded, his gaze shifting back toward the stove as he mixed in some salt and olive oil to the cooking pasta.

"That's good."

The conversation only seemed to drag. It felt dull and forced; something they never experienced before. A long silence ensued. She listened to the boiling of the water on the stove and the wind hollering outside as a tough breeze brushed through, shuffling a few brown leaves past the window.

Turning back to face her as the pasta sat and waited to cook, Zack was the first to interrupt the silence. "So, how are you and Adam?"

"Huh?" She was taken aback by his question, better yet the mention of that name. "He, uh... He and I don't speak anymore. In fact, I don't even think he's in town anymore."

Zack held a confused expression. "I thought you two were still—Sorry."

She shook her head. "No, no. It's okay. I think the last time I really spoke to him was before—" She paused. She wanted to say *Sky's funeral*, but respectfully refrained. "But yeah, I still see Kayla every week and last I heard, he went back to visit family again."

"Oh, I guess I didn't even notice his absence."

Adalyn let out a singular *ha* as her eyes drifted off once more. "How are you?" she finally asked, recognizing she hadn't even bothered checking in on him.

"I'm well."

"Anything new in your world?"

His gaze met hers for a moment as he attempted to recollect over the previous month. As much as life had changed since he'd last seen her, so much almost felt like nothing at all.

Aside from weekly therapy to not only heal from Sky and Mia, but his own childhood trauma, he carried on with life as normal. After enough of staring off into space, he eventually looked back over at her and shrugged. "Just normal life, really."

She simply nodded, not bothering to deep dive too much into that question. "Did you see Vi recently?"

"No, why? I actually don't think I've talked to anyone much recently." He turned back to face the stove. Stirring the pasta, he popped the tray of meatballs into the oven to reheat. "How is everyone?"

"Well, Vi's new baby is probably the cutest thing to ever exist. He's learning to grab things. Mainly hair, which really is becoming a problem... But I'm stunned you haven't met him yet."

"Oh, Mitch? I met Mitch."

"You did?"

"Yeah. Not recently or anything, but one of the first weeks after she got home, I went to visit her."

"Oh. Good." She fell silent, uncertain what to say next. Taking a deep sigh, she set the keychain she'd been fiddling with down on the counter, creating a rather loud *clinking* sound. "So, you're probably wondering why I'm even here..."

"I assume it's not for dinner?" he chuckled, keeping the air light. A soft smile tugged at the corner of her lips, and she shook her head. She wanted to laugh, but her nerves prohibited doing so. His face grew serious at that notion as his attention pinned on her and he motioned her to continue.

"Alright, Zack... I have a confession." She took another deep sigh, really expressing the exhale. "Okay, I know it's been forever ago, but I thought about giving *us* another shot. I know this is so random and crazy, but I started thinking about us more and I miss it... I miss the old times." Their eyes met for an instance before she nervously dropped her gaze.

His expression went wide with shock. Even shielded under the terrible kitchen lighting, his eyes pierced her. "Huh... Well, I'd be lying if I said I didn't like you still..." She let out an audible sigh of relief, and he couldn't help but produce a friendly grin. "And random and crazy doesn't do this justice."

"You still like me?" She couldn't hold back a faint smirk as she asked.

"Why wouldn't I?" Briefly turning around, he gave the pasta another stir.

"I dunno... I suppose after everything that's happened lately, I was probably the last thing on your mind." He shook his head, but refrained from further explanation. "Okay well, I guess I did have one concern..."

Zack quirked an eyebrow. "And what's that?"

"Well *if*, and I say *if*, anything were to happen, I don't know..." She returned to restlessly fiddling with her keychain. "I'm just afraid it'll be a month or so later and suddenly everything will repeat itself."

The timer on the oven dinged right at that moment, forcing him to turn away from her. Setting down the tray on the countertop, he immediately twisted his focus onto the pasta that was still cooking. With a few strings in his hand, he tried one, and upon recognizing they weren't completely finished, he took the other two and playfully tossed it at her. One happened to land in her hair as she squealed. A giggle filtered through her lips for the first time since she'd arrived—something he really missed hearing. She was easy to distract; easy to make happy, too. However, their bout of playfulness didn't distract them from the pressing topic at hand.

"You had a valid worry, there," he eventually spoke as the laughter died down. Even he couldn't deny that that worry hadn't crossed his own thoughts on an occasion. "I gave up too soon—for a good reason, but too soon."

His redirection of topic caught her off guard, and she stopped laughing completely. Staring at him, she asked, "What do you mean?"

"Okay, I know what I will say isn't exactly going to be comforting, but I can promise you that what happened won't repeat itself—if I can help it."

"Yeah?" Her tone held disbelief. "How?"

His back was now turned to her again as he drained the pasta in the sink. Taking a deep sigh in, he let out the exhale and turned to her with the pot in his left hand. "It's done."

"What? I—"

"No, dinner. It's done. It's ready."

"Oh..." She immediately fell silent, really uncertain where she *thought* the conversation was headed.

"And, I admit... I can be childish and emotionless at times..." He paused as he set down two bowls on the island counter for them. "But I'm a lot better now than I was back then." He faltered again, finding his words. Taking a deeper sigh than before, his eyes met hers. "And I actually really want to try and do the things that I should've done, and tell you the things I should've told you before. I think you deserve that."

A smile boiled at the surface, as she was at a loss for words now. "Alright." She finally mustered up dialogue to respond with, and *alright* happened to be the best she got out. Choking on air, she struggled to finish that sentence. "Alright... You have to try this time."

He vigorously bobbed his head up and down. "Alright," he responded back. "I will."

Producing a grin, she picked up her bowl of food and began to walk to the dining table, only to halt. Turning around, she looked up at him. Her gaze brushed over his tanned skin and hazel eyes, and with the delicate smirk that rested on her lips, she kissed him. All the worry that she'd come there with seemed to float away.

CHAPTER THIRTY-SEVEN

April 2, 2016

Trickles of rain fell from the sky and bounced off the canopy of leaves that shielded Kane Park that late morning. As the first weekend of the Farmer's Market was in full swing, the grounds flooded with residents who gathered in the park to scale the never-ending aisles.

With nothing in mind to shop for, Zack and Adalyn wandered the galleries, frequently stopping to examine whatever caught their attention, then continuing onward.

"Love, come try this!" The pet name rolled off his tongue like sweet maple syrup as she nearly skipped over to him.

"What is it?"

He stepped aside to make room for her beside him, unveiling a small cheese stand. Holding a toothpick with a tiny cheese cube pierced at the end of it, he handed it to her. "Apparently it's made of goat." Zack's tone held some sort of bewilderment, as if he'd forgotten the existence of *goat* cheese, though she let him have his moment. His enthusiasm made her smile.

Taking a bite of the small block, she lit up with merriment. "Wow," she exclaimed. "This is—"

"Should we take some with us?" With her mouth still full from the bite, she eagerly nodded.

Shoving the larger block of cheese in her bag, she glanced over at Zack, who's attention was already drawn to the next thing. It was out of his peripheral that he caught a glimpse of a kid—fitting, of course.

A faint *baaah* cooed in the distance as Zack made his way through the crowd. Like metal to some magnet, he was off to the next best thing.

"Zack, wait up!" She pushed through the crowd, blindly following behind him. Coming to an abrupt halt in front of a stand, she gasped. *Baby farm animals.* It was the first one she saw that season. Ranging from ducks and chicks to goats and pigs, the booth stirred with life.

"Is this some sort of petting zoo?" Adalyn inquired, though the man only shook his head.

"They're all buyable," he spoke. "The name's Dave."

"I'm Adalyn." Her tone was wary. Inching closer to Zack's side, she felt rather out of place. There was something strange about being the only ones standing at that booth, while everyone else moved past; something off-putting, but Zack didn't seem to notice.

"Are you here every weekend?" Zack asked.

"No, sir. Jus er'y first a' the month." For so far north, his accent was interesting to her—distracting, really.

"Oh, okay." Zack bent down to pet the baby goat which initially drew his attention to begin with. "What're they raised for?"

"Whatcha mean, boy?"

"Well like, are they for eating, or pets, or..."

"Ya can raise 'em as pets, I s'ppose," the farmer said as he rose from his seat. "Most o' my buyers raise 'em for their own farm. You got a farm, boy?" Zack shook his head and the farmer grunted. "Well, I suppose, they get 'em for just about anythin'."

"Do they make good pets?"

The farmer shrugged and grunted again. "'Pends. Which one?"

Zack looked around at all the animals, though Adalyn knew he was about to go for the goat, and she really didn't want that. "The chicks," Adalyn intruded, hovering over a brooder of baby chicks.

The farmer glared at Adalyn for a moment before he spoke. "They'd be fine for pets, but ya got a place to keep 'em?"

"Does inside work?" she asked, really having no clue what it took to tend to a chicken.

The farmer only laughed. "Not a chance! Not 'less you want them ruinin' ya home and runnin' amuck."

"What does it take?" Zack asked.

Twisting his direction to Zack now, the farmer glanced over at him as he made his way toward the brooder. "Ya need protection from wildlife like foxes, and up 'ere, you outta be crazy thinkin' somethin' could survive in the forest."

"Then why'd you bring them here?" Adalyn contested. The farmer just grunted loudly, and she took the hint. Spending a few more moments inspecting the baby animals on display, she finally turned to Zack. "Ready?"

"Uh, yeah." He didn't want to go quite yet. Perhaps the farm animals reminded him of his childhood, or maybe he was being sucked in by the adorableness, but he was hesitant to leave. Following her only steps into the crowded aisle, he stopped. Zack watched as Adalyn inadvertently continued walking on, gaining distance in between them, but he couldn't seem to continue on. "What if—" he spoke up.

She halted in her tracks. Recognizing his voice had become muffled against the masses, she turned around. "Don't tell me..."

"What do you think they do with the animals if no one buys them?"

"Zack... I'm sure someone buys them. We do *not* need any more pets!" She knew he would do this; she knew he would fall in love.

"I saw it in your eyes when you were looking at those chicks."

"Y-yeah, so?" She stuttered when she spoke. A part of her wanted them too, but the difference was, she knew that they did not have what it took to tend to a farm animal.

"I already have names picked out..." A sly smirk arose on his face as he stepped closer to her, something she couldn't resist smiling back at. She let out a loud sigh, followed by an eye-roll, but it was his signal to continue. Holding his hand out to her, she reached for it and he led her back to the booth.

"Y'all didn' make it far," the farmer commented as he stumbled back to his seat from tending to a pen.

"I think we wanna give the chicks another look," Zack responded as he gently squeezed Adalyn's hand. The farmer motioned to the chicks as if to grant them permission.

Hovering over the brood, they looked at the chicks. Under that red light, they all looked the same to Adalyn. She leaned in closer, examining for any identifying qualities, but the dimmed light made it nearly impossible.

"They all look the same," she finally said aloud while looking over at Zack.

He audibly gasped. "Don't let them hear that. They'll be hurt!"

"Oh yeah? Tell me one that stands out," she spoke through faltered giggles.

"Well," he pointed to a baby chick in the far corner, "I've named that one Fabio."

"But he's all alone in the corner," she protested.

"Well, the other ones annoyed him." She laughed, realizing he, too, couldn't tell any of them apart, but she missed his quipping humor. It had been almost a year since she'd truly seen him this genuine—since she'd seen his alluring smile.

"Okay, how about that one?" She pointed to another random chick.

"That one? That's—" he paused, pondering a random name. "Pete."

"Pete?" she playfully questioned. He nodded, pridefully. "Alright... So, say we adopt Pete..."

Zack quirked an eyebrow. "Oh? Am I hearing you coming around to this idea?"

"I-I didn't *quite* say that..."

He slowly nodded his head. "Okay. Say we adopt Pete?"

She just shrugged, pondering it a moment longer. "Who gets custody when we aren't together?"

A rumbled chuckle emitted from his throat as he glanced down at the baby chicks. "Split custody?"

A smile snuck on her face as she followed his gaze. "Okay... Then, let's get him."

Simultaneously, they peered over their shoulders to the farmer who'd dazed off, twirling a toothpick in his mouth. Catching their gazes out of his peripheral, he cleared his throat. "Ya folk finally made up ya minds?" Adalyn nodded as she waited for him to walk over. "Aight, which one?"

"This one." Zack pointed to the chick he'd randomly named Pete, though at that moment a cooing erupted from the chick nearest, as if it called to them.

"Oh! Zack, I think that one likes us," Adalyn spoke with awe.

Following her gaze, he stared at the chick that had cooed. "Well, now, is Pete the one you want? Because I kinda had my eye on Caiden."

"Oh, is that one now Caiden?" She raised an eyebrow, knowing well of the game he was playing; tugging at her heartstrings with a subtle reference to the chick she'd won during their first carnival. He exuberantly nodded, and she let out a ceding sigh.

"We'll actually take that one, good sir."

The farmer grumbled as he mumbled, "*Whatever*," under his breath. Plucking the young chick from its flock, he placed it in a breathable cardboard box and handed it to Zack. "Ya gonna need supplies?"

"Uh," he glanced over at Adalyn, who quickly nodded. "Yeah. What do ya have?"

Walking back to the front of his booth, he groaned as he bent down. Standing back up, he handed Zack a care box for new chicken owners. "All the info ya need is in 'ere, and anythin' else is what Google is for. 'Ere's my card." He handed Zack a business card. "In case anythin' major goes wrong. Don't call if ya can Google it!"

Zack nodded while he flipped through the folder of care, as if he was actually consuming the information on the page. "Thank you."

The farmer groaned again. "Good luck." He mumbled, "*weirdos,*" under his breath.

Adalyn innocently smiled, as if to pretend she didn't hear him clear as day. Wrapping her arm around Zack's, she reached for the folder in his hands to read over as they slowly began wandering away.

Just hardly out of earshot now, she turned to Zack with a glistening, toothy grin. "We got a chick," she spiritedly exclaimed. Zack returned her enthusiasm with an equal amount of excitement as he peered in the box, down at the nesting baby.

"Welcome to your new family, Caiden."

CHAPTER THIRTY-EIGHT

June 8, 2016

The arched windows in Adalyn's abode made for a perfect spot to watch the summer storm blow through. Like a blackout curtain, blocks of solid gray clouds barricaded the day's sunlight, plunging the town into a gray haze.

Inside, sheltered from the storm, the atmosphere was hospitably pleasant, like a heated blanket on a cold day—exceptionally comforting when the rest of the world was but a cold, bitter blurb. In the corner, a warm glow emitted from the fireplace while the television whispered in the background.

Positioned on the sofa, Adalyn glanced over her shoulder at Zack, who stood on the opposite side of the island. "I don't think we ever finished our conversation," she announced.

Fiddling with miscellaneous items on the counter, he froze with concern. His mind raced, trying to recollect *what* conversation she was referring to. "Oh, we never did talk about that..." he responded, pleading that she would clue him in.

"Indeed." She paused as she reflected, though her faltering drew out his concern even further. Taking a deep breath, she finally continued her statement. "Well, I suppose if you actually decided to stay here, then within the community, you'd have some benefits by association..." She wavered for another moment before adding, "To a degree!"

An uncontrolled smile crept onto his face. "You don't—" His voice cracked, and he cleared his throat. He felt undeserving of her offer.

She pleasantly nodded as she carried on. "Plus, I feel like there's a lot more benefits, too. Like we'd have more room for the dogs, Caiden wouldn't have to be transported back and forth all the time, no more long night drives home for either of us, a quicker commute to work—oh, we could even carpool!" Enthusiasm grew in her tone.

Adjusting his composure, he looked over at her. "I'd love that."

"Really?" she asked with eagerness. "Does that mean a yes?"

Meeting her gaze, he hastily nodded. He was sure of his answer since the moment he'd lightheartedly brought it up to her days prior.

She beamed a smile brighter than he'd ever seen. Excitement overtook her as she was in disbelief of what was happening—she never thought she'd see the day. *They were moving in together.* Attempting to regain composure, she took a deep inhale. "Okay, well, I got to thinking," she began.

Moving over toward the couch, a hint of nervousness returned to the pit of his stomach as he questioned what she was about to say next. "What's up?" he casually asked.

"I was just thinking how we could redesign the place once you move in."

Taking a seat across from her on the coffee table, he grinned with relief. "Okay, shoot!"

"So, for starters, I was thinking we rearrange the upstairs. Ya'know, like take out one of the guest bedrooms and replace it with a study, or a game room, or something." He internally visualized her idea for a moment before nodding along. "Then maybe we find a way to merge our furniture?"

He interrupted her there. "I don't have a whole lot to bring over. I don't need to bring over the living room furniture, or the bedroom furniture..."

"But I don't want it to be all *my* stuff. I want it to be a perfect blend." He lightly chuckled at her vitality. "Oh! Maybe we can start hanging up some of your decorations on these walls?" She glanced around at the cream-painted walls, cringing to its emptiness.

"Sure, we can do that," he responded with a faint grin, though pleased that she was so concerned.

"Fantastic!" Her elated expression never left as she exclaimed, "I'm so excited!"

He watched with admiration to this sense of marvel that washed over her—an expression unmirrored by anyone else. He was indubitably in love.

"Should we celebrate?" he finally asked. "Maybe martinis at La Regale? It is a special occasion, after all!" As he offered, his gaze slowly wandered over to the arched window, where the evening break in the clouds arrived and shed light into the room for the first time all day.

"Hmm," she contemplated aloud, churning over ways to celebrate such an event, but hesitant to leave home. "You know, this storm has really been making me crave milk and cookies..."

He grinned at her wholesome response, though it quickly faded. "I—My baking skills are lacking. I'm not sure how the outcome of the cookies will be..." Zack stuttered, as he stood up, meandering back into the kitchen to fetch a drink of some kind. He pressed his lips together as he considered alternative options. "But I can go buy some from Cathy's?" he proposed.

Her face lit up with interest as he mentioned Cathy's infamous freshly-baked cookies. Momentarily shifting her gaze toward the large window, she pressed, "Drinks too?"

"Ah, you cannot forget drinks," he said in jest. "What kind, my dear?"

"Any kind. Surprise me, Love!" Her tone remained playful as she watched him fetch his coat from the entryway. "Oh, I don't think I have milk..."

"So, should I go out for milk as well?"

Both of their eyes drifted toward the refrigerator, and he hesitantly walked back into the kitchen to examine the bare shelves. Looking back at her, he shook his head, and she produced the best puppy eyes she could possibly give. "Please," she coaxed. "It wouldn't be the same without milk."

She played a dangerous game with such an expression; it was his Achilles' heel. He let out a soft sigh before nodding in agreement. "Alright, I'll be back soon." Collecting his belongings from the counter, he leaned over the back of the couch and gave her a soft peck on the forehead, then proceeded down the hallway.

"Thank you!"

"Yes, you're welcome, dear," he hollered back as he disappeared through the front door, leaving only a bluster of chilly wind in his place.

It was but a swift ride into town from her abode, though the moments felt like hours to her impatient mind. During the time of his absence, Adalyn mindlessly surfed through the television channels, seeking anything to ease her eagerness and growing hunger.

Forty minutes felt like a lifetime as a soft knock erupted on her front door. She furrowed her brows with confusion as she began to unravel the blanket to stand. Before her concern grew further, the door pushed open and he walked in.

"I'm back, and I come bearing milk and other things," he hollered as he shut the door behind him.

"Why did you knock?" she questioned as she positioned herself to face the hallway.

"It wasn't opening for a moment. I thought that for once in a blue moon, you might have locked it," he teased.

"Oh!" To his prediction, Adalyn hadn't moved from her spot on the couch since he'd left, but his presence was enough motivation to get her up. Bouncing off the couch, she slid across the hardwood floor to assist. "What other things did you get?"

"Just some odd assortment of cookies, a bag of chips, gummy bears... You know, necessities." He chuckled as she took the bag from his hands and made their way into the kitchen.

"You bought *gummy bears*? I couldn't love you more right now!"

"I'm glad gummy candy is the source of at least fifty percent of the love in this relationship," he quipped while fetching two cups from the cabinet.

"Oh hush." She rolled her eyes as she unbagged the items and laid them across the counter. Pouring milk into two glasses, he slid one across the countertop. Gliding like a pad of butter on a hot pan, it stopped just inches from the end of the table. An audible gasp left her lips as she prepared for the glass to shatter across the floor, but it never came. He'd been a bartender most of his life, where that risky move was performed nightly, and though she was impressed, she hid it well.

Snatching up the milk and assortment of cookies, she sauntered back to the couch with Zack following close behind. The fire still crackled as she plucked the blanket from the back of the couch and pulled it over the two of them. Gazing up at him, she returned to their previous banter. "I love you for *you*." Biting at her bottom lip, she curved them into a delicate smile.

CHAPTER THIRTY-NINE

June 27, 2016

"How long will you be gone?" she asked. Reaching for her glass of water, she took a long sip.

Zack looked up at her from his plate. He must've been similarly upset, as he had taken his fork and aimlessly shuffled the food around. "Only a month or two," he finally replied while he took a small bite. She nodded. "But once I get back, we'll work on moving stuff in!" His voice aimed to be lighthearted. A faint smile appeared across her face, but she struggled to mean it.

"Everything tasting alright?" Ruby asked, coming by the table to check on them.

"Yes, thank you." Adalyn nodded as she took a bite of food to show she was enjoying it. Turning back to Zack, she let out a gentle sigh.

"It won't be for long," he promised. "I just have to go tend to some things in New York, then I'll be back."

She smiled again, though even he could see through its facade. "I'm sorry I'm such a bummer—"

"Don't be," he interrupted, taking another small bite.

She set her fork down, letting it clatter against the ceramic. "I just am awful at saying goodbye."

"But, it isn't *goodbye*. I'll be back before you know it." He extended his hand across the table, reaching for hers to console her.

She took his hand. "I know," she conceded, letting out another faint sigh.

"Aren't you going to be traveling, anyways?" He chuckled, attempting to lighten the mood.

"Well, sure, but it's not the same."

"You'll be having way more fun in Europe for a month with Joyce than I will in New York with my god-awful family."

"I know." She looked up at him with a playful smirk. Letting go of his hand, she reached for her glass and took a gulp of water. She wasn't sure what to say anymore.

"When I get back, maybe we can figure out what we wanna turn that extra guest room into?"

"Sure," she shrugged.

"I liked your idea of a game room."

She giggled. "Sure! It's your room to design."

"Or, what about a pet room? Ya'know, for the dogs and Caiden."

She shook her head as she continued to laugh. "When we get back, we need to figure out what to do about Caiden."

"What do ya mean?"

"Well, he can't stay inside forever. He needs a coup to roam in."

"Yeah..." Zack sipped his water. "We'll build one when we get back."

They fell into a bout of silence as Adalyn munched on her lunch. Admiring the warm weather that finally hit town, she gazed off to the forest that lined Granny's Diner.

"So, when do you have to leave?" she asked.

He paused, not wanting to answer. Wiping his mouth with a napkin, his eyes avoided contact. "Uh... The car is already packed..."

"You're leaving *now*?" Her voice raised as she nearly spit out her food.

He nodded.

When he arrived at Dawn Hills in the summer of '14, he didn't expect more than a small town and boring individuals, but instead was introduced to a world of extraordinary residents that held more meaning and insight than anyone could possibly compare to back in New York. Being shown a world that coexisted with nature and a wild sense of compassion for one another, he wasn't sure how to return to the city without an underlying hatred for the apathetic people that wandered those downtown streets.

His deepest desires begged him to stay, but woefully, he knew his obligations were back in the city—at least for a month or so.

Unable to find her appetite anymore, she swallowed her last bite and looked at him. Tears welled at the bottom of her eyes, seconds from dropping. "I-I didn't know it was so soon..."

"I didn't mean to not tell you…"

"Why didn't you?"

"I didn't expect to leave so soon, but I forgot to filter in the travel time."

"So, how much time do we have?"

He let out a soft sigh. Letting his fork clink against the plate, he leaned back in his seat. Perhaps he was holding back tears of his own, but it took him a long moment before he looked at her again. "However long you want."

Her heart sank. She knew she was keeping him, but she didn't want to let him go. Adalyn wanted to stall; she wanted to sit at that diner all night with him, but she knew better. Another silence fell upon the table as they were both unsure how to walk away. They remained that way for a while. Playing with the food on their plates, they peacefully sat there in each other's presence for as long as they could.

Forty-five minutes passed of sitting like this, and eventually, as Adalyn downed a third glass of water, she looked up at him. Meeting his hazel eyes, she faintly grinned; she knew it was time. Without a singular word, he understood, but he couldn't get himself to get up; he couldn't bring himself to leave her.

Only a month, he told himself.

She nodded, as if to have heard him, but he knew she was nodding to tell herself that *it'll be okay*.

"Okay," she spoke, breaking the bout of silence. "It's time…" The confidence in her voice masked her true feelings; however, they both could see right through it.

He simply nodded and took a deep sigh. "I'll be back before you know it," he repeated as he slowly gathered his things.

"I'll race you home?" she teased.

"With how long the drive back is, I think your plane will win," he jested for her amusement.

Standing now, they still didn't leave the table, though conversation was scarce. The only thing left to do was say goodbye, something neither of them wanted to do. "When do you leave?" he asked.

"We leave on Wednesday."

"So only two days, and by the time you get back, I'll almost be drivin' back, myself!"

She smiled, and with a singular nod, his words almost eased her. But just as quickly as the wave of calmness came, it left and the pit in her stomach returned. "What if you have to stay longer?"

Sensing her concern, he stepped closer and gently grabbed her, pulling her in for a kiss. Melting in his arms, she relaxed her tensed posture. She felt safe with him, as if the world was nothing but them, and all dangers were but a mere concept.

Finally, he spoke in yet another light-hearted way. "Then, you'll get home to the pets before me, which I'll be jealous of! And we'll call every night until I come home."

She bobbed her head. It didn't ease her, but she knew once they were back, everything would be okay. "It won't be bad," she announced, though she said it to ease her own mind.

"It won't be bad," he echoed. "I promise, it won't be."

She hadn't even noticed that they'd walked to the front door now. Standing at the entrance, the only thing left was to pass through the threshold. Reaching for his hand, she squeezed it as she took a deep sigh and motioned for him to open the door. She was ready—well, she was trying to be.

Pushing the door open, scents of the fresh summer air struck them and a gentle breeze blew through her hair. He looked at her. Radiant as ever, he pulled her into his comforting embrace one more time, kissing her as though she was the only thing that mattered.

Letting go, he brushed a strand of hair out of her face and gave her one final peck on the forehead. "I'll be back before you know it," he recited for the fourth time. A wide smile crossed her lips, and though she wasn't happy about his departure, she refused to be remembered as anything but a bright face.

Standing on the porch, she watched him as he descended the staircase.

Capturing one last glance of the town, he turned to her once more and waved. Taking in her alluring beauty one last time, he jumped into the Jeep and she watched as it slowly drove off.

CHAPTER FORTY

August 1, 2016

New York's lights and urban nightlife were not enough to keep Zack sticking around for much longer than needed. The unpleasant stench of car exhaust and unidentified burnt meat permeated the city like an uncontrollable gas, while perpetual screams infiltrated the streets. From the moment he stepped foot into the city, he yearned for his return to that tucked-away town that smelt of savory maplewood and conifer pine.

After his lengthy and insufferable visit, his facial hair had become a bit rugged. Uneven stubble overtook his face and the unpalatable stench of the city still lingered on his body, bonding to him like blackened gum on the filthy New York sidewalks.

It had been just over a month since he'd left, and far too long since he'd arrived at the doorsteps of his parent's Bronx apartment. Passing his days tending to his ill mother, he whittled away under the dingy, amber lights that lit up that callus apartment she'd called home for so many years.

Longing for his own home, he missed the clear blue water that splashed against the lake's shore and the fresh air from nearby pine trees, but most of all, he missed Adalyn. Recently returned from Europe, he imagined her spirited smile as she pranced around the countryside. He imagined her delicate voice as she called for him, and the elation as she ran into his arms.

"Zack," Beka's voice tugged him back to the present. Looking over his shoulder, Beka approached with a large box in her arms. "It's the last one. Where do you want it? Should I put it in your car?"

Being pulled down by the weight of a box in his own arms, he glanced around. Standing dead center in what was now his mother's empty apartment, he fumbled for words. "Uh... Let's just get it down to the moving truck." He followed his sister down the building's steep stairs and into the main hallway.

"Do you think she'll like the place?" she asked.

"I-I don't know..."

"Their brochure looked really friendly. Shuffleboard every day, plenty of arts and crafts... it's right up her alley!" Beka pushed the front door open as it swung and slammed against the back wall.

Throwing the two boxes into the back of the moving truck, Zack let out a hefty cough before clearing his throat. "Beka, I think she'll be fine. You can go visit her every day."

"What about Dad?" she questioned, abruptly.

"What about him?"

"Do you think he'll come around?"

"Does it even matter anymore?" Zack retorted.

She simply shrugged. "So, when do you leave—like, what time?"

Closing the back of the truck, he glanced over at her. "In a couple hours. I'll help get Mom moved, then I gotta take off." His voice was colder now, stunting the conversation.

"Okay," she replied. "How was Adalyn's flight home?"

"Huh?" He was taken by surprise with that question.

"Well, you said she was just getting back from Europe. How was the flight? Have you spoken to her at all?"

"Oh, yeah. We talked earlier. It was good, normal."

"Where did she go, again?"

"All over." Zack chuckled to himself as he tried to recollect all the places she said she was venturing off to. "I believe she went to Greece, Netherlands, Italy, Germany, Sweden, and one other place I can't quite—oh, Croatia."

"Wow!" Beka was taken aback. "Have you spoken much to her?"

"It's been difficult with the time zones, but we started talking more when she got back home last Wednesday."

"Ah! So, she's waiting for you." Beka playfully nudged him, and he rolled his eyes.

"Are you ready to go?" He twirled his keys around his middle finger, motioning to the car.

"Fine," she groaned. "But I'm just saying, I want partial credit for this set-up!"

"How did you partake at all?" Zack contested.

"Well, remember that first time I came into town? Yeah, I *totally* gave away how you felt about her, and look! The next day, you two were dating."

He rolled his eyes once more. "Just get in the car," he chuckled.

The Doting Tree was an assisted living facility, aiding in the care for ill patients of all kinds. Just outside the city limits, its pictures portrayed sunny skies and clean air, something that didn't seem to disappoint upon arrival.

Stepping from the car, Beka's eyes nearly went wide with amusement. As they met up with the transport bus, she grabbed hold of their mother's wheelchair.

"What do you think?" she asked. She didn't expect a response, though a glistening smile crossed the woman's face.

"She can't understand," Zack argued.

"I beg to differ." Beka motioned to the woman's expression.

Taking their first steps into the facility, a cool breeze chilled them as goosebumps formed on the surface of their skin. Their gaze trailed around the inside, admiring the pastel colors that seemed to lighten the rooms. Zack's eyes roamed over to the clock that hung on the far wall. Mentally analyzing the travel time home, he completely spaced as they were invited up to the front desk.

"Zack," Beka's voice called for him. Following his gaze to the clock, she let out an audible sigh. "You know, I got it from here if you want to get home."

"Huh? Wha—No, no. I want to help."

"I know it's a long drive back, and the only thing left to do is get Mom checked in. Seriously, it's no big deal if you want to take off."

"I—" Zack glanced back at the clock again, recognizing that even if he didn't stop to rest, he still wouldn't make it home until late the following day.

Kneeling down in front of his mother's wheelchair, he looked at her. Withering away, her radiant beauty he'd grown up knowing had faded, leaving a thin, frail woman in its place. With the illness came silence, as she no longer could speak, and as the days passed, the sickness ate away at her cognizance. He looked into her eyes, but there was nothing except her dark brown hues staring back at him, like he was a stranger.

He could've cried—he wanted to cry, but he didn't. Kissing the top of his mother's forehead, he whispered his final words to her. "I love you."

Standing up now, he turned to Beka with open arms. "Take good care of her."

She simply nodded. Unlike him, she wasn't stoic. Tears gently trickled down her cheeks as they hugged. "You'll be back, right?"

"Of course," he replied, though even he subconsciously knew that was a lie. "You're always welcome to visit, too," he added.

"I will," she said, letting go of him. "Okay, loser! Get going before it gets too late."

A faint grin appeared across his lips, and he nodded. Walking out, he turned back one last time to wave goodbye as he passed through the glass doors.

The moment he was able to escape the clutches of that repulsive city, he'd hastily flung the last of his belongings into the car, unsteadily stacking them on top of one another. Sleep was a nonexistent concept in his head as he craved the snugness of his cozy cabin, though there was one more stop before departing. One more stop, and then he was headed home.

Off Elm Boulevard, just outside the Bronx, rested a small paint shop. A stifled ding rang throughout the shop, alerting the owner of a customer. Clattering in the back room grew louder as the man walked onto the floor.

"Ah, you're just in time, Monsieur!" The man greeted Zack with a feeble French accent and vivacious hand gestures. Zack smiled and strolled over to the front desk. "Just one moment," he spoke before disappearing behind the draping curtains that sectioned off the art studio. Quickly returning, he held out a medium-sized framed painting. "What do you think?"

Taking it in his hands, Zack peered through the frame's glazing, admiring a painted recreation from the afternoon on the pier, up at Logan's cabin. He gaped at the painted Adalyn, who, even in a picture, glistened brighter than the sunset behind her.

"Your thoughts?" the artist repeated.

Zack's eyes shifted over to the man as he grinned. "I like it!"

"Wonderful! Then, you are all set."

"Thank you," Zack beamed as he turned toward the front door.

Sitting idle in his car for a moment longer, he taped a singular piece of paper to the back of the frame and set it in the passenger seat beside him. *Home*, he thought as he started the car.

The drive was upwards of three days if he chose to appropriately stop, though Zack had other plans. Eager to get home, he drove on through as long as he could, resting few and far in between.

Meandering through the lonely backroads of North America, his engine roared, disrupting the tranquil afternoon in August as it passed under tunnels of foliage with greenery towering as tall as the eye could see. The scent of pine trees permeated the air and birds chirped above, encompassing him with the comforting memories of home.

CHAPTER FORTY-ONE

August 3, 2016

The reflection of a tired woman in ruffled white stared back at her as Adalyn grasped the glass doors to the hospital. It was a quarter after six in the morning when her plane landed in rural Wisconsin, and only thirty more minutes before she approached the doors to the Emergency Ward. Taking a deep inhale, she shoved them open and rushed inside.

Approaching the front desk, the atmosphere was filled with the bustling *hum* of activity, perplexing her already fragile mind.

"Zack," she managed to get out through panting breaths. "Where is he?"

The nurse behind the desk glanced up and immediately took note of Adalyn's panicked state. "What's his last name, ma'am?" she asked calmly.

"Sorry," Adalyn gathered her composure and took a deep breath. "Zack-Zackary Blake."

Returning her gaze to the keyboard in front of her, the nurse tapped away on the computer. "And you're..."

"Adalyn Dawn. I guess I'm listed as his emergency contact."

"Do you mind if I grab an ID from you?"

Frantically pulling out her license, she unintentionally slapped it down against the top of the desk. "Would you happen to know if there's anyone else of his family coming?"

"Uh," more tapping continued, "it doesn't seem like there was anyone else to notify, ma'am."

"Oh... Okay." She scanned the waiting area around her, perhaps looking for any familiar face, but there wasn't anyone.

A few moments passed before the nurse looked up again. "Alright, he's still in surgery if you want to take a seat in the waiting area."

"Umm, okay. Thank you."

Taking a seat in a bench that faced out toward the horizon, it was the first time since she'd left home that she'd had a moment to think. After receiving a midnight call from the local police department who told her that Zack had been in a serious hit and run accident, she was throttled into what felt like a never-ending whirlwind.

The sun was growing in the sky, currently reaching her line of sight and causing her to squint. She took deep breaths, trying to calm herself. *He's okay*, she kept repeating in her head while she watched the world drone on in the distance. As the last of the adrenaline drained from her body and her racing thoughts dissipated, her eyes grew heavy.

"Ms. Dawn?" A different nurse tapped her shoulder, shaking her wake. Disoriented, she wasn't certain how long she'd been asleep for. "Ms. Dawn?" the woman repeated.

"Huh?" She rubbed her eyes.

"He's out of surgery and stable, ma'am."

"What time is it?"

"Just past two," the nurse replied.

"Oh, gosh." Adalyn jolted upright. "I didn't mean to sleep this long..." Peering around at the nearly empty waiting room, her attention jerked back at the nurse. "He's awake?"

Kneeling down in front of Adalyn, the nurse sighed and shook her head. "He is stable though, if you'd like to go see him."

"O-oh, okay." Gathering her belongings, she followed the nurse down the maze of corridors. Counting room numbers as she passed by, she caught fleeting glances inside each.

"Here we are," the nurse said as she stopped outside of room 822.

"Thank you."

Adalyn took a deep breath and held it as she slowly brought her hand up to the doorknob. There was hesitance to enter; fear to see what lay behind this door. Finally, after exhaling her stalled breath, she warily pushed the door open. The curtain was drawn, still blocking her view, though the beeping of the machine grew louder as she neared.

Her heart raced as she gripped onto the curtains. Another deep breath and she hastily pulled them back, revealing Zack. She gasped.

Sound asleep, he laid motionless in the bed. His chest moved up and down as he breathed and his eyes unconsciously fluttered, perhaps adjusting to the sudden change of lighting.

Adalyn rushed to the bedside, daring not to touch him in fear of moving anything, then looked back at the nurse still in the doorway. "Is he—"

"He's in a coma," she calmly replied.

With disbelief, Adalyn choked on her breath. "How?"

The nurse heaved a sigh of sympathy as she grasped on to the clipboard beside the sink. Taking a seat in the chair beside his bed, Adalyn impatiently watched as the nurse scanned his record. "He got wheeled in late last night after a car accident." She paused, continuing to flip through doctor notes. "He was in surgery for impalement and stab wounds in several places, broken ribs, internal bleeding, and an intracranial hematoma."

"A what?"

"A brain hemorrhage," the nurse clarified.

Tears began welling in Adalyn's eyes as her gaze drifted over to the sleeping Zack. Sniffling them back the best she could, she peered up at the nurse. "W-what does that mean?"

The woman sighed once more and took a couple steps toward Adalyn. Perhaps she felt for the woman. "There was a collection of blood in the skull. It's usually caused by a blood vessel that bursts, pools in the tissue, and presses on the brain. In this case, that was caused by the trauma of the car accident, then being left hanging in the car for hours."

"Hours?" Adalyn hysterically screamed.

The nurse remained calm as she handed the woman a small packet of paper. "This is the police report, if you care to read it."

Taking it from the woman, Adalyn blankly stared down at the papers in her hand before looking back up. "How long will he be like this?"

The woman gave her a sympathetic look as she shrugged. "We aren't sure."

"Is he in pain?"

"In this state? No. But, if he comes out of a coma, he probably would be." Adalyn shot her a confused stare, begging her to explain, to which she did. "Due to his history, there is nothing we could do about his pain. I don't think he'd want to be awake right about now."

Glancing over at Zack, Adalyn just simply nodded. She peered back at the paperwork that rested in her hands. She attempted to survey it, though her racing mind wouldn't let her.

"And there's no one else coming?" Adalyn asked.

She shook her head. "No one else is listed, except you."

"Not even his sister?"

"No one else is listed, except you," the nurse repeated.

"Thank you." Adalyn's tone sounded defeated.

She nodded as she dismissed herself. "I'm gonna leave you two be. If you need me, just give me a ring on the remote."

Closing the door behind her, she left Adalyn alone in that dreary, dull room with nothing but the faint sounds of beeping.

CHAPTER FORTY-TWO

August 8, 2016

Nearly a week ticked by since the accident, and still no signs of life. Zack was completely unresponsive.

That morning, as the nurse took vitals and started the feeding tube, Adalyn blankly stared at his limp body. No matter how long she looked, or how many times she was told, her mind simply could not wrap itself around the concept that *this* was where she was.

A pit grew in her stomach. Boiling with sadness, it rolled up her center until it sat like a lump in her throat. She felt nauseous. Perhaps it was her body's way of shutting out the truth, but it forced her to turn away.

Returning her attention to the book in her hands, she struggled to read the words. Heaving a heavy sigh, she bookmarked the page and set the novel down on the rolling tray table. *It was no use.*

"Can I get you anything?" the nurse asked, having caught her uneasiness.

"Huh?" Adalyn jolted her attention to the corner of the room, where the nurse trifled with Zack's cords. "Oh, uh... No. Thank you, though." Looking back over in his direction, the pit returned and she instantly turned away. She couldn't bear to look at him today—not like this.

A long beep emitted from the blood pressure machine and the nurse worked to take off the cuff. Switching over to the other side of the bed, she fiddled with the feeding tube again. "Mind my intrusion, but I've been in this field a while now, and as heartbreaking as every case is, I feel for you." For a fleeting second, the nurse glanced over at Adalyn, then quickly returned her focus onto the tubing. "Sometimes, we get these horrible accidents in our ward and—"

A tear trickled down Adalyn's cheek before the woman could finish. She'd been holding onto it all morning, just waiting for the perfect moment for it to fall. And just as the singular tear escaped her walls, more soon followed. Cascading to the floor like a rushing stream, she cried. It had been a couple days since she'd done so last; a couple days since she truly allowed herself to *feel* the pain that she was suffering.

Unable to see past the glaze of tears, Adalyn began hyperventilating.

"O-oh, ma'am, I didn't mean to make you cry! I-I'm so sorry..." the nurse apologized as a singular beep drew her back to Zack's feeding tube. Tending to it, she quickly returned to the woman's side. "L-let me—uh..." The nurse glanced around the room. "Let me go get you a box of tissues. I'll be only a moment."

"W-wait..." Adalyn mumbled, though the nurse was already gone. Taking choppy breaths, she froze in her seat. This was the last thing she wanted: to be alone with him.

To her, he was no longer *Zack*, but rather a ghost of his former self; an empty vessel. Logically, she knew that wasn't the case. *It was Zack. Her Zack.* The man she loved lay only feet away, fighting for his life.

Taking another deep breath, she forced herself to look his way. Climbing out of the chair, she slowly crept up to his bedside. He was paler than she remembered, sicker maybe.

Sniffling, a few more tears dropped onto his bedding, leaving behind tiny puddles that soaked into the blue fabric.

"Why can't you just wake up?" she asked.

Staring at him, a tense sensation grew in her chest, constricting her. As if someone had ripped her heart out and was squeezing it. It wasn't shattered, it was suffocating. *Being here was suffocating.* She was drowning in a sea of sorrow and a prisoner inside those gray hospital walls.

Time no longer made sense to her. It felt as if it all happened yesterday, yet at the same time, it felt like a lifetime ago.

Her breaths came quicker, now. Grasping at her chest, she was struggling for air. Tears streamed down her cheeks as she stumbled backwards. Her world was equally crashing in on her, and bouncing out; the room throbbed around her in a wave.

Two knocks pounded in the distance, but she couldn't seem to find them.

"Adalyn?" A distant voice hollered, but all she could see were the walls of the room.

Everything past that point had faded into black, and by the time she'd come to, she was sitting in a room.

"Where am I?" she asked, sitting up.

"You had a panic attack," a voice to her left spoke.

Panning her vision toward the noise, she furrowed her eyebrows. "Max?" Adalyn questioned. "What are you doing here?"

"My flight just got in. I was coming to check on how he was doing, and came in to you on the floor, gripping your chest."

Adalyn's expression turned to shock as she began to assess herself. Hooked up to a heart monitor, she sat in a hospital room of her own. "Where am I?"

"They had to admit you, but you're free to go once you feel better."

"How long have I been out?"

Max lifted his arm to check his watch. "About an hour." Exhaling a defeated sigh, she began ripping off the machine's stickers. "Wha-what are you doing?"

"You said I'm free to go. I'm going!"

"I-I think you should give it a moment," he protested. "Zack isn't going anywhere."

"And how do you know that? You've been here with me," Adalyn defensively hissed. Recognizing her tone, she backed down. "I'm sorry... I just—"

"It's alright," he interrupted. "I can let you have some time, if you'd—"

"Actually, I could use the company... I sort of feel like I'm going insane, being here." He nodded and took a seat on the bench that rested under the large windowsill. "Thanks for coming."

"I wouldn't miss being here."

"You're actually the first visitor we've had."

Snapping his head in her direction, a look of disbelief washed over him. "Not even Beka?"

She shook her head. "I talked to her the other day and she said she was just figuring out some things, then taking the next flight out. That was on Thursday." Max bobbed his head in response, though seemingly just as disappointed with her as Adalyn was.

"I talked to the nurse today," Max began, switching topics.

"Oh?" Adalyn wasn't certain where this was going.

"They mentioned that Zack can't take anything for pain. Did you know anything about that?"

"Uh... They mentioned it to me when he was first admitted. It was because of a prior addiction issue, I think."

"I don't get why something that was over a decade ago is still affecting him. Unless... Is he still—"

A wave of nervousness rushed over her as she began picking at her fingernail. "Last I heard, he stopped when Sky came... But I-I didn't know about any of it until after he stopped..."

Max let out a thick sigh as a tense air washed over them. "I just don't get why he didn't tell me..."

"Did he in the past?"

Max nodded. "I was the first one to have known; the one to help him through it the first time."

"Maybe that's why? He didn't want to disappoint you."

"Maybe." Max cut the conversation short, though Adalyn saw it in his eyes that it gnawed at him.

Changing the topic, she asked the question not many dared to ask. "Do you think he'll make it?"

Max furrowed his eyebrows as he glanced over at Adalyn. "He's a fighter."

"What if he doesn't make it?"

"Don't t—"

"No! I keep hearing that, but what *if*? He hasn't been getting any better; he hasn't woken up."

"Then I—" Max paused. "I don't know…"

A long silence followed, leaving the room stale. Breaking it, an airy chuckle left Max's lips, causing Adalyn to glance over in confusion.

"You know that time that you went over to his house after he got back from New York and told him you still loved him?"

"How did you know—" she started. He raised an eyebrow, as if to ponder why it was even a question, and she sighed. "Yeah. Why?"

"He wasn't supposed to stay in town."

"What do you mean?"

"He'd came back to pack his stuff. He was supposed to move back to New York. He'd gotten this great job offer in Manhattan and planned to live with Beka, but then you waltzed in his front door, confessing your love for him and he couldn't do it."

"Wha-what?" Adalyn was baffled, though before she could press any further, a soft ping emitted from Max's phone, interrupting them.

"Oh, it's Maddie. I'll need to call her back. She's flying in today."

"Maddie is coming?" A bit of glee returned to her voice.

"It was supposed to be a big surprise, but it seemed like you could use some good news." Max hopped off his spot in the windowsill.

"Thank you." A faint smile tugged at the side of her lips. Taking a deep breath, she stood up. "Okay, I'm ready."

"Huh? Ready for what?"

"Take me back to his room."

"Are you sure? You could come run some errands with me, then pick Maddie up from the airport in a couple hours. You know, get you out of here and back into the world..."

She stubbornly shook her head. "I want to go back now."

"Are you sure you'll be fine?"

Adalyn confidently nodded. "And if not, I know you and Maddie aren't far away."

"Alright," he complied, hesitantly. Reaching for the door handle, he held it open for her. "He's just a floor up. I'll walk with you."

"Thank you," she replied, following him.

Back in the room, light shone through the open window, illuminating everything as she glanced around.

"Are you sure you're okay?" Max repeated.

"Yes." Feeling more relieved than she did that morning, she feigned a smile as he suspiciously eyed her. "I promise, if I need anything, I'll call."

Dithering in the doorway for a moment more, he finally ceded. "Alright. I'll be back later tonight with Maddie."

Smiling more sincerely to that response, Adalyn nodded as he turned to leave.

Taking her seat in the chair, she opened her book once more, though her mind wandered so far, it was nearly impossible to focus. Her gaze drifted over to the bed as she stared. *This isn't the end*, she repeated over and over to herself.

A tear welled in the corner of her eye, and with a deep inhale, she flipped to the back of her book, took a pen, and turned to what she knew best.

"Dear Zack," she read aloud as she sat in the small chair beside his bed.

Dear Zack,

This is everything I wished I could've said to you.

With everything we've been through over the last few years, I don't think I've experienced love like this; I don't think I've loved like I love you.

Through your optimistic enthusiasm, your endless jokes, and your caring nature, you've shown me trust, support, and comfort. And when I needed it, you've also shown me space. All of which taught me what true, healthy love was really like.

You once called me a Once in a Lifetime Girl, and of course when I heard that for the first time, I felt special. However, I've since come to realize you were wrong. You are my Once in a Lifetime Guy. You are my mere ray of light through that never-ending tunnel of haunting shadows and whispering voices. That hand that reached out for me when I was surrounded by rubble and ashes and coughing for air. Inevitably, you were there for me, by my side, when I felt my most alone. For that, I am forever grateful.

I can't even begin to find the words that express how I feel when I think about you, about us. What I wouldn't give to just hop back in time. Back to two years ago, when we first met, or to the time of our first kiss, or when we would stay up all night, doing nothing but chatting.

Your mere existence brought this sort of light to my world; this inspiration that motivated me to keep going. And even with your most stupid, simplistic of jokes, you forged a smile on my face, reminding me that above it all, I'll be okay.

Zack Blake, I love you. I have from the day I met you, and will until your last breath.

CHAPTER FORTY-THREE

August 10, 2016

"Wait up," she hollered. Even to her, her voice sounded like a distance scream. "Zack, wait!"

Running through a field of high grass, she stumbled onto the dirt path. He was only walking, why hadn't she caught up to him yet? Running on top of dry land, she felt like she was trudging through thick mud. Tears were strolling down her cheeks now, frustrated that he wasn't acknowledging her. Squeezing her eyes shut, she opened them again, this time only inches from him.

She grabbed his wrist, yanking him back.

"Why?" she screamed at him. His face was dry, emotionless, stale. "Why won't you just tell me the truth?" Tears rolled down her cheeks, blurring her vision.

Finally, he spoke. "What do you want to know?" His voice was monotonous.

Letting go of his arm, she wiped her tears away. Staring at him, he didn't look like himself. "Tell me the truth!"

He blankly stared at her. Perhaps it was because she was making a scene, or that he didn't understand why she was so hysteric, but he had no reaction. His attention left and he slowly spun back around. Letting out a gentle sigh, he continued walking without another word.

"Zack," she yelled again, though he wasn't stopping. "Zack!" Tears returned to her cheeks. "Please," she begged.

Reaching out, she grabbed his arm again, and he stopped. Turning to her, his hazel eyes were soulful this time.

A soft beeping echoed in the distance, removing her from the field and dirt path. Tugging her from it like a camera falling out of focus, it became a hazy blur of green.

Pulled from her slumber, Adalyn gasped for air as she assessed her surroundings. The dream had startled her. *It felt so real, like a distant world,* she thought to herself, attempting to understand its meaning. Perhaps her insecurities were beginning to take a toll on her.

Working to gather her bearings, her eyes drifted across the room, inevitably landing on the bed. She let out a melancholy sigh. It had been over a week that she'd been there, though in her mind, it felt like months. The same dreary walls encompassed her like a tomb; except it wasn't her tomb.

Taking one more look at Zack, she nestled into her make-shift bed in the recliner and slowly shut her eyes again, drifting back into dream-land.

Sprinting down the hall, she leapt into his arms, tackling him to the floor. "You're back," she screamed with joy. "I've missed you!"

Zack let out a chuckle as he fell back with a *hmpf*. "Oh, I've missed you too, love."

Rolling off him in a fit of laughter, she stood up and held out her hand. Reaching for it, he pulled himself up, brushed himself off, and smiled at her. She wrapped her arms around his neck and kissed him, though as she pulled back, her expression changed to a solemn frown. "Have you actually missed me, though? You left me!"

"I have actually missed you. No need to second-guess that." Gently grabbing at her waist, he drew her in and kissed her cheek. "I did but I'm back now, the past is the past." Letting out an airy chuckle, he brushed a piece of her hair aside.

Glancing down at the floor, she watched as red flowers sprouted around them, covering the hardwood with their leafy stems. Letting out a sigh of relief, she looked back at him. "I hope you'll stay a while before you leave me again." She paused, smiling once again at his smooth complexion. "I really have missed you! Catch me up. What's new? Where've you been?"

"Oh a lot of places, doing my *Zacky Thing*. How've you been, love?"

"I've been well," she beamed. "It's been too boring without you around."

"Well, hopefully I'll bring some fun back now that I'm here."

"Sounds *perfect*!" Her eyes glistened at the sight of him. "We can stay up till all hours of the night, talking. Like the old days."

"I'll start the coffee," he teased.

Giggling, she leaned in to kiss him, though another incessant beeping drew her away. Grasping for just a minute more in that field, the dream was swiped from her as he faded into a blurry haze.

The beeping grew louder, causing her to stir. No longer fighting it, she slowly began opening her eyes. Curious as to why the machine hadn't stopped yet, her focus trailed over.

Letting out an audible *gasp*, she froze. Her hands slowly carried up to her mouth, covering it as her heart raced. The sound had altered from its rhythmic pattern, to a long, continuous *beeeep*.

Flatlining. It—he's flatlining.

Adalyn watched from the chair as a group of nurses ran into the room with a crash cart. Numb in her seat, she couldn't move; she couldn't blink. Her worst nightmare was unfolding in front of her own eyes, and she was frozen. Unable to move and unable to look away.

"Code Blue," one of the nurses shouted into their radio, yanking her into reality.

"Stand clear," another announced as the machine charged up. It jolted him. No response.

"Going again," the same nurse said. Another jolt. No response. Again. No response.

The rush and urgency slowly left the room as he continued to lay there, lifelessly. His chest was still. No longer slowly bobbing up and down as he breathed, it was stagnant.

Her stomach lurched as a tense sensation washed over her chest. This time, it felt as though someone had squeezed her heart until it exploded. Muffled voices from the nurses droned out into a faded *hum* as her world began spinning again. She couldn't feel it, but tears began streaming down her cheeks, and she couldn't remember it, but she was wailing in agony.

The truth was inevitable, and though she couldn't recall much else of what happened during those fateful early morning hours, it became clear that the moment in the diner all those months ago, was their final goodbye.

CHAPTER FORTY-FOUR

August 14, 2016

Four days were not enough time for Adalyn to process her loss. Locking herself away in her room, she fell bedridden since her return home yesterday. Staring at the urn that rested on her dresser, a tear trailed down her cheek. Then another, and another, until a puddle turned into a pool amongst her bed sheets. Just when she thought there were no more tears left to cry, more fell.

There was no longer a pit in her stomach, but rather a void. Her thoughts traced back on meaningless little moments with him as she listened to his hearty laughter ring in her mind on repeat. His dopey, puppy-esque smile crackled in her mind like a home video and his hazel eyes stared back at her.

She couldn't help but smile for just a brief moment, until she was pulled back to the reality that that was all that was left of him; a memory. Taking a deep breath, she held it for a moment, perhaps to try and calm herself, though it did just the opposite. On the exhale, a long stream of tears followed as she sobbed.

Plucking a tissue from the box, she blew her nose and threw it onto the floor, where a graveyard of tissues had been slowly piling up. She wasn't sure if it was therapeutic to cry this much, but nonetheless, she couldn't help it even if it wasn't.

Continuing to weep, her mind shifted again, this time recollecting on their last fight. An awful memory to have, but yet one of many that made their relationship all the more real. Angry at herself as she thought back, she wished so deeply that she'd done differently, said differently. Perhaps if she didn't fight him that time, he'd still be here.

You'd be better off without me, his voice rang in her mind. It enraged her when he said it back then, but now, above all else, she was angry. Angry that he thought that, angry that he said that. Perhaps he was using it as ammunition against her in that brief moment, but here she was, forced to experience life without him, and she was miserable, empty.

Burying her face in her damp comforter, she screamed, "You're so fucking stupid!" Muffled against the sheets, she lifted her head and cried. Something about this felt good. Imagining it was him, she screamed some more. "I hate you! I hate you, I hate you, I. Hate. You!"

Sitting back up, she sniffled and wiped away her tears. She didn't care anymore. There was no meaning, no purpose, no care. She was numb, at least for now.

"Are you ready?" Maddie's solemn tone asked from the doorway. Sophie and Rocky perked up to the voice, just as startled by it as Adalyn.

She jolted, surprised by Maddie's presence. *How long was she standing there?* Peering over, she shook her head. "I-I can't do it…"

Simply nodding, Maddie slowly walked across the carpet of tissues that sprawled across the floor and sat on the edge of Adalyn's bed. "I understand."

Sniffling, she fiddled with a tissue in her hand, occasionally shifting focus between it and Maddie. "How am I supposed to get over this?"

She shrugged and exerted a sympathetic sigh. "One day at a time. You take it one day at a time, and slowly, it'll get better."

"What if I don't want to?" Adalyn asked, a singular tear strolling down her cheek.

She wiped it away with her finger and presented an optimistic smile, attempting to cheer up her friend. "That's what your friends are here for. We're here to get you through the tough spots, like today."

Taking a deep breath, Adalyn looked her in the eyes. "I just don't think I can today… It's too new."

Maddie nodded once more. "Alright, then we don't today."

"What about everyone else?"

"They will be fine at the service without you, and when you're ready, we can spread the ashes on our own time."

Nodding, Adalyn produced a half-assed, synthetic smile. She wished it was genuine, because her friend's kind support was all she could've asked for, but at such a time, smiling wasn't an option.

"I'll go let the dogs out and feed Caiden, and you continue resting. I'll be back up to check on you after. Okay?" Adalyn just nodded as Maddie disappeared down the stairs.

Returning to her thoughts, she recalled the more pivotal moments of their friendship. From crashing his car, to stealing Logan's boat and taking it for a joyride, there was their first date and the time they took Sky to the lake to feed the ducks. There was Ragnar's marriage and both Halloween celebrations. There were so many pivotal memories that flashed through her mind like a slideshow. Each, a scene with its own brief trailer.

If she could do it all over again, she'd do it no differently.

"Hey Adalyn," a voice spoke from the doorway, though this one built rage in her heart.

Turning her head toward the door, she scowled. "What are you doing here?"

"I'm here for the funeral."

"Yet, you couldn't have been there when he was in the hospital, when you promised you were coming? Where were you then, Beka?" she snapped.

"I know, I know... Things came up at work, I couldn't leave. I know it's no excuse, but I really do regret not making it to the hospital in time. But I'm here now. I'm sorry for your loss."

She simply raised an eyebrow as she repeated, "He was in there for over a week, and you said you were coming."

"I know..." Beka responded. "Are you coming to the funeral?" she asked after a moment of silence.

Adalyn shook her head. "No."

"Why not?"

"I don't want to," she protested like a child.

"I think it would be lovely having you there," Beka urged.

"I, quite frankly, don't care what you think. You lost my respect last week."

"I understand."

"You made it clear how little your brother meant to you; how you prioritize family."

"I—That's not it *at all*," she exclaimed. A hint of pain wavered behind her voice.

"Really? Because you didn't bother being there when he was on his deathbed. You couldn't bother caring about him. You're just like the rest of your family; selfish and heartless. Did you ever care about him?" She didn't know if she meant what escaped her lips, but in the heat of the moment, she simply didn't care. It felt good to yell, to blame someone else.

"Okay, Adalyn. I get you're hurt, but that just isn't true. I love my brother very much, more than I love any of my other family. I regret not being there, I will always regret that. Please don't make me feel worse than I already do." Adalyn rolled her eyes, not budging from the animosity that boiled in her chest. "Please come to the service," Beka repeated.

"No," Adalyn responded. "Why does it matter?"

"It would matter to my brother."

Adalyn huffed. "You don't get to say that."

Making her way across the floor of tissues, Beka took a seat at the foot of Adalyn's bed. "I do. My brother loved you very much, more than I've seen him love anyone. If not doing it for me, or anyone else, do it for him." She paused for a long moment and let out a quiet sigh, noticing Adalyn wasn't going to budge. Pondering for a moment, she peered over at her in a serious manner. "You know, Zack didn't always used to be this kind. Before he moved here, I hadn't seen him smile since we were young, back in North Carolina." Allowing a brief pause to take hold, she asked, "You remember that day I came to you in the diner and we traveled to the lodge?"

Adalyn furrowed her eyebrows. "I suppose so... Why?"

"I came there under false pretenses..."

"Of course you did," she said, rolling her eyes.

"Can I explain?"

"Do I have a choice?" Adalyn sarcastically argued.

"No." Beka coldly stated. Taking a moment to gather herself, she continued. "It began this one morning, early in that week, when I'd taken a stroll to the French Express. I ran into your friend, Ragnor?"

"Ragnar," Adalyn corrected.

"Sure. Ragnar. I don't know if it was me he was looking for that day, or if it was all by happen-chance, but he came to me in that coffee shop with a file folder—very old school, if you ask me. It was a small folder of letters you'd written to Kayla about my brother."

It took a moment, but it all began to click. It all began making sense now; that encounter in the back of Kayla's bakery when they helped unload the large truck, Ragnar stole the letters from the back office.

"He had this plan. He knew you'd never tell Zack how you felt and I knew my brother loved you so much, he bit his tongue in fear of losing you. So, your friend had a plan to talk you two into dating."

Adalyn wanted to be shocked by that, but she wasn't. She knew Ragnar's habits of meddling. Rolling her eyes, she simply asked, "What was your gain?"

"Happiness for my brother," she instantly replied. "And clearly, that worked, because not even a day later, he finally got the courage to ask you out and you said yes. So, tell me I don't care again, because not only do I care about him, but I care about you. Yes, I couldn't make it to the hospital, and I'll regret that, but you'll regret not making it to the funeral."

Adalyn huffed again like a child who didn't get her way, but deep down, she knew Beka was right. "Okay," she finally conceded.

"Good. Now, when was the last time you showered or brushed your hair?" Beka asked, to which Adalyn just shrugged. It was sometime before Zack's passing, that's all she knew. Exhaling a gentle sigh, Beka nodded. "Okay, I'll go get Maddie and we'll get you cleaned up."

Standing up, she headed to the doorway and called for Maddie, who came jogging up the stairs almost immediately. Chatting briefly in the doorway, the two ladies exchanged fleeting smiles.

"I'll be downstairs, waiting for you," Beka spoke as she stepped out of the room, leaving just Maddie now.

Adalyn's attention turned to her best friend. "I really don't want to go..."

"I know. But it'll be good, I promise."

"I guess."

"Okay well, let's start with a shower. I'll even sit in the bathroom with you and you can cry the whole time."

Adalyn groaned, though inevitably agreed. It took nearly a village, but eventually she got cleaned and prepped for the first time in days.

Standing in front of a mirror, she stared at herself. To her, she looked sickly. Thinner than before, she was frail in comparison to when she left, though living on only hospital cafeteria snacks could do that to a person's complexion.

"Are you ready to go?" Maddie asked, standing beside her in the mirror.

"Just a moment." Walking to her dresser, she pulled out the necklace that Zack had gifted her on their first Christmas. Placing it around her neck, she dropped her hands by her side and just stared. Memories of that Christmas flooded her mind. *If only I hadn't bought him that car,* she thought, though she knew that wouldn't have changed anything.

"You look beautiful in that, Adalyn," Beka complimented from the doorway.

Swiveling her head in the direction, Adalyn faintly smiled. "Thanks."

"Are you ready?" Beka held her hand out for Adalyn, who after a long moment of hesitation, nodded.

CHAPTER FORTY-FIVE

December 16, 2016

It had taken Adalyn a while to compile her belongings, but to reward herself for her accomplishments, she brewed a cup of tea and watched the sun rise across the tree line for the last time. Harboring dynamic colors painted across the clouds, this occasion seemed more magnificent than the others.

Staring out for quite some time, her tea grew cold and she returned the cup to the sink. Glancing up from the island counter, she scanned her abode again. Tidied and cleaned, the place seemed untouched, barren. A heavy weight grew in her chest, one she couldn't quite pinpoint. With a mixture of surprise and anxiety, she was shocked by what she was about to do, though it was far too late to turn back.

When will you be back? Adalyn recalled Maddie asking at her farewell party the night before, to which she'd simply replied, *I'm not sure I will.*

Where will you go? Maddie's voice echoed once more, which muted her. Even Adalyn was oblivious to what lay ahead. Her plan was to travel south and meet Beka in Cherokee, North Carolina, where Zack had grown up. There, they would send him off with a proper goodbye in a site he'd cherished most. After that, it was only onward.

Pulling her from her thoughts, the clock in the entryway struck nine and a solemn sigh left her lips. Only an hour until Vi's infamous SUV tore up the mountainside to take her away, though perhaps this was all a good thing.

Four months had come and gone since Zack passed and nothing had gotten any easier. To her, the world was meaningless; it was nothing without him. The smile that had persistently coated her lips vanished and the laughter that emitted from the heart of her soul, dissipated.

Leaning against the kitchen counter, she stared out the arch windows while sunlight crept in, illuminating the room with its blinding beams. Closing her eyes, a fit of laughter cracked the still air, and she jumped at its foreign sound.

The warm sun washed over her, numbing her senses as she was suddenly transported. Standing in line at Cathy's Ice Cream Shop, she recognized it was *her* laughter that had startled her.

"I'm Zack. Zackary Blake in full," he spoke, drawing her attention to him. His voice was crisp, as if he was truly beside her.

A delicate smile tugged at her and she eagerly opened her eyes, only to be terribly disappointed. Standing alone in her abode, her heart immediately sank. As the lump grew in her throat, she swallowed it down and closed her eyes again.

This time, soft dings of carnival games rang through the air and lights flashed in the hazy background.

"Whatcha gonna name it?" His gaze drifted down to the stuffed chick in her hands.

"Not sure. Do you have any cute ideas?"

"Caiden!" he declared with such enthusiasm.

"I like Caiden!"

The memory began to fade out and she fought it, wishing to stay just a minute longer. Faltering in the black void, a soft whimper left her lips. Opening her eyes, she drew herself back to the present.

Moving toward the window now, she glanced over the heart of Dawn Hills, though from the treetops, she could only faintly make out the tip of the Architect Building. Emitting a deep exhale, she painted a map of the town in her mind, walking down every street of the place she'd called home.

This world was all she knew, yet time and time again, it proceeded to break her. There was nothing left for her here, and it felt almost freeing.

Sophie and Rocky barked in the distance, plucking her from the trance she'd sucked herself into. Advancing toward the back patio, she paused when she heard a car ascending her driveway.

Vi's early.

Redirecting her steps, she walked toward the front door, opening it just as the person knocked.

Adalyn froze in the doorway.

"Ms. Dawn?" an officer asked. His tone was soft, but she remained uneased.

"Yes," she hesitantly replied. "What do I owe the visit to?"

"I'm just returning something that I believe belonged to you." The officer held out a large, orange envelope.

"Uh, thanks..." Furrowing her eyebrows, she took it and turned it in her hands. It felt heavy to the touch, and the name *Adalyn Dawn* was written in sharpie across the back.

"I hope you have a great day, Ms. Dawn," the officer spoke as he began to descend down her pathway.

"Y-you as well..." Still standing in the doorway, she watched him return to his car right as Violet's SUV swung into the driveway beside him.

Reluctant to open the envelope quite yet, she hid it behind her back as Vi made her way up the path.

"What was that about?"

Adalyn shrugged. "Something about a stray dog in the area," she replied as they walked inside.

"Oh. He was cute," Vi jested. "Are you ready?"

Taking one final glance around the living room, Adalyn nodded. "Definitely."

"North Carolina, here we come!"

"Thank you for doing this with me."

"Of course. Where's your stuff?"

"It's at the front door," Adalyn replied, motioning toward the three large suitcases that rested in the corner of the entryway.

"Okay, I'll load these into the car, you grab the dogs, and then we're off."

"Are you sure you don't want any help loading the luggage?"

Violet shook her head. "Nope, I'm all good. Get the dogs and meet me at the car," she replied as she stepped out the door with a suitcase in her hand.

As she disappeared down the pathway, Adalyn's smile faded. Her attention drew back toward the envelope that she'd set down on the counter. Touching its edges, she stared at the ominous envelope. Holding it in her hands for a moment, she listened as Vi came inside to drag another bag out. "Two more, then I'm ready!"

"Ready whenever you are," Adalyn hollered back.

Taking a deep breath, she tore into the sealed flap.

"A picture?" she questioned aloud, though it took her a moment before she pieced the image together.

A hand-painted photograph of her and Zack rested inside its frame. Holding Adalyn bridal-style on the pier in Lake Shasta, it became a moment forever frozen in time. It was the moment that she knew she'd fallen in love with him, and perhaps the moment he knew it too.

Letting out the air she'd unconsciously pent up, tears began welling at the corners of her eyes. The pier flashed back in her mind like a movie clip, and all she wanted to do was go back to it. She felt his warm embrace encompass her along that salty lake.

Sniffling back the tears, she twisted the frame in her hand and felt something bunch up against her palm. Curiously, she flipped the painting around, revealing a thick piece of cream-colored paper tucked into the back of it. *A note.*

"Adalyn," Vi called. "I've got everything loaded up, are you ready?"

"Huh—oh, yeah!" Sticking the frame back in the envelope and the envelope in her bag, she reached for the dogs' leashes and her purse.

Adalyn walked out of her front door, closing it behind her as if she closed away a piece of her past once again. Stopping at the end of her driveway, she turned around to stare at the place she'd called home, though it didn't feel like *home* anymore.

"You okay?" Vi asked. Adalyn turned her head toward her, and with a forced smile, simply nodded.

Settling into the car, she grasped for the envelope as a deep sigh escaped her lips. Fraught with wonder, she twisted the frame in her hands while the car passed under arches of foliage that paved their way out of the forest.

Dear Adalyn,

To celebrate the new chapter that we're about to embark on, I encapsulated the most pivotal moment in our past, where I first truly knew I loved you. Last spring, as I picked you up in my arms on the pier of Lake Shasta, you glanced up at me with this look of pure adoration, and in that moment, I knew that I never wanted to let you go.

As we go into this next journey together, I want our last goodbye at the restaurant to mark the ending of an era. And looking ahead, I know that with you, I don't want to be just another ending.

Forever Yours,

Zack Blake

ACKNOWLEDGEMENTS

This is a huge thank you for Isak, Genna, and Thomas, who not only stood beside me as I poured my heart into words, but supported me through every step.

This is also a time to acknowledge my family and friends who, though this is not their genre, read it anyways.

This is to younger me, who was always writing and coming up with stories, well here you go!

ABOUT THE AUTHOR

Finding her aspirations to write at just five years old, she picked up the idolization of becoming an author at a young age.

After graduating in 2021 with an Undergraduate degree in Criminal Justice, minoring in Sociology and Literature, she finally decided to take the plunge and dedicate her time to cultivating her passion.

Following her life-long dreams, she introduced her first novel, *Memories of Yesterday*, in August 2023, a book loosely written about her own first love story.

When not writing and working her day-job as an Analyst, Rynn can be found cuddled up with her pets, or traveling the world.